DIRTY
LITTLE
SECRETS

JO SPAIN

DIRTY LITTLE SECRETS

Quercus

First published in Great Britain in 2019 by

Quercus Editions Ltd
Carmelite House
50 Victoria Embankment
London EC4Y 0DZ

An Hachette UK company

A CIP catalogue record for this book is available
from the British Library

HB ISBN 978 1 78747 432 1
TPB ISBN 978 1 78747 431 4
EB ISBN 978 1 78747 430 7

10 9 8 7 6 5 4 3 2 1

Typeset by Jouve (UK), Milton Keynes

Printed and bound in Great Britain by Clays Ltd, Elcograf S.p.A.

Dad,
Look how far I've come!
Miss you x

PROLOGUE

Death stalked the Vale.
In every corner, every whisper.
They just didn't know it yet.

The bluebottle had no idea it was about to die.

It zipped upwards in the blue sky, warm sun shimmering on its wings, bright metallic stomach bloated with human skin cells and blood.

The bluebottle didn't see the blackbird swoop, beak open in anticipation. It didn't hear the satisfying crunch that brought an untimely end to its short, blissful life.

The blackbird continued its descent. There, just beyond the sycamore, streaming from the chimney of the cottage, were more mid-flight snacks. Hundreds of them – fat, juicy, winged insects.

The bird didn't see the boy, with his Extreme Blastzooka Nerf gun and the bullets he'd modified to cause maximum damage from what was supposed to be a minimum-impact toy.

When the missile hit, slate-coloured feathers exploded in all directions. Death and gravity cast the bird onto the top branches of the tree, from where it *thump, thump, thumped* the whole thirty metres down to a soft patch of grass below.

The boy, breathlessly running towards his felled prey, didn't see his mother throw open the kitchen door and bear down on him — the bird's squawk and the boy's squeak had jolted her from all thoughts of her absent lover.

Instantly, she saw what her son had done.

But before she could grab him, the boy pointed up and said, with more awe than even the dead bird had incited: *'Fuuuuck!'* And despite the itch to now punish him twice as hard, the mother's eyes were drawn to the cloud on the periphery of her vision, a black, menacing, humming mass of bluebottles rising out of next door's chimney.

The mother clamped her hand over her mouth. That swarm could only mean one thing, and it wasn't anything good.

Whatever had happened next door, the mother certainly hadn't seen *that* coming.

Once upon a time, they'd all tried to be more neighbourly. As recently as a couple of years ago, that effort had taken the form of a street party.

Nobody could remember who had suggested it. Alison, a newbie at the time, reckoned the street party was Olive's doing. Chrissy thought it was Ron's. Ed presumed it was David's. Nobody supposed George had come up with it. Not because he wasn't a nice guy, but he was painfully shy and you just couldn't imagine him saying, *Hey, let's have a bit of a party, mark the start of the summer hols!*

George, though, had put in the most effort. His house, number one, was the largest on the Vale and, therefore, he clearly had the most money (well, his family did – they all knew his father owned the property). That day, George, very generously, brought out four bottles of champagne, a crate of real ale and giant-sized tubs of American toffee candy and wine gums. They were added to the haphazard mix of sweets and savouries already laid out on the trestle table. The sugary wine gums sat between the large bowls of Jollof rice and fried plantains that David had provided.

The adults had floated around each other nervously, despite the fact that most of them were professionals, used to networking and performing. Matt was an accountant. Lily a school teacher. David worked in investments. George was a layout graphic designer. Alison owned a boutique. Ed was a retired something or other – whatever he'd done, it had left him very wealthy. They all had money, in fact. Or at least appeared to. They were social equals and the majority of them had lived in proximity for years.

And yet there was a shyness amongst the grown-ups of Withered Vale. In a domestic setting, out of the suits and offices, metres from their own private abodes, each of them felt an odd sense of discomfort, like they should be more relaxed than they were. Like they should know each other more than they did.

The children, forced into being the centre of attention and with far too much responsibility on their tiny number, had awkwardly played football in an attempt to entertain. The twins were useless. Wolf kicked the ball with such intensity it was like it was diseased and he needed to clear it as quickly as possible. Lily May, his sister, defended herself, not the goal, twisting her body in knots any time the ball was aimed in her direction, at all times nervously sucking the ends of her braids. Cam, a couple of years older and many degrees rougher, was brutally violent, with John McEnroe's indignant temper whenever he was called to order. And Holly – well, she stood slightly aside, old enough to babysit, too young to be in the adults' company, painfully self-conscious and bored and mortified.

Somehow, despite the alcohol, the generous food portions, the sun's gentle warmth and Ron's best attempts to get an adult football game going, the party just didn't come off.

If you'd asked any of them why, they'd have all shrugged, unable to put a finger on it.

But if you'd made them think hard . . .

Olive Collins had moved from group to group, chatting to the women, harmlessly flirting with the men, trying to amuse the children, generally being a pleasant, sociable *host*.

Of all the seven homes in the privileged gated estate of Withered Vale, Olive's was the smallest and the one that stood out as the most different. Of all the residents, she was the one who probably belonged the least. Not that anybody would think that. Or say it, when they did.

The horseshoe-shaped street was a common area. And with the exception of Alison, nobody believed the party had been suggested by Olive.

Olive preferred one-to-ones.

But she'd taken over. Olive, Withered Vale's longest resident, had an awful tendency to act like she owned the place.

Slowly, they peeled off. Chrissy, a reluctant attendee in the first place, steered Cam firmly by the shoulder towards home; Matt sloping loyally behind his wife and son. Alison linked arms with her daughter, Holly, smiling and thanking everybody as they left. Ron, the singleton, made away with two bottles of ale and a cheeky wink. Ed half-offered to keep the party going in his house until his wife, Amelia, reminded him loudly that they'd an early flight the next day. David, eager to return to his own kingdom, brought the twins Wolf and Lily May home, all walking in a row like ducks.

Lily told David she'd follow on shortly and offered to help George carry the remains of the crate back to his house. Of all the residents, these two had managed to strike up an unlikely but genuine friendship – just chit-chat on the footpath, little more, but some neighbourly engagement in an otherwise very private estate.

Only Olive was left, folding up the chequered tablecloths she'd supplied.

'Olive looks a bit sad,' George remarked, when they were out of earshot.

'Does she?' Lily said, casting a discreet backwards glance at their neighbour, the ponytail of dreads she was wearing in her hair that day swinging on her bare shoulders as she turned.

Olive was pulling together the corners of the cloth, mouth turned down, fringe falling into her eyes, her cardigan buttoned up to the neck. A lonely figure.

'Well, you're an eligible bachelor, George,' Lily said.

'And you're the neighbourhood saint,' George retorted.

'I have to put the twins to bed.'

'I have to put myself to bed. Alone.'

They both smiled tightly. Neither could bring themselves to invite Olive over for a nightcap.

Their neighbour was always perfectly amiable but both Lily and George knew the wisdom of the saying 'if somebody is gossiping to you, they're gossiping about you'.

'Maybe Alison . . .' Lily said, catching sight of Holly's mother making her way back down her drive towards Olive. Alison hadn't yet got the measure of everybody but everybody reckoned they had the measure of her. She was a soft soul. Kind.

'Ah,' George said. They were off the hook. Alison chatted away to Olive and the other woman nodded happily. Then the two women made their way into Olive's cottage.

Thank goodness for lovely Alison.

Poor Olive. She was so very hard to relax around. Even then.

Even before she properly began to wreak havoc on the lives of her neighbours.

NEWS TODAY
ONLINE EDITION

1 June 2017

The body of a woman found in her home yesterday may have been in situ for almost three months, according to a police spokesperson.

The gruesome discovery was made after a resident in the wealthy gated community where the woman lived contacted the emergency services citing concerns about her neighbour's property.

Local officers had to force entry into the woman's home to ascertain her whereabouts and safety. After finding her body, a police forensics unit was summoned to the scene.

The woman's identity has yet to be disclosed. It has been revealed that the deceased was in her mid-fifties and lived alone. Cause of death also remains a mystery and will be determined by a post-mortem, due to be conducted later today.

The woman's home is situated in a quiet residential area just outside the village of Marwood in Wicklow. This morning, locals reacted with horror to the news that her death had gone unnoticed for so long.

At time of printing, nobody from Withered Vale itself has been willing to talk to the media.

OLIVE

No. 4

At first, there was just me. Before my house had a number. Before the others arrived.

I hadn't intended to live on the outskirts of the village on my own. I'd ended up there by chance. I couldn't afford any of the houses on sale on the main street. Or the side streets. Or the streets off the side streets. My income from the health board, where I worked as a language therapist for children, was good. Just not good enough.

Priced out of buying a house where I'd grown up, one day in 1988 I drove over the bridge and out past the pretty woods that dotted most of my home county.

Just beside the woods and before the fields that made up John Berry's land, I saw the cottage. Its owner had died months earlier and we all knew his son, by then an illegal immigrant in the States, had no plans to return. A home wasn't much use when you couldn't get a job for love nor money and anyway, nobody left America once they'd got in.

It was just a matter of the estate agent phoning and telling him somebody was willing to take it off his hands. I got it for a song and a promise to ship some personal belongings over.

'Withered Vale?' my mother said, eyes wide and appalled. 'Why would you pick there, are you mad?'

'It's picked me,' I laughed. 'It's the only place I can afford.'

My parents only knew the Vale because of its history. At the start of the twentieth century, an over-enthusiastic and most certainly drunk farmer had decided to tackle pests on his land by going hell for leather with arsenic spray. He poisoned all his crops in the process – they withered and died in the fields.

'But it's miles away,' my mother protested. 'How will I get by without you?'

'The cottage is minutes away in the car,' I said. 'I'm twenty-six. I can't stay living at home forever!'

In truth, it wouldn't have mattered if I'd gone to live on the moon. I still had to call around to my parents' every evening on the way home from work, at least until they both died, a year apart, a decade later.

After the initial period of grieving, I realised I was glad to be able to go directly home each night. The remoteness and the single life didn't bother me at first. I was exhausted from all the running about, before and during my parents' illnesses. I could imagine nothing nicer than arriving home from work to a lovely, clean house, with a takeaway, a video, a bottle of wine; nowhere to go, no duties to fulfil. I happily went on like that for, oh, I don't know, at least a year.

It's true what they say. What's seldom is wonderful and my routine soon became, well, routine.

And as time wore on, I became lonely.

I'd no siblings and no close friends and I hadn't planned on being a spinster. There was no revelatory moment, no decision, when I thought, I'm so thrilled with this life, I think I'll just stay on my own.

If anything, I'd been convinced I'd follow the traditional route.

I wasn't a dainty and pretty woman exactly, but I certainly wasn't ugly and boyfriends were never a problem. For whatever reason, though, I never met anybody I was willing to settle with, or for. I was destined to be *just the one*.

But I did enjoy company.

So, in 2001, when John Berry sprang it on me that the land under my cottage actually belonged to him and he'd sold it to a property developer to build on, the only concern I had was whether my home would remain standing.

'Of course!' he assured me. 'You don't have the freehold, but you've bought the place and it's yours. This fellow would have to buy you out but he has no plans to. He's going to build around you. He's not going mad, either. Just a few houses to see how it goes. It's going to be an exclusive development – large, fancy homes for rich, important types. The ones who like their privacy. Withered Vale, right next door to Marwood, a whole village on your doorstep. Everybody will want to buy a place.'

'Is he really keeping the name?' I asked, amazed. Pockets of these developments had begun to spring up all over the country at the turn of the century, copycat American-style estates for the privileged few. But they all had names straight from the LA handbook: *The Hills*; *The Heights*; *Lakeside*.

'Oh, he's keeping it,' Berry said. 'He loves it. Thinks it will make the place unique. He reckons he's going to blow the property values around here out of the water.'

One by one, I watched the houses go up around me in a semi-circle. While they were big, each one was different, and all had a quality of design. And the fact each house was unique meant my cottage, despite its far smaller size, didn't stand out quite as much. In fact, when he brought the landscapers in, the developer added the same hedge border as mine around all the properties. It gave the Vale a feeling of continuity, he said.

Sadly, it was just a tad too tasteful for him. He lost the run of himself and turned us into a 'gated' community. He hung a big wrought-iron sign over the railings in case anybody struggled to find Withered Vale, the only outpost for miles between Marwood and the next village on the other side of the woods.

I'd gone from being a one-off cottage on the edge of civilisation to part of an elite club.

As the families moved in, one by one, I greeted them generously and genuinely. The homes were numbered one to seven and my cottage, after some initial wrangling with the developer about where I would sit on his patch, was number four.

Right in the middle of everything.

Some of them came and stayed, some of them moved in and moved out and we got new neighbours. They were all blow-ins to me.

I tried to be friendly with everybody. I hope people remember that. That I tried very hard.

The police men and women beavering around my body right now don't know anything of my story yet. They don't know anything at all, really. They've spent the last twenty-four hours trying to rid the house of flies and maggots and the pests they know are here but can't see — the mice and rats. The gnawing at my fingers and toes speak to their existence. It's amazing there's anything left of me.

It's the heat, you see. After an unusually cold spring and early summer, I was doing okay, sitting there on the chair, silently decomposing. The same chair Ron from number seven bent me over for three and a half minutes of mind-blowing passion the night before I died, leaving with my knickers scrunched up in his pocket.

I hope, for his sake, he's got rid of them.

Then late May came and the weather turned on its head, sending temperatures soaring and bringing all sorts of nastiness into my living room.

It's amazing how long they left me, my *neighbours*. Not one, not a single one, came to check on me. Not even Ron. And Chrissy only rang the police when my cottage looked like a public health hazard.

Was I really that hated?

Those poor detectives. I almost feel sorry for them. It's going to take them forever trying to figure out who killed me.

FRANK

Frank Brazil had never claimed to have a strong stomach. And he wasn't going to start pretending now, in the presence of this body – this carcass. Every time his eyes happened on the blackened, liquefied lumpen form, bile threatened to explode from his oesophagus.

Even his partner Emma looked slightly less orange than normal, her naturally fair skin a few notches paler under the caked foundation cream.

'It's utterly disgusting,' she said, decisively. She hadn't stopped talking since they'd arrived. Frank prided himself on being a modern man – he held to the philosophy that there was no difference between men and women, that the fairer sex were equal – in fact, *superior* – to men in almost every way. First his mother, then his lovely Mona, had kept him right in that regard.

But, Christ . . . Emma. He could not get his head around the girl. So young, with so many opinions and all of them so fixed!

'The poor woman. What has happened to *community*? How could her neighbours not notice she wasn't around? You'd think one of them would have knocked and raised the alarm. You should see what they're saying on social media about the people who live here. And where are her family?'

Frank shrugged. It wasn't that he didn't agree. Frank's home was in an old council housing estate that had been gentrified and while many of his neighbours these days were students or young professionals, there was still a community feel to the place. Only last week they'd had a football tournament of sorts on the green that the houses surrounded. Dads, city-boys, students and children alike all joined in.

If one of his neighbours died, he'd notice they'd gone missing in action and there were far more than seven houses in his estate.

'It's just plain wrong, elderly people being left alone like this,' Emma continued. 'I hope the government runs those ads again, the ones about checking on vulnerable pensioners. They'll have to, in the wake of this.'

'Elderly? Emma, she was fifty-five! That's two years older than me.'

'Well, I'm not being funny, Frank, but you *are* retiring in three months,' Emma said, and Frank clamped his hand to his forehead. How could you ever explain to a twenty-eight-year-old that fifty-three was not old? That he was retiring because he was tired and sad and no longer cared? He'd been working in this job longer than she'd been alive and he'd seen too much. He'd lost empathy. When that went, you had to go too. Every sensible copper knew that.

He turned away from Emma and peered through the window. Somebody had raised the blinds to let light into the room. The entrance gates had made it easy to isolate the crime scene – there was no press throng, it was just the police and emergency vehicles inside the perimeter. And the neighbours, who were still holed up in their houses, having woken up to a shitstorm of epic proportions.

Forensics had taken initial DNA from the scene. There was plenty. Too much, in fact. If it wasn't accidental death or suicide, if it turned out Olive Collins had been murdered, they had tonnes to work through. They'd even, according to the speculation of the forensics team, potentially picked up traces of semen from the floor beside the body.

'She must have had a chap,' he said aloud, to himself and to nobody.

'Do you think so?' Emma said. She pulled on her gloves and picked up a framed photograph from the dresser. Crime Scene was finished in the sitting room – every surface dusted and swabbed, every inch photographed – but the detectives still wore baggies over their shoes and blue rubber gloves on their hands. The picture showed a younger Olive in a large-collared blouse with a striped jumper last seen circa 1985, sporting a bowl haircut. 'She wasn't particularly attractive. And she was . . .' Emma trailed off like she'd thought better of her next sentence.

He shrugged.

'If she was willing . . . That's usually enough for most men. Anyway, I wouldn't go judging her looks on a thirty-year-old photograph; the entire population looked ridiculous in the eighties. Or on what's in the chair, there. Let's find a more recent picture of her.'

The deputy state pathologist appeared in the doorway.

'I'm ready to move the body.'

Hovering behind him was the head of forensics, the likeable, down-to-earth Amira Lund. Frank had a lot of time for Amira, and he liked to tell himself it wasn't just because she was a very attractive woman – big almond eyes, dark skin, long luscious black hair (that he rarely saw, to be fair, given all their interactions took place with her ensconced in a white suit).

'Frank, got a minute?' she asked.

'They're about to move the body,' Emma said.

'Abso-fucking-lutely I have a minute,' Frank said. There wasn't a chance he was hanging around to see Olive Collins' corpse being shifted from the chair into a body bag. Christ knew what was under that saggy mess. His skin crawled just thinking about it.

'You're in charge,' he told Emma, who struggled to hide her delight before she realised what she was about to witness. The smile died on her face.

Frank followed Amira out, ducking his head under the door frame and emerging into the small hallway that ran between the sitting room and the kitchen. He knew already that it led off towards the two bedrooms and bathroom. The cottage didn't have an upstairs but it had a large enough ground-floor footprint.

'Through here,' she said, bringing him into the kitchen. Frank stood aside to let one of her team come out first, his large hands filled with evidence bags.

'Has God said anything yet?' Amira nodded back in the direction of the sitting room.

'He deigned to tell me when I arrived that it's difficult to pick up anything from a body in that state – truly, a revelation of biblical proportions – but there are no bullet or knife wounds, no old blood stains. Nothing you don't know yourself. However she died, it was gentle enough. Maybe she'd a heart attack. Or she took a bottle of pills and just sat down to watch telly, drifted off. The lads who found her said the television was on stand-by, like it had switched itself off after a time but was ready to go with a flick of the remote.'

Amira shook her head.

'I don't think that's what happened.'

Frank sighed. Sudden death was always treated as suspicious. They had to examine all the angles, tick all the boxes. But in the end, all it really created for the police was paperwork. Lots and lots of it.

He'd been happy to come out here this morning because admin was all he was good for. Emma wanted complex, high-profile cases. Day-long interrogations. Sensational trials. She was young, she had the energy for it. Anybody who looked like they got up at the crack of dawn every day just to apply make-up had the energy for anything.

All Frank wanted was an eight-hour shift where nothing of note happened, after which he'd head home to a frozen pizza, David Attenborough on the TV and a good night's sleep free from nightmares.

'What is it?' he asked, tentatively.

'The boiler was pumping carbon monoxide into the house.'

Frank cocked his head, raised a hand, pulled at the tuft of reddish-brown hairs over his upper lip.

'Accidental death from ingestion of poisonous gas. Very sad. They should make those CM alarms obligatory.'

Amira shook her head again.

'Nope. Not accidental. Come over here.'

Frank followed her to the kitchen door, every step heavy and resigned. He watched as Amira stood on a chair and traced blue-gloved fingers around the vent over the door.

'What's that?' she said.

He took his place on the chair.

'Tape,' he answered, and his stomach felt funny.

'Tape,' she repeated. 'Every vent. The doors and windows are well insulated, nothing needed there.'

'What about the front door? Didn't the neighbour say something about the letter box being taped off?'

'It was just the letter box and it was masking tape, not clear tape. And there are fingerprints on it. A couple of sets. One is probably the neighbour who found her. The other, if I were to hazard a guess, is probably the victim's. She had a postbox attached to the front wall, maybe she didn't need or want people sticking post in the door.'

Frank, drowning, clutched for the lifebuoy.

'So, either Olive Collins had an aversion to fresh air or her death was planned. She wanted the method she chose to be effective. She knew the boiler was leaking or she blocked the pipe. Is it an old one?'

'No. It's fairly new. It's in that cupboard on the wall behind you. It's not long since it was serviced, according to the sticker on its front. But the caps were unscrewed and the flue stuffed with cardboard. Manually.'

'Well. Suicide it is, so. She taped up all the air vents. I'm surprised she didn't block the chimney. That's what drew the neighbour's attention – the bluebottles.'

'There was nothing in the chimney,' Amira clarified. 'But that wouldn't have mattered. The chimney flue is narrow and not sufficient to empty a home of carbon monoxide. She had a painting propped in front of it as well. There was some ash in the fireplace from paper she must have burned, but no open fires for her.'

'Sorry, Amira, what's the point? Something is giving you itchy knickers.'

'I'll tell you what's upsetting me, Frank. This house is crawling with DNA. For a woman who was left dead in her sitting room for nigh on three months, it looks like she had an awful lot of visitors in the run-up. The only place we haven't picked up fingerprints is on the tape over those vents. Nor from the pipes attached to the boiler. They were cleaned.'

'Shit.'

'Yeah.'

'But – come on, it's still more likely she'd have done it herself. How could somebody have taped up all the vents without her noticing?'

'It's not like it would take that long, Frank. And, as you can see, it's clear tape. I didn't notice it until we checked the boiler and I started to look closely.'

'I don't know, Amira. As a manner in which to murder somebody, it's fairly diabolical. I'd go so far as to say it's a little over-imaginative for this day and age.'

Amira shrugged.

'Some people aren't into knives and guns, Frank, and not everybody has the strength or capacity for strangulation, despite what the movies tell us.' She hesitated. 'There's more.'

'You're upsetting me now,' Frank sighed.

'Wait for it. Her phone was beside her when we arrived. We dialled the last number. She rang *us*.'

The colour drained from Frank's face.

'No.'

'Yep. I've done your homework for you. She dialled the emergency services. 3rd of March, 7 p.m. You might want to sit down for the next bit.'

'I think I might.' Frank pulled out a faux-leather brown chair from the kitchen table and plonked his arse on it.

'It was recorded as a distress call. Two uniforms were sent out. They got in the main gate, knocked on the door.'

'They knocked on the door?' Frank felt like Alice, plummeting down the rabbit hole.

'Blinds were drawn. Nobody answered. No obvious sign of distress. They were going to go around the back but the man next door pulled up and the three had a little tête-à-tête. The neighbour said he hadn't seen or heard anything unusual and that if the blinds were down she was most likely away. So they put it down to a hoax call and left. And the blinds stayed down for another three months, until we arrived. Here's another little tidbit for you – the Champions League was on the night she phoned. Kick off was 7.45 p.m. Do you think the lads might have had an interest in the match?'

Frank laughed. It was nervous and it was involuntary.

'I've never been so glad to be retiring,' he said. 'Country cops cock up again. There's your headline. What did she say in the call?'

'In a very agitated tone, she said, and I'm quoting, *I think something is very wrong.* Then she hung up. Abrupt.'

'Clearly just a hoax, then. Idiots.'

'Yeah,' Amira said. She pulled out the chair beside him and sank into it. 'You're screwed, aren't you? Sorry, if I'd known earlier, I'd have rung and told you to call in sick. Fancy a drink later? I'll buy.'

Frank shook his head. Like that would make up for it. Three months. That was all he had left. And now Emma would be foaming at the mouth. There'd be an incident team. Press conferences. Weeks of interviews. Unpaid overtime.

Unless . . .

His only hope was that the bosses wouldn't want him to immediately classify it as murder. Resources were tight, statistics were everything, and a lack of fingerprints wasn't an absolute indicator of criminal intent. He and Emma could spend a couple of days looking into the dead woman's life, interviewing the neighbours, that sort of thing, while they waited for the post-mortem and forensic results. Try to determine if there were any actual motives for somebody to want to kill the woman.

With any luck, she'd be whiter than white and the coroner would record it as death by suicide.

Frank almost laughed at his own desperation.

GEORGE

No. 1

Wolf Solanke was in George Richmond's back garden again. George could see his little head of tight Afro curls bobbing up and down as he laboured at the patch of earth he'd chosen to transform that morning.

Lily had bought the twins gardening sets for Christmas last year. But George knew Wolf's father David had OCD when it came to *his* lawn. Everything in the Solankes' backyard might look as if it was thrown together devil-may-care, but it was a cultivated chaos. There was no way David would let his kids muck around out there with mini trowels and spades.

So Wolf liked to play in George's extremely expensive land-scaped flower beds and George didn't mind a jot. The gardeners came, they did their thing, he was grateful and oblivious at the same time.

It was nice to have a little company, even if it was an eight-year-old kid.

He sauntered across the lawn to Wolf, who was so focused on

whatever he was up to with his small rake that he didn't notice George's approach.

'It's hot today, isn't it?' George said.

Wolf jumped.

He looked up at George with big brown eyes, then looked away again, scratching at his dark cheek with mucky nails.

'It's very warm,' Wolf said. 'The weather woman said twenty-eight degrees by noon.'

'Wow. A heatwave.'

'That is not a heatwave,' Wolf replied.

'Well, technically, no . . .' George trailed off. He'd learned early there was no point having arguments with Wolf about specifics.

'Fancy a drink, kiddo?'

'No, thank you. Mr Richmond, you really need to put something down for these begonias. The slugs are eating them.'

George, while impressed by Wolf's knowledge of his shrubbery, merely shrugged.

'Circle of life, pal. Slugs have as much right to eat as you and I.'

Wolf looked aghast.

'But you'll have no flowers.'

'I'll tell my gardener to grow some that aren't so slug-friendly. 'Course, then I might get other bugs. On the scale of things, I don't mind slugs. I've heard whitefly are like locusts. Eat everything they see. Bloody insects, eh?'

George was shocked to see tears well up in Wolf's eyes.

He dropped to his hunkers so he was level with the kid.

'Hey, pal, what's the problem?'

Wolf didn't answer. Instead, he rubbed angrily at his eyes,

gathered up his equipment and started off down the garden, disappearing into the gap in the hedge he used to transport himself home.

George stood there, metaphorically scratching his head.

Alone again, he turned and made his way back into his house and climbed the stairs. His destination was the landing window, the one that gave him the best view.

The Vale was normally so tranquil. Nothing ever happened in it. Nothing anybody talked about, anyhow.

But right now, it felt like bedlam. There wasn't a single person George knew out on the road. Just lots and lots of police.

He rested his head on the cool glass, the rich net curtain leaving triangular indents on his forehead, and closed his eyes. The familiar anxiety began to bubble, a feeling that he could only respond to in one way.

A door banged outside and George's eyes shot open, just in time to see a flurry of activity at number four. They were bringing out her body.

He shook his head. It was her. Really her. He was watching his dead neighbour being wheeled out of her home on a stretcher and what did he feel?

Nothing.

But then, George was never very good at proper emotions.

That's what his father had told him when George had lost his job – when he'd been fired from the newspaper. It had taken all of the great Stu Richmond's power to keep what had happened quiet. And George hadn't even seemed upset. Or grateful. So Stu said.

He'd been almost right. George's main emotion had been relief.

Not because he'd been *saved*, but because he no longer had to keep up the lie.

Any one of his journalist 'friends' would have happily run with the story, that's what George's dad had said. He was probably right.

Luckily, management were terrified of falling out with Stu Richmond. George's father was the country's leading music mogul, the Irish Simon Cowell, and a big deal in the States. If his artists boycotted the paper's entertainment section, well . . . It was decided that George losing his job was punishment enough.

His father had done him that one favour and then more or less washed his hands of him. Bar the house and the monthly cheques.

'Don't ever embarrass me again,' he'd said.

George had tried. He'd gone to counselling when he'd been fired, attempted to get to the bottom of what it was that made him such a screw-up. He went weeks without leaving the house, not reaching for distraction with his computer or TV, meditating even, in an effort to fix himself.

At one point in his sad little existence, he'd considered putting a dating app on his phone and trying to find a girlfriend. He wasn't a bad-looking man and he was still youngish, only thirty-five. The counsellor said he had to stop shying away from intimacy. There was still time to come back from the brink.

But no matter what he did, it crept in again.

People had no idea.

George reckoned what was wrong with him was worse than being addicted to crack cocaine.

Just looking at all the activity outside was too much for him.

Olive bloody Collins.

George felt the familiar urge come over him. The stress, the desperation. He could think of nothing else but doing what he had to do. Right there, right then.

He reached for the wipes on the windowsill.

Good riddance to bad rubbish, he thought, as he scrubbed the wood clean.

OLIVE

No. 4

When Stu Richmond moved into number one, it was very exciting. In a country of B-list celebs, he was a shining star because he'd made it *in the States*. The man who'd launched many a career and garnered millions in the process. He was more famous than half the bands he'd founded, probably aided by the fact they had a habit of crashing and burning when the egos properly landed.

I insisted on calling him Mr Richmond. I did it partially because I was old-fashioned, but, if I'm honest, mainly to annoy him. He was one of those people that just provoke the rebel in you. 'Stu' fitted the image he was trying to project and that image was of a man that wasn't out of place with a girlfriend who was younger than his adult son; a man who had a red Porsche in the driveway; a man who routinely flew 'Stateside'; and, God bless him, a man who had a personal trainer and hair plugs.

First the girlfriend departed. Then Mr Richmond headed back to his US home. The charming countryside and fabulous Withered Vale lost its allure over the course of one damp winter.

It was George's turn to live in the mini-mansion.

George was far quieter than his father. A real lone wolf – isolated even, you might say. We were such a small community, it was a terrible waste.

At first I thought he might be gay and a little shy because of it. It was clichéd, I know, but he was young, handsome, kept the exterior of his home immaculate, and I never saw a girl call to his house, never saw a woman on his arm.

That summer, I stuck a Pride sticker in the sitting room window to show some solidarity. Maybe that was all he needed. Some outreach.

I watched to see if he'd do the same. He didn't.

It turned out George wasn't gay.

George was something else altogether.

LILY & DAVID

No. 2

She couldn't think about what was happening outside. She'd no energy for it.

Lily Solanke was exhausted. Utterly exhausted. She always felt like this as the summer term drew to a close. The energy it took to entertain children and keep a class relatively calm for those last few weeks – when lessons were done, the sun was shining and patience was wearing thin, for staff and pupils alike – was immense.

Even her fingers felt tired as she made her way through the pile of reports that awaited her signature on the kitchen table. She'd already written one for each member of her own class but, as Year Head, she had to countersign Mr Delahunt's batch as well. Her eyes paused on one, declaring a student below average in all the English disciplines – reading, writing, spelling, enunciation. Her colleague had scrawled *Delsia must try harder* in the comments box, along with some equally unkind remarks that she knew did not come from a good place.

Lily had to resist adding underneath *Mr Delahunt must try harder*.

Delsia was a ten-year-old from Malawi who'd only arrived in their school at the beginning of last year. She was a gorgeous little thing, friendly and happy, displaying no signs of the trauma she'd endured in her passage to Ireland.

Lily made a note to put in a funding request for additional language support for the coming September.

She left the report aside. She wanted to ring Mr Delahunt and give him an earful for making such insensitive and unthinking comments. She'd be assertive, yet diplomatic.

But she knew she wouldn't make the call, because, apparently, you couldn't be black *and* objective about racism.

Lily was on track to make headmistress.

All she had to do was not rock the boat.

And that was tough going, when end-of-year energy levels were low and nerves frayed.

Each year, when June approached and the tiredness hit, Lily wondered anew why she hadn't chosen to teach secondary level, the twelve-to-eighteen age group. Their school days were longer during the year, but they finished at the end of May. Imagine that. Three whole months off for summer.

But she couldn't bring herself to retrain. She loved small children. She loved the imaginations of the seven-year-olds in her class. Their little personalities, already individual, so unintentionally funny and naïve and open.

She was too good with small children to give it all up for an extra month off each year.

Her job was also one of the reasons she refused to move – anywhere. In the early days of their relationship, David used to joke about building her a palace in his home village of Calabar in Nigeria, where she could buy and run fifty schools if she wanted and not have to work even half as hard.

'Life would be so easy,' he would say. 'We're rich, we'd be even richer there, and nothing else matters. You wouldn't have to prove yourself. There's no such thing as *colour* in Nigeria. We are the norm, not the exception.'

She couldn't understand that concept. She'd lived in a mainly white country her whole life – her colour defined her.

And, anyhow, she knew he was joking about the move. David had fled Nigeria after his father had been involved in a failed military coup that had temporarily put his whole family under threat. David, the eldest, had emigrated on a student visa, sent abroad to earn for the family. And earn he did. He clawed his way to wealth and respectability, despite everything stacked against him.

His family were long since clear of danger but had never regained favour. David's weekly payments to his father's bank account kept them going but the shame of dependency meant their relationship was strained.

Nigeria was her husband's past, a romantic pipe dream. A land Lily would probably never see. And she didn't mind. Her job and her children were her life. They took all her time, which meant she had nothing left to deal with other drama.

She'd taken the day off when she realised what had happened in number four. But she still had work to do, she still had to keep on top of things.

She was really only there for Wolf.

Her son needed her today. And Lily was good like that, when her kids needed her.

She was good. That's what she told herself.

The phone rang.

EMMA

'The neighbours are gathering outside.'

Emma had found Frank in one of the bedrooms – the dead woman's, by the look of things. The dressing table was heaped with perfumes and creams and nail polish – Anais Anais, Pond's, Rimmel pale pink. A book lay open on the bedside locker, *The Moonstone*. One of Emma's favourites.

'The body's been moved. The other residents must have seen the activity. Jesus, it was awful. They had to bring the entomologist back in.'

'Don't.' Frank was sifting through hangers in the wardrobe. 'No men's clothes,' he said.

'Why would there be men's clothes?' Emma asked.

'The semen. A steady boyfriend and there'd be something in here. A shirt. A pair of boxers. An extra toothbrush in the bathroom. There's nothing.'

'Maybe it was just a one-night stand,' Emma said.

'Even at her age?' Frank replied.

He picked up another object and peered at it, every innocuous item seemingly holding some sort of meaning only Frank could interpret.

'There's a box of old letters and certificates in the wardrobe,' he said. 'We need it all bagged up and brought back to the station. And *read*. Actually examined. Make that clear to the team. And we need to find out about this woman's life. Talk to her neighbours, track down family, see if she'd any enemies, any scorned lovers . . .'

He muttered to himself again.

Emma felt her cheeks reddening. She hated when he did this, got on with the job without telling her what was really on his mind. When she'd been assigned to work with him, late last year, she'd thought she was being placed in the safe hands of a mentor – somebody who'd be willing to impart all his experience and knowledge before going off to pastures green.

She knew he'd been a good detective in his day, however she felt about Frank Brazil now, with his silly moustache and monosyllabic utterances. But instead of teaching Emma things, talking her through his steps, he spent most of their time together mumbling under his breath. Which meant she had to keep repeating 'What?' so she sounded like an absolute idiot all the time.

Frank, sadly, seemed to bring out the worst in Emma. She knew it was ridiculous, that she was carving a career based on her own merit, but she was desperate for him to tell her she was *good*. She wanted him to see beyond her age and her accent and, while maybe not treat her as an equal, at least view her as a protégée.

She wanted to have that conversation with him, honestly, openly.

She couldn't, though. In her head, she couldn't find any combination of words that didn't make her sound like a clingy lunatic.

So, in the absence of some emotional honesty, she found herself being petulant and angry and insecure around Frank.

'What did Amira Lund say?' she asked.

Frank mumbled.

'What?'

'Jesus, Emma. She. Said. It. Looks. Like. Olive's. Death. Might. Have. Been. Suspicious.'

Emma bristled.

'Right. I was worried about that.'

Frank stopped what he was doing and looked at her.

'Really? With everything pointing to sudden death or suicide, you immediately leapt to the conclusion this could be a murder?'

'It's what she's wearing.'

Frank's eyes widened.

'What she's *wearing*?'

'Yes. She's dressed like she was in for the night. PJs, slippers, no jewellery. The remote control was on the arm of the chair beside her, the phone next to her hand, a cup of what was probably tea on the table. If I was committing suicide, I'd be wearing something nicer and have my full make-up on. I'd lie on my bed, or maybe get in the bath. I wouldn't boil the kettle and turn on the TV. And I'd make sure I was found.'

'I don't mean this to sound insulting, Emma, but most people aren't you. Why would anybody give a toss what they were wearing when they were discovered dead?'

'You wouldn't even be thinking it – not consciously. You're a woman; it just comes naturally, to put on your best.'

Frank snorted.

'Right. Well, if you ever find yourself some evening picking out a nice dress and putting on more lipstick when you've nowhere to go and nobody to see, do me a favour and give me a call, won't you?'

Emma chewed the inside of her cheek.

'There's also the fact that every single air vent in this house is Sellotaped – I guess that's what really set alarm bells ringing for me. But I suppose you only see those things if you're looking. Anyhow, should we go out and talk to these neighbours of hers?'

Emma spun on her heel before Frank had the chance to reply. If she'd hung on, she'd have seen his jaw drop.

GEORGE

No. 1

It seemed like the right thing to do, once the body had been removed.

To come out and see if the police knew anything.

George was putting all his effort into being normal.

Show concern. Gossip with the neighbours. Act like everybody else, not like somebody with something to hide.

He'd rung Lily, so now the Solankes had come out too.

George shot her a friendly smile. They had barely exchanged a hello in weeks and George missed her company. He missed everything, these days.

Lily seemed bored, verging on irritated, like she'd no interest in standing out on the road and it was only David's big arm around her waist that had propelled her from the safety of her home. She'd tried and failed to contain her curls beneath her headscarf and was now brushing them off her face like they were one more nuisance on a day full of inconvenience.

David was perfectly relaxed. Now, *that* was unusual. The man was typically wound up like a coiled spring. David could wear chinos morning, noon and night and grow all the organic veg in the world and he would still send off a predatory vibe. David was an alpha male, and George could readily admit he didn't like being around his sort. Too much effort to prove yourself and when it came to that, George always fell short.

There was no sign of Wolf and Lily May.

He hoped Wolf was okay. It had only dawned on him afterwards why Wolf had been crying in his garden. George had mentioned bugs and they all knew now that Olive had been a bit of a breeding ground these last few months.

Jesus. It didn't bear thinking about.

Poor Wolf.

Alison and Holly Daly approached their neighbours hesitantly. Alison's arm was wrapped around her daughter, but to an observer it was Holly propping Alison up. Even though Holly looked particularly young today, dressed in three-quarter-length jeans and a plain white tee shirt, her long dark hair plaited chastely down her back.

When George first met Holly, he'd thought she was nineteen or twenty. He'd been shocked when he discovered she was only fifteen. She'd dressed older, back then, and there'd been something about her, something that spoke to maturity.

But as the years passed, she seemed to regress, like she'd decided to hang on to her youth. Or get it back. One or the other.

Alison looked up and caught George looking at them. He turned his head quickly, blushing.

The door to Olive Collins' house had opened again and the two detectives came out. A man and woman – him, middle-aged, built like a tank, red brush-like hair and moustache. Her, younger, dyed blonde, enough make-up to plaster a block of apartments. At the same time, Ron Ryan from number seven made an appearance.

Chrissy and Matt Hennessy were staying put in number five. Chrissy was still traumatised, according to David, who'd apparently called over last night bearing gifts of herbal teabags and kind words about how they all should have known and it shouldn't have been left to her to ring the police. Like green tea would soothe the nerves after realising all those bluebottles you'd just seen had been eating your neighbour's corpse.

She and Cam had been the first to notice something was up.

With any other eleven-year-old, you'd wonder if that discovery would have a long-term effect on them. Not Cam. George had caught the youngster out in his back garden one day, standing on a decaying tree trunk. He had the sights of what looked like a plastic Uzi machine gun trained on Lily May next door.

'What are you doing, Cam?' George asked.

'Shush. You'll alert the prey.'

And George thought *he* had issues.

'Ladies and gents.' The older detective was talking. They gave him their full attention.

'I'm Detective Frank Brazil and this is my colleague, Detective Emma Child. Thanks for coming over and showing your concern for Ms Collins.'

George raised an eyebrow. The detective had to be patronising them. Nobody had shown concern for Olive in months.

'I appreciate how shocking this is for the whole community, especially for yourselves as the deceased's closest neighbours. We realise also that our presence here will cause you some inconvenience and that you will have to contend with the curiosity of the media beyond the gates. Some of you, we understand, have already taken the day off work. So, conscious of how much this is putting you out, we're going to try to conduct our business as seamlessly as possible.'

What was he going to say? George wondered. That Olive had had an accident? That she'd killed herself?

'While I cannot discuss details of Ms Collins' death at the moment, I do want to tell you that we have opened a case file. We would like to speak to you all individually and we will be calling house to house. We'll try to get these interviews done today so you're free to return to your normal routines ASAP. If anybody has pressing appointments, just let us know and we'll schedule you for this evening or over the weekend. But please, everybody, I'd like you to try as hard as you can to cast your minds back three months ago, to 3rd of March, to be exact. Check diaries, phones, social media, that sort of thing. Were you at home and if so, did you see or hear anything out of the ordinary? Did anybody call into Ms Collins', were there any strange cars on the road, that sort of thing.'

'Wait a minute,' David interrupted. 'Are you saying something untoward has happened? That she didn't just die?'

Untoward. Who used words like that? George frowned. The detective had probably already drawn conclusions about the Vale's residents on the basis of the size of the houses. For some ridiculous reason, it was important to George that this cop, who he didn't even know, didn't see him as some sort of privileged little tosspot. As Stu Richmond's son, he'd had a lifetime of people making that assumption. George moved further away from David Solanke, shifting his feet until he was closer to Ron, who seemed to be positively humming with nervous energy.

'As I said, I can't discuss details of Ms Collins' death. Now, is there anybody among you who can tell us if Ms Collins had any family? Mrs Hennessy in number five was in quite a distressed state last night when the body was found. She wasn't able to tell us if there was anybody we should contact.'

'She didn't have anybody.' Alison spoke up. She was pale, her eyes wide. An older version of her daughter, with classy, strategic clothing and immaculate hair and make-up. 'She was an only child and her parents are dead.'

George noticed Lily flinch. His friend was definitely not herself.

Alison, too, looked very anxious, he thought. But then, he'd noticed that in her before. It was unusual, given she was such a successful businesswoman, that Alison could be so nervous and so . . . lovely. Neither seemed to really fit.

George knew what it was to be a mass of contradictions. But right now, his neighbour seemed completely out of sorts.

'I see,' the detective said. 'Well, that's useful. Okay, folks, right now, I suggest you return to your homes and we'll be around to you shortly. Maybe Ms . . .?'

He looked at Alison questioningly.

'Alison. Alison Daly.'

'We might come over to you first, if that's okay, Ms Daly?'

Alison nodded, reluctantly.

'I'm in number three,' she said.

And with that, they began to disperse.

Each wondering, when will my turn come?

LILY

No. 2

'We need to discuss what we're going to tell the children.'

As soon as they returned to the house, David had picked up where he'd left off – washing thick muck from the carrots he'd pulled from the vegetable patch. He'd abandoned them seconds after George rang. Lily had no interest in going out but David said it was important they all show some neighbourhood solidarity . . . after the fact.

Turns out, the detectives were going to speak to all of them.

And now Lily was really on edge.

'. . . maybe she fell over and gave herself an aneurysm or something?' David was still talking. 'You can imagine her doing something so bloody stupid, can't you. Idiot woman.'

Lily made balls with her fists and released, trying to squeeze and expel the tension from her body. Quietly, she began to collect the piles of reports she'd left on the table, hoping her husband would understand that she was in no mood to talk.

About anything, let alone about death.

David had never lost anyone. Both his parents and his many

brothers and sisters were alive and kicking over in Nigeria. Too alive and kicking, a daughter-in-law might say, though at least the distance meant contact was restricted to phone calls, emails and the occasional, painful Skype session.

Lily had felt grief not once but three times in her life.

The first occasion was when she was seven.

Her parents had brought her to the seaside, bought her an ice cream and told her she was adopted.

Lily had always known she was different. From the moment she realised that the girl in the mirror was her – with those huge brown eyes, brown skin and hair that grew in electrified corkscrew curls, so unlike her pale, blue-eyed, straight-haired friends. Yes, right from the point of consciousness, Lily had known she was *other*.

As a child, she used to ask her parents all the time why they were a different colour to her, why she was a different colour to everybody. When she was seven, they gave her the answer she knew and had probably always suspected was the truth.

'You mean,' she'd said to them that day, 'my mother didn't want me?'

'I'm your mum!' her mum had protested, adding to the confusion and general chaos of the conversation.

It was like a death – her own – the end of the person she thought she was.

When she'd got over the shock, she'd gone over the subterfuge with a fine-tooth comb. It was fascinating, the attention to detail those around her had paid to the lie that was her fake family. All those aunties who used to say, *Oh, that's so like her dad!* The neighbours, who'd nodded wisely and said, *You get that from your mother.*

Initially, in her innocence, Lily had wondered if everybody

around her knew her real parents and had been referring to her actual inherited genetics.

Then she realised every adult she knew had been just as convincing about Santa Claus and the tooth fairy and God. Grown-ups excelled at charades for children, even when it came to untruths about their very existence.

It took Lily years to recover from the rage she felt at being conned.

But, after some fantasising about a famous, wealthy mother who'd been forced to give her up, followed by the deluded and depressing years imagining her adoptive parents had stolen her from an impoverished African village, Lily realised that her second mother and father were as good as it got.

Later, she learned the truth about her birth parents and it wasn't anywhere as fascinating as she'd imagined. Lily's father had been an immigrant doctor who'd slept with a local nurse then high-tailed it to a hospital in London when he realised a few dates and one night of passion now required a lifelong follow-up. The nurse had given Lily up when it dawned on her she'd be raising a mixed-race child alone in a judgemental rural village.

Lily had tried and failed to build a relationship there, but its lack of success wasn't as distressing as it could have been. She loved her mum and dad. They'd never seen her colour as a problem – in fact, they'd fostered the absolute opposite belief in her; that she was as special as it got.

The three of them were all they needed.

Which made it all the worse when her parents died, one after the other. Cancer in both cases. She had never been able to forgive her dad for smoking outside the church at her mum's funeral, when he'd just borne witness to his own wife's failed battle with lung cancer.

I need one of you, she said, her plea falling on not unsympathetic but ultimately deaf ears, as he used one smoke butt to light the next.

'It's my nerves, my little flower,' he'd said. 'I'll just have this one. For your mum.'

Lily had been eighteen when they buried her mother, twenty-four when her dad went. Lily was left feeling adrift, an orphan, without the anchor of family or place. It drove her to work even harder to create a version of herself that felt stable, secure. She was a human Build-A-Bear, stuffing herself with opinions and ideas and putting on the clothes that suited the filling.

She knew she'd done that, she wasn't stupid. She'd drawn herself and clung to the image.

Which made it all the more unsettling when David, a man she'd fallen in love with precisely because he was so very different to her, a man who seemed completely comfortable in his own skin, started to copy her. Like he too was looking for security, when she'd married him on the basis that that was one of his chief offerings.

Growing vegetables out the back – what on earth was that all about? Gardening had been *her* thing. When they got together she'd have laid money on David being the sort of man who dug up grass to lay all-weather decking, the sort of guy who saw the garden as somewhere to have a barbecue on a Saturday. She'd loved that. They were yin and yang but they'd make it work.

'Did you hear me, Lily? I said I think we should discuss . . .'

'I heard you!'

She didn't mean it to sound so abrupt and instantly regretted it.

David turned around, shocked. He put down the carrots and

dried his hands on a tea-towel. He crossed over to where she sat, flicking on the kettle switch as he did, one fluid movement.

'I'm sorry, beautiful. I should have asked how you were doing. I'm an idiot. I'm shocked about Olive but I know you saw her much more than me, o. I was just thinking of Wolf, you know. I'm sorry.'

He squeezed her shoulders and kissed the top of her head, the garlic from last night's dinner still smelly on his fingertips.

'I'll make you some peppermint tea,' he said. 'Remember, it's not your fault, my love. We live busy lives. It's not like the old days. You can't keep checking on your neighbours every five minutes. There's nothing to feel guilty about. This is the world now.'

'Maybe some real tea?' she said and David took a step back. If that was how he reacted to a request for a mildly caffeinated beverage, she could only imagine what he'd have said if he'd followed her upstairs last night and seen her slugging from the miniature bottle of vodka she'd hidden in her knickers drawer.

She still had no idea what had come over her. She wasn't the sort to hide in her room and throw bad things into her body to make herself feel better. She'd go for a run, or do pilates, or sit by the seafront and breathe.

But something had happened to Lily over the last couple of years. The greener David had become, the more she'd felt herself slipping over to the dark side.

She looked the same. She still dressed in flowing print dresses and wore her hair natural, not relaxed or weaved, though she did tuck it under a headscarf so as not to scare the horses at work (after her dreads of last summer, her Afro was huge). She went to school, she smiled and cooked and helped the children with their artwork and shopped ethically and was . . . decent.

There was no explanation for stealing the vodka from the hotel minibar at last Christmas's work party, or for the two pairs of ripped jeans she'd bought in Topshop, or for the covert trips to TGI's for plates of greasy bad stuff, or the . . . Well.

Best not to go there.

'Real tea coming up,' David said, in full St John Ambulance mode, his other latest fad. 'And maybe even a sneaky sugar, o? For the shock.'

Lily took a deep breath.

Shock? She wasn't shocked *at all* that Olive Collins was dead.

Something was very wrong with Lily Solanke.

OLIVE

No. 4

The Solankes moved into number two next.

The city slicker and the school teacher, the twins following a few years later. Gorgeous little babies, then darling toddlers – well, they grew into their own people. And Wolf was my favourite.

It wasn't his fault he was caught in the middle. Not his fault at all.

When Lily had the twins, we were all thrilled. Nobody more so than their father, who seemed to have been planning those children for quite some time. He'd told me once that they'd lived in an apartment in the city before they moved to the Vale. It wouldn't have been safe for children, David said. Not with an eighth-floor balcony.

Bear in mind, this was a few years before Lily conceived.

He did add – to clarify the move wasn't just about future children – that he knew Lily wasn't happy with urban life. She was a free soul, he said. She needed gardens and trees and wide open spaces.

I got the distinct impression Lily had come home one day to find all their possessions in a moving van and David holding a set of keys crying *Surprise!*

They didn't have a house party to get to know the neighbours, but I called over anyway with a welcome basket and they were perfectly friendly.

Friendly, but distant.

I kept trying, though.

And I endeavoured not to make judgements. Lily wasn't exactly my type of woman – that New Age hippie thing, floaty dresses and hand-woven scarves, yoga and quinoa – that whole lifestyle has never appealed to me. But she was educated and smart and seemed like a good person.

Too good.

I guessed that there was more to Lily, funnily enough, by her kids. Let's be honest, nobody names a child after themselves unless there's real vanity there. Lily May, forever a tiny derivative of her mother, denied an identity of her own. A daughter and a twin, not a whole part at all.

I wasn't as quick figuring out David. He was very jovial, very pleasant. He'd sometimes call over with vegetarian recipes and baskets of vegetables he'd grown in his garden and he'd chat away.

It was unusual, he informed me, for a Nigerian man to choose to not eat meat.

'When I go home, my brothers laugh at me,' he said. 'And yet, much of our national cuisine is based on beans and vegetables and rice. I might retire there one day and open a thriving vegetarian eatery for returnees. Would you miss me, Olive, o?'

'I'd miss the free veg,' I'd say and he would fill my porch with a barrel laugh.

And he was a very handsome man, not to mention a good father. I'd often see him on a Saturday taking the children off towards town for a walk on the strand, or to see a movie, tall and strong, wearing his white linen shirt and beige chinos. He smelled of incense and kept his dark hair tight. An Idris Elba lookalike, a couple of doors down.

I couldn't believe it when I found out the man worked for a bloody hedge fund.

A hedge fund.

His job was to bet against people about to get screwed and earn money off their misery. Every time I looked at him after that I pictured Michael Douglas in *Wall Street* spouting his *Greed is Good* quote.

When I first met the Solankes, I really did think that they were people I had to impress. I wanted them to know that I understood culture and international affairs and that I wasn't some middle-aged country bumpkin.

But I realised after a while that not only were they a mass of contradictions, they were also quite boring. When you're partial to a nice glass of Merlot and don't mind eating a tray of burger and chips on your lap while watching the soaps, it gets tiresome, somebody relentlessly pointing out how healthy and clean-living they are.

I don't think I'd have had much to do with them except for their one winning, endearing point.

Wolf.

HOLLY & ALISON

No. 3

Holly wished she could wrap her mother up in cotton wool.

She knew it was the wrong way round. That it should be her mother who worried about her all the time.

But it wasn't that way. And Holly was used to it.

'Mam, stop. Sit down. I'll do it.'

Alison was straightening the cushions in the sitting room like a woman possessed. Her greatest skill was her ability to present things nicely. Make everything look beautiful. One misshapen corner, and the two detectives about to call would arrest her for sure.

Holly guided her mother to the comfortable armchair and plonked her down in it.

'Every time I think of her rotting in there . . .' Alison's face was blank, shocked. 'I can't believe it's real. Do you think she tried calling out at all? Oh, God. And now the police are coming.'

Alison's eyes began to water.

'Mam, stop!' Holly said. 'Your mascara is running.'

Alison blinked and looked at Holly like she was seeing her for the first time.

'I don't think my mascara . . .'

'Those two detectives will be here any second. You need to pull yourself together. Look,' Holly lowered her voice. 'She could have been yelling her head off in there and we wouldn't have heard her. But it wouldn't matter if we had. She was an awful woman. You should be glad she's dead.'

'Holly! You can't say things like that. When somebody dies . . .'

'They're still the same person. Oh, Mam, don't look at me like that. I'll stick the kettle on, okay?'

By the time Holly got to the kitchen, the detectives were knocking on the front door. She sighed and flung a handful of teabags in a pot, put a few cups on a tray, and fetched a half-pint of milk from the fridge.

'There was no need,' the man detective said, when Holly brought in the tray. 'But thank you. Holly, isn't it? Your mum said you've just finished up for the summer holidays. You'll certainly have something to tell everybody when you go back to school in September. It's your final exams next year, isn't it?'

Holly flashed her mother a look, then nodded mutely at the detective.

School? Jesus, she couldn't leave her mother alone for five seconds.

Holly tried to read him. Older men were usually easy. Depending on what she guessed they liked, she either played it mature and sensible, or tugged on her hair like an innocent little school kid. She instinctively knew neither approach would work with this one. He looked like the sort who could see through anybody. He looked like the sort who *suspected* everybody.

'So, you were saying, you run D-Style?' The woman detective had barely glanced at Holly, just a mere up and down to acknowledge her presence.

Alison nodded.

'I own it. I opened my first store in 2015. I've three now. I run the one near the marina. You should pop in, I'll fix you up with something nice.'

Holly's jaw clenched. Why did her mother always say that? It was like she had some form of Tourette's except, instead of swearing, she was habitually generous.

Luckily for the business, most people were too polite to take her up on it.

Most people.

'Oh, thank you,' the detective answered, looking flustered. 'We can't avail of gifts from the public, I'm afraid. My mum shops there sometimes. It's older women's clothing, isn't it?'

'Em, not really,' Alison said, too politely. Holly's mother designed clothes so classy they looked good on women of any age.

'Have you had a chance to look back through your diary?' the man asked. Frank, was that his name? And his surname, was it a country? Holly tried to remember. She was terrible with names.

Faces she could pick out anywhere. Thankfully.

Alison shook her head.

'Sorry,' he said. 'Of course you haven't. We came straight over. Would you like to do a quick check?'

'What date was it again?'

'3rd of March.'

Alison picked up her phone and scrolled through her calendar.

'I flew to London that night. Oh.' She placed her hand on her chest. 'I'm so relieved. I had an awful feeling that Olive might have been shouting for help and I didn't hear. I could never have forgiven myself if . . . actually, what did happen to her, Detective Brazil? Did you . . . did you find anything suspicious in her house?'

'Like I said,' Frank answered, 'we can't disclose any details just yet. What time did you fly out that evening?'

'Um, seven-ish? I'd have got to the airport about five, I guess. No, wait, I remember. I went straight from the shop in Wicklow town that day and got caught in traffic. I made it there just before six and was a bit panicky. But I'd checked in online, so I went straight to the gate and it was fine in the end.'

'I see. And you were here during the day, were you?'

'Well, up until I popped into the shop at about twelve, yes. As normal. But why . . .?'

'You didn't notice anything off next door? You didn't see anybody calling in or out?'

'No. The Vale is always so quiet, you really do notice anybody or anything out of the ordinary. The postman has the gate code, and the emergency services, the electricity providers, companies like that. We tend to see the same service men come in and out. Nobody ever came to visit Olive. If somebody had called in – if there was a strange car parked outside her house – I definitely would remember. If I'd seen it, that is.'

'And you, Holly?' Frank turned to her. 'Were you here on your own when your mam was away, or was your dad here? Excuse me,' he looked back at her mother. 'Is Dad on the scene?'

Alison shook her head.

'I was on my own,' Holly said.

'And no brothers or sisters?'

'It was just one night,' Alison jumped in. She was twisting her hands nervously and Holly noticed a sweaty sheen breaking out on her mother's forehead. She knew exactly what was going through Alison's mind – can they arrest me for leaving a seventeen-year-old home alone overnight? Holly was sure they couldn't but she felt a little prickle of fear, too. They should have talked about this stuff. Not plumped the cushions and made tea.

'I was back the next evening,' her mother continued. 'Normally Holly would come with me but she wasn't feeling well. As soon as I landed, I rang her and then again early the next morning, didn't I?'

Holly nodded.

'Mam FaceTimed me, to make sure I wasn't having a party.' She smiled. Normal. Everything must seem normal.

'What was wrong with you?' the woman detective asked.

'Migraine.'

'And you didn't bring a friend over just to keep you company? When I was a teenager, if my mum had left me home alone for a night . . .'

'With a migraine?' Holly asked, eyebrows raised. 'I could barely answer the phone that evening, but I knew Mam would fly home if I didn't.'

'So, you'd have had a party if you'd been well?' Frank smiled.

'No,' Holly said. 'I'd have been with my mother. London? Shopping?'

'Of course. Excuse my ignorance. And did you hear or see anything strange that day, when you were here alone?'

'Yeah. My ears were buzzing and there were lots of tiny white dots floating in front of my eyes.'

Frank looked to Alison, who stared at Holly, beseeching. Don't be a smart-ass, her mother's eyes pleaded. Let them leave here and forget about us.

'Sorry,' Holly said. 'I don't mean to be facetious. It's just, I spent the whole day in bed and didn't get up until nearly midnight, when I made some toast and then went back to my room to watch TV. I'd the curtains closed and, to be honest, our house is so big I can barely hear what Mam is doing if I'm upstairs, let alone anything from next door.'

Frank nodded.

'Facetious. You're a clever kid, Holly. What did you think of your neighbour, Olive? How did people in the Vale feel about her in general?'

Be kind, be kind, be kind, Holly's gut told her.

But what was the point of that? The cops weren't idiots. Not everybody who died was liked. They knew that.

'How did I feel about her? She was a total cunt.'

Holly instantly regretted dropping the c-bomb. The woman spat a mouthful of tea back in her cup and Frank's eyes grew so large the rest of his features nearly dropped off his face.

It took a couple of seconds for her mother to lift her jaw from the floor.

'Holly! What's got into you? I'm so sorry, Detectives, I . . .'

The detective raised his hand to quiet Alison.

'It's okay, Ms Daly. It's refreshing to hear some brutal honesty. But perhaps you'd expand a little, Holly. What was it about your neighbour that made her so . . . unpleasant, in your eyes?'

'Oh, she wasn't unpleasant, not really,' Alison interrupted. 'She just didn't think sometimes. I don't . . .'

'Ms Daly, please, let Holly tell us.'

'Oh. Sorry.'

Holly shrugged.

'How long have you got?'

FRANK

'That made no sense,' Emma said.

Frank barely heard her. He was two steps ahead of her as usual, his long legs covering in one stride what she could only manage in two.

'I suggest we do the remainder from the start, one to seven,' he said, pointing at the house nearest the entrance to the Vale. It was another monstrosity, probably seven bedrooms at least. It seemed to be the recurring theme of this development. With the exception of the dead woman's cottage, the rest of the houses were all pointlessly oversized.

Frank lived in a three-bed terraced house. He and his wife, both from proper working-class families where the kids outnumbered the adults by roughly four to one, had thought that was huge when they bought it. All that space for two people!

He and Mona were going to have two kids, a bedroom each, and the four of them would live happily ever after.

Unfortunately, there were no kids.

'I mean, it happens all the time. But to blackmail somebody, you

have to have something to blackmail with.' Emma was still bab-
bling on.

'What?' Frank stopped and turned to her.

'What Holly Daly said. How could Olive Collins have been
blackmailing her mother if her mother has nothing to hide? Is the
mother telling the truth? Did Holly pick it up wrong? You heard
Alison. We'd only come in the door and she was offering me something out of her shop. She probably just said the same to Olive
Collins and Olive took her up on it. I mean, who in their right
mind would blackmail somebody for free clothes?'

'You reckon Holly picked it up wrong because she's a kid? I
would have thought, given you're not that much older yourself,
you'd have had natural sympathies. Shouldn't it be me who thinks
Holly is a silly little girl?'

Emma frowned.

'I don't think she's silly and I'm not dismissing her because she's a
child . . .'

'But you are believing her mother when she says she has nothing
to hide. That's nonsense. If Olive Collins was blackmailing her,
Alison Daly is hardly likely to tell us why. She'll be thanking her
lucky stars that Olive is gone and her secret is safe. And, though it
pains me to say it, now we have a suspect and motive for somebody
wanting Olive dead.'

'But Alison Daly went to London on the night we believe Olive
died.'

'Even if Alison is telling the truth, she left that evening. She
could have messed with Olive's boiler earlier that day. Which – ah
fuck – would also explain the method of killing. Whoever did it
wouldn't have to alibi themselves for any specific time.'

'Statistically, most killers are . . .'

Frank snorted, cutting Emma off.

'Save me from the numbers. I know, most killers are men. And every time a woman murders somebody, it makes it easier for her to get away with it because the statistics magicians are jumping up and down saying, *No, look over there, at the man, not the woman holding the knife dripping with blood.* It wasn't a violent attack, Emma, which means it's far more likely a female may have done it.'

'Right, well, tell me this,' Emma snapped. 'Did Alison Daly strike you as a cold-blooded murderer? Because I'll tell you what she struck me as – a mild-mannered woman who's absolutely devastated her neighbour has been dead next door these last three months.'

'Not devastated enough to go in and check on her, though, as you were quick to point out earlier. These houses might be detached, but they're not surrounded by fucking moats. And, pardon my ignorance, Emma, but if Olive was deliberately whacked and we encounter the person who did it, are you expecting them to act *guilty*? You think somebody capable of leaving the woman rotting for three months has a conscience?'

'Jesus, do you really think one of her neighbours would have killed her and just left her sitting there?' she said. 'That's not just lacking in conscience. That's psychopathic.'

'*If* she was killed, it may well have been by somebody outside of here, somebody from her past, say. But, we've only talked to one set of neighbours and already we've been told that the woman had no family and didn't seem to have visitors, either. So, if you lived next to somebody like that and suddenly there was a car outside her house or you saw somebody call in or leave, wouldn't you remember that? Rest assured, Emma, if somebody outside of this little conclave came in to murder the owner of number four, someone will have noticed.'

Emma frowned.

'Right,' Frank said, taking the point as won. 'Are we calling in to number one or what?'

Emma pouted and marched ahead of him.

He caught up in seconds.

'And you missed the most important thing,' he said.

'Oh, there's more?'

'Yeah, there's more. Whether Holly Daly made sense isn't important. What she and her mother said isn't important. It's what they didn't say that matters. They're hiding something. What, I don't know, but five minutes in their company was enough to know it's something very, very big.'

Emma kept her eyes straight ahead. She hated when he was right.

OLIVE

No. 4

The Dalys only moved into number three a couple of years ago. Before that, a lovely Iranian man lived there with his wife and son. The father was a doctor, a surgeon, I think. I didn't see much of the wife. She kept to herself but when she did leave the house, she was always dressed beautifully. Long, glossy, coiffed hair, tanned skin, real jewels, designer clothes. A little aloof, but boy, was I jealous.

Their son was an odd one. I sometimes found him watching me, disdain all over his face. Probably because I was a woman, and independent and, well, white. Put it this way – I always worried that his hobbies might include listening to rap music, skate-boarding and training to be a jihadi. But still, if I spoke to him, he always answered very politely. Lovely manners.

When the Dalys came, I was really happy to see another woman on the Vale. I got on well with Amelia Miller in number six, but I hadn't gelled with Lily or Chrissy and, to be honest, I was disappointed at how much everybody kept to themselves. Very little effort was made to interact. People seemed to have different ideas of what constituted a neighbourhood and the fact we were all behind a gate together didn't seem to matter.

Alison and Holly were quiet to begin with, but I suggested a street party shortly after they arrived to help them mix and, later that day, Alison called over to say thanks.

We opened a bottle of wine and sat in the front garden, the evening sun still warm, the smell of late blooms in our noses. I told her how long I had lived there and how different it had been.

'You must have been terribly lonely,' she said.

'I guess I was,' I admitted. 'Not that I realised straight away. I was working full-time – I only do two days a week now and I'm retiring next year. But back then, with the commute home from the capital and seeing my parents each evening, I got in late most nights and that was five days a week. I was so happy to be home, I didn't notice I was home alone, do you know what I mean? When I learned other houses were being built I felt . . . I don't know. I was looking forward to seeing people outside of work. Having neighbours over for a drink every now and again.'

We clinked our glasses, smiled.

'Yes,' she said. 'It's easy to slip into a routine and not realise you're unhappy.'

'I'm so glad you're here,' I said. 'The family before you – they were lovely, but they kept to themselves. The wife was like a supermodel. Very beautiful, but distant. A bit like Lily.'

'I never met her,' Alison said. 'The wife, I mean. I did see the husband at the solicitors when we signed.'

'Yes, well, they were Iranian. Very patriarchal society, I think he did all the business. Nice man but . . . At least she wasn't in a burka. It would have been a shame to hide that gorgeous hair.'

'Oh, Olive, I'm not sure they have to wear burkas in Iran.'

'I'm joking,' I said. 'Sort of.'

She tutted at me, then we sat and drank in contented silence for a while.

'Where were you living before?' I asked.

Alison pursed her lips and stared out at the street. The night light had just popped on outside my garden and we watched the moths fluttering, dangerously dive-bombing the glass.

'Just outside the city centre,' she said.

I found it a little odd she wasn't more specific. I worked in the capital; it wasn't like I didn't know the geography.

'And Holly's dad? Sorry, tell me if I'm being intrusive.'

Alison smiled tightly and shook her head.

'No, of course not. You're just making conversation. I, em, I will tell you, when we've more time. I think I should get back to Holly. She won't like being in the house alone now it's getting dark.'

'But she can see you from the window. Have another glass, go on. I enjoy your company.'

'No, really, I mustn't. You're so very kind, though. Can we say we'll do this again soon?'

I nodded, eagerly.

And we did, and the next time, she talked a little more.

There was something about Alison and Holly that made me feel very protective. Like they needed somebody to put their arms around them and keep them safe.

It's astonishing how easy it is to pull the wool over somebody's eyes. Even mine, and I'd always considered myself a good judge of character.

FRANK

Number one, the house with who knew how many bedrooms, was home to a single man. Frank gave George Richmond a brief hand-shake and watched, amused, as Emma stuttered over her introduction. He was a good-looking guy, this George chap.

He invited the detectives in and offered them seats but didn't suggest refreshments. Frank looked around the lounge. It was a typical bachelor pad. Black leather couches, a forty-inch smart HD Sony hooked up to an Xbox, the latest Apple Mac laptop sitting on a table in the corner. Beside, oddly, a packet of baby wipes.

A clean freak, Frank guessed. Unless he'd a kid who visited on the weekend or something. No children lived here full time. It was far too ordered, too sanitised.

'Nice place you have,' he said. 'You must have one of those jobs where they actually believe in rewarding their employees. Don't ever join the police, George.'

The younger man smiled, but it was more of a grimace. He was nervous, but Frank didn't mind that. With the presence of detectives in his living room, suddenly George Richmond was remembering that speeding fine he'd never paid, the prostitute he'd been with in Prague, the tax return he'd fiddled. Everybody was the same.

'I'm not actually working at the moment,' he said. 'Not properly, I mean. I was in graphic design but I just do a little freelance layout work now.'

'Lose your job?'

George shrugged.

'Sort of. I'd a little disagreement with my employers. Anyway, my father owns this house so I'm luckier than most.'

'Oh.' Frank could see the light die in Emma's eyes. Fired, and living on daddy's dollar. No matter how handsome George was, it didn't quite compensate for being a thirty-five-year-old loser. 'Dad has a few bob, does he?'

'You could say that. He's Stu Richmond.'

Frank shook his head. He'd never heard of him but he must be somebody because George looked embarrassed and like he was waiting for . . .

'No way!' Emma said. 'You're Stu Richmond's son?'

'Yeah.'

'Wow. That's . . .' She looked at Frank, who just held out his palms to indicate they'd lost him at hello.

'He's like Ireland's Simon Cowell?' she said, her voice going up at the end in amazement. 'He managed Sequence and Missy B and W-Squad?'

'Any Beatles? Fleetwood? Rolling Stones?'

George smiled while Emma tutted, exasperated.

'Yeah,' he said. 'More my thing, too. My dad is all pop, though. Where the money is. He scouts for major labels now.'

'Right. Brilliant. Anyhow, what we really want to talk to you about is your neighbour, Olive, not Top of the Pops.' Frank had to move the conversation on. Emma looked on the verge of going home for her back catalogue of *Billboard* magazines to get them signed. 'Did you know your neighbour well?'

'Not very. I like to keep to myself. It's the only way when you live in a cut-off community like this. Smile, make small talk, but keep your hedges high and your door closed. We used to make an effort – parties on the road, New Year's Eve get-togethers, that sort of thing – but it sort of died a death. Olive probably tried more than most, God love her. She called over here once looking for something and asked would I take a key for her house in case she ever got locked out. I thought it was a bit unnecessary. Around here – she could have just left it under the mat. But she wanted us all to be those kind of neighbours, if you know what I mean.'

'So, you have a key to her house?' Frank said, his ears pricking. 'Have you ever been in there?'

George blinked.

'No, never. And I can't imagine I'm the only one on the block who has one. She had a key to mine as well. I was wondering, actually, if I could get it back? Now she's dead?'

'I'm sure that can be arranged, later. But tell me a bit more about this key you have.'

George opened his mouth to speak, then closed it again. His cheeks flushed red.

'Ah,' he said. 'I see. I swear, I've never touched that key. I've never been in her house, not even once. It's hanging in my hall; you passed it on the way in. Eh, what, exactly, do you think happened to her?'

Frank shifted on the armchair, the leather squeaking as he moved. The afternoon was getting warmer as it progressed. So were Olive's neighbours.

'Did you have any unusual interactions with Ms Collins? Not all of the residents seemed to find her . . . well, she may have had a fractious relationship with at least one household on the Vale.'

'The Dalys?' George asked.

'You know about it?'

'No. But it's the only house you've been in.'

Frank cocked his head. George had him there.

'I can't go into details,' Frank said.

'I get that,' George nodded. 'It's just, with all these questions, and your going around the Vale – it seems like you might be worried something bad happened to her.'

Frank pursed his lips.

George waited, then gave up.

'I got on fine with her. I can't speak for my neighbours, but I never had a run-in with her.'

'And on the 3rd of March, you were . . .?'

'Here. I don't do much these days, just work from home. I mean, I might have popped out to the shop or something, but I wasn't away or at day-long meetings or anything. And I didn't see any-thing strange, if that's your next question.'

'Right,' Frank said. He'd nothing else to ask. But he didn't want to leave. He wanted to keep sitting there with George Richmond. See if he'd add anything more.

Frank hated it when his interest was piqued.

CHRISSY & MATT

No. 5

When Chrissy and Matt Hennessy had moved into number five, just under twelve years ago, one of the first things Chrissy had done, heavily pregnant, was throw a party for her new neighbours.

She'd read all the manuals. It took a village to raise a child and Chrissy didn't have enough people locally to fill a three-man tent, let alone make up a community. Matt worked ridiculous hours. Chrissy's family, consisting of her dad and two brothers, were as useful as chocolate teapots when it came to babies. And her friends weren't the sort to travel far outside the inner-city flats where they'd all grown up together and most of them still lived.

She'd gathered when she and Matt moved in that there were some women living in Withered Vale. Nobody with any small children, which worried her a little. But the black family in number two were young enough and the husband, David, had mentioned they were trying for a baby.

Mrs Kazemi, the Middle Eastern-looking woman in number three, had a teenager, so at least she'd been there and knew what it was like. Olive Collins next door was child-free and older but seemed very friendly – she'd spoken to them at length when they'd viewed the house. And Amelia Miller on the other side was equally child-free and older but also seemed nice.

Perhaps, lacking kids of their own, the new neighbours would be perfect target babysitters. Chrissy was determined to cultivate all of them as friends and insidiously inveigle them into helping her rear her child. She was bloody terrified she'd screw it all up if she was left to do it on her own. Let's face it – her own runaway mother hadn't exactly been a role model.

Operating around Matt's put-upon sighs and groans about finances, Chrissy went online at Tesco's (her bump was so large, if she leaned into an actual trolley, she was likely to tip over) and ordered their entire party range. Chrissy's cooking skills extended to frozen waffles and curry-flavoured instant noodles, but she reckoned even she could lay out a platter of mini-muffins and make it look good. And she instinctively knew this party had to be posh. If she was going to fit in, a tray of cider and packets of Pringles weren't going to do it. So she also ordered a box of champagne (Matt nearly had a meltdown) in addition to the cases of beer. Voilà. An instant party from the back of a delivery van.

She thought the house looked tremendous by the time the professional cleaners had been in and out and she'd decorated. It was close to Hallowe'en and Chrissy had set lights in pumpkin heads and strung up some festive lanterns. Plastic spiders were dotted around the plates of food; she'd even got her hands on some cotton webbing.

Chrissy was thrilled and Matt was impressed at her efforts, despite the cost.

'How lucky am I?' he said, embracing her from behind, his hands protectively wrapped around her stomach. 'I have a wife who is not only an amazing host but also a beautiful, sexy, fertile goddess.'

Chrissy had laughed.

'I just farted when you squeezed my tummy there, Matt. Sexy might be stretching it. And if the baby shifts on my bladder again, I'm going to wee on your shoe.'

'Who says I wouldn't find a bit of Chrissy wee sexy?'

They were like that, then. So in love.

It should have been a wonderful party. The neighbours seemed to be up for it.

Olive Collins arrived early with two bottles of wine and cooed enthusiastically about how much work Chrissy had put in.

Chrissy was a vodka-tonic sort of girl, but she had poured herself a single glass of champagne to relax into the evening. She'd spent €600 on six bottles; it didn't seem like the crime of the century to have a little taste.

Even still, she confided in Olive that she wasn't sure what people might think if they saw a pregnant woman drinking so she'd planned to have just the one glass prior to everybody arriving.

'Don't be so silly,' Olive scoffed. 'It's your party. And it's 2005, for goodness' sake. Everybody knows you can have a glass or two without harming the baby. Honestly, when my mother was pregnant she had a glass of port every night. Though, that might explain my wonky eye.'

'You don't have a wonky . . . Oh!' Chrissy laughed.

She decided to take Olive up on her advice. Matt was equally blasé about her having the odd drink. All Matt cared about was Chrissy's happiness.

When the other guests arrived, she poured her second glass

and joined them in a toast. Then she did her utmost to ensure everybody enjoyed themselves, moving from small group to group, offering the finest of Tesco's freezers and refilling glasses.

Despite her best intentions, and even with Matt pulling along, there was an odd atmosphere at the gathering. Nobody seemed to really connect. Where Chrissy had grown up, parties like this usually ended up with everybody sitting around the living room enjoying a sing-song, or, on alternate nights, the police being called after somebody had thrown a punch and broken a window.

Chrissy's first proper grown-up party never took off. The Kazemis from number three were kind but kept to themselves. Stu Richmond had sent his apologies and a hamper of fruit (who sent fruit to a party?). Lily and David had seemed put out that most of the party food was meat-based – but Chrissy hadn't known they were vegetarians and, Jesus, there was cheese and crisps. Not to mention fruit. The Millers spent the bulk of the night talking to each other, or to Olive, and not really mingling. Olive herself was at pains to be sociable and kept offering to help. Only Ron from number seven was truly lovely, funny and flirty.

As the night wore on, Chrissy began to get a bad feeling that she hadn't landed in a neighbourhood that was going to be too involved in the upbringing of her baby. In fact, she'd started to wonder if any of them would even send a card when the child was born, let alone turn up with casseroles and offers to do the washing while she slept (the manuals had promised this would happen and insisted the new mother avail of *any and all offers of help!* which Chrissy had absolutely no problem with).

Chrissy found herself pouring a final half-glass of champers – she'd been eating like a horse and it was hours since her last – and assessing what she'd garnered from the party.

Olive. That was her best hope of a new, helpful friend.

With that in mind, Chrissy made a beeline for the little group containing Olive, David and Lily Solanke.

They didn't hear her approach so she got the full benefit of the hushed conversation.

'Oh, I suppose it's no big deal to have a few drinks when you're expecting. And it's not like I can judge, I've never been pregnant. But it does look a bit off, I do agree.'

This was Olive.

'I know, I know, we're being all judgemental – but I'm surprised her husband hasn't said something. He seems like a good, straight-forward man. I'm not saying I'd mind if you'd a rare glass, Lily, if we were expecting – you're your own woman after all – but three or four seems excessive.'

This was David.

'Well, I don't drink at all and I certainly wouldn't if I was preg-nant. But she seems fine. The real concern I'd have about this house and a child coming into it is the lack of books. Who gets a TV that size and doesn't build a single bookshelf? I don't think I've ever seen a house without one. I can't even imagine not reading to a child.'

Lily had added her two cents.

Chrissy turned on her heel, her face burning.

Ron Ryan had seen her leaving, her face red, tears in her eyes, and asked if she was okay.

'Hormones,' she squeaked and fled upstairs, mortified.

The old, non-pregnant Chrissy would most likely have marched over to the little group and given them a right talking-to for being so bitchy. At her own party in her own home, no less. Chrissy wasn't a shrinking violet and she'd grown up in an area that taught her how important – how necessary – it was to be tough.

But pregnant Chrissy felt vulnerable and lonely and humiliated.

When she broke it down in the days afterwards (and she thought about it a lot) she decided that Olive was trying to impress the Solankes who, if Chrissy was honest, seemed really up themselves. She just couldn't believe that anybody would be so two-faced as to encourage her to drink and then say it looked bad. Chrissy herself had been in situations where she'd found herself nodding along to a group's agreed wisdom, even though she didn't quite believe it. Some people had that effect on you.

But it still meant her neighbour couldn't be trusted and loyalty was important to Chrissy.

When Matt came to bed the night of the party, he asked her why she'd disappeared without saying goodnight to everybody.

'I wasn't really enjoying myself,' she said. 'It was a bad idea. I'm not sure I like our neighbours and I'm tired and hormonal and just . . . just not myself.'

'Well, the whole point of moving here was to have some privacy,' Matt said. 'You don't need to talk to anybody if you don't want to.'

Then he rolled over and fell asleep.

Chrissy listened to his snoring, her head whirring. She hadn't wanted privacy. She hadn't wanted to shut herself off from her neighbours.

But it looked like she might have no choice.

EMMA

The Solankes' house could have been lifted from a suburb in Sydney and transported to Ireland. It belonged beside the sea, not in the middle of a country valley. It was fine for the summer but in the winter? Too much glass and not enough radiators.

That's what Emma thought as she sat in Lily and David's bright, spacious kitchen. The whole back wall seemed to be open, the garden an extension of the room. Sun splashed onto the distressed wood table and teak floors. The windowsill over the sink was chock-a-block with plants and herbs in multicoloured pots. Wind chimes hung from the ceiling at the open patio doors and every so often jingled in the gentle breeze.

Emma looked over at Frank and gave her head a quick shake. He pursed his lips, frowned.

Emma had just come in. She'd been on the phone, checking in with the IT guys back at the station. A cursory preliminary trawl had thrown up nothing on Olive Collins to indicate anybody had cause to harm her. No run-ins with former work colleagues, no family to speak of (which they'd already established), no public order offences, no . . . anything. Olive Collins was clean as a whistle and even her social media accounts – which, luckily, she'd left logged in – didn't have much interaction with anybody outside of her neighbours and some old friends who seemed to mainly live abroad.

If the woman had secrets, they were well kept. If they were looking for suspects in her murder, perhaps it was somebody closer to home.

David had served Earl Grey tea on a table decorated with pots of jasmine, along with a plate of what he proudly declared were his home-made, gluten-free, dairy-free brownies.

Taste-free too, Emma thought, biting into one and nearly choking on the cardboard-like texture, realising too late it would require a whole lot of liquid to swallow it down.

Frank was already red-faced, still getting his head around the perfumed mouthful of liquid he'd just supped.

Of the two of their hosts, Lily Solanke looked like she should be the one making vegan brownies and knocking back herbal tea. She had the smooth skin and healthy glow of a woman who rarely let an additive pass her lips. Emma could imagine Lily getting up at 6 a.m. each day to run forty-seven miles as the sun rose.

But today she was sitting in front of them, ramrod straight and uncomfortable, like somebody had shoved a broomstick up her back.

It was three o'clock and Emma and Frank had skipped lunch in their eagerness to get around the neighbours'. They'd phoned HQ and their boss had told them not to worry about coming in for a case meeting until they were sure they had an actual case. She was relaxed like that, happy to let Frank use his investigative discretion and, therein, keep resources to a minimum.

One more house after this, they'd promised themselves, then

they'd call it a day and head home. A body could only sustain itself on fragrant tea and fake cake for so long.

'So, you didn't notice anything unusual at all over at the cottage in the lead-up to your neighbour's absence?' Emma trotted out the line, while discreetly placing the rest of the brownie on the side of her saucer.

'Nothing at all,' David said. 'Of course, I'm a little oblivious like that, truth be told. I work in the city all week and on the weekend I'm mostly doing things with the children. The only neighbour I see a lot of during the week is Matt Hennessy from across the way. We both work in the city centre, so occasionally we car-share. Though not as often as I'd like. I think everybody commuting should do it to cut back on air pollution. But Matt gets up too early, even for me. It's amazing. The guy is the hardest-working account-ant I know. If we ever move back to Nigeria, I'm definitely hiring that man as my general manager. Anyhow, sometimes I just drive to the station and go in on the train instead. I'm in the International Financial Services Centre.'

'What do you work at?' Emma asked. She was a bit surprised that this seeming latter-day hippie worked in the IFSC. Unless he was some sort of designer or something. That would make sense, she supposed. An artist, but in the modern computer sense.

'Oh, it's boring. I just work with numbers.'

The detectives waited.

'He's a hedge-fund manager,' Lily said. David smiled rigidly.

Knock me down with a feather, Emma thought. Did Mr Solanke take off his beaded necklace when he went to work, or just wear it under his suit shirt? Or was he one of these über-modern capitalists, channelling the whole Mark Zuckerberg vibe? Look at me, I might

77

be worth millions and impoverish nations, but I wear Nike into work! I'm a hip finance vulture!

'Eh. Right. Wow, that's . . . interesting. And you, Lily? What do you do?'

'I'm a primary school teacher.'

'Of course,' Emma said, because that made absolute sense. The household wasn't completely on its axis.

'Did you see more of your neighbour, then, than your husband?' Frank asked. 'You'd have shorter days, I'm guessing.'

'Yes. I definitely saw more of her.'

'But not in the last few months?'

Lily shook her head, unable to meet their eyes.

'It's been an awful shock,' David said, taking his wife's hand, before turning back to Emma and Frank.

'I suppose I thought Olive had gone off on holiday or something,' Lily offered, realising she should justify herself. 'Ed and Amelia – they live across the road – go off on these month-long cruises all the time. And Olive told me once that she took early retirement from the health board when the government were paying those huge tax-free lump sums, so she had money.'

'And did she really never have people around?' Frank asked. 'Other than her neighbours, I mean?'

Lily and David looked at each other, and shrugged.

'She didn't actually seem to have anybody in her life,' David said. 'I don't think she's had a visitor since we moved here.'

'Were you friendly with her?' Emma asked.

'We weren't, like, living in each other's pockets,' Lily said. She was squirming under the gaze of the detectives. 'I can't pretend otherwise. Clearly that's the case, or at some point over the last three months I'd have called over there.'

'I got on very well with her,' David said, a little defensively. 'I didn't see her that much, but I always exchanged pleasantries with her when I did.'

Lily frowned, and laughed a little, a sound of surprise.

'David, you shared all of about an hour's conversation with her over the past ten years.'

There was a flash of something dark on David's face. Barely there, but Emma caught it, and his wife did too, by the looks of it. She opened her mouth, looked taken aback. Whatever it was, it was gone as soon as it had appeared. It seemed David was good at keeping his emotions in check.

There's the hedge-fund manager, Emma said to herself.

'So you weren't bosom buddies,' Frank said. 'Fair enough. Did it go beyond that? Did you ever have a falling-out with Olive Collins? Mrs Solanke?'

'I . . .'

It looked for a moment like Lily wasn't planning to answer truthfully. Just a moment.

Then she nodded, ever so slightly.

'I wouldn't call it a falling-out as such, just a disagreement.'

'It was nothing,' David interrupted.

'Indulge us,' Frank said.

Lily looked uncertainly at her husband, then back to Frank.

'She . . . eh . . . she gave Wolf meat.'

Both Emma and Frank frowned, but David smiled, rolled his eyes dismissively — *nothing to see here.*

'I know,' Lily said, her colour heightening. 'It sounds silly. But it wasn't the first time, either. We're vegetarians, see.'

'Back up a minute,' Emma said. 'Wolf – who's he? Your dog?'

Lily and David glared at Emma, horrified.

'He's our *son*,' David said.

'Oh.' Emma felt heat creeping up her neck and around her ears. 'I'm sorry, I just . . .' There was no completing that sentence.

'And then what happened?' Frank asked, moving it on. 'Did you think she'd done this – given Wolf meat – just to piss you off or something? Because presumably, if it was just a one-off misunderstanding, you'd have mentioned it to her, she'd have stopped and everybody would have gone about their lives, no hard feelings.'

'Well . . .' Lily said. 'I don't think her motives were innocent.'

'Oh, Lily, she didn't do it to irritate us,' her husband said. 'We were annoyed by it, but that doesn't mean that was her rationale. Olive Collins was a little lonely. Wolf liked her and she enjoyed his company. He used to call over there a lot. We let him. And she let him eat there. Ultimately, Wolf needs to take a little personal responsibility here.'

'David, he's eight!'

'Mr and Mrs Solanke,' Frank interrupted, to Emma's relief. 'If we can just stay with the story. What happened? Did you have words?'

'It really does seem so silly now . . .' Lily said.

'Not that silly. You thought she was deliberately using your child. I know that would make *me* very angry – most people, in fact. So what did you do about it?'

Lily baulked. Emma could see her mentally backtracking, perhaps thinking she never should have mentioned the whole thing at all. But she had, which hopefully meant Lily Solanke was naturally honest.

'Well, I went over. I told her to stop giving Wolf meat.' Lily was firm, using her best teacher voice. Even Emma knew she'd obey that voice and she'd left school quite some time ago.

'So it didn't cause a rift, but it left things a bit sour, is that it?' Frank kept pushing.

Lily blushed. David was starting to look distinctly uncomfortable.

Frank sat forward.

'I see this kind of thing all the time. Mostly, when adults disagree over children, there are a few harsh words then everybody gets on with their lives because, in truth, people know it really is a stupid thing to fall out over. But sometimes things escalate. Nobody can help it, or really know why it goes in that direction. There can be underlying causes – sometimes people never liked each other anyway and suddenly there's something to focus that animosity on.'

Frank paused, let that thought fester.

'Was there more going with you pair and Olive?'

The Solankes shook their heads in unison.

'God, no. And we didn't fight afterwards either. It was like you said. I just . . . told her she'd crossed a line and pulled her up on what she'd done.'

'But *why* had she crossed the line?'

Lily was beginning to look flustered. She held out her hands, shrugged, completely at a loss.

'I think this is all a distraction,' David said, curtly. He took his wife's hand, stared at the detectives. 'Would it have mattered if we'd had a yelling match with Olive on the street? Unless you're saying somebody did something . . .'

'Is Wolf here?' Emma cut in.

'Why?' Lily asked.

'We'd like to talk to him,' Frank said.

The Solankes exchanged a glance.

'Right now?' Lily said.

'Yes.'

'I'm afraid that's out of the question,' David said. 'Wolf is very sensitive. We haven't told the children yet what's happened.'

'How old did you say your children were again?' Emma asked. It had just dawned on her that she couldn't hear kids. Were they even in the house?

'They're both eight.'

'Twins?'

'Yes.'

'And where are they?'

'They're here. They're reading upstairs.'

'Reading?' Emma said. 'They must be great kids. Smart. I'm sure they won't mind chatting to us for a couple of minutes.'

'I'm sorry, I have to insist,' David said. 'Wolf will take this very hard. We need to give him a little time. How you impart this sort of thing is really formative for a child.'

Emma couldn't help but notice Lily's short flinch.

'Look, we're back tomorrow. We'll give you until then. We need to speak to the kid, okay? Both of them, in fact.'

The parents nodded.

David resignedly, Emma noted.

But Lily – she looked scared.

OLIVE

No. 4

I didn't deliberately set out to upset the Solankes.

You can parse it in a way that makes it sound like I did, but it's simply not true. I have my faults but I would never manipulate a child. People who use children, in my opinion, are the lowest of the low.

It all started in my garden last summer. I was strategically placing slug pellets around my dahlias (the little buggers won't leave them alone until they're at least six inches high) when a shadow fell over the bed of earth I was working on. I looked up and there were the twins, leaning over the small hedge by the front gate.

It wasn't the first time we'd spoken. But normally our exchanges were silly chit-chat, the sort you have with children, nothing deep. *Why is your house so small? Do you prefer dogs or cats? How old are you? That old!* That sort of thing.

'What are you doing?' Wolf asked.

'I'm putting down poison for the slugs,' I said. 'They're eating my plants.'

'Oh, that's awful,' Lily May squeaked. Her braids bounced as she spoke, colourful beads clicking.

'Don't worry, these little blue things will kill all the pests,' I said. 'But make sure you never pick any up or put them near your mouth. They're very dangerous.'

Lily May's big brown eyes widened.

'But . . . but, that's what I meant – the blue things are awful. Papa says we have to be very careful on the land all around here, that we have to treat it with respect. There was a silly man who put poison down and then nothing could be grown here for ages.'

I sat back on my hunkers. I bit my tongue. It was hard not to point out that her daddy, given his job, seemed to care more about soil than people.

'I know all about the poison, Lily May. But these won't harm the soil. Just the slugs. They're destroying my flowers. And they are very pretty flowers. What do you suggest I do about the slugs to stop them from eating them all?'

'You could pick them up?'

'The plants?'

'No, the slugs.'

I tried not to laugh. She was a sensitive little soul. Sensitive and a bit thick.

'Or,' Wolf said, 'you could pour salt on them. Dry them out until they die.'

'Wolf!' Lily May cried in distress.

'Well, you said you were worried about poison,' he shrugged. '*She* can't stand out here all night picking up slugs.' He nodded his head at me.

I smiled. I liked how his mind worked, even if it was untenable.

'I'm afraid there's not enough salt in my kitchen for your solution either, Wolf.'

He shrugged again.

'Do you have any biscuits?'

'I might do.'

'Can we have some?'

'Are you always this direct?'

'Don't ask, won't get.'

Beside Wolf, Lily May was getting agitated.

'I don't think we should . . .' she said. '*You know*. Mummy might get angry.'

'Are you not allowed to eat biscuits?' I asked.

(See? I actually checked. I know some parents have a thing about sugar. Nonsense, but I dealt with many an odd parent in my day.)

'We are allowed,' Wolf said. 'She means our mummy might get annoyed because I asked you for something instead of waiting to be offered. That's very rude. Mummy says, anyway.'

'Ah. I see. Well, I don't think it's rude, as such. I think you're right. Don't ask, *don't* get. Come on, I'll root something out for you.'

They followed me in and I set them up with a small plate of chocolate digestives and glasses of milk. I didn't stock up on things like diluted juice in those days. No need, when it was just me. The Ribena came later.

And then I stuck the TV on. They'd got comfortable, you see. I assumed if their mother let them out on the street unmonitored, she wouldn't mind them being in my living room. I'd seen them go into Chrissy's house next door often enough.

I'd just left my job in the health board the previous week and I was still in the process of extricating myself. I'd been their most indispensable employee, it seemed, something I'd suspected myself even when they weren't giving me a whole lot of thanks for it. While the children watched TV, I sat there replying to my successor's multiple emails (mainly telling her I no longer worked there and she should direct her endless stream of questions to someone who actually did). When I'd finished that, I just browsed on Facebook and Twitter, CBeebies in the background.

The window was open in the sitting room; if their mother had called for them, I'd have heard her.

The twins sat there for a full hour, barely speaking, just absorbed in the cartoons.

Then Wolf asked me the time and said, 'We should go back,' and off they went. He thanked me on the way out. Such a polite little boy. Very exact, very proper. Given I'd been teaching children how to speak *exactly* and *properly* all my working life, I warmed to him almost immediately.

Lily Solanke hadn't come looking for them once.

This became our pattern that summer.

I never, sadly, became attached to Lily May. She talked too much and had a habit of criticising and making prissy observations. Wolf, though. He was clever. And hilarious. Often unintentionally, but sometimes he would tell me a joke and later, I'd think about it again and laugh until I cried.

They were always two-liners: *Why did the chicken cross the road? Because the green man told him to.*

Priceless.

Lily knew I'd worked with children so I don't think it bothered her that the kids spent time in mine. But it was the TV that set her off.

I mean, I couldn't have known, could I?

The first time she came around, it wasn't that big a deal.

Lily May had ratted, of course she had. I'm sure Wolf would have carried on without uttering a word. I doubt he'd have brought his sister with him at all, except they were twins and their parents expected them to do everything together. Wolf had no more in common with his twin than Lily May did with the teenage Holly Daly.

'Olive, em, have you been letting my children watch television?' Lily asked, when I let her in.

'I . . . Yes, I have. I presumed you knew where they were?'

'Oh, of course. We like to give Wolf and Lily May their freedom. It's important they have a sense of independence and learn to handle responsibility. And we know the Vale is safe, so they're never at risk.'

Even as she was talking, I noticed she kept saying 'we'. Like she and David were as one. I wondered if she was even conscious of it.

'We don't mind them dropping in on people or having the odd sweet treat as long as they aren't making a nuisance of themselves,' she went on. 'But Olive, they are only allowed set hours of television viewing. One hour a day. So they've been having their hour at home and then coming over to you and watching for hours on end.'

'But I . . .'

'Did you not think it was strange that they would want to visit your house and just watch TV? Most of the time children want adults to talk to them. You didn't find it unusual that they were coming in here and sitting there quietly for hours?'

'I genuinely didn't think anything of it,' I said. 'They didn't say anything. I supposed they just liked coming in for the biscuits and juice.'

I was disturbed by how panicked Lily looked when I mentioned juice. You'd swear I'd said Coke and McDonald's, the funny thing her face was doing.

'I'm sorry, is there something wrong with juice?'

'I . . . no, I guess the odd time won't rot their teeth. It's just, working in the school you get these notices all the time about what the kids should and shouldn't eat and drink. Dilute squash is the devil.' She smiled, like it was really nothing, when I could see it was very much something.

Lily caught me on the back foot that day. I didn't want to fall out with her. I enjoyed Wolf's company and I didn't want her to ban him from dropping in. So I nodded along contritely and promised that I wouldn't let the children watch any more television but they were more than welcome to call by just for a chat.

'Well, school starts back next week and it won't be long before the evenings lengthen, so they won't be out as much in any case,' she said.

I tried not to show my disappointment but she must have seen something in my face.

'I know you meant no harm, Olive. Really. I'm not going to stop them visiting the odd time but I don't want them in here every day trying to hoodwink you into giving them something they're not allowed at home. Children are clever like that.' She smiled at me again.

I found it utterly patronising. She would have known, as a professional who worked with children herself, that I was quite aware of children's ways and means. I didn't say that, though. I just smiled back, biting my tongue so hard it could have come off in my mouth.

Whatever control she thought she had over those kids, Wolf hadn't received the memo.

The very next day, he called over. Minus Lily May this time. The penny had dropped and I admired him even more for it.

'I'm sorry, I can't let you watch television, Wolf,' I said. 'Your mother wasn't best pleased with me yesterday. You might have mentioned you weren't allowed too much TV time.'

He shrugged.

'I didn't tell her what we were doing. Lily May did. And I don't call over to watch your TV. I call over because you are a nice lady. Can I just have something to eat?'

'Does Mum know you're here?'

'She said we weren't to be in here every day asking could we watch cartoons.'

I studied his face for any giveaways. I'd have laid money on Lily telling the twins they were to give my house a wide berth for a while. Wolf had obviously taken what suited him from what I imagine was probably a very long rant.

'Just give me a second,' I said.

I rang Lily.

'Oh, hi, Lily. I just wanted to check – Wolf is here and I want to make sure you're okay with that. I don't mind at all. I have some colours and paper he can draw on. The TV will be off.'

I'd caught her off guard this time.

'Um, yes, of course,' she said, too polite to not return my politeness. 'Just tell him to come home in an hour.'

I smiled at Wolf after I'd hung up.

'You can stay,' I said.

'And have something to eat?' he asked, big eyes staring up.

'Maybe not biscuits or juice,' I said. 'What about a sandwich?'

'Thank you,' he said.

So I made him a ham sandwich.

I might as well have strapped dynamite to the child, the furore that caused.

HOLLY

No. 3

Holly had gone for a hike in the woods behind their house.

Well, that wasn't strictly true. Holly had gone just far enough into the woods to make sure she was obscured from view, should her mother decide to look out the back bedroom window in her direction.

She reached into the hollow in the tree roots where she'd hidden the pack of cigarettes. They were still dry and Holly thanked her lucky stars. She climbed up onto the highest root and made herself comfortable against the tree bark. She could still see the back of Olive's house. It sent a shiver down her spine.

She pulled out her lighter, sparked up her cigarette and sighed.

It amused Holly that her mother never asked why she had a lighter in the pocket of her skinny jeans. There really could only be two reasons — one, Holly was a secret smoker, or two, she was an arsonist — either of which should surely worry Alison. But who knew what went on in her mother's head? They'd been through so much together and sometimes it was still a mystery.

Like that time Alison had unintentionally clipped a car in the village.

It had been a total accident. The road was narrow and they'd both heard the little bang and been shocked.

'Probably just a scrape,' Alison said, calmly, though her voice held a note of panic. Holly didn't suggest they check. She just agreed with her mother.

Then the car's owner had walked into the cafe where Alison and Holly were having lunch and asked if anybody had seen who'd broken his wing mirror.

Holly had expected Alison to own up, be mortified, explain and apologise profusely. Alison was the sort of person who'd say sorry to somebody who'd bumped into her on the street.

But her mother had just stared down at her cappuccino and said nothing. Odd, Holly thought.

She asked her mother on the way home why she hadn't said anything. Alison had shrugged and kept her focus on the road ahead, not meeting her daughter's eye.

'I don't know, love. Sometimes, it feels like the best thing to do is deny, deny, deny. If they didn't actually see you do it . . .'

Holly got it and didn't get it. She knew her mam had been conditioned to lie. When she needed to.

Holly took a long drag from the cigarette.

Her mother was definitely lying about something now.

CHRISSY

No. 5

Chrissy Hennessy couldn't remember the last time she'd felt this relaxed.

It was probably the valium.

She smiled and sipped her coffee, took a bite of the bagel she'd smothered in Nutella. Tried not to think about . . .

Yesterday had been quite distressing.

When they'd seen the flies.

Her stomach lurched at the memory.

Flies laid maggots. And maggots ate . . .

Chrissy felt the bagel hit her stomach hard.

It wasn't a good idea to think about dead bodies while eating your lunch.

'Get inside,' she'd said to Cam, when they'd seen the insects.

But he'd taken off at a sprint in the direction of Olive's house and what could she do but follow? She hadn't even been wearing any shoes.

'Shit. Come back here!' she'd yelled at him, muttering 'you little devil' under her breath. When had that become his moniker? It used to be 'Mammy's little pet' and 'My favourite little man'.

Because of the angle of their house, Cam emerged at the front of Olive's home. He'd climbed over the small fence that sat where Olive's hedge didn't meet her boundary wall and Chrissy scraped her leg badly doing the same. She caught him at the door, trying to spy through their neighbour's letter box.

'There's tape blocking it off, I can't . . .' he'd said, poking his fingers in. It was at that moment Chrissy noticed that the postbox affixed to the front wall had letters sticking out of it – the box was too full to shove them all the way in. You'd think the postman would have noticed . . .

'We can't be here,' she said to Cam, yanking at his shoulder, just as his fingers managed to push through the masking tape on the other side of the letter box.

Her son had recoiled and fallen on his backside when the smell hit him, but she'd assumed it was her pulling at him that caused it and instantly felt awful.

'Oh, Cam, I'm sorry,' she said. Then the smell hit her too and she felt herself gagging.

'Eughh, gross,' Cam had said, holding his nose. He stood up and pelted back in the direction of their house.

His mother was slower to follow.

On automatic, she walked back to her house, taking the front garden route this time, one foot moving in front of the other. She knew it was all going to kick off, then.

Back home, she'd rung the police.

Chrissy had told the officers last night that she was too shocked to talk. In truth, she was trying to process that, from now on, everything would be different, everything would be *easier*.

The police agreed, she was in a state. They recommended strong, sugary tea and a good night's rest.

She hadn't slept a wink. She'd lain awake all night, thinking.

Imagining her lover's arms wrapped around her, lying on his chest, the hairs there a soft cushion, listening to his heartbeat.

She didn't have to worry any more about seeing him. The threat was gone.

But her husband had decided to stay home. Matt, who usually went to work on a Monday morning and put in so many hours until Friday night that it was like he lived elsewhere during the week.

Matt, who'd awoken this morning and announced he was taking the day off because Chrissy and Cam needed him and the police would probably be round.

Need you? Chrissy had said, amazed, in her head. We haven't *needed* you in years.

She had, once. Needed and wanted. But she'd learned the hard way to rely on herself. Slowly. Like a lobster in a pot of gradually warming water.

Two weeks after Cam was born, Matt had gone back to work. They'd shared a workplace before the baby, so she was supposed to appreciate how busy he was, how he couldn't take any more time off than his two weeks' holidays.

As if in the world of accountancy somebody would die if Matt was out of the office a single second longer with his wife and new baby. Matt Hennessy, hotshot numbers man, ready to HALO-drop into your business and sort out your debit and credit columns.

While she was on maternity leave, Matt had started the campaign. He didn't want his son raised in a crèche. He was glad she was home. And she'd gone along with it, taking on the full burden of childcare. Even now, she couldn't figure out what had been going on in her head. Fair enough, accountancy wasn't her dream job but she'd worked bloody hard to get where she was. Almost everyone else she'd gone to school with had ended up single-parenting, in shit jobs or living on the dole. Working was her identity. She'd had a baby, not a lobotomy.

But soon, there she was, a full-time mother, her days filled with Cam, only Cam. As it turned out, Matt didn't want his son raised by strangers but he also hadn't planned to be too involved himself.

At three years of age, Cam caught meningitis. That had been the test – and the final straw.

Matt had been concerned, of course he was. The man was human. But not as worried as she'd been. Her heart had almost stopped beating when the doctors told them what they suspected.

Chrissy had convinced herself she was overreacting to the little rash and the flu-like symptoms and was sure that they'd laugh at her in the A&E department and send her home. But she'd arrived not a minute too soon.

A couple of days after Cam was admitted, Matt said he had to go back to work. Chrissy was shocked, and then she remonstrated with him. Who cared if the work piled up, if Matt lost an account, if the whole bloody thing imploded? Their son was ill.

But he was so calm and practical. Every day he went in, not returning to the isolation ward until late in the evening. He slept there every other night, which Chrissy presumed was to ease his conscience.

Because it was she who stayed with Cam in the small hospital room all day long, every day. She held his tiny little hand for what felt like weeks while they pumped him full of drugs and painkillers. She barely left to go to the toilet, let alone eat or drink or do anything more than breathe.

Her family were no help – she'd one brother travelling in Australia by then and the remaining one, Peter, had always been useless. Her dad called by with a giant teddy, then said he'd a darts tournament to get to. Bloody *darts*. She'd never in her life missed having a proper mother so much.

Chrissy was on her own.

When she snapped after the long weeks and read Matt the riot act for abandoning her, he reacted appallingly. He accused her of being a drama queen, and started ranting and raving about him being the one who was paying the hospital bills. Before she had a chance to reply, he walked out.

Yep, Matt had a terrible habit of disappearing when the going got tough.

Her feelings about that had morphed from frustration to sadness, to confusion, to resignation to outright anger. She was, to all intents, a young, frustrated single mother, trapped with a middle-aged man who more and more didn't even seem to *see* her.

It wasn't the only reason she'd started having an affair, but it was certainly a major contributory factor.

These last few months, though, her husband had been acting very strangely.

It was like he was having some sort of mid-life crisis. He was leaving work at odd hours, ringing her during the day to see how she was doing, all out-of-character stuff.

And then there was the inexplicable decision to stay at home today. She wondered if he was on the verge of a breakdown or something. He *had* been working an awful lot. Apparently.

Chrissy exhaled loudly. Oh, Ron. I wish you were here, she mouthed silently into the empty kitchen.

Chrissy wasn't perfect. She knew she was weak. Lots of people had flaws. Hers was needing to be loved. And she'd do anything to get it.

Olive bloody Collins.

Chrissy realised her coffee had gone cold.

It was time to stop thinking about that horrible woman. She was gone.

OLIVE

No. 4

When Chrissy Hennessy moved into number five, so pregnant it looked like a sneeze would send the child skidding into the world, she'd seemed really eager to be friendly.

She threw a party not long after they arrived and it was great fun – apparently she couldn't cook to save her life but, my goodness, she went all out catering for us with shop-purchased fancies and expensive champagne. She obviously didn't come from money and, to be honest, it was refreshing. She was a laugh. And the party was a lovely effort and greatly appreciated.

Then she had Cam and she just disappeared.

I called over with baby gifts in the first week or so and she opened the door, big bags under her eyes, looking like she wanted to kill me for knocking. I wasn't to know the child was asleep. And if she was that desperate for some shut-eye, all she had to do was ask me in and I've have minded the little man for her.

She didn't want to know any of us.

Well, all but one of us.

I was never able to understand what my Ron saw in her.

She's pretty, I'll give her that. That waif-like charm, loose blonde curls, big, vacant blue eyes. The type men lap up, a virginal quality, even while pushing a buggy. But so little to talk about. So lacking in desire to improve herself or have any sort of independence.

See, if Ron had just had sex with her and walked away, I think I could have come to terms with it.

But he kept going back. That hurt. It really, really hurt.

And the awful thing was, when I knee-jerked and pushed him away, Ron went over there more. I created a vacancy which she happily filled.

There's always one, isn't there? The woman who has it all but still isn't happy and needs to have what everybody else has, too.

Always one.

FRANK

Halfway through their chat with the Hennessys, Frank was ready to call it a day. His feet, swollen from the heat, were pinching in his shoes and his shirt was starting to give off an entirely unprofessional odour.

They were sitting in the lounge, a comfortable space filled with expensive modern furniture designed to make the room look seventies-chic. The windows were adorned with patterned curtains, not the plain blinds of most of the neighbours' houses. The carpet was some sort of animal print. And the couches were covered with faux-fur throws. Money, but not a lot of taste.

Chrissy was a good-looking woman. She reminded Frank of his wife. Big blue eyes and blonde curls, dimples in both cheeks that dipped when she smiled and frowned so she was never able to pull off a stern look, even when she was properly angry.

'So. We've established this isn't the closest of neighbourhoods,' Frank said.

Matt shrugged.

'I suppose it's natural to presume we would be, living the way we do.'

The husband had decided to do the talking. He'd punched well above his weight when he'd landed his wife. Here was a case of the school nerd winning the beauty queen. Matt was a head shorter than Chrissy and thinning on top, though he could only have been late thirties at most. Money, Frank thought.

'You think because we live in an exclusive development we're all in here like one big family, shutting the world out. It's not like that. Sure, we know our neighbours. We've made efforts with the odd joint social occasion. There was one year we had drinks, wasn't there, Chrissy? Some of us try to be a little more sociable than others. But generally, nobody chooses to live behind a gate because they want to live in other people's pockets.

'At least, that's not what my family wants. You live in a place like this for privacy, Detective. If Olive Collins didn't feel like being out in her garden or taking a walk around the Vale, that was her business. It wasn't our job to check up on her. Ed and Amelia next door have been away for months and they didn't ask anybody to water their plants or pick up their mail or anything. I only know they're gone because I'm Ed's accountant.'

'I see,' Frank said, even while he didn't.

'And your son?' Emma said. 'He wasn't kicking his ball about in her garden or having a snoop? I have two younger brothers who would have died from curiosity when they were that age if a house on our block had suddenly seemed deserted. They'd have made it their *business* to check the place out. Me too, to be fair.' She smiled. 'I'd have led the investigation.'

'Cam hasn't been near her house,' Chrissy said. Her voice wasn't what Frank had expected. She was proper working class – the grav-elly depth that said a certain side of the tracks. 'He was as shocked as I was yesterday. I hope you don't want to talk to him again. Your officers spoke to him last night.'

'Well . . .' Frank started.

'No, sorry,' Matt interrupted. 'I'll stop you there. My wife and son are extremely traumatised by this.'

Frank eyed Chrissy. She didn't exactly look traumatised.

'They've told you everything they know,' he continued, 'and I've already given you details of where I was on the 3rd of March. I had a full day of meetings. None of us saw or heard anything strange going on in number four. Do you know who you should talk to, Detective?'

Frank raised his eyebrows, waiting. And so it begins, he thought.

'Ron Ryan in number seven. He was in and out of Olive Collins' quite a bit. Through the back door, if you know what I'm saying.'

Chrissy's eyes had almost doubled in size, while her mouth formed a small 'o'.

'You weren't aware of this, Mrs Hennessy?' Frank asked. 'It's just, normally it's the spouse at home who picks up on the comings and goings from neighbours' houses.'

Chrissy shook her head, mute. Weird, Frank thought. She seemed more shocked by the fact something had been going on she wasn't aware of than the fact her neighbour had been dead next door for three months.

'It's amazing I noticed,' Matt said, 'considering how little I'm here. But I saw him go in once and thought he was acting odd and it's like all these things – once you've noticed something, you see it all the time. You just have to open your eyes.'

Now Frank was really starting to worry about Chrissy Hennessy. She looked like she was about to vomit all over the nice faux-fur furnishings.

'Right. Mr Hennessy, one more thing. The night Ms Collins died, she rang the emergency services. Two police officers were called out to the house. They didn't get an answer. They were going to start looking for alternative entry points to the house when you pulled up. You told them you hadn't seen or heard anything out of the ordinary, even though you've told us now that you were out all day.'

'Well, I hadn't. And I meant in the days previous as well. Everything seemed absolutely fine.'

'And you also told the officers that she was probably away. Why did you say that?'

'The house looked empty, the blinds were down. There was a lamplight on, but everybody in the Vale has automatic timers for our lights at night.'

'You never told me any of this,' Chrissy interrupted.

'Bloody hell, Chrissy. We don't tell each other everything, do we? Anyway, I told the police we all kept to ourselves but I was sure everything was okay and I'd check in the next day.'

'But you didn't.'

'No. I completely forgot. And your lot seemed happy. To be honest, there was a match on that night; we were all eager to get away for it. I didn't see her the next day or the day after and then it went clean out of my head. We weren't friends. She wasn't missed. I mean, it was hardly my job to worry, was it? If the police weren't even that concerned . . . They could have come back and checked again, but they didn't.'

'Okay, we'll leave it there for now,' Frank said. There was no way he was following that line of logic with a civilian. The shit was going to hit the proverbial fan for the two lads who'd failed in their duties that night.

Matt walked the detectives out to the front door, but Frank stopped in the hall.

'Your neighbours in number six – Ed . . .'

'And Amelia. Their surname is Miller.'

'You said they've been away for a few months.'

'Yes. They're an older couple; they go on cruises, rent villas in Spain, that sort of thing. Live the high life.'

'And you know all this because you're their accountant?'

Matt smiled.

'Sure. We know where all the bodies are buried.'

As soon as the words left his mouth, he realised what he'd said.

'It's a turn of the phrase. I didn't mean . . .'

'No, of course not,' Frank said. 'Do you do anybody else's accounts in the Vale?'

'No. I'm a partner in Cole, Little & Hennessy. We mainly do corporate accounts. But Ed approached me personally and he was willing to pay the higher rates we charge, so I took him on.'

'They've a bit of money, then?'

Matt smiled thinly.

'I'm sort of like a priest. We don't reveal the secrets of the confessional. But I'll put it like this for you, Detective – nobody in the Vale is struggling. Even Olive had a little nest egg.'

'Right. Anyway, do you know when they'll be back next door?'

'No. Open-ended this trip, I think. They've been gone three months now, though.'

'Three months?' Frank frowned.

'Yes.'

He and Emma looked at each other.

'Are you saying they went at the start of March?' Emma said.

Matt opened his mouth, then shut it and nodded.

'Yes. I guess so.'

ED & AMELIA

No. 6

Cadiz, Spain

'Are you coming in, or shall I set dinner out on the balcony?'

Amelia's voice drifted out through the open sliding doors. Ed Miller was sitting in his favourite sun lounger, an American spy novel in one hand, glass of Johnny Walker's in the other. He'd read the same page three times now and still had no clue as to who had just revealed what. That was the problem buying books in a foreign country. You were limited to whatever English editions you could find and this one was . . . well, pulp.

He dropped it on the ground.

'Let's eat outside,' he called to his wife. 'It's balmy.'

The temperature had dropped from its earlier intensity. Not that it was ever too warm here. He liked that about coastal Spain. There was always a gentle breeze from the ocean, so even when the sun was blasting its rays, you just had to walk along the strand and the faint spray from the water and the soft sea breeze would cool the skin.

Amelia came out carrying a large dish of paella. It smelled divine, all saffron and paprika and mussels. Ed knew that when he took his first bite, he would lavish praise on his wife for another delicious meal cooked with gorgeous, fresh local produce.

What he would definitely not say was that he really, more than anything in the world, could have murdered a lamb chop and some buttery jacket potatoes that evening.

'Will you grab the salad and a bottle?' she said.

He pulled himself up from the lounger, a simple task that was getting harder and harder these days. He was sixty-five, soon to be sixty-six, and he'd begun to suspect retiring young had prematurely aged him. He'd had notions he'd go on all these hill walks and maybe take up some sort of activity, bowling or ballroom dancing, something that would keep him active. Instead, he'd slipped into a quiet contentment with life, happy to sit and drink and watch the world glide on by. He liked to walk when they visited new cities. Best way to see them. But their holidays had become more sedate this last while.

He passed Amelia as she brought out the plates and cutlery, giving her ample bottom a little squeeze through her flowing cotton skirt.

'Now, now, you dirty old man,' she grinned. 'Something just beeped, by the way.'

'That was me saying hello.'

'Ha! I think it was your computer.'

'Ah. An email. Give me two minutes.'

Ed found the laptop on the table in the sitting room, beside Amelia's bountiful collection of magazines boasting pictures of beautiful homes and beautiful people. He spotted the price sticker on one of the covers. Six euro! You'd buy a paperback for that. His wife was keeping the whole women's glossy print operation in business.

He brought the screen on the computer back to life and saw an email from his neighbour back home, Matt Hennessy. Also his accountant. And a bloody good one, too.

He read the few lines and a smile started to break on his lips.

'Well, well, well,' he said.

In the kitchen, he saw the bottle of Cava that Amelia had taken out and left beside two flute glasses. Instead of grabbing it, he went to the fridge.

There it was. The bottle of champagne he'd bought in the little off-licence they'd found. It had been five times more expensive than the Cava but still half the price you'd pay in Ireland for a good brand.

'You never know,' he'd said to Amelia when she'd raised her eyes as he put it in the basket. 'We might have a special occasion to celebrate.'

They were trying to watch their money. They were wealthy but they weren't that old. The lifestyle they'd chosen cost a lot – it was important to be judicious in terms of outlay. Of course, now he'd seen what she spent on magazines, it put the exchange in a whole new light.

Well, it didn't get more special than this.

Amelia blushed like a girl when he emerged onto the balcony. He'd walked through the swaying white curtains with the bottle of champagne like he was the Milk Tray man.

'Ooo,' she said. 'Are we celebrating?'

'We are indeed,' he said.

He wouldn't tell her why until he'd popped the cork and filled the two glasses, holding the bubbles up to his nose and wafting the dry, sparkly aroma up his nostrils.

'Mmm,' he said, like an expert. 'Excellent vintage.'

'Ed Miller, are you going to keep me in suspense all night?'

Ed smiled. Amelia's eyes were bright with anticipation, her big round face beaming from ear to ear even before she heard the news.

'That email I got. It was from Matt Hennessy. He was wondering when we're coming home.'

His wife's smile faltered a little.

'We discussed that, Ed. Can we ever go back there now?'

'We can go back, my dear. Straight away if we like. They found Olive Collins dead yesterday.'

'Oh, my goodness.' Amelia's hand flew to her breast, her heart thumping visibly. She could barely contain her glee, but she had to ask the next question.

'What did he say happened to her?'

'Matt reckons it might have been a heart attack or something. The police don't know anything.'

Ed raised his glass to his wife.

He loved when he had good news for her.

And she didn't really have to know everything.

'We're going home, my love.'

'We're going home,' she said. And they clinked their glasses and raised them to their lips, eyeing each other as they drank the champagne, thinking nothing had ever tasted sweeter.

GEORGE

No. 1

An eerie quiet descended on Withered Vale that evening.

The police cars had cleared out and a rudimentary cordon had been placed around Olive Collins' house, consisting of bright yellow tape across her door and tied to either side of the garden gate.

The purple and white stocks in her garden still scented the air; everything looked the same but it had all changed.

George shuddered as he looked out his window and across the road.

Would he die alone like Olive? If he had a sudden aneurysm or fell and cracked his head on the glass table, would he be left lying inside his house for months, his body just a writhing mass of creepy-crawlies by the time the police found him?

He hadn't heard from his father in . . . when was the last time he'd heard from the great Stu Richmond? Had he sent a card at Christmas?

They'd never been particularly close. George's mother had succumbed to breast cancer before he'd had a chance to even know her. He felt grief for the idea of her, more than for the actual person.

Lily next door had sympathised with him when he'd confided in her, telling him her parents had died from cancer too, but he didn't feel any camaraderie in their shared experience of loss. Her pain ran deep. George felt like bereaved child was a role he had to play – the little boy who'd lost his mum when he was only four.

His father had stepped into the shoes of both parents in the way he approached all problems – financially. Their housekeeper was the only female George had known and, unluckily, he'd ended up in the care of the single least maternal woman who'd ever walked the earth.

George finally understood the full extent of Susan's uselessness when he turned ten.

She (most likely under instruction from his father) had organised a birthday party in the local soft-play centre and had also been delegated the task of buying and giving George his gift from his father – who was off in Amsterdam, where his acts were performing in some outdoor festival.

Perhaps she'd been guided to the correct aisle in the toy store by a knowledgeable shop assistant or maybe she'd stumbled upon it by accident, but she'd somehow picked out the absolute best present George could have wished for – a Tamagotchi. While his friends oohed and aahed, George threw himself at Susan and hugged her tightly, gushing his thanks.

She stood there stiffly then removed his arms from around her waist.

'I'm glad you like it,' she said. 'Your father said money was no object. You should go play now. I need to organise the chicken nuggets.'

There wasn't an ounce of warmth in her, not even the slightest hint of affection. She'd only let him hug her because she'd been taken by surprise and even that she'd managed to make excruciatingly painful.

A therapist would say (a therapist had said) that it was the absence of women in George's life that had caused his problems. It was a cliché dripping in a stereotype.

George sighed. Maybe it was true, too. There was no great groundbreaking, psychoanalytical moment to be had. His brain was mortifyingly banal.

A knock on the door shook him from his reverie.

George blinked. He'd been staring out the window. How had somebody come up the footpath without him noticing? What kind of a neighbourhood voyeur was he?

The surprises kept on coming. Ron Ryan from number seven was standing in his porch.

'Hey,' he said, when George opened the door. 'Fancy a beer?'

George did a quick mental calculation. He had plans for the evening. Did Ron want one beer, or was he the sort for whom 'a beer' meant *let's get hammered*?

And he hadn't even had the courtesy to bring some beer.

Still. The day had been an odd one. Maybe George should just go with it. Who knew what Ron had to say for himself?

'Sure,' he said. 'Come in.'

Ron walked ahead of George towards the kitchen, which was amazing considering it was the first time he'd ever been in his home.

'I think I have some in the fridge,' George said.

'Fuck me,' Ron said, not even hearing. 'My pad is nice but, George man, they must drop their knickers on the spot when you bring them back here.'

George looked around the kitchen. It was impressive, in a style only his father could conjure. Monied minimalist – cupboards hidden in the walls, a large island with its own sink and chopping area, a low-hanging art deco light. At least it was easy to keep clean.

'Eh, yeah,' he said.

George had only chatted with Ron a few times. He found the other man odd. He had at least ten years on George but spoke to him like they were buddies on the same football team; given much of Ron's chitchat was locker-room stuff, that was an appropriate analogy. George only had a vague idea what his neighbour did for a living. Reading between the lines, it sounded very much like sales, but Ron had done a number on his CV and now it was senior commission executive or some other such nonsense.

And he was an out-and-out ladies' man. He dressed like a ladies' man. He spoke like a ladies' man. He even smelled like a ladies' man. George got the impression that while other little boys had grown up wanting to be Indiana Jones or Maradona or Axel Rose, Ron had decided early on to model himself on Julio Iglesias.

'You been away, Ron?' he asked, handing the other man a bottle of Heineken and nodding at the deep tan on Ron's arms. It had been freezing up to a couple of weeks ago – not a hint of summer in the air.

Ron looked down, puzzled, then got it.

'This? God, no. That's from sunbeds, man. You should check them out. You look a bit pasty. You still have to get the girls to come home with you, before you get their knees trembling with . . . all this.' He circled the air with his hand, indicating the luxury modern kitchen. 'Though I suppose Daddy's money helps.'

George watched as Ron necked half the lager that Daddy's

money had bought. It was the same banter mixed with casual jealousy that he was used to.

But Ron seemed on edge this evening.

Well, they all were, weren't they?

'So, Olive,' Ron said, and took another gulp. 'Mad, huh?'

George nodded.

Ron ran his hand through his dark hair, giving it a vigorous shake.

'Have they said anything to you?' he asked. 'The cops, I mean?'

'They called over,' George said. 'But they didn't say anything more than what they told us on the street. Have they not been in with you?'

'No. A uniformed one called in. He was looking for samples to rule out fingerprints and shit like that. I mean, I was in her house before. Obviously. Weren't we all? Anyway, he just said that detectives would call by tomorrow. Suits me. I mean, it's Saturday anyway. I wouldn't be able to take another day off work. Quotas, you know.'

'Of course,' George said, and took a sip from the bottle. Just one of the lads, shooting the breeze with a beer, talking about work and the weekend.

George only cared about two sets of figures these days – the amount his father deposited in his bank each month and the gigabyte speed of the broadband that connected him to the outside world.

'Did they take samples from you?' Ron asked.

'Yeah.'

'Oh. Good. Not just me then! So, we still don't know if they think she died naturally?'

George shrugged.

'There's nothing to say anything out of the ordinary happened to her. I think the police just have to go through the motions. Why? Are you worried?'

Ron stroked his chin and drank again. He was very fidgety. It was unsettling. Before tonight, if you'd asked George to come up with a word for Ron, it would have been 'smooth'. Cheesy, a given, but still smooth. *Philadelphia.*

'I was just thinking, if something did happen to her, you know, we'd be like . . . suspects.'

'Suspects?'

'Yeah. Because we're the two single men.'

George shook his head. 'I'm not sure that's the determining criteria for the police when they're arresting somebody. Find the local single man. If you don't mind me saying, Ron, you seem a bit jittery.'

Ron put his bottle down and placed both his hands on the marble counter.

'Yeah. I guess I am a bit.' He looked up. George was still standing by the fridge, resting against the counter, ready to fetch more beers if the situation required it.

'I was sleeping with her.'

George blinked.

'What?'

'Making love, having *intercourse.*'

George gave a nervous laugh.

'Wasn't she like, in her fifties or something?'

Ron shrugged and half-smiled, his cheeks red.

'She was fifty-five. Don't be so ageist, mate. Your sex life doesn't stop when you hit the big five-oh. Anyway, she had a lovely body. You get to a point, George, you learn to appreciate a cougar. She was fun. Not needy, just up for a giggle. In the beginning, anyway.'

George had to take a sip of beer to stop himself from gagging. Sex with Olive? The image of her rotting in her house flashed into his head. Christ.

And then George looked at Ron and frowned. It looked like he was trying to play it cool, but it was apparent to George that Ron was actually quite upset.

Ron and Olive. Who knew?

'Eh . . . sorry for your loss,' George said, trying to sound casual.

'No, that's not what I'm bothered about. Here's what's on my mind – I had sex with her the night before she died. If it was the 3rd she died on. I had sex with her on the 2nd.'

'Oh.' George paused. 'Shit.'

'Yeah. I have a bad feeling about this.'

'I'm sure there's nothing to worry about. I mean . . . did you kill her?'

Ron screwed up his face and shook his head, then laughed thinly.

'Of course I didn't fucking kill her. Not much of a criminal master-mind, am I? Sitting over here and chatting with you about my worries over a beer.'

'Maybe you're double-bluffing.' George took another sip. His bottle was nearly empty. 'Do you want another one?'

Ron was looking at him oddly.

'No. No, I'd better not. I just wanted to see if they'd said any-thing to you.' He stared at his Heineken. 'Eh, we should do this more often. The lads, you know. You only live across the street.'

George smiled and nodded. This wouldn't become a thing. He was sure of that.

'No, I mean it,' Ron said. 'Sometimes I get a bit caught up with other things, you know? It's nice to have a few mates you can drop in to. Someone to talk to. And you remind me of . . . ah. Nothing.'

George studied Ron, puzzled. He seemed unusually sincere.

'I'll walk you out,' George said, breaking the moment. He had become obsessively paranoid about people being in his house when he couldn't see them. He always hid everything away, but you never knew.

They left the house and strolled down the footpath to the end of the garden.

Holly Daly from two up was standing at the kerb, her hand resting on the bin she'd gone out to retrieve. She was staring over at Olive's cottage.

Ron raised his hand and waved at Holly.

'Hi there! You and your mum okay?'

Holly turned towards them, her features distorting from reflective concentration to seemingly blank and bored in the space of a split second.

She barely acknowledged the two men before she turned on her heel, dragging the bin in behind her.

George watched Ron watching their neighbour walk up her garden path. Ron said nothing. He didn't have to.

Then he gave George a half-hearted clap on his back and strolled off into the night.

George headed back to his own house.

Ron Ryan had been having sex with Olive Collins and was, in

all likelihood, sleeping with half a dozen other women at the same time. He had quite openly been staring at Holly Daly's arse, and he knew she was only seventeen.

And yet, George was the one who'd been called a dirty little pervert.

OLIVE

No. 4

George Richmond.

Lovely, shy, kind, funny George Richmond.

The man nobody would suspect anything bad of.

Do you know what George did when news spread that the police had found my decomposing body?

He masturbated.

Do you know what he did when they brought my body out of my house for its final journey?

He masturbated.

The fascinating thing about George is that he reaches for masturbation the same way most other people reach for a cup of tea or glass of wine. Stress sets him off.

I thought his predilection was only for teenage girls, but, as it transpires, George's perversion is unlimited.

The day I discovered what he was, I was painting my garden gate, my knees aching even though I'd found a nice plump cushion to kneel on.

I stood up to take a little break and surveyed the neighbourhood.

It was a beautiful warm day, not a hint of rain in the air. Ron in number seven was mowing his grass, a tight tee shirt paired with khaki shorts. One of the kids, Cam from next door, I think, was orchestrating a mass battle on the kerb outside his house. Toy soldiers had been ordered to carry out red-clover-mite genocide.

Just over the hedge in the garden beside mine, Holly was lying on a blanket, book open, wearing a yellow bikini top and white denim shorts. She was dozing, not reading.

Despite my friendship with her mum, Holly kept to herself. That hadn't stopped me becoming fond of her. She was a quiet thing, even though she was stunning and like all teenage girls, aware of it. Back then, she used to wear make-up all the time, and those barely-there clothes young girls seem to think are an expression of feminist leanings.

As time wore on, Holly shed that skin. She became more natural-looking and if anything, more beautiful. For that summer, she was all about the misplaced girl power as dictated by the latest blogger, vlogger or whatever those opinionated minxes call themselves.

That day, my eyes wandered further down the Vale.

It was the movement that caught my eye.

The curtains had blown aside in the wind and there was George, standing at his upstairs window, his face expressionless, blank. He was peering over at the Dalys' garden, his body rigid but his arm jigging up and down.

I'd always had excellent eyesight. And I knew immediately what he was at.

I saw him, but he didn't see me.

I didn't react. Not that day. I was too shocked.

It took me a while to get my head around what I'd witnessed.

A few days later, I put on my nicest dress, a pretty red one with a large white daisy print, and called over to ask George if he had any flour.

'Flour?' he'd said, like I'd just asked him for a gram of cocaine. I stood on his step, waiting to be asked in, but he'd barred his door like a man with something to hide.

'Yes, flour,' I laughed lightly. 'To bake with?'

Of course, he was wondering why the hell I'd called in to him and not one of our female neighbours. But he was too polite to ask.

'I don't think so . . .' he said, shaking his head. 'I can look?'

'Lovely,' I smiled, and clapped my hands like a girl. 'If you do have some, I can't promise to return it, but I will throw on an extra batch of scones just for you.' I winked, as coquettishly as my self-respect would allow.

And that got me in the door. I led the conversation, talking about having good neighbours and the friendliness of the Vale and how we were all like one big family looking out for each other, while he opened cupboard after cupboard, unable to meet my eye, nerves turning into beads of sweat all over his forehead. Then I apologised for not calling over more and asked would he take a key for my house in case I was ever stuck? I was *more* than willing to do the same for him.

'Are these spare?' I said, picking up the keys with the blank fob from the shelf in the hall on my way out, flourless. I dangled them from my little finger and pulled in my lower lip with my teeth. 'Gosh, it's hot, isn't it?' I traced a hand down my neck to the line of my cleavage and rubbed my chest so vigorously my breasts wobbled. His eyes never left my hand.

'Yes,' he said, distracted, cementing the image on his brain for later, I imagine. Like putty, he was. I don't think he even realised I'd left with the keys until I was gone. I'd always thought of myself as an excellent actress. Turns out, I hadn't been deluding myself.

It may have been a stupid plan, but I wanted to get inside George Richmond's house when he wasn't there. I needed to make sure he had nothing to hide.

The developer had built a set of gates around us to keep the danger outside. But if a grown man could stand at his window masturbating as a fifteen-year-old girl sunbathed in her own front garden, then maybe the danger was inside the gates.

HOLLY

No. 3

Holly slammed the front door with such force, the framed photo on the telephone table in the hall fell over. She righted the picture of herself on her Communion day, catching sight of her reflection in the mirror as she did.

Despite having very little outlet or desire to show it off these days, Holly still knew she was very beautiful. She could look at herself for an age and not grow bored, tucking her hair behind her ears and pulling it up into a messy bun, while pouting with her perfect mouth; catching her side profile to admire her pert nose; sucking in her face to admire her high cheekbones, arched but not angular; making herself look happy, look sad, look angry, but always delightfully cute. Narcissus has nothing on a female teenager.

Yep, she was beautiful. And Holly knew it gave her power, a power she liked to play with sometimes – stretching its boundaries to see how far it could go before it snapped back.

There was never enough power. That's what she'd learned.

And worse. Being pretty attracted all the wrong sorts of attention.

Take George Richmond. What was his problem? He was good looking, for an older man. Wealthy, too. Why didn't he have a girl-friend? He wasn't gay, that was for sure. She'd seen the way he looked at her. Ron Ryan, too.

And they were just the men who lived in the Vale. It had been so much worse when she had to interact with boys her own age.

Holly couldn't put a finger on the exact moment she realised for certain she was gay. It had been too early for her to accept it, that was for sure. She'd pretended, like all teenagers did. She'd wanted to fit in.

Thankfully, the mistakes she'd made in doing that had been few and far apart. Though, ultimately, they had been big.

Huge, in fact.

She hadn't grasped cause and effect. She was surrounded by girls just like her at the time. Later, when she understood what she'd done, she'd smartened up, but it hurt her to hear girls talking like they knew everything, like they were in control. Like they owned the world and were untouchable.

When they'd moved to Withered Vale, she'd been eager to get along with the girls in her new school, as though if she resumed life as it had been, everything would return to being okay. She spent hours shopping in outlet malls with those girls, trying on various lip glosses and bodycon dresses that were too old for them, drinking Starbucks and talking with semi-American accents.

Once – and only once – she'd gone to a disco with them.

In the taxi on the way to the new venue in town, the Mezzanine, they'd explained to her the concept of snowballing.

'It's what you do at the Mez,' they'd said, speaking to her like she was the village idiot.

'I'm sorry,' she'd said. 'Run that by me again. You have sex with a guy . . .'

Theresa had shaken her head adamantly, her glorious red hair whipping back and forth and filling the cab with the scent of honey shampoo and hairspray.

'Jesus, Holly. How many times? You do not have sex. You give him a blowjob. And then you kiss a girl.'

'With his semen in my mouth?'

'Yeah. It's snowballing – get it? You kiss a girl, she kisses another girl. The boys love it.'

'I fucking bet they do. I am *not* doing that. I'd rather have sex with somebody.'

'Don't be such an idiot. Nobody shags these days. You have to respect your body.'

Holly had shaken her head quietly while the other girls laughed along with their leader. They were all sixteen and thought it was fine to give boys their own little porn movie and believe the girls were the ones having fun.

They were still labouring under the illusion prettiness was a superpower.

The innocence.

'Holly? What are you doing out here? It sounds like you're smashing the place up.'

Alison walked out of the kitchen, her hands still in oven gloves.

'The picture fell over,' Holly said.

'Come in and have some pizza. It's just out of the oven.'

Holly followed her mother into the kitchen and took a seat at the breakfast bar, while her mam rolled the pizza slicer through the thick rounds of pepperoni.

Alison had poured herself a large glass of wine, and left the bottle open on the counter. Holly picked it up and poured two fingers of wine into a tumbler meant for Coke.

'Holly,' Alison admonished.

'It's been a long day,' her daughter replied, raising the glass to her lips, daring her mother to forbid it.

Alison sighed, but let Holly take a sip.

Holly viewed her mother sideways, wondering how to start the conversation. Then she just blurted it out.

'I mean, school, Mam? Why did you say that to the detectives? What were you thinking?'

'I had to say something. They asked if we were going anywhere on our holidays and I . . . just said it. You would have finished school yesterday if you were still going.'

'What if they check? Why didn't you just tell them the truth? We're not breaking the law, me homeschooling. You've told them a lie and that's going to make them suspicious.'

'They're not going to check something like that, Holly. And homeschooling *is* unusual. We don't want to stand out. Everything has to seem ordinary.'

Holly took another sip of the wine, the tannins making her tongue feel thick. It was too dry. She preferred sweeter wines like the dessert wine in the back of the cabinet that she sampled whenever her mother left her alone for a night. If Alison ever decided to open that Sauternes, she was in for a shock.

Her mother slid a plate with a pizza slice towards her.

'Perhaps, Holly, you should think about going back to school.'

The sentence hung in the air like an unexploded bomb.

'I can't go back,' Holly said, quietly.

'Just for the final year. For your exams. We don't have to keep hiding . . .'

'I can't go back!' Holly blinked and took a deep breath. 'That's how he found us last time,' she said, calmer.

Her mother shook her head. 'That won't happen again.'

'Yes, it will. I can't be in a school and not register on the roll, Mam. I can't fake my name. God knows how many schools he rang before that stupid secretary said, "Oh yes, we've an Eva Baker here." '

Her mother stared at the counter, tracing circles with her finger, not able to look up at Holly. She really was acting very peculiar today.

'We could speak to the school, Holly. Explain.'

Holly shook her head vigorously.

'No. Don't you see, Mam? Can't you imagine what that took? The deviousness and persistence? Ringing place after place after place then probably doing them all again until he got somebody idiotic enough to tell him? Someone would slip up. We can't risk it.'

Alison put her glass down and reached across for her daughter's hand. She took it in hers and brought it to her mouth, kissed it gently.

'He won't hurt you again,' she said, and her tone was so assured, yet so sad, that Holly felt a lump form in her throat.

'And that's how we want it,' Holly said, gently extricating her hand and picking up a slice of pizza. 'Which is why we need to come up with a plan about what to tell the police if they ask which school I'm allegedly attending.'

Her mother pursed her lips.

'What?' Holly said.

'That's not our biggest problem, Holly. Why did you tell them that Olive Collins was blackmailing me?'

'She *was* blackmailing you!'

'She wasn't *blackmailing* me.'

Holly shook her head.

'Well, why were you giving her all those clothes, then? Out of the kindness of your heart? I know your business is good, Mam, but you're not running the Zara chain.'

'Holly.' Her mother held up her hand. 'Stop.'

Holly lowered her pizza slice, the bit she'd just swallowed making its way down uncomfortably.

'To blackmail somebody, you have to have something to blackmail them with. Your dislike of Olive is clouding your judgement. I understand you wanted to tell the detectives how unpleasant you thought she was. But you know, don't you, that you've just made them suspicious of us? Of me? What if they find out I lied?'

'Lied about what?'

Her mother blinked, then flicked her eyes sideways. Holly stared at her, taken aback. What was her mother hiding? But when Alison looked back at Holly, she was herself again.

'Nothing. Just, about our situation. You need to be more careful, pet.'

Holly felt her eyes tearing up. She'd thought she was doing the right thing, that she'd judged the man detective correctly. It would have been silly to pretend they liked their neighbour when they hadn't gone near the house for the last three months. But as soon as the word blackmail had left her mouth, she'd regretted it.

And now Holly felt like she was having an out-of-body experience.

She was used to being the grown-up, the one who told her mother what they had to do. Alison had been fragile for so long.

But something had shifted.

Her mother was looking at Holly now like she was the one who needed to be protected, like she was the one who had made the bad decisions.

Holly blinked again. This was new.

OLIVE

No. 4

I'd been watching *EastEnders*, I remember, and I'd paused it when the doorbell rang, leaving my coffee to go cold.

New Year's Day 2017 had come and gone and I'd barely seen a soul so I was happy when I opened the door to Holly Daly standing on the step.

She was shivering in the cold and my first thought was to get her inside, get her warm. I didn't immediately wonder why she was there, until I noticed she had that look about her that said she was determined to say something to me. You know the feeling, when you have to get something out of your mouth and nothing can get in the way? She looked like that.

I thought, at that point, I knew what she wanted.

It had been quite some time since Alison had paid a visit. I was hoping her daughter might be bearing an olive branch, even an apology for her mother's absence, and wanted to say it and get back to her room and Netflix as soon as possible. Odd, that Alison would send Holly, but then, I'd already begun to think Alison was a bit strange.

I led Holly into the sitting room, determined to make this foray into the world of adult politics as quick and painless as possible.

'I don't want you calling into my mother's shop any more,' she said, before I'd even offered to boil the kettle.

'What?'

'My mam is not running a charity. She can't afford to hand out freebies left, right and centre.'

'What are you talking about?' I laughed nervously. I did not like where this was going and the unexpectedness of it had rooted me to the spot, making me feel doubly ill at ease.

'You keep taking things from the shop . . .'

'I haven't taken anything . . .'

'So stop calling in there if you don't want to pay for things.'

'Holly, slow down. This is a complete misunderstanding. Are you talking about the items your mother *gives* me? That's not *taking*, not in the way you're implying. They're gifts.'

'That's a lie.'

'Holly!'

'It is. You know full well why she keeps giving you things – because you keep turning up looking for them. And we know why you're doing that. My mam is too polite to say no to you. You know that. You're letting her manners be her downfall.'

The shock of being attacked like that can only be understood if it's happened to you. When you think a conversation is going to go one way and it turns out the exact opposite . . . you can't really control your reaction. I couldn't, anyway. The adrenaline surged through me, making my tongue faster than my good sense.

'Manners?' I said. 'You come into my home and say these things and you want to speak of manners? I mean, if you think I've been somehow robbing your mother – well, let's call the police, shall we? Get them involved?'

She paled.

I was ashamed of the words almost as soon as they left my mouth.

The last thing the Dalys wanted was the police.

Neither of us said anything for a few seconds. I softened my face. I had no interest in fighting with this little girl. She didn't even realise it, but I was her friend, not her enemy. If she knew what George Richmond had been doing!

I calmed down. Holly was all bravado but it was misplaced on her mother's behalf. In a way, it was admirable that she wanted to stand up for Alison.

'Look,' I said. 'I think this is simple miscommunication. You're always welcome, Holly, to call over. We're neighbours. But really, my relationship with your mother has nothing to do with you. You don't know the full facts.'

She had more steel than I'd given her credit for.

'It has everything to do with me,' she hissed. 'You might think you can blackmail my mam into . . .'

'Blackmail! What? I've never heard the like!'

'Well, what would you call it, then? I saw her accounts – you ate into a quarter of her Christmas profits in the Wicklow shop between the dresses and the coats and all that other stuff. And you think you'll get away with it because she . . .'

She couldn't say it. Even Alison couldn't say it. It was just there, hanging over the two of them like the sword of Damocles.

But Holly was wrong. I'd never asked Alison for anything. She gave, freely. 'Oh, let me sort you out with something,' she'd say, rubbing her hands nervously, that way she does.

Maybe she saw it as a transaction, but if she did, that wasn't my doing.

Alison had told me that first time to pop down to the shop. So I did, a few days later. I bought a lovely dress and she paired it with a pretty scarf and necklace. She insisted I take them as a gift.

I was a frequent caller after that and I always bought something small but she kept throwing things on top. What was I supposed to do – hand her gifts back?

The thing is, I was mostly calling in to see her.

She'd abruptly and inexplicably cooled our friendship and I wanted to know why. *I hadn't asked for anything.*

I was willing to forgive the accusation, the aggression from Holly. We could all be friends. I'd speak to Alison. If she really had an issue with me calling in to her store, trying to be in her life, she just had to say it to me.

It was something for her and me to discuss. Not her daughter and me.

I stood aside and pointed at the door.

'I think you should go, Holly,' I said. 'We should forget all about this.'

But then Holly walked right up to me until her face was inches away from mine and I could smell the mint on her breath, the strawberry balm on her lips.

'Go into my mother's shop again and I'll fucking kill you,' she said.

RON

No. 7

Maybe it had been a mistake calling over to George's.

Ron took a drag from his cigarette and stared into the dancing flames that licked the edges of the chimenea.

He'd wanted to gauge what the others were saying. See if anybody knew about him and Olive. George had seemed like the best bet – he was the sort of bloke who noticed things. But he'd been appalled at the idea of Ron and Olive, like it never would have crossed his mind.

Ron had put it out there like it was the most natural thing in the world and he'd nothing to feel guilty about. Or hide. It had seemed like a good plan . . . but maybe he'd been overthinking things. Again.

He'd been surprised when the young policeman had knocked at the door and asked if he'd be at home the following day for a chat with the detectives. Ron had seen them making their way around the Vale and assumed he'd be getting his visit any minute. His stomach had filled with butterflies as he waited, so much so he'd ended up on the toilet, his bowels emptying while he hung onto the handrails he'd had fitted specially.

It didn't sound like they'd said anything to George to indicate they suspected Olive had been killed. It was all just routine, Ron told himself, as he flicked ash at the fire and shivered.

Christ, he'd been delighted to see the back of Olive. And he'd had three lovely months of peace, at least there was that.

At first, he'd felt nothing but satisfaction about what he'd done. But there was no denying, as time moved on, he'd started to feel a smidgen of regret.

He should have just ended it with her.

Instead, he'd been vicious. Really nasty. It took a warped brain to do what he had. But she'd brought it on herself, hadn't she? She'd been the author of her own demise. And perhaps it was because he'd had strong feelings for her, and she'd hurt him so badly, that he did what he did.

Ron took another drag.

What if she'd left a note, though? What if she had written down what he'd said to her, what he'd done?

The smoke and the fear were making Ron light-headed.

Had it all been worth it, just to get his leg over?

More and more these days, he found himself wondering that. With all women, not just his neighbours. It was like he sought out trouble, like he went looking to treat women like shit, for them to treat him like shit back. Maybe he enjoyed pain.

Because he knew he was behaving like an awful person. That it wasn't really him.

You'd think, after Olive at least, he would have learned the lesson about not pissing on his own doorstep. For a time it had seemed like fun, going from number four to number five and back again.

Olive had been his favourite. She was just pure filth. It's always the ones you least expect. He loved that about her.

Chrissy, on the other hand – she was looking for a prince. A fireman. Someone to rescue her. She wanted to talk and to be held and to cry about how her husband didn't love her any more.

There was nothing worse than a woman crying after sex.

No. He'd have to extricate himself from the Chrissy situation. It was loaded with pitfalls. But that was a problem for another day. First, he had to get through this conversation with the detectives.

Ron opened his fist. He'd had it closed so tight there were nail marks on his palm.

He looked at Olive's knickers.

One time, she'd let him stuff a pair in her mouth. Chrissy had never let him do anything like that. It was always missionary with Chrissy so she could be cuddled.

Olive had been his dream woman.

Until . . .

Ron flung the underwear into the fire and watched as it burned.

Goodbye, Olive, he whispered. *It was fun while it lasted.*

OLIVE

No. 4

Ron. My lovely man.

When did it go so sour?

Well, I know when. But why?

Why wasn't I enough?

From the moment I met Ron, I was charmed by him.

He was funny and flirty and confident – he ticked all my boxes. I'd never liked men I had to make a huge effort with; the silent ones who gave the impression of being really deep, when that was never the case.

Through many a disappointing experience, I'd learned that men who didn't talk weren't *deep*. They just had nothing to say.

With Ron, what you saw was what you got.

It took a while for me to realise that he was properly coming on to me. Ron had a way with all the women in the Vale. He would flash *that* smile and the wink, tell his dirty jokes, and we girls would blush and beam and flutter our eyelashes.

Harmless flirting.

He called around one evening and said he'd overheard me telling Ed that my boiler was broken and I needed a new one.

It was late summer, but the evening was still warm and I was wearing a cute sundress that flattered my figure from every angle. I walked a lot and I was still quite trim, even at fifty-three.

'Thought I could take a look,' he said. 'See what's up. With you being here on your own and everything.'

'Oh, right,' I said. 'You're here to *see to* my pipes, are you?'

He laughed.

'That's right. I'd like to give them a good seeing-to.'

'A proper gentleman, indeed. Come in, then!'

Once in the kitchen, he leaned behind the boiler in the cupboard, humming and hawing every so often.

'Would you like me to take off my shirt while I work?' he asked.

'You won't get me doing your laundry that easy,' I laughed.

He chuckled and ducked his head back in, pulling at various bits and examining the pipes.

'Well, my diagnosis is it's broken,' he said. 'You'll have to call somebody who knows how to fix them. Cup of tea for the working man?'

'The cheek of you,' I said. 'Run out of teabags, did you? Is that your ploy?'

He flashed me that cheeky grin.

I'm not quite sure how it happened, whether I looked at him a certain way or he at me, but one minute we were standing at the kitchen counter, laughing about something David Solanke had said about growing cucumbers, and the next thing he leaned in to kiss me.

'You are so beautiful when you laugh,' he said, and I actually felt myself melting.

Then we were wrapped around each other, his tongue one with mine, his hands, all ten of them, making their way inside my blouse, around to my bra strap, up my skirt and inside my stockings.

Our first time was exciting and sexy and fulfilling in a way I don't think I'd ever experienced. Perhaps it was the unexpectedness of it. I'd been planning a cup of tea, my book and an early night. Now Ron Ryan had me bent over my countertop, the two of us panting and sweating like animals.

His age helped, too. Ron was at least ten years younger than me and utterly gorgeous. Dark, tanned, strong. And he found me, little old me, attractive.

To begin with, I was fine with the notion of us not having a conventional relationship. I'd decided I was beyond dating – holding hands as we walked through town, that sort of thing. And I didn't want everybody in the Vale knowing my business. Ron felt the same.

But more than that – the secrecy was thrilling. It was a turn-on, never knowing when he might rap on the back door, the different things we might get up to. Sometimes, though it was rare (he had a weird thing about people being in his pad), I would call over to his on the pretext of needing a hand with something and tell him I'd no panties on and he'd do me right there, in the hallway, barely pausing to close the front door.

I had no ties, no commitments, no inhibitions. Life was short and I was going to have as much fun as possible.

It was an awakening.

We never said we loved each other. We never did anything outside of our houses. There was no explicit declaration of monogamy.

And I kept telling myself it wasn't a long-term thing and that Ron would probably settle with some young girl half his age. He'd bring her to nice places and hold her hand as they walked down the street together. Plan children and marriage.

I knew that and I swallowed it, even when, sometimes, he'd fall asleep in my bed and I would look at the dark eyelashes resting on his cheeks and run my hands through his hair and think – he's all mine.

But then I saw him at Chrissy Hennessy's when Matt's car was out.

It was morning, Cam was in school and I knew Ron was on holidays from work that week.

I'd been looking out my window and saw him come out of his house and stroll around the Vale, a hungry look on his face. I thought he was coming for me and a huge grin broke out on my face. I loved him in the morning. He had so much energy.

I turned and sprayed some perfume on my neck and wrists, but when I looked back, he was gone.

Curious, I went outside, just in time to see him saunter in next door.

I stood in my sitting room and watched out the net curtains for what seemed like an age, waiting.

A full two hours later, he came out, his face slick with sweat, that same satisfied expression on his face that I was all too familiar with. He took one furtive look around, his eyes lingering on my house, then jogged off.

The dirty bastard was having sex with both of us.

FRANK

'You'll be okay going up there, yeah?'

Frank couldn't help it. While he was all for girl power, being old-fashioned and gentlemanly was in his nature.

Emma Child's apartment block looked fairly civilised. Over-looking the harbour, the complex was well maintained, expensive. But it had all the elements of anonymity and loneliness that made Frank worry about the girl making her way inside on her own. Who knew what lurked in the stairwell?

It was, bizarrely, the first time he'd dropped her home. Nor-mally, they parted ways at the station. But it had been a long day down in Withered Vale, so they'd voted on it and unanimously decided to finish up for the evening without returning to HQ. Frank had successfully managed to delegate the bulk of the paper-work; tomorrow would be another long day.

'Eh, I think I'll manage,' Emma said, opening the car door. 'Thanks for the lift.'

She got out and trotted off in the direction of the block's entrance.

'See you in the morning,' Frank called through the window, as he swung the car into a U-turn. She was already gone.

His own estate was a hub of activity. A group of teenage boys played footie on the green, their hoodies marking the goalposts. A couple of girls sat on somebody's garden wall, pretending not to watch the game, shrieking loudly at each other's jokes and playing with their hair. Every action strategic.

The boys were oblivious.

Frank's neighbour was washing his car, the solar lights on the bush in his garden beginning to twinkle as dusk fell.

'Only home now?' he called out jovially after Frank had backed the car into the drive. 'We're away for two weeks from tomorrow. Heading to France on the ferry. Thought I'd give the car a bit of a shine. You wouldn't keep an eye on things, would you? When you're here.'

Frank walked over to the wall that separated the gardens.

'No bother. Taking the kids?'

'Unless you're offering.'

Frank smiled.

'I guess we're stuck with the little shits, then. It's a shame they don't do kennels for kids, eh? We're staying in a campsite near Normandy. Pools, playgrounds, kids' club, that sort of thing. Myself and the missus can have our fill of red wine and crêpes, as long as we squeeze it all in between the hours of 10 a.m. and 1 p.m. Might bring a few bottles back in the boot if she doesn't overpack. She's at it all day. Four suitcases! It's a car, not the bloody Tardis.'

Frank's neighbour paused, thinking.

'Hmm. We could leave the towels and bed linen there, couldn't we? Make a bit of room. We've so many towels, she'd hardly miss them.' He narrowed his eyes as he considered this and looked to Frank for guidance.

'You might need the towels to wrap the wine in for the journey back,' Frank said. 'Just in case it's a bumpy ride.'

'Good idea. I'll keep an eye out for a nice red for you. Oh, hold on, before you go.'

His neighbour dropped the sponge into the bucket of soapy water and ducked into his house. He returned with a plastic bag and a plate wrapped in tinfoil.

'Yvonne made this up for you. She did a pot of curry to get rid of the chicken in the fridge. There's some bread and that in the bag. We're getting breakfast on the ferry in the morning. No point leaving stuff rotting in the cupboards.'

'Cheers,' Frank said, taking the load.

He stuck his key in the front door, just as the evening chorus of mothers summoning their children for dinner started up.

The house was quiet and cool. Frank had installed proper double-glazing a few years ago. He worked nights back then and had to sleep during the day. You couldn't expect an entire estate to stay quiet just because you had your head down. Better to sort yourself out than get angry at the world.

He made his way into the kitchen and put away his gifted groceries – half a loaf, apples, a litre of milk, a packet of ham, four Petits Filous.

'Petits fucking Filous?' Frank said aloud, followed by a 'Sorry, Mona.'

Yvonne was having a laugh.

He wondered if she'd meant that carrier bag for him at all.

Her curry, though, was a treat. The woman could cook, no doubt about it. He took the tinfoil off, popped it in the microwave and headed into the sitting room to fetch his laptop. He stopped in the hall beside the picture of Mona on their wedding day and, now his hands were free, placed his fingers to his lips, then to her face. He did the same thing every day, entering and leaving the house. Sometimes he talked to her, too. Just to fill the silence.

'Odd day,' he said. 'Hot, too. I'm surprised the make-up wasn't sliding off Emma's face.'

He found his laptop on the coffee table beside that morning's half-drunk cup of coffee. Everything was always where Frank had left it.

Except his wife, who he'd left in bed that morning but had never seen alive again. Mona had been driving home from a late twelve-hour nursing shift at the hospital when she had the encounter with a drunk driver. When they found the car and turned it the right way up, the water in the ditch had left her unrecognisable.

She was fifteen years dead, his Mona.

He'd eat the curry in the kitchen. Mona had never liked them eating on their laps in the sitting room. It was too messy, she said, and a slippery slope to the end of a marriage.

'You think our marriage will end if we eat in front of the telly?' Frank had laughed. 'Are we that fragile?'

'First, it's watching television while we eat, and not talking. Then it's sitting in separate chairs, not snuggling up together. Then it's falling asleep with our books, instead of making love. Then it's twin beds. Then separate rooms, because I can't bear your snoring and, sure, we're no longer sleeping together anyway. Then one of us has a mid-life crisis and needs human affection, which we're not getting in the marriage. An affair starts. And *he* sits and talks to me at the dinner table. So, I have to leave you and be with him.'

'Hold up – how come it's you who has the affair? You adulter-ess, you!'

'Sit down at the table, love, and we'll not have to worry about my future virtue.'

Frank got a beer from the fridge just as the microwave pinged. He grabbed the container and sat, shoving a forkful of chicken and rice in his mouth and chewing happily as he opened his computer and refreshed the gambling website to check on that day's bets.

He'd just got settled when his mobile buzzed. It was Amira from Crime Scene.

He answered, guessing from the background noise that she was calling him from outside a pub.

'Pathology ring you yet?' she said.

Her voice was slow, her tongue thick. She was three, maybe four G&Ts in.

'Not a dicky bird,' Frank said.

'I'm in a bar.'

'I used all my powers of deduction to figure that one out.'

'I'm drinking with Ben from pathology.'

'Yeah?' Frank's ears pricked. 'What's he got to say, then?'

'I presume God himself will send you his report shortly. Hope-fully he won't smite Ben for leaking to me.'

'Hopefully you're the only one Ben is leaking to, or I'll smite him myself, never mind his boss.'

'Yada yada. It was a heart attack, if you're interested. Caused by inhalation of carbon monoxide. It was quick, though. Ben says there wasn't as much poison in her system as they'd usually see in a toxic death. Turns out, she had an undiagnosed pre-existing heart condi-tion that caused a cardiac arrest early in the process. Otherwise, she might have gone through the headaches and nausea and so on, maybe realised something was up. She was most likely phoning the emergency services in the middle of the heart attack, not realising there was even a leak.'

'I see,' Frank said. He scratched his chin as he tried to process the information. 'So, if her heart thingy was undiagnosed, then there was no way anybody would have known about it.'

'Obviously. Why? Do you think somebody could have messed with the boiler but didn't intend to kill her? Thought she'd figure it out and just get a little sick?'

'*If* somebody other than Olive messed with it—'

'Come on, Frank, you're not still beating that drum? Why did she ring us if she was trying to kill herself?'

'Aborted attempt?'

Amira snorted.

'Keep trying. Your dreams might come true. What are you doing, anyway? Do you want to come down for a drink?'

'I'm working,' Frank said.

'So am I, clearly.'

'Enjoy your night, love. Enjoy Ben.'

He hung up.

'She's just a friend,' he assured Mona, as he passed her picture on the way to the loo. 'That's all.'

LILY & DAVID

No. 2

They'd settled the children.

They hadn't told them yet. David offered some strange logic about how things would be more settled and easier to deal with in the bright sunshine of the morning. They were procrastinating, both of them, and Lily was happy to go along with whatever logic could justify it. She figured the children already knew. Telling them, telling Wolf, would make it real, so let the innocence remain a little longer.

She stood at the cooker, absentmindedly stirring and seasoning a pot of soup she'd made to use up David's carrots. Lily had no appetite. It was just a task that had to be done.

David came in behind her and placed his arms around her waist.

'Where are you, my love?'

Lily frowned.

'What?'

'Where is your beautiful head? You just put sugar into the soup.'

'I didn't,' Lily stared into the pot. 'Did I?'

David turned her around to face him.

'Forget supper. What can I do to take your mind off things?'

Lily shrugged. She seemed to have so much on her mind lately. Work, family, neighbours.

David studied her, then crossed the kitchen to his iPod dock. She watched him, puzzled, as he selected a piece of Nigerian music, a soft salsa beat. His hips started to sway to the rhythm, then his whole body was moving, coming towards her.

Lily couldn't help it; she laughed.

'Are you laughing at my moves, wench?'

Lily smiled and nodded. Her husband grabbed her in his arms and started to sway her, too, before spinning her and bringing her back into his embrace.

'Let's dance the night away,' he said, his mouth close to her ear. 'We have nowhere to go, nobody to see and nothing to worry about.'

Lily let the music take her, but still she felt the weight on her shoulders.

Nothing to worry about? That wasn't strictly true. After what had happened?

She let herself be spun again, but now the smile had slipped from her face.

Why, just why, was David so happy?

CHRISSY & MATT

No. 5

Matt wouldn't stop talking. He moved from room to room, keeping up a running commentary on the day's events, how the neighbours had reacted, who'd been saying and doing what – so much talking. Chrissy didn't think she'd heard as many words from him in years.

She really wished he'd just . . . shush. There was so much going on in her head, she needed him to be quiet for five minutes so she could think.

He was back from the kitchen, standing between Chrissy and the TV so she was forced to look at him.

'*Britain's Got Talent* is on,' she said, not moving her head from the cushion. The telly was on mute, but he didn't seem to notice. 'It's the last semi-final. You're in my way.'

'Are you serious? I'm trying to have a conversation with you.'

'You're not having a conversation with me. You're talking at me.'

'What is wrong with you? All you've done since the police left is lie on that couch.'

'It's the shock,' Chrissy said.

Matt had told them they should speak to Ron. He'd implied Ron and Olive – Ron and Olive! – were having an affair.

Could you even call it an affair? If the two of them were single? It was she who was having the affair, wasn't it?

She could hardly sit in judgement of Ron. She knew that. Not when she was the married woman. But she still felt like somebody had punched her in the throat.

The first time she and Ron had made love had been right here, on the couch.

Matt was away for the weekend and Cam was asleep upstairs. There was a gale blowing that night and Ron had called over to check if the satellite signal had gone on her telly. It had. She'd lit candles and opened a bottle of wine for herself, just for something to do. She rarely drank on her own – didn't like it, in fact – but she was quite depressed that weekend. For obvious reasons.

She invited him in and they'd ended up sharing the wine and chatting. They had so much in common. And he was so lovely. He listened to her, laughed at all her jokes. He was a charmer, she knew that, but he wasn't sleazy. He was quite smart, actually. And sensitive.

Ron had told her about his younger brother, who was severely disabled and in a home. Even though he tried to show all this bravado, like he didn't care that much, Chrissy could tell it really bothered him. Ron had spent a fortune on renovations to his house so his brother could move in with him but it had never happened. Their parents and the home's administrators had decided his brother needed full-time care in a residential setting; even the nurse Ron offered to pay for wouldn't be enough.

It was a side to Ron people didn't see and, while Chrissy knew he thought of himself as an out-and-out ladies' man, she liked this vulnerable part of him, the softness.

Ron leaned in to kiss her and she'd reacted with shock. He was very gentlemanly about it – said he'd fancied her from afar for as long as he'd known her, but that he appreciated she was a married woman. It was the way he looked at her – like he was desperate to kiss her again – that did it. When had Matt last looked at her like that? She put her wine down and pulled his face towards hers. He'd asked if she was sure and she said she'd never been more sure of anything. Then he laid her back on the couch, gently, and started to undress her. The whole time he whispered how beautiful she was and how much he wanted her. She cried some more.

In her silly, childish neediness, she'd imagined the two of them had something special. And all the while . . .

It did explain why Olive had been so utterly vicious to her that time, though.

'Hello? Earth to Chrissy.'

Matt was waving his hands at her like a traffic conductor.

'I said, what shock? You didn't actually see Olive's body.'

'You were singing from a different hymn sheet for the police,' Chrissy said.

'Yeah, well, they're not here now. And I think you need to snap out of it. Come on. You were hardly best friends with the woman.'

'You're still in the way of the TV,' Chrissy said, coldly.

Matt's mouth tightened.

'You know what, Chrissy?' he said. 'To hell with it. Let's talk about Olive. And why you should be glad she's dead.'

Chrissy's heart gave a little flutter.

'What did you say?'

'I said, you're probably glad she's dead.'

Chrissy sat up.

'What are you talking about?'

'I know she threatened you.'

'I . . . I . . . How did you know?'

She'd paled, all feeling leaking from her face and limbs like somebody had turned off a tap. Chrissy was suddenly numb, paralysed.

'I know everything,' Matt said, and the look he gave her sent shivers down her spine.

The sitting room door opened and Cam walked in.

'Are you fighting?' he said.

He was in his *Star Wars* pyjamas, the trousers shy of his ankles. They'd bought them when he was nine and they were still his favourites at eleven, despite being well worn and faded and too small for his stretching limbs.

'Why aren't you asleep?' Chrissy asked.

Matt looked at the pair of them, shook his head and walked from the room.

Chrissy felt her body sigh with relief. Good timing, Cam.

'I can't sleep,' Cam said, sitting beside her on the couch.

Chrissy studied her son's face.

She'd become used to all her interactions with her son involving pleading, screaming, cajoling, shouting. Cam had become a force who had to be dealt with. Sometimes just thinking about him gave her a knot in her stomach.

Chrissy very rarely looked at him these days. She looked *for* him. She looked *through* him. But not at him.

She was looking at him now. And while his words might be

angry and he'd got out of bed without asking, she didn't see naughtiness or cheek. She saw a distressed, frightened little boy.

She reached out her hand and touched his cheek, freckled and scratched from some escapade or other, but so soft. He still had the tiniest hint of baby in his features, the barest trace of that small toddler, blond hair standing on end and big blue eyes always smiling up at her.

She felt a lump form in her throat and the pain of how much she loved him closed in on her chest. That was the thing about being left on her own all the time with Cam from the time he was a baby – they'd cemented their bond. Matt didn't have that with his son.

'Do you want to watch *BGT* with me?' she asked.

He nodded, surprised. He'd been expecting to be yelled at, told to go back to bed, threatened with a punishment.

Chrissy held out her arm, the throw still draped over her shoulders, and Cam climbed into the cuddle. He looked up at his mother, then across at the television she'd unmuted, where a choir had started to sing 'Jerusalem'.

Chrissy kissed the top of his head, smelling shampoo and ozone and something sweet. She was content to just be with her son in that moment, not to think about what Matt had said.

'They're good singers,' he said.

'They are.'

'Can I have a Coke?'

'Don't push it.'

She felt him smile and hugged him tighter.

'Cam?'

'Yeah?'

'I'm sorry about yesterday. It must have been very upsetting for you . . . all that. And then I just let rip at you. I . . . I was in a bit of shock myself, I think. I should have talked to you. Ms Collins was our neighbour. I should have asked if you were okay.'

'I'm okay.'

'It's perfectly understandable if you're not.'

'I am. I don't care if she's dead.'

Chrissy stiffened.

'What do you mean, love?'

Cam looked up at her. His eyes were wide and his face sad and worried, like he had a terrible secret. Chrissy's heart started to pound.

'She was a bad lady, Mammy,' he said.

OLIVE

No. 4

The day I approached Chrissy Hennessy, she was standing out on her patio hanging laundry on a clothes dryer, a faraway look on her face that put her a million miles away from the pair of her husband's briefs she was loosely pegging.

She didn't even realise I was there until I reached into the basket by her feet and handed her a shirt, at which point she clasped her breast and swore.

'Jesus, Olive, you scared the life out of me.'

She laughed, this little tinkle of happiness.

'Sorry about that. Can I help you?'

I took one of the shirts and pegged it to the line while she stood there, watching me, bemused.

'Is Matt home today?'

'Mm.'

It was a loaded murmur, like she wanted rid of him. For what, I could imagine.

'That's nice. He works really hard, doesn't he?'

She picked up a towel and started to peg it, working away from me on the dryer. A nod. That was all the gratitude she had for the husband who provided for her.

'You're absolutely blessed, Chrissy, to have a man like that. I'm sure there are women who'd kill to be in your position.'

She looked at me oddly. I laughed.

'Oh, not me. He's all yours. My goodness, I'm not a husband robber!'

'I wouldn't think you were, Olive.'

She smiled. My God, it was so smug. She was free to cheat on Matt but surely he'd never look at another woman when he had her.

'I just hope you appreciate him. Sometimes I think it must be hard to marry young. I imagine some people end up feeling a little trapped. But, honestly, take it from somebody who's seen a lot more – the grass isn't always greener.'

I picked up another top, one of hers this time.

'Really, I can do this myself,' she said, a little nervously. 'There's no need.'

'Oh, I just like the company. We see so little of each other in the Vale.'

'Mm.'

I shook out the creases in the silky vest.

'I think you see a bit of Ron, though, don't you?'

'What?'

Her hand froze, halfway into the basket.

I shrugged, like I'd said something or nothing.

'I don't know what you're talking about,' she said.

I raised my eyebrows. 'I think you do.'

She narrowed her eyes, looked at me like I was something unpleasant she'd just found on her shoe.

'I mean, I'm not interfering or anything. I just thought you might need to know that it's been noticed. And if I've noticed, other people might have too.'

Chrissy turned to look back at her house so quickly, she kicked the laundry basket, upending it. She cried out. She dropped onto her hunkers, grabbing at the wet clothes, her whole face and neck roaring red now.

When she stood up, her demeanour had changed. She wasn't shocked now. She was a cornered rat. And we all know how they react.

'Are you threatening me, Olive? Because you should know that while we're all nice and polite here in the Vale, where I grew up, you learned how to defend yourself.'

I shook my head, my face astonished.

'Not at all, Chrissy. If you actually listened to me, you'd realise I'm being a friend.'

She was still staring at me, like she might have underestimated me and it was just dawning on her.

And I kept my face placid, friendly, appealing.

'You should learn to keep your nose out of other people's business if you know what's good for you,' she said, and turned on her heel.

And in that moment, I realised that I was the one who underestimated her.

EMMA

Emma loved her apartment.

She'd known from the day she and Graham first viewed it that if they ever broke up, she would be keeping it.

Prophetic, that.

Graham kicked up a fuss when she threw him out. He was the one who had heard there was an apartment on the marina for sale before it was even listed. He earned more than she did and could easily buy out her share of the mortgage.

But he didn't have a leg to stand on.

A. Her parents had given them the deposit when they'd bought the place, and –

B. She'd caught him with another woman in their bed.

Emma hadn't liked playing the family card, but she knew Graham was terrified of her father. Her dad was, understandably, fiercely protective of his little girl.

'You'll need to have a chat with my father, let him know you'll pay him his deposit back,' she'd said. 'Don't forget to mention the reason we're splitting up.'

That did it.

Graham collected the rest of his stuff that weekend. She had the mattress taken away while he was still in the apartment folding his boxers before he packed them (she wouldn't miss that little habit) and whining about having to change the names on the bills.

The fight had been worth it. Emma smoothed butter over her toast and looked out at the boats bobbing up and down in the marina, the early morning sun glistening on the water, as the world outside woke up.

One day, she might find somebody and have children and decide she wanted a garden rather than six flights of stairs and a lift that would never accommodate a buggy. One day. But not today.

Emma chewed on the toast as she carried her make-up bag and mirror over to the window. She liked to get ready in the strongest light possible.

If she could cover the scar in light that searching, nobody would be able to see it.

Graham, at his absolute lowest point, had tried to claim he'd gone looking elsewhere because she'd disappeared into herself after the attack. It was the worst, cruellest type of victim-blaming. She was glad she'd seen that in him before it was too late, before they had gone down the family route and made ties that couldn't be so easily severed.

Emma *had* been traumatised after the attack. It had taken her months to come to terms with what had happened to her – she was still getting to grips with it now.

She'd thought she was going to die. So yes, she hadn't been herself afterwards.

None of that provided cover for Graham's betrayal.

Looking in the mirror, she traced her finger down the crescent-shaped line that ran its way around her cheek and under her jaw.

And then she rummaged in her make-up bag and found her primer. She'd start with that and move on to concealer, then foundation, then her powder.

It was 8 a.m. Frank was collecting her at 9.

She had just enough time.

Emma couldn't help it. Every time she was in a car with Frank, she kept one hand on the door handle and the other on the dashboard. Her foot kept pressing the imaginary brake on her side. He didn't seem to notice. He was too busy driving like he, and any passenger he might have, was immortal. Frank had explained to her on more than one occasion that while he was fast, he was exceptionally safe. He'd had advanced driving lessons. She'd tried to explain that there was no accounting for other drivers and she really had no desire to experience his evasive manoeuvres were they to encounter somebody who wasn't as 'safe' as him, but her concerns fell on deaf ears.

The noise as his Opel Vectra hared through the countryside that morning was loud inside the car. Outside, it must have been deafening.

He talked as he tried to kill her, filling her in on the informal post-mortem report from Amira Lund the night previous. They weren't sure what relevance the new information had for their case.

They'd called in to headquarters briefly that morning and given their boss an update. She was happy for them to continue interviewing the residents in the Vale and for the team to keep up the background checks on Olive Collins, without declaring an official murder inquiry just yet.

'We'd better act surprised and grateful when God issues us with the official PM report later,' Emma said, foot jammed to the floor on her invisible brake pedal as they careered around a hairpin bend.

Frank gave her a sideways, bemused look.

'You're catching on quick,' he said. 'How do you know we call him God?'

'Neither you nor Amira Lund are particularly religious and yet you mention God quite a lot when Dr Hendricks is the pathologist on call. It doesn't take a genius.'

'Do you know what his first name is?'

'No.'

'Godfrey. Perfect, huh?'

'The road!' she replied. He'd nearly driven them into a ditch he was so far on the other side of the white line.

He laughed.

'Nothing around here to watch out for.'

'Anything on DNA?' she said, catching her breath.

'No. There's a pile of it in the house. Uniforms asked the neighbours to volunteer samples yesterday so they could be ruled out. Nobody is being difficult. Yet.'

'So, we talk to this Ron guy this morning,' Emma asked.

'Yeah. Let's see if Matt Hennessy was onto something. Maybe Ron was Olive's bit on the side.'

'Hmm,' Emma said.

'What are you hmming about?'

'That's an interesting turn of phrase you used. That he was her bit on the side. As opposed to her being his.'

'I'm a very modern man,' Frank said.

Emma turned her head so he couldn't see her smirk.

They sped north from Wicklow town and out towards the village of Marwood. It was a pretty place, the village. Emma saw some of it as they blasted through. Small red-brick houses with street fronts amid old-style butchers and grocery stores, pubs and cosy cafes. They'd seen a large Aldi on the outskirts, but it hadn't obliterated the local businesses, yet.

'It's strange, isn't it,' Emma said. 'I was reading last night about Withered Vale. You know Olive's cottage was already there when the developer built the other houses? That's why it's so much smaller than the rest. I'm amazed he kept that name. Withered Vale . . . it's not very attractive, is it? Though, I suppose it has history to it. It must have been odd for Olive, seeing all those big places going up on either side of her, and hers just this little dwelling in amongst it all. Losing all that privacy and solitude.'

They'd crossed the bridge and turned onto the narrow road that brought them towards the Vale.

'I don't know about that,' Frank said. 'You get older, you realise you like having company. I always think couples who move out to the countryside when their brood have grown up are nuts. You might think you want the peace but there comes a point where you want hustle and bustle around you. You want to know you're not alone, even if there's nobody there with you when you close the door at night. And you need to be closer to things, too. Hospitals and what have you.'

Emma said nothing. Her parents had sold their family home in town and moved somewhere more rural, an entirely isolated location. They seemed content there now. But they hadn't been happy when they first moved. She knew that.

'Maybe Olive enjoyed having all of life around her.' Frank was still talking. 'Maybe she enjoyed it too much. You heard Matt Hennessy yesterday. He had a point. You assume people living in an isolated development would be close-knit, but the Hennessys moved there for privacy. Not to know everything about their neighbours' business. Olive may have been a bit too much of a busybody.'

Ron Ryan was like a caricature of a ladies' man. From his deep orange tan and dazzling white teeth to the shiny black hair and shirt opened just a button too far.

He could have been sleazy but Emma found him kind of funny. He was nervous and kept making quips and talking flamboyantly with his hands. She didn't quite know why, but she sensed that underneath the carefully cultivated character, Ron Ryan was a nice man. Well. Nicer.

But she could tell from Frank's body language that he didn't know what to make of him.

And he smoked like a man on death row. One after the other, flicking the butts into the ashes in the chimenea in his back garden, where he'd brought them to sit. He had a wheelchair ramp leading up to his slightly raised back door, and she wondered about that. He lived alone, she knew, but maybe he wasn't the first owner of the house?

'So, eh, there's something I want to tell you,' he said. 'I slept on it and realised it was something you need to know and it might also help with your inquiries. I mean, you'd probably get there anyway, so better to tell you. Sorry, I'm rambling. I'm sort of nervous, you know. I've a feeling this isn't going to paint me in a good light.'

'Perhaps if you just . . .' Frank made a winding motion with his finger, indicating he should hurry up and get to the point.

'Oh, yeah, sure. I . . . er . . . that is, myself and Olive – we made love the night before you reckon she died.'

'You had sex with her?' Frank said.

'Um. Yes.'

'In her sitting room?'

'Eh – does that matter?'

'That's where she died. In her armchair.'

Ron swallowed.

'Shit. It was there. We had sex there.'

'Was this a common occurrence?' Frank asked. 'Were you in a relationship?'

'I wouldn't say it was a relationship, no. We just . . .' he laughed, nervously. 'Have you heard the expression "friends with benefits"?'

Frank's cheeks turned red. Emma smirked. Modern. Ha!

'I have, yes,' Frank said. 'So you and Olive, you were . . .'

'Yes.'

'And in the last three months, you haven't needed a quickie?'

'Sorry?'

'You didn't call over at any point?'

'Oh. I see what you mean. No. I can explain that, though.'

'Explain away,' Frank said, holding out his hands. 'We're all ears.'

Ron looked from one detective to the other. He oozed anxiety.

'That night I went over. Well, I went to tell her that I was done. I didn't want anything serious and she was . . . getting serious. We ended up having sex. One last time, I suppose.'

Emma cleared her throat.

'You went over to break bad news to her and ended up having sex,' she repeated. 'It doesn't seem like the normal course of events. Do you have a problem with sex, Mr Ryan?'

'Yeah. I have too much of it.' He winked.

Emma stared at him, her face blank.

Ron shifted in his chair, uncomfortable.

'Sorry. My mouth works faster than my brain sometimes.'

'Hmm.' Emma tended to agree. 'Did you tell her that you were finished after you had sex? Or had you already told her at that point and she didn't mind having this . . . goodbye shag?'

Ron's colouring was the other side of puce by now.

'I told her . . . afterwards.'

Emma raised her eyebrows.

'I appreciate this makes me look like a terrible person,' Ron said.

'We're not here to judge you on your morals,' Frank interrupted. 'Perhaps you might tell us why you decided to break it off with Olive, though? It might help us better understand things.'

Ron nodded.

'Yeah. I mean, I wasn't just being nasty. Olive had actually been pretty awful herself. She'd taken these photographs, you see.'

'What photos?'

'Pictures of me. She'd got some of me down in that new restaurant in town – you know the one the celebrity chef just opened? I was there on the launch night, brought this girl from the office. Treated her to a bottle of champagne, as it happens. Olive took photos of me through the window. There were loads like that.'

'So, she was taking photographs of you with other women?' Frank said.

'No. Well, yeah. But that wasn't the point of them. Some of them didn't have women in them at all. She had a few of me in my car, too.'

Frank and Emma looked at each other.

'I don't get it,' Emma said. 'Were you afraid she was stalking you or something?'

'Oh, she was definitely stalking me. I mean, that's the definition of it, isn't it? But the pictures, well, she took them to show I have money. That I was spending money.'

'And why would that be an issue?'

Ron coughed nervously.

'Again, I realise I'm coming across like a complete shit. I figure it's best if I'm honest with you.'

'Please, Mr Ryan.' Frank was using his *I'm patient but not that patient* voice.

'Olive took those photographs and sent them to two of my exes. I knew it was her because a couple of them were taken inside my house. Nobody is ever in my house, really, but she had been, a few times. She must have taken them on her phone. She'd got photos of me standing at the Gaggia coffee machine in the kitchen and watching the HD TV in the living room. Things like that. She sent them to my exes because I haven't paid child support in a while.'

'Ah.' Frank tapped a finger to his mouth. 'So, you didn't want your exes to know you're loaded?'

'I'm not exactly loaded . . .' Ron started, then stopped as quick. 'The thing is, I have a lifestyle and . . . other bills. I contribute to my brother's care. He's . . . Anyway. You know, it wasn't my idea to have the kids. I never wanted kids. Not after my brother. But the girls . . .' His words trailed off.

'Girls?' Emma said. 'Kids? What sort of numbers are we talking here?'

'It's just two. Two exes, two kids.'

'Why, exactly, did Olive want to get you into trouble?' Frank asked.

Ron shrugged. He looked genuinely puzzled. And, Emma thought, hurt.

'That's the thing. I don't really know. She didn't say anything when I confronted her. She just had this funny look on her face, like *I'd* let *her* down. I got so angry, I just told her to fuck right off. So, you can see why I wasn't too bothered not to see her these last few months.'

'Yes,' Emma said. 'We can see. The thing is, you've just told us that you were in her house the night before she died; you had what sounds far more like revenge sex than one last fling; and you were furious with her. Now, can *you* see how we might have a few concerns about that?'

Ron unconsciously lifted his hand to his mouth and started to chew at the skin around one of his nails.

'Yeah, but, she just died, didn't she? I wasn't to know, was I? I mean, I can't be blamed for not going over to check on her. Not after she pissed me off like that. I'm being honest with you. Would I even bother if I wanted to hide something?'

Frank sighed.

'The thing is, Mr Ryan, we have reason to suspect that somebody may have intended to harm her. That her death might not be as clear-cut as a simple accident. We're not disclosing that to the general public, but given what you've just told us – you're now a material witness. At this time, you appear to be the last person to have seen her alive.'

Ron dropped his hand from his mouth, eyes widening.

'So, perhaps you could recall for us the exact exchange you had with Ms Collins that evening,' Frank continued. 'And then we'll get somebody to take you down to the station to make a formal statement.'

'Hang on. I don't think I was the last person to see her alive.'

Emma sat forward.

'What do you mean?'

'Well, a couple of people were about that day and at least one of them went into her cottage. I was – keeping an eye. I wanted to see if she'd come over to have it out with me again.'

'Who, exactly, did you see?' Frank asked.

'I saw Ed Miller coming out her door in the morning. And Matt Hennessy outside her garden gate. And they're just the people I happened to see. I mean, I wasn't watching all day or anything. Oh, and Alison Daly was in her garden late that afternoon.'

LILY

No. 2

Wolf was in his den.

That's what Lily liked to call it in her head. David called it a fort and she supposed that was what Wolf had intended when he blockaded a corner of his room with giant stuffed animals and Mega Bloks and threw a blanket on top for a roof.

She called it his den, because, eight years later, she was still coming to terms with the fact she had a son named Wolf.

People always assumed it had been her idea. The twins' names. She was the über-trendy individual in the relationship back then. David hadn't quite found his alternative-living stride.

Things began to change while Lily was pregnant. For him and for her. She knew he'd really wanted children but she'd never imagined how all-in he would go. David bought parenting manuals and wanted to read them together. She could feel her brain seeping out of her ears any time she looked at them. She taught kids all day, every day. She didn't need or want to study the minutiae of how she would be squeezing two of them out of her vagina.

She suspected that David was trying his best to be the opposite of his father and probably a very long line of men before that. And part of her was really grateful that she had married this man, that her children's father was so engaged. Her own dad would have been so happy to see that.

Soon, David was playing music to her bump and lying with his head in her lap so he could hear the twins gurgling in the amniotic fluid. He treated her belly with reverence, gentle and worshipping. She felt like a Fabergé egg.

A Fabergé egg that wanted her husband to do her doggy-style, because she was so damned horny.

But he didn't want to risk hurting the babies. He just wanted to listen to them.

At times, she knew it was cute and loving. At times, she was too exhausted to do anything but listen as he talked at length about things like how having twins shouldn't put them off breastfeeding.

Them breastfeeding? She had been struck by that. Was David going to try to squeeze milk out of his nipples, too?

Lily was tired and felt crap *all the time*. She had just about decided that she was the worst pregnant woman ever when the doctor handed her a lifeline.

She had pre-eclampsia.

That resulted in absolute bed rest, so *their* plans of nice long walks in the countryside to keep Lily fit and healthy for the birth all went to pot. And then, on bed rest, Lily had realised she had such an intense craving for meat that she would have happily chewed on David's arm instead of the endless plates of pulses and grains he kept bringing to keep her energy levels up.

Of course, in the happy ignorance of pregnancy, when she wasn't so tired she could cry, Lily liked to imagine that she would be totally Zen about parenting when the babies arrived. She would carry them in woven organic baby slings and, sure, both of them could hang off of a nipple if they liked. She was used to kids in large numbers, two would be perfectly manageable.

None of it had happened like that.

She was sectioned at thirty-seven weeks. None of David's fancy pre-prepared birth plans came to pass. Lily had everything – the epidural, morphine, any and all of the painkillers the hospital had been willing to part with – before, during and after. She'd been so out of it that the babies' first food was not the healthy, immunising colostrum from her breasts that David had read about, but tiny little bottles of Aptamil. Then, when she'd tried to breastfeed, she'd got it all wrong. Her nipples bled, her breasts became inflamed, and eventually she'd roared at David that he could *fucking milk himself* if he wanted to breastfeed.

David had given the registrar the twins' names. He'd claimed they'd discussed them. Lily couldn't remember. All she'd wanted to do was sleep. The hospital kept her in for fourteen days after the birth and David got to go home every night while Lily was left with two four-pound babies that needed to be fed every hour or so. The nurses gave as much help as they could but she didn't have one-on-one care. It was all she could do not to kill David when he glided in fresh every morning, after his full night's sleep, trailing pink and blue balloons in his wake.

Lily had a vague notion she'd told David she wanted to name the twins after her adoptive parents, May and William. How that had become Lily May and Wolf, she wasn't entirely sure.

But David insisted she'd assented.

And she knew he wouldn't lie to her.

He was far more honest than she was, even with his chosen profession.

'You make me want to be a better person,' he'd told her once.

And she'd wondered what was so wrong with her that, lately, she was the worse person.

All of this went through Lily's mind as she climbed into Wolf's den.

Her son was reading the latest *Diary of a Wimpy Kid*, his little face stern and unhappy, not smiling like it usually was when he was enjoying the embarrassing adventures of Greg and his high-school misfortunes.

'Hey,' Lily said, squeezing in beside him and putting her arm around his shoulder.

Wolf didn't respond. He was sweating, his light brown hair stuck to his clammy forehead.

They'd told the twins about Olive that morning.

Lily May had reacted as Lily expected her to. Dramatically. She'd wailed and bawled, getting even louder when David made a fuss and said they might go out for an ice-cream treat later, because sugar might be needed for the shock. He was oddly obsessed with sugar and shock.

Wolf had scratched his nose, then retreated upstairs, wordlessly.

David said Wolf needed time alone. Lily had defied his parenting advice and come up anyway. She was desperate to speak to him.

'How are you doing?' Lily asked her son.

Wolf shrugged.

'You must be very upset,' Lily pressed on. 'I know you liked Ms Collins.'

'She was lovely,' Wolf said.

Lily pursed her lips.

'Hmm.'

Wolf turned the page. Lily wasn't fooled. She knew she had his full attention. Wolf was smart. And really sensitive. Far more so than Lily May, who liked to pretend everything in the world affected her terribly but was definitely bordering on sociopathic.

'The police want to talk to you,' Lily said.

Wolf nodded.

'You already told me that.'

'I know we did. It's just . . .' Lily swallowed. God, this was hard. There was no manual for this stuff. That was the truth of it with kids. You just made it up as you went along.

'I don't think you should tell them what happened between Ms Collins and me.'

Wolf put the book on his knees and looked up at her. He looked so sad. So weary. She was undone, seeing him looking at her like that.

'Why?'

'Well, they wouldn't understand. It was an accident. I didn't mean . . .'

'I'm not stupid.'

'I know you're not. You're a very clever little boy. Which is why I feel I can have this conversation with you.'

'I miss her.'

Lily swept his fringe sideways.

Wolf jerked his head away.

'She was really nice to me.'

Lily sighed.

'I know you think that, Wolf.'

'She *was* nice to me. I don't just think it. And if you'd been friends with her I could have kept spending time with her.'

'Honey, I know Ms Collins liked you. How could anybody not like you? But she did not behave responsibly towards you. Ms Collins had no children of her own. Sometimes, that matters.'

'It didn't matter. She was nice to me. She was nice to me.'

Wolf was trembling. He was going to lose it.

Lily's stomach knotted as she frantically searched for the right words, the right thing to do to calm him down.

The doctor had said it was important that Lily made sure to validate Wolf's feelings when he started to lose his temper. She wasn't to patronise him and she had to try to understand what he was going through, even if he couldn't properly articulate it.

She knew he was somewhere on the autism spectrum. The doctor had recently arranged tests, but he had assured her he believed Wolf's diagnosis would be at the milder end.

It could and should have been identified earlier.

That was David's fault. Lily had always known Wolf was special. He let Lily May follow him around but he never really played with her. He was always content in his own company, which had certainly been hard on his twin. And he had that way of just saying what he thought – no naughtiness in his statements, just a blank relaying of the facts. Lily May would say things sometimes to see how her parents would react, always checking for boundaries, looking to see how she was reflected in other people's eyes. That wasn't Wolf.

More than that, though, were the tantrums. Whole weeks would pass where Wolf would be off in his own little world, peaceful, quiet, content. They never knew what would set him off. The trigger could be something as small as putting butter on top of his jacket potato instead of to the side.

They could dismiss the tantrums when Wolf was small. He was a toddler. That's what toddlers did. But as a teacher, Lily knew that he should have grown out of them by now. So she'd gone against David's absolute insistence that Wolf was entirely normal and brought her son to their GP. Once again, her husband had tried to overrule her on something she had far more experience with than he had. Even if they were both Wolf's parents, she knew kids.

And she was right.

Lily's eyes started to water.

She needed another parent to help her with this. She needed David to grow up and accept their son had issues they needed to deal with together.

Wolf was glaring at her.

'You shouldn't have done what you did,' he said.

And in that moment, Lily felt the anger that seemed to pulse through her these days bubble to the surface.

'I am the adult,' she snapped. 'I can do whatever the bloody hell I like and don't you dare speak to me like that.'

Wolf blinked and then his eyes filled up too.

Lily's heart beat fast for a few seconds and she realised she needed to calm down. But before she could right the situation, before she could actually *be* the adult, her son balled up his fist and hit her as hard as he could in the face.

Lily couldn't even react as Wolf pushed past her and squeezed out of his den.

She was so shocked, she just opened and closed her mouth, tears of pain rolling down her cheek.

Then she came to her senses and stood up in the den like a giant in Lilliput, sending the blanket and Mega Bloks flying.

'Come back here, you little shit!' she yelled.

It wasn't her proudest moment.

OLIVE

No. 4

The first day I offered Wolf a ham sandwich, I thought nothing of it.

The next time he called over, he asked if he could have a chicken sandwich.

And as the days and weeks rolled by, his requests became more adventurous. Had I sausage rolls? Hot dogs? Spicy chicken wings?

I'd become the restaurant of Olive.

Our little friendship wasn't just about food. Wolf and I could spend hours together just reading or chatting. He helped me in the garden. We organised my bookshelves and CD racks into alphabetic perfection. He was generally just really good company. Uncomplicated. Unconditional.

Wolf made me wish I'd had children.

But he wasn't mine.

Now, there was no way, when I first unwittingly upset Lily Solanke, that I could have been expected to know her kids watching cartoons was *verboten*. But I can't say, following the dressing-down she gave me, that I wasn't a bit more clued in as to how smart Wolf was.

Did I one hundred per cent know that he was vegetarian?

No. Not entirely. But yes, somewhere in the recesses of my mind, I knew something was amiss. I offered him a jam scone one afternoon and he nearly recoiled.

'Haven't you any bacon?' he asked.

We probably could have kept our little secret, except for – well, there's no real plot twist here – that idiot sister of his. She called over for him one day and he wasn't quick enough with the remains of his pork chop. Lily May brushed past me and marched into the kitchen just in time to see him gnawing on the last bit of meat, juice dribbling down his chin. You could see the meanness in her eyes as she calculated how much trouble this would get him in. He'd been abandoning her for months, you see, hanging out over at mine whenever he could get away. Now she had the perfect revenge.

She ran from the kitchen and straight over to her parents.

I felt my heart flutter in my chest and wondered if the defence of ignorance would get me out of this one.

Wolf cleaned off the fat that had dripped onto his sweater and skulked off, aware he was in for a dressing-down of epic proportions.

I waited.

I wondered if David would come over. The hedge-fund manager, the man who I guessed could be as scary as hell when he put his mind to it. I certainly saw how he was with Lily. Manipulative. Controlling. Even if she was oblivious.

It was Lily who came, though, an hour after Wolf left.

This time, there was no conciliatory outreach.

'What on earth were you thinking?' she said. 'Are you really that naïve? Or are you just plain nasty?'

She was fuming. I had about a heartbeat to think: *Well, well, well. Look what's simmering in Lily!* before she resumed her tirade.

'We're vegetarians!' she yelled and then some more crap about diet and set meals and Wolf getting the best of everything and it not being my place to give her son anything, especially as she'd pulled me up on it before.

'Who's vegetarian?' I said quietly, slicing through her monologue of outrage.

'What?'

'Who is vegetarian? You and your husband? Or just your children? Did the children get to decide themselves, or did you decide for them? Or was it David? Did he decide for everybody?'

She flinched.

'That's none of your business.'

'You're in my sitting room, yelling at me, so I think we can say you've made it my business. You told Wolf he could still call over and I checked with you, on more than one occasion, whether it was okay for him to be here. You told me not to give him juice, and I didn't. Maybe you should have made a list. Wolf never told me he was a vegetarian. And if you ask me, I think you should have a little conversation with him about whether or not he wants to be. Because I'm telling you, he bloody well loves meat. If I offer him a cheese sandwich he all but spits on the table. And he probably needs meat, nutritionally. A growing boy like that.'

'What the hell do you know about what my son needs or doesn't need? How dare you?'

'How dare you come into my home and attack me like this!' I

could feel myself getting angry and I tried to calm myself down, but I just couldn't. This was the second time she'd had a go and I was fed up. 'For heaven's sake, this is a big hoo-ha about nothing. Who calls their child Wolf then says he can't eat meat? By the time he's sixteen he'll probably be on steak tartare for breakfast.'

She closed her eyes and took a deep breath. When she was satisfied she could hold it together, she opened them and looked at me like I had some sort of learning impediment and needed everything explained very slowly.

'Olive,' she said. 'It doesn't matter what you think of my parenting skills. What matters is that Wolf is my son and you do not respect my parenting rules. He will not be allowed to come over here again and I'd appreciate it if you could maintain a polite distance.'

I was so devastated, I couldn't even reply.

Lily sighed and straightened herself.

'I know you like Wolf. But I'm afraid it would be hypocritical of me to pretend that we didn't have this exchange. I'd rather we agreed to differ and go our separate ways.'

'Hypocritical?' I said, the words coming before I could stop them. I'd restrained myself once with this woman when she'd held all the cards. Now she'd upturned the table and the whole deck. I'd nothing to lose.

'Hypocritical is coming over here and claiming I've broken some sort of rule that you seem to have a pretty flexible approach to yourself.'

'Excuse me?'

'I saw you,' I said. 'In town. Down at the harbour. Stuffing a quarter-pounder *in your face.*'

I punctuated the last three words with my finger. At the same time, I noticed something moving in my eyeline. It was Wolf. He'd returned, probably to fetch his mother. Or maybe to defend me. The darling boy, so confused and worried about what was kicking off.

I knew I'd made her angry. Getting caught in a lie will do that to a person.

It was no excuse for what she did, though.

GEORGE

No. 1

Some kind of banging next door woke George. He'd fallen asleep with the window open, trying to let some air into the stiflingly hot room. He couldn't remember weather like this. It was heavy, oppressive.

The banging was followed by shouting and he realised it was Lily and Wolf next door.

He closed his eyes and tried to find sleep again. It was useless. The curtains weren't heavy enough to keep out the pinpricks of light streaming through.

What time was it, anyway? George reached for his phone on the floor beside the bed.

10.30 a.m.

He hadn't gone to sleep until after 4.

He'd been up that long, sitting in front of his computer, clicking, clicking, clicking.

No matter what he looked at, it was never enough. He had to find something else. He could have multiple windows open, his whole screen full of video squares, bodies writhing and moaning and screwing. And still, it took hours for him to find anything approximating satisfaction.

He'd overdosed on porn. His brain had seen so much of it, it did nothing for him any more. If his weakness was cocaine, he'd be dead by now. But he wasn't.

That was the horror of this addiction. It was impossible to find rock bottom.

George had felt there was hope, once.

He'd been going to counselling for some time before the Olive incident. Actually going – as in, he was in the room. Listening. Wanting help.

The counsellor, Adam, was new and apparently a leading expert on porn addiction, one of the best in the country. They'd built up a rapport, the first time George had been able to with a therapist. Nothing George said shocked or alarmed Adam; in fact, Adam was able to talk to him like he had a video set up in George's brain.

Adam didn't say stupid things like *all men watch porn* (which George's GP had actually said to him once) and he didn't treat it like it was any other addiction. In the counsellor's words, porn addiction was the most destructive because it shut down human contact. And once human contact was gone, the sufferer had to struggle on his own.

And the biggest danger was that it made you immune to extremities. Your boundaries began to shift, your concept of 'normal' became warped.

'But how do I deal with it?' George had pleaded. 'I want to stop. I need to stop.'

'And you can,' Adam had answered. 'You'll never believe this, but the way to treat porn addiction is the way we treat any addiction. We need to find the root cause. And that lies within. Once we've addressed that, then everything else is just tools we provide you with to counter the craving. Like smokers use nicotine patches. We can give you that. But we need to get to the bottom of things first.'

Then Adam had taken out this little bowl of stones. George had looked at the pebbles, the sort you'd find up and down a beach, and then at Adam like he was soft in the head.

Adam had laughed and asked George to bear with him.

'Take a stone from the bowl, one that you think most represents you,' he'd said.

So George had gone along, sifting through the bowl until he found one he was happy with.

'And now pick one for me,' Adam said.

George had dived in again.

When he was content, Adam took both the stones from his hands.

'Why did you pick this one for yourself?' he asked George.

The stone was a small grey one, spotted with black.

George blushed. He hadn't realised he was going to have to provide a rationale. He should have seen that one coming.

'Don't be embarrassed,' Adam said. 'Tell me exactly what went through your mind.'

'Well, it's me, isn't it?' George answered. 'Grey. Dull. Dirty bits streaked through. Sorry. What a cliché.'

Adam shook his head.

'Just go with it. Let me guess, you chose this one for me because it's all one colour. It's pure. You think I'm without any flaws.'

George shrugged, mortified. Was this really happening? Two

grown men having a conversation about pebbles and how they related to feelings? He was starting to feel tricked.

'You see, George, that's your problem,' Adam said. 'You think everybody else is perfect. We're not. We all have our crosses to bear. You've never asked me why I became a counsellor.'

George shrugged.

'You're good at listening.'

'Sure. But I have to do more than listen. I have to empathise. Most people become counsellors after suffering through a crisis themselves. They recover, and those that are strong enough go on to help others in the same position. Have you never found it strange that I understand your problems so well and am able to help you deal with them? It's important you know this about anybody you go to counselling with, George. Somebody who's been in your position is of far more help than somebody who can only sympathise with the aid of a textbook.'

'You were addicted to porn?'

'I was, George. I was you, only worse. I lost my wife, my children, my family, my job. I didn't just look at porn. I visited prostitutes too. I visited them so much, I caught an STD. And I gave it to my wife when she was pregnant. Imagine that. Think you can top that? Infecting your pregnant wife with a disease you caught from a sex worker?'

George's mouth fell open.

'It only eats you up when you keep it secret,' Adam continued. 'I learned that. And I was able to work my way through it. It's ten years since I acted out. I'm with a new partner now, a lovely woman, and she knows everything. And sometimes, if I catch myself looking too long at a woman in the street, or overthinking something on television, I say it to her. And she helps me address it. Because I am always honest with her. I was this stone, George.'

Adam held up the first pebble, the dirty grey one.

'And you're right. Now I'm closer to the other one. But only because I worked on myself. Every person you meet has had a dalliance with the first stone, George. We all have our problems. You're not alone.'

George had felt like crying. He had, in fact – tears spilling quietly onto his cheeks.

Because George had felt so alone, and now he didn't.

He'd left the session that night buoyed with positivity.

The next day, Olive Collins had called in to his house.

FRANK

'Well, that's given us plenty to think about.'

Frank and Emma stood at the end of Ron Ryan's garden. They'd just waved him off in the back of the squad car that was taking him down to headquarters to record a formal statement. All very casual. No need for a solicitor. He was just helping with inquiries.

'What do you think of Casanova there? Is he deflecting from himself, dropping the names of all his neighbours like that? Has he something more to hide?'

Emma hesitated.

'I don't know. Alison Daly said she went straight to the airport from her shop, so either he's lying, or she is. Either way, that's interesting. Matt Hennessy, well, he may have just been at Olive's gate. That means nothing. And we've yet to meet this Miller man. But — something is bothering me. Why didn't whoever messed with her boiler not go back and take the Sellotape off the vents?'

Frank stuck out his lower lip.

'Perhaps they didn't want to risk being seen near the house. Perhaps they thought we'd consider it suicide and didn't realise Olive would have the capacity to ring the cops. Maybe they hoped it would all just go away if they ignored it for long enough.'

'Hmm. Well, who do you want to talk to now?'

She'd no sooner said it than Lily Solanke emerged from the side of her house. The woman was in a panic, no shoes on her feet, skirt swinging wildly as she ran down her garden.

'Is everything okay, Mrs Solanke?' Frank called out.

Lily caught sight of him and came to an abrupt halt.

'Um, yes, it's just Wolf.'

They met in the middle of the road.

'We told him about Olive this morning. He's very upset. He ran out of the house.'

'Do you need us to help you find him?' Frank asked.

'No, no. I know where he's gone. The Hennessys' treehouse – I mean, Cam's treehouse. Wolf likes small spaces when he's . . . when he's in this humour.'

'I see. Well, just give us a shout if you need any help.'

Out of the corner of his eye, Frank had just spotted Alison Daly emerging from number three. He nudged Emma, who nodded.

'We'll be over later,' he said to Lily Solanke, who tried and failed to hide the worried look on her face.

Frank waved at Alison, who stood on the precipice of her front door, looking out at the scene on the road quite probably wondering what the hell was going on.

Frank and Emma walked over to her.

'Morning, Ms Daly,' Frank said. 'Any chance we could have five minutes?'

'Um, sure,' she answered. 'I need to head out shortly, but I'm sure we can manage a quick cuppa.'

She was all smiles, very friendly. Frank was more suspicious than ever.

The daughter, Holly, was curled up on the sofa with a pair of earphones in, a YouTube playlist open on her laptop.

'Good morning, Holly,' Frank said, and the girl pulled the plugs out of her ears. She sat up straighter. 'What are you listening to?'

'Pharrell,' Emma answered for Holly, pointing at the computer screen. 'Your neighbour next door could probably get him round, his dad being Stu Richmond and all.'

'Hmm,' Holly replied.

Alison hovered by the door.

'Tea or coffee?' she asked, looking from the detectives to her daughter and back again.

'Honestly, that won't be necessary,' Frank said. 'We really just want a quick word. Please, sit down, Ms Daly.'

'Alison is fine, really.'

Alison perched on the edge of the sofa beside her daughter.

Frank remained standing.

'You see, what you were saying last night, Holly, it jarred with me. That stuff about Olive Collins blackmailing your mum. We're starting to get a good picture of your neighbour and we appreciate, more than anybody, that relationships between neighbours are difficult. Just because you're all living in this community doesn't mean you're the best of friends. I actually dealt with a case once where a man was charged with attempted manslaughter after he attacked his neighbour for persistently parking his car so it made it difficult for this other guy to get into his drive.'

He had Holly's attention. And her mother's. The two were exchanging discreet glances, none of it lost on Frank.

'It strikes me that Olive might not have been very well liked, nor might she have been treated that nicely by some of the people around her. Now, just because there was discord between Olive and several of her neighbours, that doesn't mean any of you wanted her dead. But the investigation *has* moved on. And now we need people to start being very honest. So.' Frank turned to Holly's mother. 'Was Olive Collins blackmailing you, Alison?'

Alison swallowed and opened her mouth. But before she could utter a word, her daughter jumped in.

'She wasn't. I lied. I made it up.'

Frank took a deep breath.

'Why would you do that, now?'

'I'm a teenager. It's what we do.'

'Really?'

'Yeah.'

Frank shook his head.

'I just don't believe that, Holly. I think you're a bit too smart to be playing games like that.'

Holly tensed. She was panicking.

'Fine,' she said. 'I couldn't stand her, okay? She was a horrible woman. Mam is a soft touch when it comes to the store and Olive took advantage of it. I said it was blackmail but really, it was just downright robbery.'

Frank met Alison's eye.

'Is this true?' he asked.

She hesitated before nodding. The slightest beat.

'I guess so. It's testament to how good the economy is doing that I can be such a poor businesswoman and not go bankrupt.' She forced a hollow chuckle. 'Olive was a little . . . impolite. And I should have pulled her up on it. But it's difficult, when you've offered, like I did. You don't expect people to keep asking. You expect people to know how to behave. I think that was the main problem with Olive. She didn't seem to really grasp social etiquette.'

Frank said nothing. He wanted to give them every chance.

'What did you mean, the investigation has moved on?' Holly said. She eyed him curiously, agitated fingers tapping on her thighs.

'We're looking at all avenues. We haven't ruled out misadventure in Ms Collins' death.'

'Are you saying somebody might have killed her?' Alison looked like she'd stopped breathing. 'But how? Did you see something – was there something in the house? Did you know this yesterday, when you spoke to us?'

This time, Frank just shrugged.

'This is how it is, sometimes. We have to wait for the facts to be confirmed. And we don't know all the facts in this case yet. So we need to speak to people again. Is there anything you might have remembered since yesterday? For instance, you didn't call back here, did you, before you went to the airport?'

The colour started to drain from Alison's face.

But it wasn't Frank that Alison was looking at. It was her daughter. She was gauging how Holly would react to what Frank had just asked.

Holly stared at her mother quizzically.

'I – yes, now you mention it, I think I did. I'd forgotten my passport.'

'And did you call in to Ms Collins' house?'

Holly was agitated now, watching her mother like Frank and Emma, all of this seemingly new to her.

Alison shook her head. 'No. I certainly didn't.' She looked from one to the other of them. 'And if somebody said I did, then they're lying.'

Frank and Emma exchanged a glance.

Alison Daly was extremely convincing. So where did that leave Ron Ryan?

CHRISSY & MATT

No. 5

Somebody was mowing a lawn outside. It sounded like it was coming from the Solankes. In their house, the washing machine was on – who the hell had put a wash on? Had Matt?

Chrissy walked through the house in a daze. There was no sign or sound of Cam. He was probably sleeping in after his late night.

Matt was in the kitchen. It was a hub of activity – pans on the cooker, plates out, the overhead fan on the hob whirring. Chrissy took in the sight and wondered if she was dreaming.

'Can we talk?'

Matt looked over at her. And Chrissy knew she wasn't dreaming. That was the look he'd given her last night, when he'd started talking about Olive.

Chrissy had spent a second night lying awake, staring at the ceiling, but this one had been very different.

'Talk about what?' Matt grunted.

'Our son. I think something is up. I think Olive's death has affected him more than he's letting on.'

Matt slowed temporarily by the fridge door.

'He's a kid. They're resilient. And it's not like he really knew her, is it? Not like you knew her.'

Chrissy sighed. All this talking in riddles. She was too tired this morning to play along.

'Jesus, Matt, just get to the point, will you? How did you know I'd fallen out with her?'

Matt disappeared behind the open fridge door. He emerged with a tray of eggs and a packet of bacon.

'I saw you,' he said.

Chrissy's heart slowed. She could almost hear it beating.

'Saw me doing what?' she asked.

Matt placed a pan on the cooker top.

'With your lover. Well. That's not quite true. I didn't see you *with* him. I saw him leaving here one afternoon, stuffing his shirt into his trousers, a shit-eating grin on his face. That toe-rag from number seven, Ron-Ron.'

He paused to let that sink in.

'I know we accountants aren't renowned for our imaginations, Chrissy, but we're really good at putting two and two together.'

It was like a bad dream. Chrissy rubbed her temples, a pain growing so intense in her head she felt like it might explode. Why wasn't she more prepared for this – for her husband finding out? She'd fantasised about telling him enough times . . . Maybe that was it – she'd thought she would tell him. Not that he'd somehow already know.

'When?' she said.

'When what?'

'When did you see him?'

'Is that what matters? You're not going to deny it?'

Chrissy stared at Matt.

'What would be the point?'

He snorted, a crass, derisory sound. And yet, Chrissy saw something on her husband's face that took her by surprise.

He looked *injured*.

'I suppose there is no point,' he said. 'Not any more. It was months ago. And I wasn't the only one who saw it. I'd parked outside Olive's place. We were getting the drive done, remember? I walked up the side of our garden so I wouldn't stand on the cobblelock. I was just in time to see him going out the back and cutting through the Millers'. Then I looked up. Olive Collins was standing at her window. She didn't see me, but I clocked her. The look on her face when Ryan disappeared around the side of the Millers'.' Matt stared into the distance. 'She was devastated. Like, properly distraught.'

Matt resumed his activity at the cooker as Chrissy felt her world implode. She watched as he laid out bacon to sizzle in the pan. He was acting completely normal, entirely unfazed.

It scared her.

'I can't eat that,' she said.

'It's not for you. It's for that child you're so concerned about. He has to eat, doesn't he?'

Chrissy didn't react. It was Saturday morning. Matt usually went golfing and her and Cam's habit – up until recently, anyway – had been Rice Krispies on the sofa while watching DVDs. Saturday was her day off from burning stuff on the cooker. Matt didn't know that. He couldn't. He was *never there*.

'You didn't know he was sleeping with Olive as well, then?' Matt said. 'You didn't have a little chat and agree to share him?'

Chrissy shook her head. She hadn't known. She still couldn't believe it. She hadn't been able to sleep for thinking about it.

But . . . it rang true. If she really thought about it, it made perfect sense. Ron had flirted shamelessly with her, a married woman. Of course, she'd flirted right back, but she was unhappy. She'd been desperate, needy, open to it. What was his rationale? Was he so attracted to her that he just didn't give a damn that she was married?

And if that was the case, why had he never, not once, asked her to leave her husband for him?

He'd only wanted sex. It was just for fun. That's all Ron wanted. With her. With anybody.

She burned with the shame of it.

'I watched you all the time after that,' Matt said. He was plating up the bacon now, cracking the eggs on the side of the pan, the whole ritual still absurdly routine. 'You, him, her. It was like my own private soap opera. Then, one day, I saw Olive speaking to you out the back. You had that look you get when you've been caught out at something – trying to dismiss her while your little brain scrabbled for a solution. You knew I was inside the house – she knew too, I'd guess. What did she say to you? Back off, or I'll tell your husband?'

Chrissy said nothing. Her eyes filled with tears.

'It must have mattered to you, to let her wind you up like that. It must have bothered you that I might find out because you told him to stop coming over, didn't you? For a while, anyway. And then he turned up again. Where did you have sex with him, Chrissy? Where? In our bed? On that table? On the settee?'

It felt like the room was spinning.

And then, Chrissy's brain settled on one, clear thought.

'Hang on,' she said. 'All those times lately when you've come home early from work, when you've surprised me. You knew? You were . . .'

'Playing games with you?' Matt turned to face her. 'Yes. I was. It doesn't feel too good, does it? Finding out you've been lied to? Manipulated?'

'But why didn't you just confront me?' Chrissy whispered. 'Why didn't you have it out with me the first time? Oh!'

She stopped. Laughed, thinly, quietly, at the irony.

'You were punishing me. You enjoyed seeing me panic every time you turned up unexpectedly. Well played, Matt. I never knew you could be so devious. I guess that makes two of us. It couldn't have bothered you too much, then – if you were content for me to keep going with the affair.'

He turned his back on her.

She stared at him. She'd been unfaithful, but was her husband some kind of psychopath? What else was he capable of?

'Is that what you think?' he said, his voice low. 'That I was happy about it?' Matt shook his head. 'No, Chrissy. I didn't confront you because I *couldn't* confront you. I couldn't say out loud what I knew you were doing. Because that would have made it real. And I didn't want it to be real. I could hate everybody else, but not you. Never you.'

Matt started to cry.

Chrissy's mouth fell open.

OLIVE

No. 4

In the days after I'd tried to warn Chrissy away from Ron, I realised that her toughness was just for show. She'd clearly taken me seriously – for weeks after that, I didn't see Ron go near the Hennessy house. And she obviously didn't tell him about our encounter because, in the absence of her making herself available to him, he was around to me more than ever.

I'd have called that a result – except at some point, a couple of months later, Chrissy Hennessy obviously decided she couldn't live without Ron and he, like the weak, faithless man that he was, started calling back in to her and leaving me to my own devices for weeks on end.

Now, I wasn't the sort to blame it all on the woman. The problem wasn't just Chrissy. It was Ron.

How to punish him, though?

If I told Matt what his wife was up to, sure, the shit would hit the fan. But Ron would know of my involvement and that would be the end of us.

I wanted to simultaneously teach him a lesson and force him

closer to me – a willing shoulder to cry on, a woman who always had his back, who was there for him and him alone.

Not somebody who was happy to have him as just a bit on the side.

I set about planning my revenge.

I couldn't have imagined for a second that Cam Hennessy would become entangled in my war with his mother and Ron.

Cam was a funny little kid. I'd watched him grow up (from afar, Chrissy had blanked her neighbours by then). He started out as a cute little thing. I'd see him in his garden, toddling about on his little fireman truck, kicking his ball around, tripping over with chubby, clumsy legs. He was always smiling.

Then he grew. At ten years of age, Cam was a skinny, gangly lad, nearly the size of his mother. His size wasn't the only thing that changed. Cam was an angry child. You could see it in the squint of his eyes, the sulky downturn of his mouth.

I felt sorry for him. It's hard for children who don't have brothers or sisters. I knew that, as an only child myself. When the child is alone, the parents have to make an extra-special effort to provide company. My parents did. You could see Alison Daly did with Holly.

Chrissy Hennessy was too busy being an adulteress. She didn't deserve Cam, no more than she deserved her husband.

When Cam called over to my house that autumn day, even though we didn't have a relationship, I was happy to see him. I presumed he'd seen Wolf coming in and out and wanted to get in on the action, to see if he could get a chocolate bar and a Coke out of me. It made me smile, thinking I was like the aunty in the Vale, the one with the treats, the one who took the time to speak to the children.

'You upset my mammy,' he said, scratching the freckles on his nose. He was as blunt as that.

I blinked.

'Sorry?' I said.

'You upset my mammy. I saw you.'

'I didn't.'

'Yeah, you did. When she was hanging out the washing. I was in my treehouse.'

I opened and closed my mouth, unsure what to say, more interested in what he'd come out with next.

'I know something she doesn't know.'

Despite my better instincts, I asked, 'What's that now?'

'She doesn't know you're special friends with Mr Ryan, too. I saw him coming in here. He's the only one who uses your back door.'

'You don't know what you're talking about.' I laughed. It sounded nervous, even to me. But he'd taken me by surprise. I was used to doing the watching. Not being watched. 'Yes, I had a little argument with your mother but it had nothing to do with Mr Ryan.'

'I do know what I'm talking about,' he said, cool as a cucumber. I couldn't even imagine being that self-assured in front of an adult at his age. I'd have been quaking in my boots. It was unnerving. 'I know you must have said something about Mr Ryan because he used to call around to our house but then he stopped. I heard Mammy on the phone telling him he wasn't to visit her for a while. Right after you fought with her.'

'I'm sure that's to do with something completely different,' I said. 'It's just a coincidence, Cam.'

'I don't think my daddy and Mr Ryan will be happy bunnies when I tell them you made my mam cry.'

I nearly choked. That was the last thing I wanted.

I was smiling so hard my jaw had nearly locked.

'I think you're a little confused,' I said. 'I am good friends with Mr Ryan. And I know he's friends with your mother. This is grown-up stuff. It's really very silly.'

He smiled back at me.

'I need a tab,' he said.

'What?'

'A tab. A tablet? Like a computer? Mammy won't get me one.'

I knew what a tablet was.

I raised my eyebrows. Really? That was his game?

'You should ask Santa Claus for one,' I said.

'It's October. Santa is not for ages.'

'Well, your birthday then.'

'That's not for weeks.'

I shrugged.

He turned to go.

'Where are you off to?' I said, my heart fluttering.

'To Mr Ryan's.'

I let him get to the gate.

'Hey,' I called out. 'Why don't you come in for some biscuits and a Coke?'

He turned and smiled at me. Then he started to walk back up the path.

GEORGE

No. 1

The police had gone in to the Dalys'. George spotted them from the window. He seemed to be doing a lot of that lately. Staring out his window. It had to stop.

That's what had got him into trouble before.

When Olive had called over to his house that day . . . God. He'd had no clue what was coming.

She didn't even make small talk – just came out with it.

'I know what you are.'

He'd only spoken to Olive once, properly, in his life – the time she'd called over looking to borrow something or other and sat in his kitchen for an hour. He'd never warmed to her. When he moved in, Lily had warned him to watch what he said around her.

'She's very gossipy,' Lily had said. 'And very judgemental. The funny thing is, I'm fairly certain she thinks *I* have a superiority complex.'

George liked Lily. He trusted her. He gave Olive a wide berth.

So, how she knew anything about his life was beyond him.

Yet, when she'd confronted him, she started to go on about shameful secrets and a man his age knowing better.

George had stopped her there.

'What are you on about?' he'd asked. 'How do you know anything about me?'

She looked sheepish.

'I had to pop over the other day,' she said. 'You weren't in and the postman had a package for you. I brought it in . . .'

'You what?' George had felt sick. Olive's speech sounded prepared, like she'd taken days to think up what she was going to say. What package was she talking about? The book he'd ordered? But that had been on the mat in the hall when he'd got home the other day. He'd picked it up, wondered vaguely how the postman had got it in the letter box, and then thought nothing else about it.

'Well, you gave me a key,' she said. Her face was red, her words coming too fast. She was nervous and trying to stay ahead of him. Like the end had justified her means. 'And I brought it into the sitting room, and your computer was open. I accidentally brushed the keyboard off.'

George glared at her.

She'd been in his home. She'd looked through his things. George's laptop was password-protected but only with his name and date of birth. He lived alone, there was no need for complexities. Anybody could figure it out.

Somebody had.

He'd gone out in a hurry that day because he'd turned on his computer and found himself immediately looking at porn, and Adam had told him sometimes the best thing to do was to take himself out of the path of temptation. So George had jumped in the car and driven up to the mountains. He'd parked near a trail and walked for miles, breathing in fresh air fragranced with moss and pine needles and feeling alive because, for the first time in a long time, he'd said *no*.

And when he'd got home, the book Adam had recommended he buy had arrived. George had spent the night engrossed in it, reading about the stages of recovery in addiction.

It was a start. Tentative, but a start.

And now his neighbour had thrown petrol over it and lit a match.

'Who do you think you are?' he'd growled at Olive.

She held her hand up.

'I didn't come over here to have an argument with you,' she said. 'I came over to warn you. I know what you are, George Richmond. You're a pervert.'

'Excuse me? Are you serious? How dare you? You broke into my home, you hacked into my private computer, you saw some porn on my laptop and you think . . . are you insane? What are you going to tell the police when I report this? Do you think they'll let you get away with burglary because you're channelling Mary Whitehouse?'

It was so absurd, George started to laugh.

Olive pursed her lips.

'Oh, you can say what you like. But I saw you, last summer, staring at Holly Daly through your window. Pulling away on yourself. I've been watching you ever since. She's a child and you are a grown man. A disgusting man. I am telling you, you stay clear of the children on this estate. You stay clear or I'll tell everybody what you are.'

It felt like the bottom of George's world had fallen out. Because when he'd found out how young Holly was, he'd been utterly ashamed of himself. George knew Holly had tipped him into something *other*. That's when he'd gotten serious about counselling.

He hadn't even been able to reply to Olive. Olive waited for him to say something, then when she saw she'd left him speechless, she turned on her heel and let herself out the front door, a smug, satisfied look on her face.

George wanted to die. He was mortified.

He had a problem. He wasn't . . . dangerous. And Jesus, not to kids. Any man would have looked at Holly Daly in the same way. He'd had nothing to do with her and Alison when they moved in so he didn't know Holly was only fifteen. He just saw a sexy teenager. Hadn't Ron Ryan said as much last night?

He swore he wouldn't let Olive's poison fester inside him. But, that week, he missed his counselling session and slowly, true to form, slipped back into his addiction. He was only trying to make himself feel better. Even though, rationally, he knew it was the worst reaction.

Then, one night, he realised what Olive Collins had done to him.

Olive was the one in the wrong. It didn't matter if she had a key. How she'd got hold of that was a point of contention anyway.

She'd broken into his home, rifled through his private belongings.

Olive wasn't pure.

Not even close.

She was a very dirty stone.

OLIVE

No. 4

Let no good deed go unpunished. Isn't that the saying?

My mother used to say only busybodies meddled in the affairs of others. I challenged her on it once.

'What would happen in the world,' I said, 'if everybody minded their own business and didn't interfere when they saw something unjust happening?'

'Olive, pet, interfering only makes things worse.'

'I just don't believe that, Mammy. Granny didn't want to go see Dr Neely that time and you made her and if you hadn't, they'd never have spotted the cancer and Granny would have died in her sleep one night, none the wiser, but instead she had all the treatment and the care in the hospital.'

My mother started crying then.

I didn't set out to meddle. Not when it was unnecessary. Not when I thought I would make things worse. But what kind of person could have seen what George Richmond did that day in his window and not have confronted him?

It was months before I managed to get into his house after I got his keys. He hardly ever went out or when he did, it was when I was also out. I guess nerves made me procrastinate, too. It's not like I was adept at breaking into people's houses.

Then, one day, I saw him shoot out the door and jump in his car like the hounds of hell were on his tail.

He'd no sooner gone out the gates than the postman arrived.

It was raining that day and the postman stood outside George's house, holding a package and looking around like he was trying to figure out what to do with it. I went out to him.

'Can I help?' I said. 'I'm in number four.'

The postman knew me to see. He smiled, relieved.

'It's this package,' he said. 'I can't get it in his letter box and there's nobody in. I don't want to leave it on the step, not with the rain.'

'I can take it, if you like. I've a key, so I can pop it on the inside table for him.'

Have a key were the magic words.

Two minutes later I stood in George's porch, panicking.

If I was in the house and I heard his car in the drive, all I had to do was race into the hall and leave the book on his table, open his front door, step out and tell him I was just leaving something in for him.

If I was caught.

George's laptop was open on his couch. Password-protected.

That was probably where I crossed the line and once I'd done that, well, there was no stopping me.

It took me a few goes and if he'd had any sense, I wouldn't have got anywhere. I knew the year he was born. His father had told me once that, despite his youthful looks, he had a son who'd been born in 1982.

So, I chanced my arm and typed in his birthday. Then his surname and birthday. Then his first name and year of birth and, hey presto.

Filth. Windows and windows of it.

As well as on the computer, he had shelves and shelves of the stuff in a room upstairs. And not all normal – well, what I'd consider normal – either.

But you'd want to see the kind of thing he was looking at online!

My God, I'm no innocent, but talk about disturbing. S&M, violent sex, gang-rape fantasies, snuff, that kind of thing. None of that upset me as much as the page he had open that claimed to show older men with teenage girls. Barely legal, it was called.

That's why I went upstairs. It wouldn't have surprised me if he'd had a woman chained up up there. And a gimp in his closet.

I know the girls in these videos are usually of age and made to look younger.

Well, that's how it's supposed to be.

But having seen George in action watching Holly Daly, there was no way I was taking the chance.

I couldn't go to the police and tell them what I'd seen because then I'd have to say how I'd seen it. I had no option – I had to confront George. He could have been planning to groom Holly, for all I knew. They say it's often somebody the victim knew.

They also say it's always the person you least suspect.

HOLLY & ALISON

No. 3

Holly had abandoned the earphones.

She lay on her bed, staring up at the stars she'd stuck on the ceiling when they'd moved in. Music blasted into the room, lyrics that meant everything and nothing, depending on her mood. Today, they'd no relevance. It was all just noise, drowning everything else out.

The stars hadn't been bought for Holly. But they'd come in her bag anyway, when her mother had packed in a rush that night. She didn't know if Alison knew they were on the ceiling. She hadn't said anything if she did.

As if summoned by thought, Alison appeared in the doorway.

'Can you turn that down?' she called.

Holly sighed. She reached for the remote control somewhere near her fingertips and banged at the volume button a few times.

'Aren't you going in to the shop?' she asked her mother, and resumed staring at the ceiling.

'Change of plan,' Alison said. The sudden dip in the bed told Holly her mother was now sitting on the edge. Not content there, she sidled up beside her daughter and lay down, a hand behind her head, mirroring Holly.

'I thought you were the one who said we had to be normal?'

'Did I? Normal is overrated.'

Holly gave her mother a sideways glance. It wasn't happening again, was it? She couldn't bear it if Alison had to go away. It had been so hard the last time, even though it had just been for a few days.

It wasn't her mother being in hospital that had been the worst bit. It was when she came home. Holly had tiptoed around on eggshells, terrified. But Alison had seemed remarkably philosophical about it all. She'd even stitched her breakdown into jokes, with throwaway lines about having to go back to the funny farm when she did something silly or forgot something.

'Too soon, Mam,' Holly would say, and Alison would purse her lips and nod apologetically.

She didn't joke about what the breakdown had really been like. The screaming and crying and smashing things. After so many years of holding it together, of being quiet and calm and gentle, Alison had snapped and it had been terrifying.

Holly never wanted to witness that again.

Alison turned her head and looked at her daughter.

'What was all that about with the detectives?' Holly said. 'I never knew you came back to the house that day.'

'It was nothing. You were up in bed. I called in, got my passport and ran. It just went clean out of my head.'

'Did you go near Olive's?'

'No, for heaven's sake.'

'But why do you keep asking them what they found in her house?' Holly persisted.

Alison threw her hands in the air, exasperated.

'I'm curious! I know they think she was murdered. I'm just wondering how.'

'Really? Are you okay, Mam? It's not ... Should I do something?'

'I'm absolutely fine, Holly. It's you I'm worried about.'

'Me?' Holly frowned. 'Why are you worried about me?'

'Love, I think we have to tell the detectives why we're here. It was okay to think we could hide before, when the Vale was anonymous. But the way we're acting now, we're drawing attention to ourselves. And they might think it's because we'd something to do with Olive's death. Because they don't know otherwise. If we're honest with them, then they'll know we're good people. That we've nothing to hide.'

Holly clenched her teeth.

'You just want to tell somebody,' she said. 'That's why you spoke to Olive in the first place. Why, Mam? Did you really think you could trust her?'

'Yes, Holly. Yes, I did.'

'But why?'

'She was another woman. An independent woman. She seemed strong. She was nice to me. And I *did* need somebody to confide in.'

'You had me!' Holly didn't mean it to come out as whiny as it sounded. She wasn't a kid. She hated sounding like one.

'I know I had you. I *have* you. But there are some things you shouldn't have to shoulder, love. You've been through enough. Too much. What he did to us – what he did to me – you never should have seen that. You should never have been exposed to it. To any of it, including how I handled it, afterwards.'

Holly said nothing. The lump in her throat was too big. She had to swallow a few times before she could trust herself to speak without sobbing.

'I do get it,' she said, quietly. 'I understand wanting somebody your own age to talk to. Well, not your own age. You know what I mean. I suppose you weren't to know that Olive was such an evil cow.'

Alison inhaled deeply.

'Holly, listen to me. You have to stop saying that. Olive didn't appreciate what we'd been through. I could have tried telling her, but hearing something is very different to actually understanding. You have to experience that kind of life before you can know why we ran. And, to be fair, I didn't try very hard to make her understand.'

'What do you mean?'

'I didn't even try to tell her the whole story, Holly. I told her we were running. I told her who we were running from. I didn't think I needed to fill in the rest. I assumed she'd get it, as a woman. But she didn't. She drew her own conclusions. Too late, I realised she wasn't what you'd describe as a woman's woman. I'm not sure which of us was more stupid, her or me. I should have told her to stay out of the shop ages ago. I knew what she was at when she kept coming in. I'd get a knot in my stomach every time I saw her. She knew what she was at as well, even if she couldn't admit it to herself. I should have been more assertive. That's my problem, love, isn't it? I'm scared of my own shadow.'

Holly didn't reply. Instead, she squeezed her mother's hand. Only Holly realised how hard her mother fought timidity every second of the day.

'They're beautiful,' Alison said.

213

'What?'

'The stars.'

Holly followed her mother's eyeline.

'I . . . I stuck them up when we moved in,' she said. She could barely breathe. What would Alison say next? How would she react?

Would the tears start again?

But Alison just sighed. A deep, heartbroken, painful sigh. No tears.

'I miss her,' she said, squeezing Holly's hand back.

Holly closed her eyes then looked back at the stars.

'Me too.'

They lay there for a minute, silent bar the low strains of music in the background.

'Mam?' Holly said.

'Yes?'

'I did something.'

Alison sighed.

'I know, love.'

EMMA

They'd called in to the Solankes' at number two, only to discover that Lily was still out looking for Wolf.

'He's probably in the treehouse,' David told them. 'Lily went after him.'

'We'll pop over and see what's going on,' Emma said.

They walked out of the garden, Frank tutting as they went.

'Such an ado about nothing,' he said to Emma. 'Is it just me or do parents these days make bringing up kids seem like such an *effort*? There's so much thinking and talking. All this family politicking. That pair are going to screw up their kids no matter how much they dance around it. All parents do.'

Emma smiled grimly.

'Do you have kids, Frank?' she asked.

He bristled.

'No. But I don't see how that precludes me from having an opinion.'

'I never said it did,' Emma said. But it was too late – he'd stormed off again, walking at a pace he knew she couldn't keep up with.

That bloody man. It was like Frank made it his life's work to always misunderstand her.

They were able to access the Hennessys' back garden via the side of the house. At the bottom, Lily was standing beneath a huge tree and calling up into the branches, fists balled tight at her sides.

Emma stepped on something soft as they approached. She looked down.

'Arghh! Jesus fucking Christ!'

Frank nearly leapt three feet in the air beside her. Even Lily's head spun around.

'What the hell?'

Emma pointed at the dead bird on the ground. She'd crushed its stomach and some of the maggots feasting there had spilled out onto the grass.

Frank, to his credit, didn't make a joke.

'I'll get a bag,' he said. 'Can't leave that there. You need to clean your shoe?'

Emma turned green at the thought of what might be on her sole.

She reached into her bag and pulled out a pair of skinny ballet pumps she kept there for driving.

'You know what?' she said. 'Get two bags.'

She held onto his arm as she stepped out of her block heels and slipped on the pumps.

'I feel like I'm bringing my niece to dance rehearsal,' Frank joked.

'I'm really not that young,' Emma said. 'And if I'm not allowed to remind you how old you are, I don't see why you get to keep making jokes about my age.'

Frank looked puzzled, but he said nothing. Instead, he walked up to the Hennessys' back door and rapped loudly.

Emma left her soiled heels in the grass and continued down the garden to Lily. As she approached, she could see the wooden contraption high up in the branches.

'What was it?' Lily asked.

'A dead bird.'

Lily wrinkled her nose.

'Is your son up there, then?' Emma asked.

'Yes. He won't come down. I don't want to go up. He gets . . .' Lily threw her hands in the air.

Emma stared at the red mark on Lily's cheek. She hadn't noticed it out on the road – maybe because Lily's dark face had been flushed from running.

'What happened there?'

'What?' Lily's hand flew to her cheek.

'Did Wolf do that?'

'It was an accident.'

Emma nodded.

'What if I climb up? It's different when it's a policewoman and not your mum who wants to have a chat.'

Lily looked like she was about to protest, but gave in almost as fast.

'He has to come down,' she said, defeated. 'I'm afraid of heights. Which he knows, full well.'

Frank was at the dead bird now, two plastic Tesco bags in hand. He scooped her shoes into one.

Emma found the first branch and started to haul herself up into the tree.

She was good at climbing. She'd forgotten. It came naturally to her. She'd small feet with surprisingly high arches. The flexible pumps helped. They slotted into the best nooks and crannies, and she was nimble. She reached the house in no time.

She allowed herself to bask in the achievement for a moment.

The kid was sitting on the floor of the treehouse, knotting reeds together in some bowl shape. The floor was full of them. Whether they'd been there already or he'd brought them up was a mystery.

He didn't look at Emma as she crawled onto the boards beside him. But his fingers, and his breathing, had slowed.

Emma sat and crossed her legs. She picked up three long strands and started to plait them.

'I'm Emma,' she said.

Wolf said nothing.

'I'm a policewoman. A detective. Like on the TV.'

Silence.

'I love what you're doing there. I'm no good at building things. I'm pretty good at taking stuff apart, as it happens. It's probably what makes me a good detective. Getting into things.'

Wolf's fingers laboured slowly on his design. He wasn't just tying the reeds together, Emma noticed. He was fashioning an intricate nest. It was beautiful.

'Your mum is down there,' Emma continued. 'She's a bit worried about you. I guess you know that. You can probably hear her calling. She doesn't want to climb up here, though. She thinks it might upset you. That, and she's scared of heights.'

The kid shrugged.

Emma reached the end of her plait.

'Do you want to use this?' she said, and offered it to him.

He looked at it.

'It's good,' he said, meeting her eye, then looking away as quick.

Classic symptoms, Emma thought. But mild.

'I used to do this a lot with my brother,' she said. 'He's grown up now. He's studying to be a scientist. He's really clever. I have a feeling you're very clever, too. Am I right?'

Wolf shrugged again.

'My parents say I am. My sister thinks I'm not.'

'Your sister, Lily May? She's your twin, right?'

'Yeah.'

'I always wanted a twin when I was growing up.'

'It's not fun.'

'Isn't it?'

'No. She follows me everywhere. She wants to do everything with me. I read a magazine article once. I don't think I was supposed to see it. It said a baby ate her twin in the womb.'

'Lucky you didn't eat Lily May.'

'I'm lucky she didn't eat me.'

'It's okay to want to be on your own. I live on my own at the moment. I never thought I'd enjoy it but I really do. Nobody is in the loo when I want to go. Nobody uses the milk or eats the treats I buy. And I can have a whole bath without wondering if my housemates have left enough hot water.'

'Yeah. We used to share baths but we're too old now. I like being on my own but . . .'

'Yes?'

'I like having friends. Lily May is not my friend. She's my sister. I wouldn't choose her as a friend.'

'I get that. I think it would drive me nuts too, if somebody never left my side and I didn't want to be around them all the time. I suppose Ms Collins understood. She lived on her own. She'd appreciate somebody wanting time for themselves. But then, you were great company for her, too.'

Wolf started to nod, then stopped, looking like he was trying to decide if he'd just been tricked.

'You don't have to talk to me about anything you don't want to,' Emma said. 'It's just, because I'm a police detective and because Ms Collins died, I need to chat with everybody who knew her. To see if anything was wrong. We were coming to talk to you today, anyway.'

Wolf hesitated on the next knot. He was considering.

'Is everything okay up there?' Lily's voice rose up through the leaves.

Emma cursed. That would end it, she thought. She shouldn't be having this little chat with Wolf, as informal as it was, but . . . the mother had given her permission to go up and get him.

'I'd like to talk to you,' Wolf whispered. 'But Mummy says I can't.'

'Oh,' Emma said. 'I see.'

Her heart gave a little flutter.

'Just a minute,' she called down to Lily.

'I feel really bad,' Wolf said.

'Why?'

'I wish I'd called over. Then I might have saved her.'

'Oh, Wolf. You couldn't have. When she died, it was very quick. Calling over wouldn't have changed anything.'

'She wouldn't have been left on her own, though. What did she look like when you found her? Did she have bandages on her?'

'I'm sorry?'

'Like *The Mummy*. Daddy said she must have been mummified

and then Mummy said she must have looked awful because of all the bugs.'

Emma shook her head.

'No. She just looked like she'd fallen asleep. And she seemed very happy.'

'Oh.'

Wolf didn't quite smile but he seemed a little less worried.

'That really is a lovely thing you're making,' Emma said. 'Do you think you could make me one?'

'Why?'

'I could use one.'

'For what?'

'Little trinkets.'

'Oh. Well, not this one. Stuff could fall out through this one.'

'That's what I was thinking.'

'I'll do you a tighter one.'

Emma smiled.

'Thanks. I'll pop down and tell your mum you're doing a job for me. We'll go over to your house, okay? Come down when you're ready.'

Wolf nodded. He didn't say anything else. He was already busy selecting fresh reeds from the floor.

Emma tried to get back down the tree as gracefully as she'd climbed up but gravity added unwanted impetus to her descent, making it artless and clumsy; she bruised her shins and grazed her knuckles in the process.

Once she'd straightened up, she met Lily's questioning gaze.

'He's fine up there,' she said. 'He'll be down in a bit. But I think we need to have a little chat.'

Lily's face crumpled.

ED & AMELIA

No. 6

They'd been so excited by the news, they'd got a flight home that morning, a ridiculously expensive indulgence.

The apartment was only let out for another week, anyway, and then Ed was facing a lengthy negotiation with their landlord. They would likely have had to move someplace else – Spanish rental prices for short lets were increasing by the day as they approached the summer months proper.

Amelia had her heart set on another cruise in July. She'd spotted one that took in Dubrovnik and the Greek isles. Ed fancied trying the famous Chios Mastiha liqueur. He wasn't going to argue with his wife's choice.

Now they could go home, get the house aired out and lived in again – maybe rented, even – then fly out in July for three weeks on the Med. After that, they could think longer-term. Their house in Withered Vale had nice equity in it. If they sold it, they could buy a little place in Portugal, maybe, where prices weren't so high and there was a large population of British and Irish ex-pats to live amongst. If they hung on a bit, maybe Brexit would mean all those

Brits had to sell up and they could end up getting somewhere very cheap indeed. The capital release from the house, combined with their savings, would allow for a very comfortable lifestyle.

The world was their lobster, as Ed liked to say.

The first sign that they might have made a miscalculation was when the taxi pulled up outside their house and Ed saw two strangers walking with Lily Solanke to her house across the way. It wasn't the presence of a man and woman he didn't know that alarmed him. It was the gait on the fellow – the hunched-over shoulders and determined stride of a man on a mission. A man who was there to ask questions.

Ed's eyes took him in and then flicked to the yellow tape that had come loose from the gate of Olive Collins' house and was now flapping in the breeze.

The man stopped and looked over at Ed and Amelia, as they waited for the taxi driver to take their suitcases from the boot so they could pay him.

It was a look that said, *You're people of interest*. Ed knew it, because somebody had looked at him like that before. Another detective, another time.

Amelia had paid the driver from her purse before Ed could tell her he'd changed his mind and they were going straight back to the airport. She didn't even see the policeman, who'd halted his progress towards the Solankes' and was now ambling towards them.

'Mr and Mrs Miller, is it?' he called out.

Amelia nearly dropped her handbag.

'That's right,' Ed said, acting suitably suspicious, because who wouldn't, being accosted outside their own home by some stranger who evidently knew them.

'I'm Detective Frank Brazil. That's my colleague, Emma Child, over there with your neighbour. Listen, I'm sorry to just land on you like this. I don't know if you heard, but one of your neighbours has passed away.'

Ed nodded. He wouldn't be caught out in a lie. Matt might have been asked to contact them, as opposed to just taking it upon himself.

'We did, sadly. Matt next door let me know. Awful news to get. We were due back anyway but at least now we'll be here for the funeral.'

'Right. Anyhow, we're just popping around to everybody. We'd like to have a chat with you about Ms Collins. Could we call over to you when we're finished with Mrs Solanke?'

'We've only just got back,' Amelia said. 'I've got nothing in. No milk or teabags. The house will be covered in dust.'

The detective dismissed her concerns with a shake of the head.

'Please, don't worry yourself. It's just a quick chat. We aren't expecting hospitality. You'll be able to get back to your unpacking in no time at all.'

Amelia looked like she was going to protest some more but Ed cut her off.

'No problem, Detective. Sorry, we're both exhausted. It's been a long morning.'

'Totally understandable. We'll see you shortly. Perhaps your neighbour might lend you a pint of milk so you can have a cuppa and relax. It looks like you need it.'

Ed smiled. When the detective walked off, he turned to Amelia.

'Leave those there,' he said, indicating the suitcases. 'I'll do them in a moment. I'm just popping in to Matt. To borrow some teabags.'

Amelia nodded.

Ed made his way to the Hennessys', marched up the front steps and rang the bell twice, before hammering on the oak door with the side of his fist.

Matt opened it, looking fit to kill.

'Ah. Matt. There you are. I'm back.'

Ed's neighbour looked surprised, then puzzled.

'Ed, yes, great. Good to see you. I'm sort of in the middle of something here. Is there anything you need?'

'Is that any way to greet your neighbour who's been away for three months?'

Ed smiled. Nothing to see here. We're all friends.

Matt opened his mouth, then shut it again. He forced a smile in return.

'Sorry. No, of course. I'm distracted. Under a bit of pressure, you know how it is. I wasn't expecting to see you. Were you due back? You didn't respond to my email yesterday.'

'That's why I'm here. We were flying back anyway, but I saw your email right before we left. What a tragedy. The police just collared me as we were getting out of the taxi. They want to have a word. What happened to her? Olive?'

Matt shrugged.

'Like I said. They don't know. Or at least, they haven't said anything.'

'But wasn't it natural causes? That's what you implied in your email. Why do they want to talk to everybody?'

Matt was getting impatient. Ed could see the sweat breaking out over his upper lip. He did look stressed. And he'd lost more hair since Ed had seen him last. He'd want to be careful about that. That Chrissy one was a looker. She hardly wanted to be married to some old codger who was bald at forty.

'It's just what they do, isn't it?' Matt said. 'Sorry, Ed, I'm really up against it in here. I have to . . .'

Ed nodded. He turned and walked back towards his house.

It wasn't *just* what they did. The police never did anything without good reason.

Of all people, Ed knew that.

OLIVE

No. 4

Oh, Ed.

My poor old pal.

When Ed and Amelia moved in, I genuinely thought I'd found some good friends. They'd ten years on me, but they were more my kind of people than the others who followed into the Vale. Ed and Amelia travelled. Ed was intelligent – a big reader, which is always a plus for me. Whenever I met somebody who told me they didn't read, I used to smile and nod and deduct thirty points or so from their IQ.

Ed and I used to swap books. Neither of us did Kindles, so we were in the lovely position of being able to not just recommend a great novel, but actually lend one.

Amelia was quiet, happy to potter in the kitchen and join us for coffee or wine when we'd exhausted the topics of genre versus literary, the classics versus modern sensations. She wasn't as well read, but she was still clever, still interesting.

The Millers talked me into taking my first package holiday. It didn't matter, they said, that I was going alone. On those trips, you often found single people who wanted to see the world but weren't intrepid enough to go off on one-man travels. Meals were shared occasions and people liked to chat, but of course I'd have my own room if I wanted peace and quiet.

I did it, too. I'd only been on holiday outside Ireland once before – two weeks with the women from work at a resort in Tenerife. It wasn't my sort of thing. All they wanted to do was sleep by the pool all day while they worked on their tans, then drink cheap, acid-inducing Tinto de Verano all night. I liked to see where I was staying. Visit the sights. Have wine that didn't give me an ulcer, not get sunburnt.

The holiday that Ed and Amelia recommended was a tour of the Alps, beginning in Salzburg and ending in Chamonix. I'd been addicted to the *Chalet School* books when I was young, something I'd completely forgotten as I grew older. The thought of seeing the region, its snow-capped peaks and edelweiss, drinking mulled wine in Christmas markets and eating roasted chestnuts, made my heart soar.

And it was almost as good as the Millers had recommended. The others on the package tour were very friendly, but they were all older. Much older. Not like the Millers, more like pensioners. They took me under their collective wing and I was grateful, but it would have been nice to meet somebody my own age.

It only served to strengthen my friendship with Ed and Amelia, however. We were able to talk about the holiday at length when I returned and they started to get excited about where I, and they, could go next.

Many bottles of Bordeaux were consumed while we planned.

Everything was fine, until that fateful day.

It's really shocking to find out somebody you think you know is an absolute liar.

And not just a liar about something small.

Yes, I can see how detectives wanting to talk to Ed would make him nervous.

GEORGE

No. 1

George had left the Vale. Well, technically speaking. What he'd really left was his computer. A necessary escape.

He'd been in the Horse and Hound pub before; he'd bumped into Lily in the village once and they'd grabbed a coffee there.

But George wasn't the sort of man who went into a bar and ordered a pint on his own. He wasn't entirely sure what the protocol was. Should he buy a paper? Would there be sport showing on a giant TV? Was it okay to order whiskey at lunchtime or would people look at him like he was an alcoholic? Ha! Better that, than what he really was.

Considering he'd left the house on instinct, he put an awful lot of thought into what came next once he was in the village. He opened and closed the car door at least five times before he made up his mind.

Eventually, he ducked into the bookshop a few doors down from the pub and picked up the latest literary release from a big pile on a table by the door. He'd arrived at the conclusion that people would have no problem interrupting somebody reading a paper, but perhaps they'd think twice if he was engrossed in a book.

'You reading that?'

The barman was young, twenties maybe.

George looked around to see if the question was addressed to him.

The pub was populated (some sports team was playing later, judging by the amount of red jerseys on display), but George was the only one sitting at that section of the counter.

'I just bought it,' he said, hesitantly.

The barman shook his head, sympathetically.

'Got it for my mother's birthday. She said it made her want to slit her wrists. She's a big fan of Lee Child, though, so it was probably a bad choice on my part.'

George turned the book around and read aloud from the blurb.

' "*One man's journey into his innermost thoughts and feelings, transcribed across decades, transcending class and place, this is an existential analysis of the human mind.*" Yeah. A bit of a change from Jack Reacher. I think I'm with your mother on this one.'

The barman laughed.

'Another?'

He pointed at George's near-empty whiskey and water. How had that happened?

'Eh. Yeah. Thanks.'

George looked around him while the barman replenished his glass. There were a few couples in and a family or two, but mainly it was just men and some of them were on their own, like him. So he wasn't alone. It made him feel warm inside. Though that may have been the whiskey.

The barman gave him a fresh glass and a tabloid.

'The less lofty reflections of mere mortals,' he smiled.

George grinned back, pulled the newspaper towards him.

The front page contained two stories. One about an investigation into members of the police who'd been erasing motoring penalty points for family and friends.

The other was about Olive.

George felt the acid churning in his stomach. Was there no getting away from that woman? He turned the paper over, pretended to give a damn about the line-up for that day's football match.

Within minutes he gave up and started to people-watch.

The men behind him were talking about some woman called Sarah who, by the sounds of things, had been with a couple of them at various times. And women thought men never talked about them. These guys more or less had Sarah's breast, waist, and hip measurements to hand.

George quickly tuned out of that conversation. Along the counter, the friendly barman was pulling a pint for an older man who was debating aloud who was likely to press the button first – Trump or Kim Jong Un.

The barman frowned at the pint he was pulling as the older man babbled on. George looked at the pint. It was flat. The gas was gone.

'Crap.' The barman sat the pint on the counter and looked at it.

The old man stared at the offering.

'Where's Bobby?'

George guessed – by the weight of authority attached to the name – that Bobby was the boss. The barman looked panicked now, checked his watch and looked at the door.

'He's run over to the wholesalers. He's not due back for a half hour.'

And suddenly, the world opened up for George.

'I can change over the gas for you,' he said.

The two men looked at him.

'You know how to do it?' the barman asked.

'He wouldn't have offered if he didn't, son,' the old man said.

George nodded.

'Yeah, I worked in a bar when I was in college.'

The barman looked at George like he was his saviour.

And George realised there could be life outside his house again. He didn't need or want a job that involved working with computers. He wanted a job that was pure manual labour, something he could get lost in and not think about anything or anybody else.

And he'd always been very good with his hands.

FRANK

'Where's Wolf?'

David Solanke greeted the three of them at the front door, Frank, Emma and Lily.

'Your son is over in the Hennessys',' Emma said. 'I left him on a job. He's making me something. He's a very creative little boy.'

David beamed.

'He really is. Will I make some tea?'

'Could we trouble you for coffee?' Frank said. There was no way he was drinking again whatever they'd been served yesterday.

'Oh. Sure. I have some ground. I think.'

Lily walked into the kitchen and sank into a chair. David followed his wife wordlessly, the two detectives in their wake.

She started speaking before Frank and Emma had even pulled out chairs.

'It was an accident,' she said. 'I swear, I don't know what came over me. She was taunting me, looking to upset me. I didn't mean to do it.'

Frank and Emma looked at each other. David was frozen over at the sink, kettle in hand.

'Mrs Solanke, you might need to bring us in at the beginning.' Frank stopped her from going any further. 'We're talking about this argument you had with your neighbour over your son, are we?'

Lily nodded.

'When you discovered she was giving him meat?'

'Yes. When I realised that, yet again, she was attempting to undermine me. Us. I asked David to go over and have it out with her.'

She cast her husband a sideways glance.

'I just didn't think it was a big deal,' he said, smiling. 'I thought the women could sort it out.'

Both Lily and Emma were looking at him with raised eyebrows now.

Put the shovel down and stop digging. Frank sent David a man-to-man warning glance.

'I mean,' he continued, picking up on the tension, 'I did think it was a big deal but I didn't want to go marching over there like the big bad father. A man can be very intimidating to a single woman. I'm aware of that, especially with my size. We all have to live in this community together. I thought Lily would be able to sort it out without there being huge recriminations.'

'It was your idea,' Lily said quietly.

David looked blank.

'It was your idea that our children be vegetarians. You decided. I didn't decide.'

David frowned and glanced at their visitors, embarrassed.

'That's ridiculous,' he said, nervously. 'How can they be meat-eaters when we don't buy meat? How could we let them be meat-eaters? We know what the consumption of meat does to the planet and to our bodies.'

Frank coughed to remind the Solankes that he and Emma were still there. They could have this out when the detectives had left. For now, the focus was on Olive Collins and Lily's relationship with her.

'Let's skip the virtues of why we should all be vegetarian and discuss what happened between you and your neighbour, Mrs Solanke?'

Her husband gave her a last puzzled look, then started to fuss in cupboards, searching for coffee.

'Well, the fact the kids are vegetarians matters, Detective. Because that's why I marched over there, guns blazing. I went to Olive's to tell her if she couldn't respect the choices we'd made for our children, then our children wouldn't be spending any more time in her company. And then she . . .'

'She what?'

'She called me out for the hypocrite I am.'

David stopped what he was doing.

'You didn't tell me this,' he said.

Lily shrugged.

'I told you we'd fallen out.'

'Yes, but you didn't tell me she'd called you a hypocrite. You said she was obnoxious to you. Why would she call you a hypocrite?'

Lily hesitated, chewing on her bottom lip.

'She'd seen me in town, eating a hamburger.'

Frank and Emma met each other's eyes and raised their brows. If this had been their first trip to the Solankes', they might have found it funny. Now they were versed in the food politics of the household.

David looked puzzled. Then he started to laugh.

'You? You were eating a burger?'

Lily looked down at the table.

'Yes. I was. A quarter-pounder. With cheese and onions and pickles and ketchup. It was delicious. I could murder one right now.'

Frank's stomach rumbled. And he'd an awful feeling he wasn't going to be getting that coffee.

David opened and closed his mouth like a fish.

'Wow. Okay. I'm struggling to get my head around this, Lily. I mean, *you're* the reason I became a vegetarian. You see, what you're saying about the kids there – that doesn't make much sense to me. But okay, let's pretend I decided that for them. That you'd no hand, act or part in our children becoming vegetarians. Are you going to claim now that I made you give up meat, as well? Because on our first date, I ordered a steak and you could barely make eye contact with me while I ate. Remember?'

Lily sucked the inside of her cheeks. Frank was worried about her. She looked like she was struggling to contain her breathing. She looked like she was about to blow.

'No. Of course you didn't make me a vegetarian.'

'So, could you explain what is going on?'

'Again,' Frank interrupted. 'Could we please stick to the exchange you had with Ms Collins?'

Lily squirmed. Whatever had happened between her and Olive, Frank guessed it had been stupid, and she knew it.

'She was goading me,' Lily said. 'Olive was in the wrong. But she was so bloody stubborn that, rather than accept it, she just went for me. I mean . . . I could be swinging naked from the damned light-bulb eating a leg of lamb and it still didn't give her the right to argue with me over how we're rearing our kids.'

She looked to David for confirmation of this. Frank couldn't fig-ure out what was going on with her husband. He looked confused, angry, suspicious, all at once – but more importantly, he looked like he wanted to tell his wife to stop talking. Which made Frank very curious indeed.

'And . . . I don't really know how it happened, but I punched her in the face.'

David snorted, then stopped abruptly.

'You punched her? You?'

'Yes. I am capable of bloody hitting somebody. I'm not a saint.'

David held up his hand. He couldn't help himself, Frank realised. He was *quieting* his wife.

'Detectives, why is any of this relevant? Did something actually happen to Olive – was she harmed deliberately?'

Frank sat back in his chair.

'It's been roughly thirty-six hours since your neighbour was discovered,' he said. 'It's still quite immediate. We're currently exploring all avenues, including considering if Ms Collins was a victim of foul play.'

Lily's mouth fell open.

'Oh, come on. Do you really think eating a burger and hitting somebody makes me capable of killing?' She laughed. 'I punched her. And when she started going on like she did, after, I wished I'd done it harder. But, crazy as this sounds, I managed to stop short of murdering her!'

'What did she do, after you hit her?' Emma asked.

Lily stared at her hands.

'She said she was going to report me to the Guards and to my school. It was such a nasty thing to say. She could have just smacked me back. But Wolf came in . . .'

'Wolf saw this?' David asked.

'Yes. I'd like to think she didn't hit me because he was there but, actually, when I thought about it afterwards, I decided she was far more devious than I gave her credit for. Olive Collins knew being reported for punching somebody would be terrible for me. I teach young children in a small school. They're going to make me head-mistress. We know all the parents and all the parents know us. We're supposed to be cleaner than clean. Not the sort of people who go around attacking their neighbours. And I have to be even more perfect than anybody else. For obvious reasons.'

She laughed, thinly.

'I told her to go ahead, but I felt sick. She could have ruined me.'

Emma turned to David.

'Did you know how upset your wife was about this?'

Good question, Frank thought.

David looked back at Emma, his face giving nothing away.

'She told me Olive had been awful to her – I knew that much. I comforted Lily, didn't I, darling? But I assumed it would just blow over.'

'When did this happen?' Frank asked Lily. 'When did she threaten you?'

Lily looked him straight in the eye.

'The weekend before you say she died,' she answered.

Frank noticed David shift.

He reached across and took his wife's hand.

'Lily was here, with me and the kids, on the night of the 3rd of March,' he said. 'I checked my diary. I was home from work early. It's rare for me. It was a clear evening and I asked if she wanted to bring the kids for a walk. But you were working on that project for Easter, remember? The giant egg thing for your class.'

Lily scrunched up her face, puzzled. Then she nodded, the light going on.

'Yes. I remember.'

David turned back to the detectives.

'Look, Detectives, Lily is a good mum. And she gets very defensive about Wolf. You can understand that, surely. Wolf is . . . special.'

Emma nodded.

'My brother is similar,' she said. 'He's on the spectrum. When he gets upset, it gets worse. That's probably why Wolf hit you today, Lily. He was mimicking something he's seen.'

'No, he's not autistic,' David started. 'Wait, he hit you?'

Lily nodded.

'Yes. Earlier. He is, David. He is autistic.'

'He's a tough child at times, Lily, but I think we'd know if he was autistic.'

'I brought him to the doctor for tests,' she said.

David studied his wife. Then, slowly, he withdrew his hand from hers and clamped his mouth shut.

He was furious, Frank realised. Beneath that calm, controlled exterior, David Solanke was simmering. *What else hadn't his wife told him?* he was clearly thinking.

It's what Frank was wondering, too.

That, and, what was David Solanke capable of?

ED & AMELIA

No. 6

They'd kept up with all their bills while they'd been away.

The WiFi was working fine.

Ed typed in Aer Lingus and scrolled down the options.

He hadn't noticed Amelia come through from the kitchen. She'd made black coffee and had started to draw up a list for him to take to the shops. She hadn't lied to the police. They really had nothing in.

'Are you going to bring the suitcases upstairs?' she asked him, turning on the television and flicking idly through the channels.

He didn't answer. He'd spotted a flight that had two seats on offer. It flew into Copenhagen the following morning.

'Ed? Are we unpacking the suitcases or not?'

Ed looked up.

'Maybe not, dear.'

Amelia sat down on the couch beside him.

'Copenhagen? I've never been there. It doesn't strike me as a particularly relaxed city.'

'There's the Tivoli Gardens,' Ed said. 'The Little Mermaid. Anyway, *where* is not important.'

'Are you really worried?' Amelia asked.

Ed nodded.

'I don't know why. I feel something. In here.'

He placed his hand on his gut.

She shook her head.

'I think you're letting your imagination get carried away, Ed. We can go if you're worried but really, I don't think there's any need. We haven't done anything.'

His reply never came. The doorbell rang.

'I'll get it,' Ed said.

His wife had regained the composure she'd almost lost when they were outside with the detectives. Now she was as cool as a cucumber. Good. They needed to come across like that. Nothing to hide.

He let the detectives in with the barest of polite conversation. It was important to let them know how much they were putting Ed and Amelia out.

A policeman had told Ed once that if the cops picked up four men for a crime and only one of them was guilty, there was a simple method of detecting the real culprit. They kept them overnight. And the criminal would sleep, the officer said. He knew what he'd done and he'd sleep so as to conserve his energy for the lies he'd be telling them the next day.

The innocent men couldn't sleep. Innocent men were rightly agitated when they were being accused of something they hadn't done.

So Ed was agitated when he brought the detectives into the lounge, where the laptop with the flight times had been put away.

'So, was it just a long holiday you were on?' the man, Brazil, asked.

'Yes and no,' Ed said. 'We travel a lot. We're both retired. No kids, no ties. We like to see the world but these days, mainly hot climes. We both love the more laid-back lifestyle you get in Spain, Italy, those sort of places.'

'Can't remember the last time I had a holiday abroad,' Frank said. 'I've a sister living near Curracloe beach. You know it? It's the beach they shot *Saving Private Ryan* on. I like to head down there every other summer.'

'Nice place,' Ed said. 'Good pubs. Good grub.'

He invited the detectives to take chairs.

'Can I get you a glass of water, maybe?' Amelia said.

'Oh, no, we won't be long, honestly,' the woman detective said. 'So. Did you know Olive Collins well?'

Ed and Amelia nodded.

'Very well,' Ed said. 'She spent many an evening here, as we did over there. We'd similar interests, though she didn't travel as much as we do. I suppose you could say she sort of lived vicariously through us. She never got bored of the photographs of where we'd been or my boring tales of local cuisines. I'm sorry, Detective, I hope it's not improper of me to ask, but what happened to her? She was only in her fifties, in the prime of her health.'

Brazil cocked his head sideways, like he was weighing up his answer.

'We know for certain that she had a heart attack,' he said.

Ed tried not to let the relief show on his face. A heart attack. For goodness' sake, they could hardly blame anybody for that.

The relief was short-lived.

'However, it appeared to have been brought on in suspicious circumstances.'

'I'm not following. How can a heart attack be *brought on*?'

The detective shook his head.

'That's what we're trying to establish. Did you call over to Olive at all before you left on your latest jaunt?'

Ed shook his head.

'Unfortunately, no. We were trying to get everything organised.'

'And you, Mrs Miller?'

Amelia shook her head.

'But you were such good friends,' Brazil continued. 'You didn't want to say goodbye, knowing you'd be gone for months?'

Ed shrugged.

'We feel terrible about it now. If we had known . . .'

'When was the last time you saw her?'

'Um, I think it was a day or so before we left? Did she pop over to drop some books back, Amelia?'

'She did, Ed. I remember. We did tell her we were going away, didn't we?' She turned to Frank. 'I think I said I'd see her before we left, but it went clean from my mind. You know how it is.'

The detective nodded.

Ed, despite the lecture he'd given himself, was starting to feel a little frazzled.

Had somebody seen him going into Olive's house the day they left? Was that what the questions were about? He'd been so careful, but what if somebody had spotted something from a window?

'So, you didn't fall out with Olive at all? Everything was perfectly amiable?'

'Yes. Of course.'

'And what day was this, exactly, when you left?'

'It was 3rd of March,' Amelia said, smiling. 'I looked it up. I thought you might want to check.'

'Yes,' Brazil said. 'Your neighbour mentioned something along that timeline. It's such a strange coincidence, that.'

'How so?' Ed said.

'Olive Collins died on 3rd of March.'

Ed tried not to swallow too hard. Amelia's face flushed.

'Are you sure that's the day she died?' she said. 'I mean, if she was in the house for that long, how can you determine the exact day?'

'She rang the emergency services that night,' the woman detective answered. 'And none of your neighbours saw her after that date.'

'Oh.' Amelia had nothing to add.

'By the way,' Brazil added. 'Do you need a hand with those cases in the hall? Getting them upstairs, I mean?'

Ed shook his head.

'No, really, it's fine. I'll do it later.'

'Right, so. It's just one of those bureaucratic things, but you will let us know if you're heading away again, won't you? So we can tick the boxes.'

Ed nodded, mutely.

Why, oh why, had they ever come home?

OLIVE

No. 4

When Ed called over to me on the morning of the 3rd, it was the first I'd heard of their travel plans.

He claimed they'd been in the offing for a while but I'd have bet money they'd booked the flight that very week.

How quickly everything had soured.

It wasn't my doing. And had I not been here that evening when his brother called by, I doubt anything would have changed. We would have continued on as we were. Friends.

I'd called to their house to finalise dinner arrangements for the following night when I heard the shouting. The three of us had agreed to try the new restaurant in town, the fancy Asian fusion one that apparently greeted you with a free cocktail as soon as you arrived in the door.

Naturally, when I heard the sounds of an argument, my first instinct was to jump to Ed and Amelia's defence. I was halfway up the path and I couldn't make out the words that were being exchanged but I could hear the anger in Ed's voice and in the voice of the man arguing with him — a man who sounded very similar to Ed. The same sing-song County Cork accent.

I quickened my pace up the path until I was within earshot of the open window.

I heard: *How the hell did you find us, anyway?* from Ed, before I rapped on the door to alert them to my presence.

That was all I heard. I'm not an eavesdropper.

Amelia answered, flustered and unhappy.

'What's going on?' I said, affronted on her behalf. 'Can I help?'

Instead of inviting me in, or thanking me for wanting to come to their aid, Amelia stood in the door, blocking my view.

'Now's not a good time, Olive,' she said, her voice harsh and unfamiliar.

I was taken aback.

'Amelia, if something is wrong . . .' I persisted.

'I said now is not a good time,' she snapped.

'Oh,' I said. 'Fine.'

I retreated back down the path and crossed to my house, where I went up to my room and sat at the window, looking down the street at the Millers'.

It was a dark January night, but there's a good street light just outside their house; that's where the stranger had parked. I noted his car and when he came out twenty minutes later, I saw him clearly.

No more might have come from that unpleasant evening, had it ended there.

I was certainly bruised from the brush-off by Amelia. And I didn't see either her or Ed that evening or the next day, which told me all I needed to know. Neither of them got back to me on the Asian restaurant reservation, even though I sent them both several texts.

Whatever friendship I thought we had, I'd just been made aware of its limitations.

Days later, Amelia called over. She was a different person. When I say that, I mean, she was the same person she'd always been, which was completely different to how off she'd been with me a few nights earlier.

I offered her a coffee, even though it was 6 p.m. and the perfect time for a glass of wine. If they could cool their relationship with me, I could do that right back.

She sat at my kitchen table for a good half hour, making mindless small talk and not once mentioning the awkwardness of our last exchange.

Eventually, I lost patience.

'That man the other night,' I said, slipping it into conversation like it was the most natural thing in the world. 'I hope you've had no trouble since?'

Amelia sipped at the dregs of her coffee, her body language stiff and unfriendly.

That was why she'd called over, I realised. To gauge what was going on with me. To see whether I'd want to follow up. And I did.

'Oh, him,' she said. 'A disgruntled former employee of Ed's, I'm afraid. He has it in for Ed because he wouldn't provide him with a reference. Honestly, Olive, you've no idea. At this time in our lives, we could do without that sort of hassle.'

'Oh, of course,' I said. 'Well, like I said, if you ever need me in a situation like that, just shout. I know you didn't the other night but don't be afraid to ask.'

She nodded, a tight, unreadable smile on her face.

'I'd better get back,' she said. 'I left Ed in charge of a roast chicken. Goodness knows what he'll have done to it.'

'Is it dinner time already? Honestly, I've nothing in,' I said.

'I'll see you during the week,' Amelia smiled, placing her cup by the sink.

I seethed quietly as she let herself out.

So, it was to be like that.

I couldn't figure out why, but the same pattern kept recurring for me. I tried and tried to be friendly and people always let me down.

CHRISSY

No. 5

Matt was slumped in his armchair, fidgeting with the remote control beside him. He was desperate to turn it on. Turn on the telly and turn off reality.

He hadn't opened his mouth in hours. Matt could only talk about his feelings for a set period of time. He was emotionally exhausted now. But his silence unsettled Chrissy. She'd preferred it when he was attacking her. At least then she knew what was on his mind.

Which had been a complete revelation to her.

When Matt had started sobbing in the kitchen, she'd been utterly shocked. So shocked, she hadn't known what to say or do. She was genuinely thrown by the notion that he could be so upset about her cheating on him.

But she realised she'd have to do some talking to get him to open up a bit. Who knew what else was going on with him? She couldn't quite get her head around him not having stormed out yet. Or his knowing all along. Her husband had gone from being a figure of contempt to an absolute conundrum.

'Matt. Will you talk to me? Please?'

Her husband stared at her like her very existence turned his stomach. It shocked her, that he could look at her like that.

'Do you hate me so much, Chrissy? All this time, I have never, not once, so much as even kissed another woman. And you know, I could have. I've been in nightclubs with clients, the sort of night-clubs where women just throw themselves at you if you've a few bob. It never even crossed my mind.'

Chrissy flinched.

Hadn't she, in the recesses of her brain, assumed that Matt was unfaithful? All those nights he worked late. All that time he didn't want to spend with her. And yet he seemed really tight with money – if he was working that hard, how could cash be an issue?

Would it sound better or worse now, if she told him she'd imag-ined he was cheating too?

'You thought I was with other women, didn't you?' Matt said, his voice choked. 'I don't believe this. Is that why you started it with him? Did it occur to you to ask me if I'd cheated before you sought your revenge?'

'It wasn't revenge. I was unhappy, Matt. I was lonely. I needed somebody. That's why I . . . It wasn't about you. It was about me.'

'Chrissy, if you were so unhappy you had to find solace in the arms of another man, that means it's absolutely about me.'

'Okay, fine. It's about you. Everything is about you. I am but a satellite in your universe.'

'Don't be such a drama queen.'

Chrissy bristled. Wasn't she allowed to feel emotional without being called overly dramatic?

'Fine, Matt, what do you want me to say? That maybe if you were ever here, I wouldn't have had time to be with somebody else?'

'There it is. It *is* my fault.'

Chrissy felt bubbles of rage start to pop in her brain.

'Okay, Matt. Let's think. When did I decide I wasn't happy? Perhaps it was when we moved out here, behind that gate, somewhere I would never in a million years fit in.'

'You mean, when I borrowed an absolute fortune so we could have the nicest possible house and my wife and son could be secure?'

'What? You may have seen security in this place, I saw a jail. I didn't drive when we moved here, Matt. That never even crossed your mind. I couldn't walk to a shop. I was stuck. No family, no friends. And then I had Cam and where were you? Where were you? When did we decide that I'd give up my job? Oh, that's right. We never had that conversation. It was just assumed. You said you didn't want your child in full-time childcare but *you* weren't offering to mind him. Fucking Mother Earth across the road there had twins and she still went back to work.'

Chrissy stood up. The headache was a now distant memory. She was furious. Every argument they'd never had, everything she'd ever wanted to say – it was like a great big spot had been squeezed and everything bad was oozing out.

'I mean, I wanted children. But I didn't think it was conditional. I didn't realise I was marrying into the tenth century, that I had to be the stay-at-home little woman, waiting for you to come in at all hours.'

She was in full flow now. Nothing could stop her.

'So yeah, Matt, another man, an adult, an actual grown-up, saw me and he talked to me. Not just grunts and nods and moaning about what bills needed to be paid and who'd said what in the office, but properly talking to me. And he wanted me, and Christ, I didn't even care who he was or what he looked like, I was just so happy to be *seen*.'

Chrissy took a breath. Perhaps the first since she'd started ranting. She wasn't sure.

The room stopped spinning.

She looked at Matt, who was frozen on the spot, a deer caught in headlights.

'Yes,' she said, as she sat back down on the couch. 'I guess you could say you played a part in it, Matt.'

Silence descended.

There was no sound from Cam, hiding in his room upstairs on his tablet, allegedly playing Roblox but probably watching rude videos on YouTube.

The neighbourhood outside was, as always, quiet – not even a lawnmower battling ever-growing grass or a car engine purring as its owner prepared to head out.

There was just in here, and harsh truths reverberating around the room.

Chrissy waited. Would he throw her out? She wouldn't go without Cam. And hell, why should she go at all? She was their child's primary carer. Cam had a right to stay in his own home. His mother had had an affair. It wasn't the worst thing in the world. No matter what Olive Collins tried to have Chrissy believe.

'I always knew it would come to this. I knew. You were always too good for me, Chrissy.'

When Matt spoke, it was soft, unexpected.

'I knew that, from the minute you flounced into my office, looking for a job. You had this front, this hard edge. *I'm a working-class girl, don't make eye contact with me or I'll eat you alive.* It was all bollocks. I'd never met anybody with a kinder heart, a softer smile. A more beautiful face. You were stunning. I was in love with you the moment I saw you. And I worried it would show on my face, that you'd think some pervert was offering you a job, some sleazy casting-couch director who just wanted to get you into bed.'

Matt laughed.

Chrissy held her breath.

'I wanted to give you the world. I wanted to show you I was worthy. I saw this place and thought – I can't afford it, but Chrissy would love it. I'm not an idiot, Chrissy. I know why women like you marry men like me. So I made a down payment and then I had to work fourteen-hour days to meet the mortgage repayments. We paid way over the odds. And then there was a tough patch at work during the recession but I didn't want to tell you because Cam got sick. I took a pay cut and I was so stressed. And . . . And I guess a part of me was happy that you were staying home.

'The truth is, I always knew you'd leave me. That you'd find somebody worthy of you and walk away. I'd conned myself into thinking that if you were at home, you were all for me. And I know that was wrong but I couldn't help it. I know it makes me sound like some outdated, misogynist prick, but please believe me that you're the only woman I've ever loved and I've only ever wanted you to be happy. I would do anything to make you happy.'

Chrissy covered her mouth with her hand. She didn't believe him. She couldn't believe him.

'You actually think I married you for your money?'

'Why else?'

'Oh, Matt. I loved you. How could you think for one second I was that shallow? Don't you remember how we used to laugh?

All the time. I would have lived in one of the flats with you, you fucking idiot.'

Her husband looked at her like he didn't believe her. But he couldn't ignore the earnestness in her voice. Chrissy was telling the truth.

'You thought all that and you didn't want to kill me?' she said.

'Not even once. I love you, Chrissy. I'd come home and sit out there in the car wondering if you were inside with him. I wanted to kill him, to kill myself, but I could never harm a hair on your head. I was angry at you, sure. But, ultimately, I hoped you'd get sick of him and just end it. I was waiting.'

'I had no idea. God, how has it come to this? How did it go so wrong?'

'Hell if I know. It could be worse, I suppose. We could be her next door. So few people in her life that she was left to rot in her own sitting room.'

Chrissy shook her head. 'I suppose you feel sympathy for her. Considering that what I did hurt her too.'

'No,' Matt replied. 'Don't you get it, Chrissy? I don't care what you do to me. You're still my wife and the mother of my child. It's still us versus them. When Olive became your enemy, she became mine too. Nobody threatens my wife and gets away with it. Regardless of what was behind it.'

Chrissy shuddered. She didn't like to think of the woman at all – alive or dead.

She tightened her housecoat at the belt. She was still in her pyjamas, still in yesterday's knickers. She hadn't washed her teeth or brushed her hair. And she really needed a cup of tea and something to eat.

'What are we going to do?' she said.

'What do you want to do?' Matt sounded scared.

Like the decision was hers, when she thought it was his. Wasn't it?

'Do you want a divorce?' he said.

'Do *you* want a divorce?'

'I don't even want a separation, Chrissy. I want – all I've ever wanted – is for us to work. I don't care any more if it makes me sound like a sap, but I want us to fix this. Please, whatever happens, don't leave me for him. I don't think I could bear that.'

'I'm not leaving you for him.' That much Chrissy was positive on. When she thought of Ron now, she kept imagining him with Olive and it turned her stomach.

'Really?'

'Of course, really.'

'Does that mean . . .?'

Matt got up and came over to the couch. He knelt in front of her. She could see the top of his scalp, where he'd lost so much hair it was starting to look like a monk's cap. Every time she'd seen that recently, it had filled her with disgust. Another part of her husband she couldn't stand to look at.

But right now, all that anger seemed pointless.

He was gazing at her with the love she'd stopped seeing. Even though she'd betrayed him, even though she'd hurt him. He was terrified that she would be the one to walk out on their marriage.

'I'm so sorry,' she sobbed.

His face fell.

'Is that it, then?' he asked.

'No. God, no. I mean I'm sorry, Matt, for cheating on you. For doing what I did.'

He shook his head.

'I drove you to it. You're right.'

'No. Please, stop doing that. You're worth more than that. I made my own choices. I don't want a divorce.'

'Do you want us to work on this?'

Chrissy nodded. She nodded so hard the inside of her head shook.

'I can't promise everything will be okay but I'm happy to talk things through. If you are.'

He grabbed her hands and covered his face with them. She was surprised but didn't pull back.

She let him stay like that for a few minutes before it occurred to her.

'Matt?'

'Yes?'

'When you said that when Olive became my enemy, she became yours too – what did you mean?'

RON

No. 7

There was no sound or movement from the bed. It was one of the quieter times, when Dan wasn't jerking or fidgeting, his eyes casting about like he frantically wanted to tell you something but couldn't find his voice.

Ron had always found those times the scariest. As a kid, he used to grab Dan's hands and cry, urgently, *What is it? Just tell me. I can help.* But his parents and the nurses would always explain that while he thought of Dan's mind as being trapped inside a body that wouldn't cooperate, there really wasn't anything going on in his brain at all. It was all muscle reaction and spasm.

Ron didn't believe that. He couldn't believe that. Because sometimes, Dan smiled. He smiled for Ron. And you only smile when you're happy, right?

Ron reached across and stroked his brother's hand, the skin as soft as silk.

'I'm in a bit of trouble, bro,' he said. 'Women. You know how it is. My downfall. But I messed up big this time.'

The room door was open. A female night volunteer was walking past outside, the care home's equivalent of a candy-striper. She looked in at Ron talking to Dan's prone figure and raised her eyebrows, said nothing, walked on.

'Guess you have your own problems with the girls in here, mate. How do you keep it together when you're getting bed baths from the likes of her?' Ron winked. He liked to tell himself this. That Dan had the best of everything. That he didn't feel alone and abandoned.

When Ron's parents had said that Dan had gotten too big, that they weren't young or strong enough for him any more, Ron hadn't been able to get his head around it. He'd seen it as the ultimate self-ish act. Elderly parents cared for their incapacitated children all the time, even into adulthood. Why were his parents different?

A tiny part of him understood. Especially when the doctor sat him down and showed him Dan's brain scans, talked about life expectancy (far longer than anybody could have imagined) and pointed out just how much money and care would be needed for Ron's brother. Twenty-four-seven.

But he'd railed against it, because that made him feel less guilty. Parents were shit. You couldn't rely on them for anything. In the absence of his pair stepping up for his little brother, Ron had resolved to be like a parent to Dan. He'd fight for him. And he only had time for his care. Not his own kids', who he'd never wanted to be burdened with in the first place.

'I don't want to go to jail,' he blurted out. There was a twitch in the bed, Dan's hand moved slightly. Ron reached over and flattened his brother's fringe, wiped a tiny sliver of drool from his lip.

'If I go to jail, when will I see you, mate?'

A tremor behind the eyelids.

Nothing, the doctor would say.

Everything, Ron would reply.

The faux candy-striper was back.

'Visiting hours are over, Mr Ryan.'

Ron didn't look at her, just nodded. His eyes were wet, he didn't want anybody to see.

'Sure. I'll come back tomorrow. You clocking off now, too?'

He felt, rather than saw, her flattered smile. Amazing, considering the absolute routine with which he delivered the line. Sometimes it just sprung out of Ron's mouth. It sounded fake, even to him. And yet the women always responded. Some of them, anyway. Enough.

Ron gave Dan's hand a squeeze.

Live life. That's what being Dan's brother had taught Ron. Live life for both of them. So he turned and this time he winked at the nurse. How Dan would have laughed.

FRANK

Frank wasn't sure what made him do it, but they were in the station car park and Emma was about to jump out to get her own car when the words just came out.

'Do you fancy going for a drink?'

Emma hesitated, half in, half out of the car.

'Where?'

'I don't mind.'

She pursed her lips.

'There's a bar in my apartment complex. I could drop my car home, we could have a quick one there?'

'Perfect,' Frank said.

There was a time when going straight to the pub after work had been a regular occurrence for Frank. He wasn't short on friends. Frank Brazil was well liked amongst his colleagues. A good detective, one of those rare sorts who liked his job and wasn't interested in internal politics.

But you only had to say *No, not tonight* more than a couple of times and people stopped asking. Nobody intentionally isolated him. He'd isolated himself as he came closer to retirement. He'd begun to realise that, take away the job and the obligatory drink when you clocked off and, really, workmates were just that. Mates in work. Not mates in the real world. When he left, they wouldn't see much of each other. He could count on one hand how many of them he would want to see, anyway.

Better to phase them out gradually than live with the shock when you collected your carriage clock and P45 and realised the job you'd sacrificed everything for had left you with nobody in your life.

If Emma found it odd that she was suddenly being asked to go for a drink, for the first time after months of working together, she didn't let on. Frank had been half expecting her to say she had to get home to a boyfriend or she wanted to get some paperwork done that evening. The ones on the promotion fast tracks always had *paperwork*.

Maybe he was lonely. The house was terribly quiet with the neighbours away, no running up and down stairs, doors slamming, Yvonne yelling.

Whatever it was, he just fancied company that night.

She padded off in her comfortable pumps towards her car, carrying the plastic bag containing the shoes with the remains of the dead bird still on the soles.

Frank put his car into reverse.

The bar wasn't much to his liking. Frank wasn't ashamed to admit he preferred what Mona used to call 'old man bars'. Dark, wood-panelled joints, with aged bartenders, a telly showing the horse-racing and nobody asking what you meant when you requested a pint.

Emma's bar was all fancy high stools and large windows, cocktail menus and glass bowls of water with candles floating in them.

The barman advised Frank to try one of their guest draught ales and Emma ordered a snipe of Prosecco. That was what all the young ones were drinking these days, he knew that much. Fizzy sugared muck at nine quid a glass. Five glasses from a bottle the manager was buying for a tenner wholesale.

Frank should have arrested the bar owner for daylight robbery.

He should have got Emma a flute of 7-Up.

If he threw in a packet of crisps, it would really show the age gap, which, apparently, he was no longer allowed to mention.

'Nice place, this,' Frank said, toasting the air with his ridiculously tall glass.

Emma snorted.

'Yes. I'm sure it's just like your local. Last night they had live jazz.'

Frank couldn't hide his distaste.

She laughed again.

'Do you need to ring your chap or whatever?' he said. 'You're not married, am I right?'

She shook her head.

'No hubby, no boyfriend. I had a boyfriend. Up to a few months ago.'

'What happened to him?'

'He was an asshole.'

'Well, what's it they say? Better to have loved an asshole and realise you prefer being single.'

She smiled.

'I heard about your wife.'

'It's a long time ago now.'

'You never thought about marrying again?'

Frank shook his head.

'No. Mona was the love of my life. It would have been unfair on any woman who came after her. She'd have lived in Mona's shadow.'

'Rebecca didn't mind.'

'Who?'

'Daphne du Maurier?'

Frank shook his head again. Who were these women she kept naming?

'The Daphne one sounds familiar.'

Emma laughed. 'Didn't you do the Leaving Certificate exam?'

'It wasn't called that when I went to school. We had stone tablets and an abacus. And Christian Brothers who liked to slap you on the hand with a long ruler just for fun.'

'The good old days, huh? Well, it's nice to know there are some things I'm ahead of you on.'

'I'm sure there's lots of stuff you know that I wouldn't have a clue about. You had that Wolf kid well pegged.'

'He just reminded me of my brother. He'll be fine. Justin is, anyway. But everybody around Justin is aware of the diagnosis and he's honest about it with people too, so they make allowances. When you pretend it's not an issue, that's when it becomes one.'

'Like David Solanke is doing.'

'Exactly.'

'Do you think Lily Solanke has it in her to tape up Olive Collins' house and sabotage her boiler?'

Emma ran her finger around the rim of her glass. It was already running low, Frank noted. That was the problem with that sweet stuff. Too easy to drink. Frank still had a gallon of ale in front of him. He signalled to the barman to replenish the Prosecco.

'Oh, thanks,' Emma said, distracted. 'Is there enough motive there to want to murder somebody so cold-bloodedly?'

'Is there ever enough motive? She's in line for a promotion, Olive was about to pull the rug out from under her. She sounded pretty desperate.'

'Fair enough. I don't know, to answer to your question. I think Lily's angry at herself, not her neighbour, even if that's where it manifested itself. I think she's unhappy.'

'She has a problem with her husband,' Frank said.

Emma shrugged. 'Her problem is how he sees her. It must be exhausting, to keep up perfection. Though I can't quite get my head around him. He's definitely a control freak.'

Frank rested his chin on his hand.

'Emma. Did you take psychology in college or something?'

'Yes. I'm sure I told you that before.'

Had she told him? Frank couldn't remember. Quite possibly. Sometimes she talked and he just filtered her out.

He looked at her. She seemed more relaxed than normal.

In the seconds that followed, it wasn't his own voice that filled his head. It was Mona's, pointing out that the girl was young and maybe she was nervous around Frank. Maybe that accounted for her tidal wave of chatter. And maybe Frank had been unfairly dismissive. Maybe.

'Anyway,' Emma said. 'The other reason I can't imagine Lily Solanke doing it is that she punched Olive in the face – she'd be far more of a hot-headed killer. I can picture Lily snapping and picking up a poker to batter Olive to death. Nice lady has a breakdown.

Not diligently, carefully sabotaging her boiler. And she'd need to have been in the kitchen alone to do it – can you imagine Olive leaving Lily to wander around the house after they'd fought? We know nobody saw Olive leave the Vale. We haven't picked up her car on the CCTV images in the village or Wicklow town. So we can only assume she was in for the day. No – whoever sabotaged that boiler was strategic. They were good at planning. And she let them into the house.'

Frank nodded.

'Like Ed Miller? Now there's a couple who seem to spend their lives planning. One holiday to the next.'

'Hmm. But again, like with Alison, are they lying about going into Olive's house that day or is Ron lying about seeing them?'

'Good point,' Frank said. 'They're all lying about something. That I'm bloody sure of. But are we being too quick to rule out the possibility of somebody we haven't encountered yet having it in for her and being in the house that afternoon?'

Emma shrugged.

'I don't think so. There's no evidence at all the woman had a friend in the world. Her name was in the papers today and the news hit social media early. By now we should have heard from somebody, anybody, even just wanting to jump on the grief bandwagon. And there's so much poison in that place. She'd fallen out with several of her neighbours – the Solankes, the Dalys, Ron Ryan. We don't know yet about the others, whether there's more they're not telling us. That's a lot of people with motive, if it wasn't an accident.'

'It's always the same, isn't it?' Frank said.

'What?'

'Behind closed doors. You never know what's going on. All those seemingly respectable people. Lily the school teacher punching her neighbour in the face. Olive, the retired language therapist having an affair with a toyboy and then pulling the stunt with the pictures. And all that weaselling freebies out of Alison, who, well, God knows what's going on with her and Holly. If we keep scratching . . .'

'Who knows what else we'll turn up,' Emma said.

Frank smiled, grimly.

'One of them might have killed her. The irony is, I'll bet there are plenty of her neighbours who wished the woman dead. And now that we're digging around their business and they're having uncomfortable conversations with each other – I'm sure they're thinking maybe it wasn't too bad before.'

Frank lifted his glass and looked out the window. The boats rocked gently in the harbour, the lights casting soft yellow flickers on the water.

It wasn't his favourite type of bar. But it wasn't bad either.

ED & AMELIA

No. 6

For the first time in a long time, Ed took his blood pressure before going to bed. It was high, much higher than normal. Like it had been in the bad old days, when he'd been under so much stress.

Family will do that to you. Kill you as soon as look at you.

It was ironic how healthy Amelia was compared to Ed. She'd put on more and more weight these last few years, even with their continuous travelling. She'd a healthy appetite, she enjoyed drinking and her natural pear shape and slow metabolism were not a good match for all of that. But Amelia had no blood pressure issues. Every problem they encountered, she dealt with smoothly.

Olive had been an attractive woman, Ed always thought, though a little pinched in the face. That came about because of all her negative opinions, he reckoned. Olive was a lot meaner about people than she ever realised. Judgemental. That was the word Ed would use.

On the other hand, she reminded him of Amelia. Olive, too, could be very efficient at getting her own way. Ed had often wondered what life would be like if he were with Olive and not Amelia.

But that would never have come to pass. He and Amelia had been through too much.

'Is it high again, Ed?'

Amelia came out of the en suite wrapped in her dressing gown, pale blue and getting more difficult to tie at the front.

Ed nodded.

'One forty over ninety,' he said.

Amelia tutted.

'Lie down,' she instructed. 'I'll massage your temples and you're to think of nothing, do you hear? Especially not that stupid, bloody woman.'

Ed lay back in his wife's ample lap and let her rub the sides of his head, trying not to listen as she launched into a tirade about Olive Collins, the stupid, bloody woman.

LILY

No. 2

She'd had to get out of the house.

Lily stood at the front door, breathing in the fresh night air.

When the police left, she'd told David everything. What she'd been eating. What she'd been buying.

And worse. Oh, so much worse.

What she'd been smoking.

She'd buried two parents who'd died from lung cancer. What kind of an idiot was she?

David had just sat there, shaking his head and judging her.

Eventually, she'd shut up. She'd worn herself out. She was a charlatan. All that time she'd been silently resenting him, thinking he was this big fake, and it turned out she was the one with no moral centre. The one with no core.

The absolute irony was that it had taken Olive Collins dying for all this to come out in the open. The bloody woman would have loved it.

Lily wasn't sure what it was that propelled her in the direction of Alison Daly's house.

They were around the same age, Lily and Alison. But they'd never exchanged anything more than polite pleasantries: *Isn't this weather nice? How are your children? How's Holly? You should pop into the shop sometime.*

Lily had decided Alison was a sophisticated businesswoman and they would have nothing in common. Ridiculous, considering what her own husband did for a living.

Again, she'd drawn conclusions from the penthouse of her ivory tower.

Perhaps that was what sent Lily up Alison's driveway and not George's. This masochistic urge to prove to herself that she was, in fact, wrong about everything and everyone.

It was Holly who answered the door, mouth full of food, hair bundled on top of her head, looking as beautiful as ever. Seventeen and already a head-turner. She'd have men falling all over her when she ventured out into the world proper.

'Oh, I'm sorry – did I call during dinner?' Lily asked.

Holly chewed and swallowed slowly.

'No. I'm just having a sandwich. Do you want my mother?'

Lily nodded. Holly was looking at her oddly. Of course she was. Why the hell would Lily be at their door asking for Alison?

'Mam,' Holly yelled. 'It's Lily from next door.'

Alison appeared over her shoulder seconds later.

'Eh – Hi, Lily.'

Holly appeared torn between not caring and desperately needing to know why their neighbour was suddenly at the door.

Alison was so surprised, she just stood there.

Lily shifted from foot to foot. She was lost for words, now she was here.

Holly raised her eyebrows and retreated. This was all too weird for her.

'Where are my manners?' Alison said. 'Come in.'

Lily was so grateful to be invited over the threshold, she had to stop herself from hugging Alison.

She followed the other woman through to the kitchen, where Holly cleaned away a plate while watching some show on her computer.

'Oh, Lily May has been looking to watch that,' Lily said, pointing at the screen.

'Really?' Holly said. 'I think she might be a bit young. This is *13 Reasons Why*. It's about a teenager who kills herself.'

Alison and Lily exchanged a loaded look.

'I didn't realise,' Alison said to her daughter.

'Relax, Mum. The show is a cautionary tale. Not a how-to guide.'

Alison laughed nervously.

'I'm going upstairs. If you see a body falling past the window, it's nothing, okay?' Holly said.

'Ha ha.'

Lily smiled. The interaction between Alison and Holly was so natural. And why wouldn't it be? They were mother and daughter. Shouldn't Lily have the same relationship with Lily May? Her daughter was only eight but Lily had a horrible feeling they would never be that easy with each other.

'Take a seat,' Alison said. 'Or would you be more comfortable in the sitting room?'

'Here's great,' Lily said.

Alison was still watching her closely, like she was a fish out of water. Lily discreetly studied her back. Alison looked different this evening. She was wearing a pair of leggings and a vest with thin straps. She'd no make-up on and her dark hair fell loose onto her shoulders.

Without the suit and the make-up she looked ten years younger. More in her twenties than her thirties. She could easily pass for her daughter's sister.

'I don't know about you, but it's my wine o'clock,' Alison said. 'Um – do you drink?'

The old Lily would have smiled indulgently and said, *I might have a peppermint tea but you go ahead.*

The new Lily said: 'Don't bother with a glass. Just bring me the bottle and a straw.'

'One of those days?' Alison smiled.

'One of those days.'

'I won't bother asking red or white then.'

'You can mix them if you like.'

Alison fetched glasses so big they looked like they could take a bottle each. She took an open white from the fridge and emptied it between them.

'There's plenty more where that came from,' she said.

Lily didn't reply immediately. She was drinking from the glass like somebody had just handed her a pint of water after a marathon.

'Sorry,' she said when she put the glass down. 'I actually think I woke up a few days ago and realised I was an alcoholic. I've been trying to make up for lost time.'

Alison snorted.

She sat down across from Lily.

She really was a tiny thing. She made Lily feel like a giant and Lily was only five foot seven with quite a slim build.

'You're not an alcoholic,' Alison said. 'You're speaking to a woman who has wine on tap in her fridge. It's this week, I think. The police finding Olive like that. It's been a shock for us all.'

'That's putting it mildly,' Lily said. She took another sip.

The two women met each other's eyes over their glasses.

'But she was an awful woman,' Lily said.

Alison's eyes widened.

'Oh, she was, Alison. I know you're too lovely to really see any bad in people, but trust me, there was bad in Olive.'

'She was hard work,' Alison said. She took a gulp of wine. 'I should have realised that from the beginning. You know the family I bought the house from – the Kazemis? The dad, Mahmoud, said to me: *Watch out for the racist one next door. I told her I was a doctor and she keeps telling me about her ailments.*'

Lily laughed.

'I remember him. They kept to themselves. He was a Professor of History, wasn't he? What, so she just assumed he was a doctor because he was Middle Eastern? To be fair, I never picked up a racist vibe from her. And when it comes to degrees of black . . .'

'I know,' Alison laughed. 'He was rather elitist to be honest and it was probably a bit unkind. I mean, he referred to himself as doctor, not professor, but yes – he must have picked up some strange energy from her. You should have heard what Holly called her in front of the police.'

'What did she call her?'

'Rhymes with punt.'

'Wow,' Lily said. 'She has some balls, your girl. Though I did tell the police Olive and I weren't exactly buddies. Oh, by the way, I think her actual friends are back home – the Millers. I saw them pulling in earlier.'

'Do you really think Olive had friends?' Alison asked. 'She struck me as a very lonely woman.'

'You think?'

'Yes,' Alison frowned. 'She was always trying to get to know everybody but it never really seemed to work out for her, did it? I think, in the beginning, she really did want to be my friend but she was sort of desperate with it. She had this weird neediness to her. And she was a bit of a fantasist, you know? Like, she'd tell you how brilliant she was in work, or how popular she was but . . . I was the only one who called over to her. And there was quite an age gap between us, seventeen years. Then, I suppose the Millers are a good bit older than she was, aren't they?'

'Yeah, but they're weird too, that pair,' Lily said. 'There's something creepy about them.'

'Creepy! Do you really think so?'

'Absolutely.'

'Well, I suppose the police will want to speak to them as well.' Alison swirled the wine in her glass. 'I'm pretty sure they went off on holidays around the time they're saying she died.'

'I think you might be right. Anyway, don't talk to me about the police. I feel like my life has gone into a spiral this last couple of days. Somebody on the street dies and suddenly our whole world has been put under the microscope. I may as well tell you – I had a run-in with Olive.'

'A run-in?' Alison echoed.

'Yes,' Lily nodded. 'Her face ran at my fist.'

'You didn't!'

'I know. I'm Lily the heavyweight hippie. I'm not normally violent, believe me. She just brought something out in me.'

Lily didn't know what it was but she felt the need to defend her
actions. Alison was studying her like she was suddenly wary of her.
Would that be how people looked at Lily from now on?

'It was still wrong,' she added, in a quiet voice. 'I shouldn't have
hit her at all.'

Alison shook her head, dismissing it.

'Is that what you told the police?' she asked.

'Yes. I had to. Wolf saw me do it.'

'Oh, no.' Alison's eyes widened. 'What did they say?'

Lily sighed.

'Not much, really. They think I'm crackers. David, though . . .'
She lifted her glass and drank the dregs.

Alison got up and went to the fridge, returning with a fresh bottle.

'You weren't joking about your supply,' Lily said.

'I never joke about something as important as wine.'

She filled Lily's glass, then hesitated, the bottle still in her hand.

'Why haven't we ever done this before? I mean, properly, just the
two of us? Or with Chrissy?'

Lily shook her head, unable to find an answer.

'I don't know. I really could have done with it. I got an email
from a friend before I came over here. You know what she's doing
tomorrow? She's going to an early morning rave. She's thirty-three
and she's getting up at 6 a.m. to go dancing before breakfast. Alison. Prepare yourself. There will be *no* alcohol.'

Alison widened her eyes in mock horror.

'What kind of weirdos do you hang out with?' she said.

Lily shrugged.

'I've known her all my life. Like most of my friends. I've never realised how paralysing that can be. You can't change when people have always known you. If you do something different, they think you're either having a breakdown or you fancy yourself as something special. You're in a box and you're supposed to stay there. And you know what the awful thing is? You made that box for yourself when you were a teenager. You didn't even know it was a box. I'm starting to appreciate why so many people emigrate. New life, fresh start.'

Alison blew out her cheeks.

'Wow. That's . . . deep. When you say "you"?'

'Yes. I mean me.' Lily lifted her glass. 'Hi. My name is Lily Solanke. And I'm a mess.'

Alison raised her glass and clinked it against Lily's.

'Aren't we all?' she said.

They smiled shyly at each other.

'I really want to relax my hair,' Lily said.

Alison snorted wine up her nose.

'What?'

'Relax my hair.' She ran her hands through her Afro, tugging at the tight curls, oiled to give them definition. 'It's a thing you can do with black hair. Like Beyoncé? Some women braid and sew in a weave, other women relax their curls using a lotion. It's like an anti-perm. Horrendous for your scalp. I mean, I like my hair, but sometimes I think I'd like to have it straight. Just to try it.'

Alison frowned, bemused.

'You're very, very beautiful, Lily. You don't need to do anything with your hair. But, why not make a change if you want it?'

'Because David will think I'm ashamed, that I want to look white, that I'm doing it to secure a promotion at work.' Lily threw her hands in the air. 'The thing is, he doesn't understand I've spent my whole life being proud of my colour, even though by the sounds of things, I had it harder than him. He's the one trying to be more white. What is with him being a vegetarian? His brothers nearly fell off their chairs when he told them.'

Alison laughed.

'It did always strike me as odd – just because of the bloody size of him. I can picture him chowing down on a large rack of ribs.'

Lily scoffed.

'He didn't grow that big eating ogbono seeds, I'm telling you. You know what he said today? That he became a veggie because when we went on our first date and he ordered a steak I couldn't look at him. When, the thing is, I was avoiding direct eye contact because I fancied him like crazy. Seriously.'

'Wow.' Alison looked to be considering something. 'You should call into my shop. On Monday. Call in and I'll sort you out with something that isn't floral. We can get you something low-cut. Short-hemmed. Whatever you want. Then you can go all out on your hair. Lily, don't let a man ever make you feel like you should dress or look a certain way. You do what you want to.'

Lily smiled. Maybe.

'I'll get us some snacks,' Alison said, and busied herself filling a bowl with pretzels and crisps.

Lily looked around the kitchen. It was a warm cream. Like a proper country kitchen, but neat and tidy, no mess anywhere. Not like theirs, with the pots of spices and jars of herbal tea, the kids' art stuck on the fridge, dangling wind chimes and multicoloured cushions.

Alison's kitchen still felt lived in, but she didn't need to make as much effort. She wasn't trying to make a statement about her lifestyle through her furnishings.

There were pictures on the wall. All of Alison and Holly, mostly recent. Except for the picture of the baby scan.

'David has a whole album made for the twins with that sort of stuff,' Lily said, pointing at the frame. 'Their scan photos. The bracelets from the hospital. Locks of their baby hair. You know, I used to feel really guilty about how little I cared when they were born but I realised as time went on that I was actually very depressed after giving birth. Like, properly depressed. I'd had such a difficult pregnancy with the pre-eclampsia and then nothing went to plan with the delivery or afterwards. I was overwhelmed. That was the truth of it.'

'And while you were depressed, David was doing arts and crafts?'

Lily blushed.

'I suppose I should be grateful that he did. At least the twins have it now. Did you do a book for Holly?'

Alison looked over at the picture. Her face was wistful, sad.

'No,' she said.

'Oh, well. At least her scan has pride of place.'

'That's not Holly,' Alison said. Her voice sounded funny. Like she'd something stuck in her throat.

Lily didn't know what to say.

'That's Rose.'

Alison lifted her glass and drank. Bright red blotches had broken out on her chest and face.

'I'm sorry,' Lily said. 'I didn't know you had another child. Did she . . . did something happen to her?'

Alison stared at the countertop between them.

'She wasn't mine. She was Holly's.'

Lily's mouth dropped open.

'Holly was pregnant. She was fourteen. It was just some boy. She didn't even know what sex was. Or she did, but she didn't know there were consequences. I guess she was trying to fit in, because she's gay. When she told me she fancied girls, I didn't worry about it for a second, except for, ironically, one thing – I wondered if she'd lose her chance to have a child of her own. And I worried how hard it would be for her. I suppose with everything changing so much, it will be easier than it used to be, but I still think about it. Anyway, I should have been taking better care of her. But I was . . . God love her. She was terrified. I learned my lesson then. I would never let her be that frightened again. Never. No matter what it took.'

The air had become foggy with pain. Lily hardly dared breathe.

'Did she give her up?' she asked.

Alison shook her head.

'We kept it secret for as long as we could. That was her twenty-four-week scan. She wanted to know if it was a boy or a girl. She had the names already picked out. But . . .'

'She lost her,' Lily said. The poor, poor child. To have dealt with that, so young.

Across from her, Alison had started to cry, softly.

'She didn't lose Rose.'

Lily put her hand to her chest. Her heart was thumping. She reached across and took Alison's hand.

'There's so much . . . there's so much I can't talk about,' Alison said. 'I want to. I need to. But it's Holly's decision. I'm sorry, Lily. I don't mean to sound so . . . mysterious.'

Lily shook her head.

'God, no. Please, don't apologise. We hardly know each other, Alison, you don't have to share anything you don't want to. But I'm happy to talk. Whenever you're ready. Christ knows, what you said is right, isn't it? We're all a mess. Sometimes we just need to remind ourselves we're not alone.'

Alison nodded. She wiped her eyes and stared into her wine glass.

'I'll go,' Lily said. 'Call me. Day or night and I'll pop over, okay? Promise me, you'll take me up on that?'

Alison squeezed Lily's hand back.

'I tried to trust somebody before. Olive. It didn't work, but I feel with you it might be different.'

'I'm nothing like Olive, believe me.'

The two women looked at each other.

And smiled, tentatively.

Something good might come out of the pain they were both in.

CHRISSY

No. 5

They found Cam under his duvet watching a horror movie on his tablet.

'Seriously, Cam, man. That's not on.' Matt took the tablet off their son. 'Jesus Christ, what is this? *Purged*. Have you heard of this, Chrissy?'

Chrissy shook her head, as the man on the seven-inch screen brutally stabbed some woman.

They'd been feeling guilty about leaving their son to his own devices for most of the day. Things were worse than they'd thought.

'My God,' she said, looking from the screen to her eleven-year-old. 'Cam, how did you even get this? I put parental controls on Netflix.'

Just for the moment, the conversation downstairs had ceased to matter. Chrissy and Matt were parents. And while they'd been trying to talk through the mess they had made of their marriage, their son was upstairs watching an over-18s movie that would terrify most adults.

Cam looked at them both sheepishly.

'You put controls on my account,' he said. 'Not on yours.'

'Bloody hell. I knew you were mad buying this for him, Matt.'

'I didn't buy it for him,' Matt said.

Chrissy shook her head and turned the tab off. She could barely hear him over the screams and gore.

If Cam was watching this kind of thing, well, that would explain the bird-killing at least. They would be putting a halt to this carry-on immediately.

Chrissy felt better. Better than she'd done in a long time. With each decision it felt like she was regaining some control.

She'd had a shower when she and Matt had called time for the evening. Then she'd had the tea and toast he'd made for her. While she was doing that, he'd emailed work to say he was taking a few days' leave at the start of the week.

The plan was to take it slow. Talk, find a counsellor. They'd go online and start looking at houses. They had to move, they had no choice. But it was good timing – their home was starting to regain its equity. They could sell it and move somewhere in the suburbs of Dublin and actually be quids in, with a lower mortgage on top.

Matt's shoulders had visibly relaxed at the prospect, which made Chrissy feel even worse. She'd had no idea he was under that sort of stress. She had focused on her own problems, she'd had no room to see his. But now, standing back, she could appreciate the strain he must have felt the last few years trying to keep them in the lifestyle they were used to. God, it was ridiculous how little attention they'd paid to each other.

They sat on either side of Cam. He looked absolutely terrified.

'Cam, we want to talk to you about Ms Collins next door,' Matt said. 'What you said to your mum last night about her not being a nice woman – had she said something, or done something to you that we should know about?'

Cam looked from one to the other.

'No. She was very nice to me.'

Chrissy looked at Matt over their son's head.

'Well, why did you say – wait, what do you mean, she was nice to you? What did she do that was nice?'

Cam shrugged.

'She gave me stuff.'

'Like what?'

Cam went silent.

'He probably just means biscuits and things like that,' Matt said. 'That's what you mean, son, isn't it?'

Chrissy knew there was more to it than that. She knew Cam. He was hiding something.

'What did you say, Matt, a few minutes ago?'

'What?'

'When you . . . did you say you didn't buy that tablet? Oi, where do you think you're going?'

Cam had tried to ease himself off the bed. His parents held him firmly by the shoulders.

'I didn't buy it,' Matt said. 'He said you did.'

They both looked at their son. He was staring straight ahead, trying to shrink and make himself invisible at the same time.

'Did Olive give you that?' Chrissy asked, pointing at the offending item she'd placed on top of the chest of drawers.

'Eh . . .'

'Cam! Why didn't you tell me?'

Matt shook his head.

'No, Chrissy. The question is, why did she give it to him?'

For one awful moment, Chrissy considered the worst.

Cam had been acting out so badly over the last few months. Their neighbour – a woman she had hardly known but, any time she had come into contact with her, had struck her as a piece of work – had been giving her son things.

The bad behaviour. The gifts.

Had Olive been inappropriate with Cam? Chrissy thought her heart might stop.

Cam sighed.

'I told her I'd seen her with Mr Ryan and that I knew she'd annoyed Mammy because Mammy likes Mr Ryan too. I wanted her to stop being mean to you. And I wanted a tablet.'

Chrissy clamped her mouth with her hand. Then she covered her eyes.

She couldn't look up. She couldn't look at her son or her husband.

Her child, her baby, had known she'd been having an affair. And that she was being threatened.

That was why he was behaving badly. And she'd been so quick to apportion blame to somebody else.

Chrissy could have died from the shame.

She felt Matt's hand reach around Cam and squeeze her shoulder.

'All of that is true, Cam,' he said. Chrissy didn't know how he did it. His voice sounded normal. Calm. Fatherly. Not as angry as she would have sounded. She'd have been incoherent.

'Your mum was friends with . . . that man, but Ms Collins misunderstood the situation. She was being very unkind to us. It's nice that you wanted to stand up for Mum, but not so nice that you got a tablet out of it. Do you know what that's called?'

Cam's eyes flicked sideways at them.

'Eh . . . blackmail?'

How did he even know the word? Chrissy wailed inside her head. Had he overheard her accusing Olive of it?

Don't you even think about blackmailing me.

That's what Chrissy had said to her when she called over to Olive's that last time. She'd started up the affair with Ron again and there was no way she was taking her chances with Olive.

My house, my garden are off limits. My family is off limits. And if you stick your nose in my business again, I will end you, do you understand? End you.

It had been nasty.

'Yes, it's blackmail,' Matt said. 'And it's not a game. The police can arrest you when you do things like that.'

'Are the police coming?'

Cam's voice was small. Scared.

'No. They're not coming. But you can never do anything like that again, do you understand?'

'Are they coming for you, Dad?'

Chrissy looked up at Matt.

'Why do you ask that?' he said.

'I saw you that day. When you were shouting at Ms Collins.'

Matt's mouth formed a horrified 'o'.

'What?' Chrissy said, her mouth gaping. 'You told me you hadn't spoken to her.'

Matt looked pointedly at Cam, a glance to say, *should we really have this conversation in front of our son?*

Chrissy frowned. They'd gone too far for that.

Matt sighed. 'It was nothing. I don't even want you to think about it, Chrissy. I told her to back off.' He looked down at Cam. 'But it was just a silly argument. I'm sorry you heard it. And I'm sorry you were caught up in the middle of all this ridiculous carry-on with the adults. The police aren't coming and we're not going to talk to them about any of this, okay?'

'Are we going to lie?'

'No. It's not a lie when you just don't say anything. It's not relevant to Ms Collins dying. That was, I don't know, an accident. This other stuff had nothing to do with it.'

Cam nodded, then turned to his mother to get her affirmation.

Chrissy nodded too, though with a little less certainty than her husband.

Why had Matt lied downstairs? When everything else about the exchange had been so truthful?

Cam was still looking up at them expectantly.

'There's something else we want to talk to you about,' she said, thinking it best just to move on. For now.

'I didn't steal them. Wolf said he found them in his mammy's wardrobe and he wanted me to hide them. He said his dad would be angry if he saw them.'

Chrissy and Matt looked at each other, completely at sea.

Cam got up and crossed to his chest of drawers. He opened the bottom drawer, where his winter jumpers were folded neatly, and reached into the back. He took out a packet of cigarettes.

'I haven't touched them,' he said. 'Cigarettes give you lung cancer and make you die. I read it on the packet. I'm just hiding them for Wolf because he said he doesn't want his mammy to die.'

Cam looked more panicked about the packet of Benson & Hedges than the revelation about the tablet.

'Well, well, well,' Matt said, standing up and taking the cigarettes from his son. 'It looks like – what was it you called her, Effing Mother Earth? – has secrets like the rest of us.'

Chrissy could hardly believe it. Fair play, Lily. Illicit cigarettes cast the woman in a whole new wonderful light.

'Is that all you're hiding?' Matt said, turning to Cam. 'There isn't a body in the wardrobe, is there?'

Cam shook his head.

'Thank goodness for that.' Matt was still avoiding eye contact with Chrissy and it made her uncomfortable. Just when had he had this run-in with Olive?

'Right, this other thing,' her husband continued. 'We're thinking about moving. Somewhere there might be more kids for you to play with. But we won't even begin discussing it until we know it's something you're on board with. Would you like that? If we moved house?'

There was no hiding the delight on Cam's face.

'When are we going?' he said.

His parents both smiled, taken aback.

'Soon,' Matt said. 'As soon as we can. Let's get away from this place and start afresh.'

OLIVE

No. 4

It never bothered me too much that I didn't make good friends with Lily or Alison or Chrissy. Well, especially not Chrissy.

I had the Millers, after all.

That's why the loss of Ed and Amelia's friendship hit me so hard.

I didn't think too much more about the stranger who'd caused the ruckus in their house in the days that followed the event. After Amelia's visit to me, I decided to put the man and the Millers to the back of my mind. They weren't worth it. And anyway, I had other fish to fry at the time. I'd noticed Ron Ryan coming out of next door again and Chrissy had called over to warn me to back off. That was to the fore of my thoughts.

But a week after the fight in the Millers', I was in the village picking up a packet of headache tablets in the chemist's. That's when I saw the stranger's car, the one who'd called in to the Millers', parked outside the Horse and Hound bar.

The Horse and Hound also ran a B&B. It occurred to me that if the stranger, like Ed, was from Cork City, then it'd make sense he'd book a room while in the area. But why would he still be here?

I popped over. It was lunchtime and I fancied a nice salad sandwich and a fresh pot of coffee. Why not there?

I found the stranger sitting at the bar nursing a pint and a very large grudge.

He had no interest in speaking to me initially. Not even in the small talk I was making.

Paul Miller was far more discreet than his brother gave him credit for.

But he also had a taste for drink and when I bought him another pint with my G&T after lunch, he became a little more friendly.

When I mentioned I lived in Withered Vale, his interest was piqued.

We talked a little that day – him nervous, me trying not to be too curious.

The two of us got along, that made it a little easier.

We agreed to meet again.

HOLLY & ALISON

No. 3

'Is she gone then? Your new buddy?'

Holly had come back downstairs and discovered her mother still at the breakfast bar, nibbling on pretzels and staring into the distance.

She'd heard the front door close and hadn't been able to resist coming down to find out what Lily had called over for. To the best of her knowledge, only Wolf and Lily May had ever been in the Dalys' house, never their parents.

More to the point, Holly wanted to know what her mother had said to Lily. There was something strange going on with Alison these days.

'Hey,' Alison said. 'Come, sit here beside me.'

Holly took an uneasy seat on the stool.

'How many have you had?' she said, eyeing the wine glass.

'This is only my second!'

Holly shrugged. 'I think it's good for you to have a few glasses and relax, Mam.'

'That's very generous of you.'

'You know what I mean. All I'm concerned about is that you don't relax too much. After Olive.'

'Well, that's what I want to talk to you about.'

'You haven't gone and told Lily everything, have you?' Holly was aghast. Her mother couldn't be so stupid, twice.

'No, Holly. I haven't. But this has to stop. We have to tell people what he did to us.'

Holly shook her head.

'No, Mam. We can't. He could find us.'

'Holly,' Alison's voice was firm. Tougher than Holly was used to. 'Are you sure the reason you don't want us telling people is because you're afraid he'll find us? Are you sure it's not that you don't want to say it out loud? You don't want to talk about Rose?'

Holly shuddered.

Rose. A beautiful name for a beautiful baby.

Her father had never hit her before. She was his princess, that's what he always told her. And while Holly saw the bruises on her mother and heard the shouting and violence, she knew the only thing she could do was continue in her role as a good girl – she must never do anything to upset her dad.

That got harder as she got older. By the time she was ten, she could say out loud that she despised him. Only into her pillow, but that counted. By twelve, she was smoking behind the football pitches. At thirteen, she had her first can of cider.

She wanted to talk to her mother about what her father did, but any time she raised it, Alison would soothe her and hug her and tell her it wasn't Holly's cross to bear. Alison thought she was protecting Holly when all Holly wanted to do was protect her mother.

She was thirteen years and eight months old when she got drunk on four cans of Bulmers and had sex with Kevin Robinson. He was a year older, but neither of them really knew what they were doing. He asked could he try something with her, she was too pissed to say no, then her pants were around her knees and he was pushing up against her. The next morning, she wasn't sure what had actually happened, if anything had happened at all.

She'd only been getting her periods for a year.

Her mother figured it out straight away. She told the hospital and the community liaison officer that they were in an abusive situation at home and they couldn't disclose Holly's pregnancy to her father. A care team was established to help her. Holly point-blank refused to give them Kevin's name. She insisted it had been consensual but she didn't want him dragged into it. If his parents found out, they'd never keep the secret.

When her father eventually found out she was pregnant – what was it he'd said? She was just a slut like her mother. Holly remembered the words spat from his mouth, dripping with scorn and disgust. She'd been wearing baggy jumpers and dresses and she had such a tiny bump. He hadn't even noticed. But that day she'd done something, turned or leaned back or shifted, and he saw. He saw that she was pregnant.

And he ended it. He ended it with his boots.

Twenty-seven weeks. So close.

Holly had had to deliver her baby. Stillborn. The nurses had let her and Alison hold the tiny little girl for what seemed like seconds but had actually been hours. Then Holly, only a child herself, had had to hand over her baby to be buried in a box, never having taken one breath of air, never to be held again.

The hatred that Holly had felt for her father in those moments had been pure and unadulterated. She could have killed him. She could have done what he'd done to her mother, and to herself and Rose, over and over and over, until he was a bleeding mess on the ground.

But she could do none of that because they had to run.

Maybe her mother was right. Maybe it was time to stop hiding and start telling.

Because Holly knew the rage inside her wasn't healthy. It had made her head go funny. It made her do things.

OLIVE

No. 4

I'll always regret things falling apart with the Dalys in number three. I'd cared for Alison and I thought I could take Holly under my wing.

I told Alison all about my life. And then she told me a little about hers.

She confided in me one evening over a bottle of wine. She seemed so desperate to talk.

Alison said she had run away from her husband.

She'd said the marriage hadn't worked out and then she told me what he did for a living. She said the only way she could get away from him was to run. Then she said he'd never stopped looking for them.

It had barely left her mouth before she started to backtrack. Like she instantly regretted spilling her secrets.

I felt sorry for the man. To come home one morning and discover that your wife had fled with your daughter, just because your marriage had troubles?

I mean, who wouldn't have found that disturbing?

My shock must have shown on my face and that's why she clamped her jaws shut and wouldn't talk any more.

I kept trying to reach out to her but she pulled back. I'd thought we were starting a friendship but Alison was obviously one of those people who had loose lips with a few drinks but then was too ashamed to make eye contact in the morning.

I got more and more annoyed at her. That's why I kept calling into the shop. Just to make a point. She might have been odd, but I'd done absolutely nothing wrong. I wondered what else she was hiding. I realised then that neither Alison nor Holly were on Facebook or Twitter or Instagram, something that should have alerted me to the weirdness of the household straight away. I mean, whatever about Alison, but what teenager isn't active on social media?

The fact she kept giving me things compounded my suspicions that she was quite manipulative. She was trying to buy me. That made me feel even sorrier for her ex-husband.

But I'd misjudged the Dalys.

And I had seriously misjudged the Millers.

I met with Ed's brother Paul again a few days after our first encounter. I'd gone into the village to use one of the computers in the back of the library and he'd texted and said he was back in town. He was travelling up and down, trying to get his brother to talk to him. It wasn't going well. I think that's why he opened up to me. We met back in the bar.

Paul reminded me of Ron. The same deep tan, nice eyes. Bloody hell, I was seeing Ron everywhere.

'I'll bet Ed has told you nothing about himself,' Paul said, eyeing me curiously.

'A coffee, please,' I said to the barman.

'I don't know Ed very well,' I lied. 'He's just my neighbour.'

'Nobody knows Ed well,' Paul said.

And then he started to tell me how Ed had come into so much money. It was an absorbing tale.

'There are seven of us,' Paul said. 'Most of us are doing okay now. The girls are sorted. Mary married some financial trader and moved to Dublin and Jean is working in New York. A couple of my brothers got jobs in Cork City, afterwards. When we realised that Ed had really done it, that he'd really sold up and cleared off – we all had to find other jobs.'

I swirled my coffee with the wooden stirrer.

'Were you all in business together?'

'Something like that. We worked on our father's farm. It had been the family's livelihood for decades. Then Dad got sick. We should have realised straight away. Ed and Amelia nearly killed themselves with the speed they left Dublin in order to move in with him. We'd barely seen Ed since he moved up there; Mary said she could never get hold of him. And suddenly he was hotfooting it back to Cork. His wife had been a nurse, you see, up in the capital, so in a way, it made sense that they would take care of Dad. I suppose one of the girls should have done it but Mary's chap worked all hours and she had kids, and Jean had gone to the States by that stage.'

I thought I was starting to get a handle on what had happened in the Miller family. It wasn't exactly a new story. One son moves in, suddenly the will is changed. As old as greed itself.

'Let me guess,' I said. 'Your dad died and left everything to Ed.'

'Two hundred and fifty acres of prime farmland. You know, none of us would have wanted to see the farm broken up. We'd have been happy to all be shareholders and run it together. But Ed got it all. He sold it to a developer. Got millions. The whole place is houses now. All that beautiful land gone.'

I shook my head.

'That is awful. You must be really angry with Ed.'

'Oh, that's not the half of it, Olive. You've no idea what my brother and his evil cow of a wife are capable of. Another coffee?'

I nodded.

Absolutely. I'd nowhere else to be and nobody to see.

RON

No. 7

Ron was very nervous.

The statement the cops had taken that afternoon had been more or less exactly what he'd told the detectives when they called around that morning. But when he got back from Dan's and the night hours ticked away, he could not shake the feeling that everything was going to come out.

He'd destroyed the photos. Got rid of her knickers.

The police knew he and Olive had had sex. They knew he'd argued with her.

They didn't know the rest of it.

What had possessed him?

Truth be told – he *had* been possessed. That was the problem.

He'd known for a week by that stage that Olive had been behind the photographs. He'd dodged her all that time, unable to trust himself. If he saw her face, he wouldn't be able to resist smacking it.

Who did she think she was?

Crystal had phoned him first. He'd picked up the voicemail.

'Ron, it's me, Crystal. The mother of your child. I just wanted you to know, I got your photos. I'm thrilled everything has turned around for you. So, Becky has to get braces. The dentist says it will cost four grand. Seeing as you've contributed sweet FA to her upbringing, I figured you could cover this. I'll look forward to hearing from you.'

He'd laughed nervously when he listened to the message. What was the mad woman on about?

Then Abbie turned up at his work. The girl from reception rang in the middle of an important sales meeting and suggested he get his arse down to the lobby before the shit hit the fan.

When Ron arrived downstairs, Abbie was standing in the middle of the large marble reception area with the kid in his buggy and a big suitcase.

'Take him,' she said, pushing the buggy at Ron.

Everybody was looking at them.

'What?'

'I said take him. He's your son. You can care for him now. You were quick to jump in to offer to mind your brother – well, there's your child.'

'Abbie, what are you playing at? What are you doing here?'

'The pictures, Ron.' She shoved them into Ron's hands and he flicked through them. They looked like they'd been plucked from celebrity party pages at the back of a glossy magazine, Ron being the celebrity.

'You're living the life of Riley and I'm at home in my folks' spare room. You said you were broke. You said you hadn't a penny to your name, that you were spending everything on the care home. Well, I've spoken to a solicitor. I want every cent of back money you owe me. And I am going to hound you until I get it.'

She started walking towards the door, leaving the kid and the suitcase behind. He looked at Ron with big eyes, not a clue what was going on.

Ron had run after her while the girl at reception hollered about not leaving the buggy behind.

'Abbie, you can't leave him here. I'm in work. Look, we'll talk about this. But the kid needs his mother.'

On cue, the child started to wail. She hesitated at the revolving door. Luckily for Ron, Abbie couldn't actually abandon her own baby.

Unlike him.

It was all going to cost Ron a packet.

Okay, it was true. He didn't spend *all* his income on Dan's care. He contributed about half, but it had cost him a bundle to get the house renovated. What a waste that had been.

Was it wrong he wanted to treat himself now, spend money on nice things, on living a little?

Ron spent days and nights trying to figure out who hated him enough to do what they'd done. Eventually, he had to call around to the girls to see the photographs again.

Crystal's pictures gave it away.

There were images of him inside his home. And only one person had been in there with him often enough to have taken photos. In one of them, he could even see her coat hanging over a chair.

He didn't know why she'd done it. But he knew he was going to get her back for it.

Ron stewed over his revenge for weeks.

Then it had come to him one night.

A revenge so sweet, he laughed out loud when it landed in his head.

Two could play at that game.

He'd teach her.

OLIVE

No. 4

The first time I saw Ed and Amelia after that night with Paul, I couldn't even look at them.

We'd ended up in bed together, Ed's brother and I. He was a good-looking man but the real reason – on my part anyway – lay in a combination of the multiple G&Ts that followed the coffee and the hurt I was still feeling over Ron. That's what prompted me to go back to Paul's two-star hotel room, with the dated striped curtains, foot-worn carpet and smoke-stained ceiling. The bed springs creaked and the sheets felt scratchy on my skin and the whole time I wanted to cry for everything I'd had with my younger lover. I'd have given anything to have him hold me again, to wipe clean from my head the images I'd conjured of him with Chrissy Hennessy.

Paul, the gentleman, made me tea from a kettle that took eons to boil, then sat in the bed with me while I gently probed him further on what he'd started to tell me in the bar.

'Dad had cancer, sure. He was dying. None of us denied that. But he had months, maybe a year left in him. Ed probably had plenty of time to get him to change the will but even then, he was at it

304

post-haste. His own father. He raced to his sickbed and set about isolating him from his family, until he left everything to Ed and then — you know what he did then? — he murdered him.'

'What?'

I suppose I'd been expecting it, given the way our conversation had been going. But the way Paul had been telling it in the bar, I thought Ed and Amelia had been negligent. That they'd let the old man die. Not that they'd ended his life.

It was all I could do not to faint with the shock.

Ed and Amelia, my friends.

Ed and Amelia, murderers.

'Yeah. They killed him. There was an investigation and every-thing. The detective they put in charge — he told me, he said, *I know what that pair did*. But they couldn't prove it. None of us could. That's who you have living next door, Olive. Two killers.'

His story put my problems with Ron right out of my head.

All I could think was, somebody should punish that pair.

RON

No. 7

Olive had initially been off with him when he called over that evening of the 2nd March. She kept making snide remarks about him disappearing and ignoring her.

He spun her some crap about being busy at work and very stressed. He even dropped in a line about having some personal issues with an ex, to see if she'd bite.

The wicked cow didn't even blink.

Ron ate the takeaway he'd brought over, every mouthful tasting like dry chalk, and drank wine that ran down his throat like acid, all the while smiling and laughing and trying to warm her up. He put aside everything he felt and worked on her like he'd never worked on a woman before.

It was an effort. Now he knew what Olive was really like, he could see all the unattractive things in her that he'd either never noticed or hadn't minded. He could see her age. The lines that puckered her mouth. The loose skin sagging at her neck. The nasty little glint in her dull eyes.

She started to relax, eventually. By the time they were a

bottle in, she was laughing with him. Two bottles and they were kissing.

He struggled to get turned on, laughed and blamed it on the alcohol.

Overall, though, it was the best performance he'd ever given.

When he started to undress her, she wanted to lie on her back.

He shook his head and tutted.

'No, from behind,' he said. 'You're so sexy from behind.'

As soon as it was over, he reached for his phone and started snapping away.

She turned her head. The smile died on her face when she saw what he was doing.

'I'm just taking a few for the family album,' he said.

She yelped, twisted around and pushed him away, horrified.

'Stop it, Ron,' she said. She was still unsure what was happening, still unclear whether he was joking.

But there was a little bit of her that already knew. The guilty bit of her.

'Now, Olive, they're just for the record; I don't actually know if you have any exes that I can send these photos to,' he said as he stood up. He slipped the phone in one pocket, her pants in the other and zipped up his fly. 'You seem to be fairly bereft of friends and lovers. But that doesn't really matter. Because if you ever take a picture of me and send it to one of my exes again, I will plaster this lot all over the internet and auction your knickers alongside them. Sure, I might get arrested. Sure, I might even go to jail. But to see your face when I expose what you are – I'll take that chance.'

Her first instinct was to fly at him. She started clawing at his trousers, trying to get the phone out. Olive was feisty, he'd give her that.

But she didn't have his strength.

When she realised she was beaten, she'd started to cry and there was no denying Ron had felt bad. He wasn't a monster. He had absolutely no intention of sharing those photographs with any-body, ever. It would be more trouble than it was worth. But she couldn't know that.

He had to punish her. Protect himself.

It was important, that night, that she knew what he was capable of.

Had she lived, he would have eventually told her it was quits between them. Maybe she would have told him why she'd done what she had. Perhaps they even would have made up, but he doubted it.

It didn't matter, anyway. She didn't live.

He'd warned her to leave him in peace.

But Olive always knew how to take things to the next level.

EMMA

It was a new morning. A new dawn.

The previous night had been brilliant.

The fact Frank had asked her to go for a drink in the first place had thrown the rule book out the window (the book he'd never shown her but had clearly written).

And then his face when she'd suggested the über-hip Harbour Bar in her complex. Jason behind the bar had recommended a Rebel Red for Frank and Emma knew it was the first time Frank had encountered the ale in his life. She'd thought he might balk at the first glass and order a Guinness.

But no. From the off, he'd proved her wrong.

She'd had to phone a taxi at 1 a.m. to take Frank home. They'd been drinking for six hours straight. Well, Frank had. Emma had moved on to water at eleven, conscious she wanted to call into the office the next day, even if it was Sunday. She'd advised Frank to do the same but he'd insisted on buying shots.

Shots!

Jason had helped her deposit him in the cab, Frank riffing and singing Fleetwood Mac's 'The Chain' the whole way out of the bar. They could still hear him caterwauling through the car's open window when the driver turned out of the car park.

Emma was now en route to pick up her boss. It was early, but her head was clear and she felt relaxed and happy. She'd stuck *Rumours* in the CD player to wind him up and 'Dreams' blasted out of the speakers as she drove, so loud it drowned out the air conditioning.

The call had come from Alison Daly at 9 a.m. She'd been full of apologies for ringing on a Sunday. Emma had explained that detectives were never off during an active case (though she had been planning on putting in a short day and she guessed Frank hadn't been planning on anything).

Emma would pick up Frank and then they'd pay a quick visit to the Dalys.

Frank's home was in one of those sprawling, gentrified council estates built in the sixties. The roads were filled with three-bed terraced houses with space for one car in the drive and a large green in the middle for all the neighbourhood children to play on.

These estates hadn't been designed for the modern age of commuting and the weekend bore testament to that, cars parked up left, right and centre. No household had just one vehicle any more.

Except Frank, who currently had no car. It was still parked outside Emma's apartment.

He got in, cast her a wary glance and fidgeted with the passenger seat until it shot back and he had leg room.

'What time did you get up?' he asked, as she inched carefully down the narrow road that led out of his estate, avoiding the cars on all sides.

'Just before Alison rang.'

'You look very fresh for somebody who was out on the booze last night.'

Emma checked her lipstick in the rear-view mirror. She rubbed her chin.

'I just had a shower and a shave, Frank,' she joked. 'You could have tried it.'

'It was all I could do to lift my head off the pillow. What were we drinking last night?'

'Sambuca.'

'What?'

'It's a liquorice liqueur. It was your idea. You had two. And then you had my two.'

'Christ. Can you turn that down a bit? My head is still banging.'

'I thought you loved Fleetwood Mac.'

Frank stared out the window.

'I don't remember telling you that.'

'You told me plenty last night. But I worked out your love of Fleetwood from the fact you wouldn't stop singing their songs.'

He chuckled, half embarrassed.

'"Landslide".'

'Sorry?'

'That was the song myself and Mona danced to at our wedding. Stevie Nicks.'

'Oh.'

Emma smiled, sadly. He'd talked a lot about Mona last night, but hadn't mentioned that. It was obvious Frank was still madly in love with his wife.

But he had talked a little about Amira Lund in forensics, too.

Emma didn't know the Pakistani woman that well, but she seemed very nice.

Maybe Frank would move on. You never knew.

'What do you think she wants us for?' Emma asked. 'Alison?'

'A confession, hopefully. She killed Olive Collins. Case closed. The mild-mannered businesswoman. They're the ones you have to watch.'

Emma said nothing.

She drove slowly out to Withered Vale, resisting the urge to put her foot down and scare the life out of Frank, like he did to her regularly. She didn't want to risk him throwing up on her upholstery.

The Vale was quiet in the Sunday morning sun. Alison Daly had coffee on for the detectives and had put out a plate of fresh pastries. Holly was there too, in a head-to-toe pink onesie. She looked different, Emma thought. More subdued.

'Thanks so much for coming out, Detectives,' Alison said. She kept wringing her hands. 'You're so good. Let me pour you some coffee. Will you have a Danish? A pain au chocolat?'

Emma said yes to a coffee. Frank hesitated then said he'd take one, too, strong and black.

'You didn't have to do this,' Emma said. 'Lay all this out. We're not doing any favours. This is our job.'

'But it's very kind of you,' Frank said. 'That's what my colleague means to say.'

'Of course,' Emma said. 'That's what I meant.' Why did he keep correcting her like that? She was going to have to have a word with him.

Alison looked at each of them, then poured the coffee.

'Eh . . . yes. Of course. It's just, well, I've something to tell you.'

'Go ahead,' Emma said.

'I haven't been entirely honest with you.'

'Okay.'

'About Olive Collins.'

Emma nodded. They'd guessed that already.

'Are you going to sit with us, Holly?' Frank asked.

Holly looked belligerent. Her mother cast her a beseeching look.

'Fine,' she said, and pulled out the fourth chair at the kitchen island.

'So,' Emma said. 'What happened with Olive?'

Alison took a deep breath.

'Look, I'm not sure you could classify it as blackmail. And I genuinely don't think Olive had a clue how others saw her. She was quick to jump to conclusions about everybody else but was very lacking in self-awareness. But – well – Olive *was* pushing it at the shop. She kept calling in. After the first time, she'd pick up the smallest or cheapest item and then start talking about how this dress or that top would go lovely with it but she couldn't afford it. She was absolutely brazen. She never said anything overt. It was never a quid pro quo. But I definitely felt I had to keep giving her stuff or she'd . . . she'd tell people our secret.'

'Which is?' Frank asked.

Alison looked like she was in pain.

'I don't go to school,' Holly interrupted. 'I mean – I do study here at home, but I'm not in school.'

'Okay.' Frank turned to Emma, who shrugged slightly.

'You're seventeen, Holly,' she said. 'You're not breaking the law.'

'I can't go to school. Last time I went to school, he tracked us

313

down. We moved all the way over here, all the way from Galway and he still found us. My name is not Holly. And her name is not Alison. We're not even Dalys.'

Frank and Emma were listening properly now.

'You're on the run?' Frank asked.

Alison nodded.

'Your husband?' Emma said.

'Yes. He . . . he was very violent. He had been, for years. I took it. I always thought Holly was sheltered from it but . . .'

'I went a bit wild,' Holly said. 'Drinking. Smoking. I knew what he was doing to her and it messed me up. I started hanging around with lads. I got . . .' She took a deep breath. Then another gulp that turned into a sob.

Alison put her arm around her shoulders and squeezed.

'She was expecting. He didn't find out until she was nearly seven months. I was saving as much as I could and it was hard because he took everything. I'd won a scholarship to the London College of Design just before I met him. I was designing clothes for a top fashion outfit. I earned plenty. But it took me months of squirrelling away money to plan our escape. I've no close family, you see. Nobody who would believe me. Nobody who'd help. You wouldn't believe the sort of stuff I had to do. Buying cheap bread and putting it into Hovis wrapping paper; getting toilet rolls from Poundworld, putting them all out and burning the plastic.'

'We've seen it all before,' Frank said, gently.

'Yes. I guess you have. Well, none of it mattered. He found out she was pregnant before we could leave. He didn't say anything at first. He waited. That night, he brought me home flowers and a bottle of wine and said we were going to celebrate. I said,

"Celebrate what?" And he just sat there, totally calm and said, "Becoming grandparents." He called Holly downstairs and then I realised. I . . .'

'Take your time,' Emma said. She felt light-headed. Sick to her stomach.

'I screamed at Holly to get out. But he hit me on the head with the wine bottle. I was lying on the floor and I couldn't get up and she wouldn't leave. It was my fault – that's what he said. I hadn't taken care of her.'

Alison looked at her daughter.

'You wouldn't leave,' she said. Emma watched as she touched Holly's cheek tenderly. Holly's eyes were dry now but Emma had never seen anybody look so heartbroken.

Alison turned back to them.

'Holly yelled at him to get away from me. She cursed and yelled and lashed out at him. It was the first time she'd actually seen him hit me. He punched her in the face. Then, when she fell, he kicked her in the stomach.'

Emma closed her eyes. The room was starting to spin. She was holding onto the countertop so tightly, her knuckles had turned white.

It was too vivid. Too . . . familiar.

But she knew it wasn't happening to her. This was somebody else's story. She had to pull herself together.

Frank was speaking.

'. . . horrific. I understand why you ran. Sometimes that's the only way. I know I shouldn't say that, I should be able to tell you the justice system will deal with him but the sad truth is—'

'Yes, but that's the problem, isn't it?' Holly cut him off. Emma opened her eyes.

On Holly's face, she saw anger so raw, it looked like the girl could kill.

'He nearly beat my mother to death. He killed my baby. And it wasn't that you fuckers couldn't do something. You *wouldn't* do something. Fine, he lost his job. But he was still one of you shower, wasn't he? Still in the fold. Still protected. He never went to jail. A suspended sentence. That's all he got. Because, whatever happens, you can't go sending a cop to prison now, can you?'

'Holly,' Alison said, her face white.

'He was a policeman?' Frank said.

'He was a fucking policeman,' Holly spat. 'We have to live in hiding. Mam should be running international clothes stores but she can only have a couple of small ones in case he makes the link. I can't go to school. And he's walking around, not a care in the world. You're all bastards. The whole lot of you.'

She jumped off her stool and stormed from the room.

'I'm sorry,' Alison said. 'Please, just give me five minutes. She didn't want me to tell you, for that reason. Just . . .'

'Of course,' Frank said.

When they heard her footsteps follow her daughter's angry stomping up the stairs, he turned to Emma.

'Are you okay?' he asked. 'You've gone very pale.'

Emma nodded. She felt terrible. Her skin was clammy and she was having palpitations.

'It's rough, isn't it?' Frank said. 'Hard to believe. I mean, I've seen enough domestic violence victims in my time to believe the pair of them, but one of our own? Animal.'

Emma nodded mutely.

The scar that ran along her cheek itched horrendously. It was all she could do not to tear at it. It always did that when she thought about him.

She'd been so lucky. So, so lucky.

Alison came back after a couple of minutes.

'I'm sorry,' she said again. 'She won't come back down. It was very traumatic for her, that whole period. We left afterwards, but then I got ill. I had a breakdown. She had to cope with an awful lot.'

'I understand,' Emma said. 'You need to wrap that girl in cotton wool now. Really, Alison. It's important you do that.'

Alison looked at Emma curiously, then nodded.

'I know.'

'So you told Olive Collins all this and she was using it against you?' Frank asked.

'No. That was the problem. I didn't tell her everything. I think that was my mistake. I started to tell her but she seemed a bit – how can I put this – *over-eager* to know my business. I'm naturally cautious, for obvious reasons. I pulled back when I saw that. I think that put her nose out of joint.'

'Still,' Frank said, shaking his head.

'I know. I spoke to Lily last night. That was what encouraged me to tell you. It seems like Olive was clashing with a few of us, but I don't think any of us were particularly good neighbours to her either. I didn't kill her. But there's more I should have told you.'

Alison took a deep breath.

'Holly went over and gave Olive a piece of her mind. And Olive said if she did it again, she'd call the police. It was a nasty thing to say and Olive realised it herself. She came into the shop some time afterwards and told me what had happened. We had . . . words.'

'I see,' Frank said. 'There's nothing else?'

Alison shook her head.

'Are you ready, if he ever turns up?' Emma asked.

Alison blinked. She stared at Emma, something unspoken passing between them. Then she lowered her eyes.

'We've alarms inside and out. He'd have to get in the gate, obviously, but assuming he did that, we keep everything locked day and night. We've both been to self-defence lessons.'

'You probably know all this already,' Emma said. 'Don't have anything he can use against you. No knives or guns. Have something you can reach for easily. Pepper spray, that kind of thing. That's what I'd advise, if I wasn't a policewoman, I mean. Do you want to tell me his name and I'll find out what he's doing?'

'I . . .' Alison seemed lost for words.

'Just think about it,' Emma said. 'Don't be afraid to ask for help. Remember, isolating yourself leaves you more vulnerable.'

Alison nodded.

They finished their coffee and made their way out, promising to be in touch.

Once in the garden, Frank turned to Emma.

'You're very knowledgable on that stuff,' he said.

'Shouldn't I be?' Emma said. 'I'm a female detective, Frank. One in every two women murdered in Ireland is killed by their partner.'

'I know the numbers. You just seem . . . I don't know.'

Emma said nothing.

'That stuff about the pepper spray,' he continued. 'The completely illegal pepper spray.'

She shook her head.

'It's a long story. Not now, okay?'

Frank nodded.

'Sure.'

She started to walk down the path.

'Emma,' he said.

She sighed.

'Yeah?'

'I just want to say that, now you know my Fleetwood Mac secret, I'm here if you ever feel like confiding.'

She smiled.

'I'll bear that in mind. Hang on, Frank. Holly?'

Holly had opened the door and was running down the path behind them.

She waited until she was beside them before she spoke.

'Mam didn't kill Olive,' she said.

'Okay,' Frank said.

'I didn't kill her either. I know Mam said I'd gone over there but it was worse than that. I threatened Olive. I told her I'd kill her if she didn't leave Mam alone. But I wasn't serious. I just said it. It wasn't something I'd actually do. I couldn't.'

The girl was getting frantic.

Emma took her by the shoulders.

'Holly, it's okay. Calm down. Nobody is accusing you of anything.'

Holly nodded.

'I know you think somebody killed her. I just wanted to say, I think you should speak to George Richmond again.'

Frank looked over at Emma.

'Why's that, Holly?' he said.

'He had a big falling-out with her. I heard him, yelling at her. Mam thinks I'm being daft but George sounded like he actually wanted to murder Olive. And it was around the time you're talking about. I don't think it was that exact day, but it was sometime around then. Late February, early March.'

'What was he arguing with her about?' Frank asked.

Holly shook her head.

'I don't know. But there's something not right with him. He's . . . I've seen him looking at me. I don't like the way he looks at me.'

'Holly,' Emma said. 'This is important. Where did this fight happen? Where was George when he was yelling at Olive?'

Holly shrugged.

'I'm not sure. It might have been on her porch or in her garden. I didn't look out, but I could hear them.'

'Okay,' Emma said. 'Look, we'll speak to him. You go back in to your mam.'

Holly nodded.

Emma turned to Frank when she'd left.

'Can your hangover take another interview or do you need a cure?'

'I'm grand,' Frank said. 'But just let me make a phone call first.'

GEORGE

No. 1

When his home phone rang, George had been filled with relief, not irritation. It was like God had sent another intervention, a human being who wanted to talk to George to remind him that he was still connected to the universe. That he was still a person.

Adam had promised to book him in for a counselling session during the week but maybe, even though it was Sunday, he was ringing to tell George he had an opening. George would go now. He'd go at any time. He'd go anywhere Adam wanted to meet. If he could just start talking and get back the magic power that Adam had bestowed on him. The ability to be normal.

But it wasn't Adam ringing. It was Ron. And he was ringing with bad news.

'She was definitely murdered, mate,' he told George. 'I'm just giving you a heads up. Like I said, they're already eyeing me for it. You know what these fuckers are like. You weren't – you didn't have any run-ins with Olive, did you?'

George had been appalled.

'No,' George lied. 'I got on great with Olive. What are they saying happened to her?'

'They're not. But they had me make a formal statement and said I was the last person to see her alive, all that crack. They don't do that when it's accidental. I'm speaking to a solicitor.'

When George got off the phone, he got his laptop out.

And went straight back to masturbating.

ED & AMELIA

No. 6

Amelia was sitting at the window upstairs, looking out across the road.

Ed placed the tea on the sill beside her.

'They're back,' she said, nodding at the two detectives, who'd just emerged from the Dalys' garden.

Ed sighed. So they were.

'It doesn't mean anything,' he said. 'We went away the day she died. So what? That's just coincidence. If they thought we were responsible in some way, they wouldn't be out there sunning themselves and chatting to the neighbours.'

Amelia glared at him.

'You don't think that, Ed. No more than I do. You know what it was like last time.'

She was right, of course. Last time, the detectives had spoken to everybody in the family before finally pulling Ed and Amelia in for questioning.

It was disgraceful, what his siblings had alleged. But Ed and Amelia had told the *truth*.

Ed's father had grown weaker over the weekend. They'd called the doctor on Saturday evening. He'd arrived and spent some time with Edward Senior. When he was leaving, he insisted that Ed's father be put on strict bed rest and if he couldn't eat, they were to put him on the drip. The doctor had given Amelia a supply of morphine for any pain. The doctor said all this in front of Edward Senior.

Ed had noticed his father seemed very depressed after the doctor left, despite all the reassurances from the medic that he would return on Monday and expected that Edward would be much recovered by then. The hospital had given Edward months, if not a year. There was no imminent danger of him dying.

But Ed's father had begun to make comments about being a burden and not wanting to live the rest of his life confined to his bed.

They'd pooh-poohed that nonsense away and made Edward comfortable. Because they were concerned, Ed and Amelia had agreed to take turns sitting with him that night.

Yes, Ed's brother Paul had rung saying he wanted to visit. But by that stage, their father had finally slipped into much-needed, peaceful sleep and Ed suggested Paul call in on Monday, when he would hopefully be up and about again. Paul had argued with Ed. Their father had tried to contact Paul during the week and he wanted to see him.

Eventually, Paul accepted it would be wrong to wake their father and agreed to visit on Monday when the doctor was there.

Amelia told the police that at some point during her shift on the Saturday night, she had fallen asleep. When she woke, startled to realise she'd drifted off, she saw Edward was still sleeping. She noted that he'd turned onto his side and was facing away from her. She picked up her book and read in the lamplight.

It wasn't for another hour, just before dawn was breaking, that she decided to wake Edward for some breakfast and to check his vitals.

Ed was awoken in the bedroom next door by a scream. He jumped out of bed and ran in to find his wife kneeling on the floor beside his father. Edward Senior had a syringe in his arm, the full vial of morphine attached. As Ed and Amelia told the police, he'd clearly taken the opportunity of Amelia sleeping to grab the medicine the doctor had left and inject himself.

Edward had been diabetic all his life. Nobody doubted his ability to use the syringe.

More importantly, he'd left a note in handwriting verified as his. It was on the dresser on the other side of his bed.

It said: *To my children, I'm sorry for what I've done. I had no choice. Please forgive me.*

Ed had summoned the emergency services immediately and Amelia tried to apply CPR. It was too late.

At the inquest, the doctor who'd attended Edward Senior said he had found his patient to be very 'down in the dumps' that Saturday. It was his opinion that Mr Miller had become very depressed over the previous few months. Edward had expressed distress about being stuck indoors all the time and losing his independence.

The whole affair would have been considered a terrible tragedy, and was, right up until Edward's will was read. He'd changed it two weeks before he died. His new will included a note to say that, as Ed and Amelia were now his sole carers, it was only right and proper that he leave them the house and farm. He feared if he left it to all his children they would squabble over the management of it. He trusted Ed to run the farm successfully and they could all keep their jobs.

Ed's siblings had reacted with horror.

Two of his brothers decided to go to the police. The detective in charge of the initial inquiry into the suicide already had his suspicions. He spoke to all the family members outside of Ed and Amelia; all of them took turns to stick the knife in. They claimed that once Ed and Amelia had moved back to Cork the pair had steadily isolated their father. Edward had become more withdrawn and unwilling to see his family. He also seemed to have deteriorated faster with Amelia as his nurse.

Ed and Amelia fought back, saying that once they'd taken over Edward's care the other family members had abandoned their responsibilities. His brothers and sister Mary had returned to their respective homes and Jean hadn't even visited once from New York to see her father before he died, believing Skype to be an appropriate alternative. Ed and Amelia were left to cope with both the business end of running the farm and Edward's health.

According to Paul, the suicide note from his father was actually the beginning of a letter apologising to his other children for changing his will. He suspected Ed and Amelia of abusing Edward and forcing his hand. The solicitor who'd changed the will, however, said his client appeared in the full possession of his senses when he made the alteration and, in fact, had been jovial. It was a practical step, Edward Senior had said. He'd realised that trying to divide the farm amongst seven siblings would lead to chaos.

In the end, while the police had been curious about the whole affair, and a file was opened, there simply wasn't enough evidence to prove anything untoward had happened in Edward's room that night.

So Ed had inherited everything. He'd gained money, but lost a family.

Wasn't it always the way?

He and Amelia sat together now on the windowsill, staring out at the detectives.

'Olive was a stupid woman,' Amelia said, breaking the silence. 'I never liked her.'

'Didn't you? I used to think she was good company. Once.'

Amelia pursed her lips. She straightened her peach striped skirt over her knees.

'You were flattered by her, Ed. She flirted with you. But she gave me the creeps. She wanted to jump on our lives. All those comments about travelling on her own and how nice it would be to have somebody to go with. That was all intended to wring an invitation out of us. It wasn't our duty to keep her company. It wasn't our fault she didn't have a family of her own. She made stuff up as well.'

'What do you mean?'

'That holiday she was always going on about. The one with the women from work. She claimed they asked her to go away several times after that but she declined because it wasn't her sort of thing. Well, if what she said was anything to go by, she was a total wet blanket on that trip. Can you imagine those women ever asking her to go anywhere with them again? And where were those friends who always wanted her to join them? We never saw them.'

Ed nodded. Amelia was good at seeing through people. She'd known how his siblings would react when his father died. She'd predicted to the last word what they'd say and when.

'You're telling me the truth about everything, though, aren't you, Ed?' she said. 'You didn't hit her or do anything silly when you were over there?'

'No. I told her we were off on a last-minute trip but as soon as we were settled I'd be in touch. And I told her Paul was a malicious liar.'

'And you said she could come out to join us this time.'

'Yes. I told you all this, Amelia.'

Amelia shook her head. He knew she was thinking she should have gone herself, that she would have been far better at reading Olive's thoughts.

'Fine. I've a pile of washing to get on. Did you take all the mail in from the box, by the way? You need to give me a hand, Ed. I can't do everything.'

Ed sighed.

'I was busy getting the shopping in last night, Amelia. I've to sort out the car today; I'll get the post in when I'm ready.'

Amelia tutted.

Why didn't she ever believe him?

Ed thought he'd done a good job with Olive, though. To begin with, anyhow.

She had been mortified when he told her Paul had been in touch to say he'd spoken to her when he'd been in Wicklow that time.

'I can imagine what he told you,' Ed said. 'It's nothing he hasn't said to others before. It was a horrible lesson for me, Olive, discovering what money does to a family. I know I shouldn't complain. I became a very wealthy man, after all. But I did lose all my siblings in the process. That's hard to get your head around, that people you love can hate you so much.'

She'd smiled and he'd thought he was winning her round.

Then she hit him with it, while she still had that simpering, friendly look on her face.

'But Ed, when you sold the farm, didn't you ever consider giving your siblings their share of the profits?'

He'd tried not to let anything show on his face.

'Well, at first I thought, this is exactly why Dad left me everything. Because of this sort of fighting. I did consider splitting it when it got bad, but by then, everything had soured. Too much had been said. There was no coming back from it.'

'Oh, of course. I understand.'

She didn't.

Ed and Amelia had chosen the right time to clear out of Withered Vale.

It wasn't that he thought anything could be opened up with the police again. The file on his father was closed. Game over.

But Ed did not want the rumours about what they'd done following them to Wicklow. They'd lived here for years, peacefully, undisturbed. He'd no idea how Paul had found them but, when he'd turned up at their last place in Dublin, he'd kicked up such a stink that Ed had handed over thousands just to get rid of him.

Ed knew how it worked with blackmailers. You just had to keep paying out. They were never happy. That's how it would have been with Olive, too.

Ed had done exactly what Amelia had suggested. Bar one thing.

He couldn't tell his wife.

She'd kill him.

FRANK

'I don't like stating the blindingly obvious, you being a detective and all, but you do realise it's Sunday?'

'I do, Amira. I also know if this were any other lab in the country, there would have been nobody to answer the phone. You're one in a million, you know that?'

Frank could feel Amira's blushes down the phone.

'If you're dropping compliments already, you're definitely after something. What can I do you for?'

'The DNA from the Withered Vale place. Have you made any matches to the neighbours yet?'

'I'd love to rant and rave, tell you how busy I am and that I'll call you when I have results but yes, I have, actually. I've been matching samples all morning.'

Frank smiled at Emma, who was idling outside the Solankes' house, waiting for him to get off the phone.

'And?'

'And the whole neighbourhood more or less was in her house at some point. Lily Solanke, David Solanke, Alison Daly, Holly Daly,

Ed Miller, Amelia Miller, Ron Ryan – it's his sperm, by the way – George Richmond, and . . . okay, nothing from the Hennessys, as it happens, but that doesn't mean much. They could have been in and out and didn't touch anything. There's some more DNA we couldn't ID. Possibly friends, tradesmen, that sort of thing. You just let me know when you've new samples for me to test against. I'll drop everything.'

'Sounds like you've let nothing drop, Amira. That's fantastic. And that's all DNA from inside the house, is it?'

'It would be a bit difficult to lift it from the garden, Frank.'

'You know what I mean. It's not from the front door, window frames, that sort of thing?'

'No. This is all internal samples. I'm moving on to fingerprints now, so I'll probably have more as we go. In fact, I think I've something interesting but I won't say more until I'm sure.'

'You're such a tease.'

Frank thanked her and hung up. He pulled at the hairs of his moustache and pondered the new information.

'Well?' Emma said.

'George Richmond lied to us. He said he'd never been in her house, even though he had a key. Turns out, his DNA was in her home.'

Emma clapped her hands.

'Brilliant. Let's go.'

George Richmond was in.

He greeted them warily at the door.

'Eh, Ron rang,' he said. 'He says you think something might have happened to Olive. Didn't she just die? I mean, is it true, was she killed?'

'She died from a heart attack,' Frank said. 'But we don't know yet whether or not there was foul play.'

George blinked as he tried to process what that meant.

'We want to talk to you, George, because you told us that you'd never been inside Olive Collins' property. Is there anything you'd like to clarify in that regard? Have you remembered any additional information since we spoke to you yesterday?'

'I . . . eh . . .'

'Because it's never too late to make us aware of the full facts. It doesn't automatically cast you in a suspicious light. Lying to us, however . . .'

'I'm not a liar.'

'Could you have been in her house and forgotten?'

George reddened.

He sat down on the couch. Frank and Emma sat, too.

It was confession time.

'I didn't want to tell you about it.'

Frank leaned forward.

'Tell us what? Did you visit her on 3rd of March, perchance?'

'God, no. It was – I think it was weeks before that. I called over. I was only in the hall, I didn't go right in. The front door was open.'

'Oh. I see. So now you were in her house. Why not tell us?'

'I . . . look, I went over to have it out with her. She'd accused me of something – when actually it was her who'd done something very wrong – and I wanted to confront her.'

Frank sighed.

'Which was it, George? Had you done something, or had she done something? What was she accusing you of?'

George took a deep breath.

'She let herself into my house when I wasn't here and went through my possessions. She saw some things, stuff that I'm not proud of. I have a . . . I have a problem. I'm getting help for it, but I still have stuff in the house.'

'What sort of problem?'

George stared at the floor.

Suddenly, it was so obvious to Frank.

George's father was a music mogul. Sex, drugs and rock and roll.

Drugs, that's what Olive had found. And that would explain why George was so edgy all the time.

'I appreciate if you're worried about admitting to something illegal,' Frank said. 'But we're not here to catch you out. If Olive had, let's say, spotted a few joints or that . . . well, unless you're running a heroin lab out of your basement, it's not a huge cause of concern for us. Do you understand what I'm saying, George? We're not going to bust you for drugs for personal use. The only relevance for us is if that's what you fought with Olive over.'

George looked at him, aghast.

'It's not illegal. I don't take drugs. God. I wish drugs were my problem.'

Frank was puzzled. What was worse than drugs?

George kept throwing nervous glances at Emma.

Frank made a quick decision. She could chew the ear off him for it later.

'Emma, sorry, I'm parched. Is there any chance you could stick the kettle on?'

Emma frowned. He stared back, apologetic but firm.

'Fine,' she said. She left the room with as much bad grace as possible.

'Thanks,' George said. 'Speaking about this in front of women —
they just won't get it.'

'I'm no closer to knowing what you're on about, son.'

George met Frank's eye.

'I'm addicted to porn.'

Frank tried not to laugh.

'Is that it? Aren't we all?'

George shook his head.

'No, man. I mean, properly addicted. I could sit in front of a
computer for twelve hours straight and masturbate about twenty
times. I masturbate so much it hurts. And it means every other area
of my life is messed up. I can't have a job. Well, not one that involves
computers, not yet. I can't have a girlfriend. Some days, I can't even
leave the house. I'm not alone. There are loads of men like me. I
swear, I'm not kidding.'

Frank sat back and rubbed his jaw. George's face was grave. He
believed he was addicted to porn, whatever Frank thought.

'So, Olive Collins let herself in, rifled through your — what,
magazines? — and was purer than pure herself, was she? What did
she say to you that upset you so much?'

'She . . . and this was completely off the mark, but — she accused
me of being a paedophile.'

Frank shifted nervously and sat forward in the seat.

'George, don't lie to me now. This stuff is easy to check. Do you
have images of underage girls or boys in this house or on your
computer?'

George groaned and put his head in his hands.

'No, of course I don't. It was in her head. She was a poisonous old
bat. Crazy. She made stuff up.'

'Why would she make stuff up?'

'I don't know. That's why I went over to have it out with her. I told her if she broke into my house again, I'd report her to the police.'

'Is that all you said to her?'

George bit his lip.

'George?'

'No. I lost it a bit. I threatened her.'

'With what?' Frank asked.

'I said if she said anything about me to the neighbours . . . she'd, eh, regret it.'

'Hmm. And all this over a few naughty pictures?'

George stood up.

'Where are you off to?' Frank said.

'I need to show you something.'

Frank followed George upstairs. He could hear Emma in the kitchen banging around sulkily. She was probably spitting in the tea.

The stairs ran for two levels and opened out onto a huge landing area, cream carpets and large glass windows, with rooms off to either side.

'I've started throwing a lot of this stuff out,' George said, pausing outside one of the rooms. 'There used to be more. It takes a while to get rid of it because, well, you don't want the bin men clocking it.'

He opened the door.

Frank walked in.

Frank's brother was a big Beatles fan. He'd a room like this – floor to ceiling shelving with every record, book, magazine and collectible that the band had ever released. A museum dedicated to the Fab Four.

George had a museum of porn. It was how the storage rooms in a Playboy mansion might look, Frank thought. Rows and rows of adult DVDs and magazines. All neatly stacked and stored. They even looked to be in some sort of order.

'And this is just the hardcopy material,' George said. 'With the internet these days, you don't even need this stuff any more. I haven't bought anything online in years. You know, they say most teenage boys don't even know women have pubic hair. That they think anal sex is totally normal. That's how prolific and normalised porn is. The line between reality and fantasy becomes blurred. That's what it's doing to our brains.'

Frank couldn't speak. He just stood there, opening and closing his mouth like a fish.

Eventually, he pulled it together.

'Eh, right. Yeah. I can see why you'd have taken issue with Olive Collins seeing all this.'

George nodded glumly.

'Did you take it further, son?'

'What?'

'Did you go beyond threatening her?'

George shook his head.

'No. I swear. I wouldn't harm a woman. I know porn can be violent. It desensitises you. I think that's why I yelled at her, why I thought it was okay to scare her. But when I saw how upset she was, I backed off. I swear.'

George's eyes flickered sideways. Frank caught it, tried to assess what it meant. Had George been happy to see Olive scared? Had he gone further?

'Okay,' Frank said. 'And you're getting treatment for this – addiction? What does that involve?'

'Counselling, mainly. Getting rid of everything, obviously. Which I'm trying to do. It was working before – well, before I had that fight with Olive. It set me back. But I'm going to get into it again.'

'I see. Well, good luck with that. Right. We'd better go back downstairs before my partner reports me to our human resources department.'

Frank closed the door to the room. He had to resist the urge to offer to take a few DVDs off George's hands. He didn't think it would go down too well.

As they walked down the stairs, he looked at the back of the younger man's head. You'd never know, to look at him, what was going on in there. He came across so . . . nice.

George Richmond was very good at hiding things.

EMMA

Emma was not happy with Frank.

He hadn't even made a pretence of drinking the tea he'd sent her on the fool's errand to fetch.

She stomped down the garden path ahead of him and didn't stop until she'd reached her car.

'Seriously, Frank?' she snapped, as he arrived beside her. 'Tea? You know, I was actually starting to like you.'

'Starting to like me? I thought I was your hero.'

'Very funny. Yes. Starting to. Stockholm Syndrome, I think they call it.'

'What's your problem with me?' Frank exclaimed.

'What's my problem with you? Isn't it more what's your problem with me? You know what, cards on the table, Frank. You think I've got where I am because I'm a pretty face and a young woman, that I tick all the politically correct boxes, don't you? I mean, if you respected me as an equal, you wouldn't have asked me to make bloody tea in front of a suspect. But you haven't a clue, Frank. You haven't a clue what I've come through, how hard I've had to work.

And I've noticed things on this investigation that you haven't. You've said that yourself.'

'Emma, any chance I can get a word in? Look, get in the car, will you?'

'I'll get in the car because I want to get in the car and not because you're telling me to get in the car.'

Frank shrugged and walked around to his side. She heard him mutter, 'Just as long as you get in the fucking car,' as he went, which did nothing to improve her humour.

'Now,' he said, when he'd closed the passenger door and she'd slammed hers.

Emma stared out the windscreen, refusing to make eye contact.

Frank sighed.

'Emma, don't tell me it didn't dawn on you in there that he wanted to talk to me alone. He says he's a porn addict. He was too embarrassed to say it in front of you. You being a young woman with a pretty face and all. And, if we're being totally honest, you do have an awful tendency to open your mouth without thinking. Chances are, at the first mention of his penis, you'd have arrested him for indecent exposure.'

Emma blushed.

'I do not say things without thinking.'

'I don't think you mean to. But I do think you're sometimes not entirely aware of your tone.'

'Well, that's rich, Mr New Man. You think you're a barrel of self-awareness yourself, do you? Everything I say you pick up wrong.'

Frank sighed.

'Maybe it's a bit of both. The point is, I wasn't looking to upset you in there. If it had been a delicate female matter, I'd have cleared out. Without having to be asked, I might add.'

Emma said nothing for a minute. That, she could believe.

'Is he?' she asked.

'What?'

'A porn addict?'

'He sure has a lot of material in the house. I didn't know there was such a thing, but if it does exist, I think George is one, yes.'

'It *is* a thing. They say it's the number one addiction in people presenting for treatment these days. I can't believe you don't know that. And I can't believe I didn't pick that up off him.'

They said nothing for a minute. Then Frank puffed the air out of his cheeks.

'I'm sorry if I've been unfair to you,' he said.

'No *if* about it,' she snapped. 'Get your own tea next time.'

'Not just in there. In general. You must have realised by now, Emma, I'm nearly finished. I'm tired. I want out. You're the new wave. You've plenty of energy. I just want to get the job done and dusted and go home. You want promotions and praise and awards. We're a mismatch. I know I'm an irritable old codger but don't take it personally.'

'How do you know I want all those things?'

'What?'

'Promotions and praise and awards.'

'Well, you know. The way you turn in for work, for one thing. The make-up and that.'

Emma snorted.

'You think I wear all this on my face because I want a top job? Because I'm some vain bimbo?'

'I didn't say you were a bimbo.'

Emma reached across him into the glove compartment. She took out a packet of wipes and pulled at the top one.

She scrubbed and scrubbed, discarding the wipes as she went, a little brown pile building on her lap.

Then she turned to face Frank.

His shock, when he saw the scar that ran around the side of her cheek and under her jaw, was palpable.

'Jesus, Emma. I never noticed.'

'You're not supposed to. That's the point. Sure, I'd like a promotion. Do you have any idea how much MAC foundation I go through in a month? I'm spending nearly a second mortgage on make-up.'

Frank shook his head.

'What happened? Is it . . . When we were talking to the Dalys . . .'

Emma sighed.

She pulled down the sun visor and flipped up the mirror, reached into her bag for the foundation. She'd only cleaned her cheek, she didn't need to reapply her eye make-up or lippie. The problem, of course, with changing your skin tone was that you then had to ramp up all the other make-up as well, or you looked like you'd no eyebrows, lashes or lips. It was a vicious circle.

She felt Frank's hand on her arm and stopped.

'You don't need to wear that crap.'

Emma looked away before he could see the tears that had filled her eyes.

'Please, Frank,' she said. 'Don't be nice about it. Not when I was feeling so annoyed at you.'

She turned back to the mirror. She spoke as she massaged the make-up in circular strokes, blending as she went.

'It was an ex-boyfriend. I'd already broken up with him, as soon as I realised how possessive he was. I was stupid to begin with. I was in Garda training college, for crying out loud – of anybody, you'd think I'd have seen the signs. He would never come out with my friends; when he did he was quiet and sulky. But when we were on our own he was great fun, really attentive and loving. I figured he was shy, to start. He was clever like that. But then it progressed. He started whining when I went out without him. That turned into asking what I was doing and who I was with. Then – ah hell, you don't need to hear all this. You know exactly how it goes.'

'Tell me anyway,' Frank said.

She glanced sideways at him.

'I'll parse it. The last weekend we were together as a couple, we had a fight and I went to bed not speaking to him. I knew I was going to end it. I figured he'd sleep on the couch. But he came in and, during the night, I woke up and he was trying to . . . you know. I was well able for him. I kicked him in the balls. He swore and went mad, especially when I pointed out that technically, what he'd done was attempted rape. Then I said it was over and he started crying. I threw him out. I was so relieved that he'd gone. I just wanted to put it behind me.'

'He wasn't gone, though?'

'No. We were living out west at the time, where I'd got my first posting. He started calling to the house all the time, hammering on the door, ringing me non-stop.

'The bosses were great. They gave me a transfer home and I moved back in with my folks. I figured he wouldn't come near me there and I was right, for a while. I even started seeing somebody else. Graham. We moved in together, eventually. He was a total plonker in the end, but it was good for me to jump back in, you know. So, anyway, it turns out the arsehole was stalking me. I hadn't a clue. He followed me home one night to my parents' house. They were away, so he knew I was on my own. And he broke in. He slashed my face and told me he was going to kill me. He beat me until I was unconscious.'

She said it matter-of-factly. The counselling had given her the strength to do that. It wasn't that it didn't affect her. She just didn't feel the need to start blubbing every time she told somebody. She saved the crying for when she was alone at night – when she woke up sweating and cowering in her bed and had to get up and check her bedroom door was locked, then her front door, then all the windows, even though the apartment was on the sixth floor.

'My parents had to sell the house, afterwards. They said they couldn't live there any longer, knowing what had happened to me in my own room. Our family home, where they'd lived all their married life. He destroyed more than just my face.'

The car was silent.

Emma waited a minute before turning to look at Frank.

He was clutching the dashboard, his face ashen.

'So, yes, I understood what the Dalys were talking about.'

Frank shook his head.

'I'm sorry. I'd no idea.'

Emma shrugged.

'Why broadcast it? It doesn't make me a better detective. If anything, it probably makes me sound a bit shit. Who'd trust somebody who couldn't even protect themselves?'

'Where is he now?'

'Prison. I like to call in there sometimes.'

'You visit him?'

'Are you mad? I visit the guards. Without my make-up on.'

Some colour had made its way back into Frank's cheeks.

'Good woman,' he said. 'Is there anything . . .?'

Emma held up her hand.

'I really can't talk about it any more, Frank. It's in the past. I cover this up every day so I'm not reminded of it. Maybe one day I won't feel the need, but for now, I do. Hey, what the hell is going on there?'

She leaned around Frank so she could get a better view out the window.

Matt Hennessy had marched up Ron Ryan's driveway and was hammering on the door like the house was on fire.

The two detectives got out of the car just as Ron answered. They were crossing the road when the shouting began and had entered the garden by the time Matt threw the first punch.

'Woah!' Frank yelled, running up the path. Matt had Ron in a headlock and was trying to land another dig to his face. Ron was attempting to twist out of Matt's grasp and pulling at anything he could find – in this instance, the other man's trousers. They were starting to come down.

Emma stopped halfway up the garden. Frank had this one. There was no way she was throwing herself into the melee. In any case, she wasn't worried about Matt or Ron's safety. That first punch might have hurt, but now it was a proper middle-aged-man fight. The pair were doing more damage to themselves than to each other. Ron was so red, it looked like he'd given himself a hernia.

Chrissy Hennessy appeared at Emma's side. She'd run from her house in a panic, if the slippers were anything to go by, but now she stopped and dropped her hands to her sides.

'Sweet Jesus,' she said. 'Look at them.'

Emma tried to look stern and not laugh.

Frank had managed to swing Matt away from Ron, who, now he was free, was dancing on the spot with his fists raised.

'Come to my house and start throwing digs at me,' he shouted. 'I'll show you.'

'Going after my wife in my house, you dirty little rat, I'll *bury* you.'

Emma turned to Chrissy, an eyebrow raised.

'I am fucking mortified,' Chrissy muttered.

'Oi!' Frank yelled. He poked Matt in the chest. 'Walk away. If you don't, I'm going to have to arrest you. Don't give him the satisfaction.'

'I want him arrested! He assaulted me!'

Frank put his hand on Ron's chest now.

'The way I see it, you two started throwing punches at each other. Let's leave it at that, shall we? It starts getting messy when a man who's already made a statement in the course of a murder investigation is suddenly getting into scraps with another neighbour – regardless of who threw the first punch.'

Ron glared at Frank.

'If he calls at my door again . . .'

'I'll be back with a warrant for him.'

'Good. You hear that, you little runt? A warrant.'

Matt tried to get around Frank.

'Get inside!' Frank roared at Ron.

The other man did as he was told, slamming his door behind him.

Chrissy walked up the path towards her husband. Emma held her breath as she watched the woman take her husband's hand and examine his bruised knuckles.

'I suggest you take Lancelot indoors,' Frank said.

'Thank you, Detective,' Chrissy said, pulling at her husband's arm.

'Sorry, I had to do it, Chrissy,' Matt said, puffing out his chest. 'I was going to beat the crap out of him. It's probably just as well the police intervened. Next time, he won't be so lucky.'

Emma and Frank watched them walk off.

'The battle of Withered Vale,' Frank said. 'It took ten men to pull Matt Hennessy off his neighbour when he found out his wife's honour had been besmirched.'

Emma smiled.

'I never realised you were such a dirty cop,' she said. 'You'd better hope Ron there doesn't change his mind and file for assault.'

'Yeah, yeah. I'm sure Matt could countersue for the damage Ron was doing to his pants. You know what's hilarious?'

'What?'

'You've just told me you had a violent stalker for years; my wife drowned in a ditch – and I don't think either of us would swap our lives with anybody in this Vale. Just goes to show you, huh? Money doesn't buy you everything.'

'True,' Emma said, cocking her head sideways.

'Hang on, who's this, now?'

Frank pulled out his phone.

'Amira?' he said, answering. 'Hmm. Yeah? No, I don't think so. Holly, yeah, but she's seventeen. Right. We will. I'll get a uniform over to do it now. Thanks.'

Emma waited until he'd hung up.

'Well?'

'That was Amira.'

'I figured that.'

'She's going through the fingerprints. The pipes leading to the boiler had been wiped clean but she picked up something on its front. One of Olive's prints.' Frank swallowed.

'And?' Emma could tell this was big.

'And she found one other partial print. She thought it would be Olive's as well, but she says now it's not.'

'Whose is it?'

'She doesn't know. But she says it's small.'

'What does that . . .? Oh.'

They were standing right across from the Solankes' house.

Neither of them spoke for a moment.

'Could be Cam's?' Frank said.

Emma nodded. She didn't think so, though. They would have taken Cam's fingerprints already, to check against those on the letter box.

If there was a kid's print inside that house – chances were it belonged to Wolf.

LILY & DAVID

No. 2

'There's a policeman at the door.'

David ignored her. He was sitting on the back step, staring off into the distance. Lily had found him there when she got up that morning and he didn't seem to have moved. He was becoming one with the step.

'David, I said there's a policeman at the door.'

'I heard you. What do you want me to do about it? Hit somebody else, have you?'

'You know, David, you might be feeling all superior because you told the detectives I was with you the night Olive is supposed to have died but, don't forget, I *know* I was here alone. Which begs the question – where were you? Maybe that's what the policeman wants to ask you.'

David eyed her nervously. Lily sighed.

'He wants to take the children's fingerprints.'

David shot up. 'What did you say?'

She followed him down the hall to the front door.

'What's this about, Officer?' David asked.

'It's just procedure,' the young lad said. He was in full uniform and had his cap in one hand, a large box under his other arm. 'We took DNA samples and fingerprints from you and your neighbours but we'd also like to take the children's. To rule them out. I have a kit here, we don't need to go to the station.'

'Rule them out of what? We told you Wolf and Lily May were in Olive Collins' house.'

The cop looked at David blankly.

'Yes. We know. That's why we need to rule them out.'

'Maybe we should . . .' Lily started.

David held up his hand to silence her. Lily's head snapped back. It was so *rude*.

And suddenly, the clouds parted. She could see everything, clear as day.

Sure, she'd been having an identity crisis of sorts, lately. A breakdown, even; call it what you will. But shouldn't she have been able to confide in David? Tell him she felt like she was going mad?

Instead, she'd taken to sneaking around like a teenager acting out. Why was that?

Could it be, just ever so slightly, that she didn't feel she could confide in David because he was so bloody sanctimonious?

She hadn't judged his lifestyle when they'd met. She'd enjoyed the differences between them.

This need to be more like her – that came from him, not from Lily.

He'd taken on her lifestyle and turned it into something that made him feel superior to everybody else. He wasn't a hippie. He was so far removed from a hippie, it was actually funny. It was just a hobby to him, one he had to be better at than anybody else because that was what he did. One they both had to be better at, because he'd included her on his team and his team always won. Nobody could ever challenge them.

David had a killer instinct.

Lily stepped forward.

'Excuse my husband's manners,' she said. 'Come in, Officer. I'll call the twins down for you.'

HOLLY & ALISON

No. 3

She refused to talk to her mother.

Holly was convinced that they were going to come a cropper now. Whatever about the woman detective, who – well, Holly couldn't put her finger on it, but she seemed to understand – the older one was a dinosaur. He mightn't deliberately drop them in it, but she could imagine him telling his police mates down the pub how he'd met two mad women on the run from one of their own.

That would be all it would take. Her father seemed to have the power to hear things that had been whispered on a different continent, let alone county. That's how it felt sometimes.

Her mother hadn't been there, that day Holly had walked out of school and saw him waiting for her. He was trying to hide in the crowd of parents for the younger kids and he looked different. He'd grown a beard and his hair was longer, more wavy. He'd always been a handsome man, her dad, tall and strong and clean-cut. Now he looked . . . like a fugitive. Funny, when they were the ones in hiding.

But she'd still seen him. She was really good at picking out a face.

He'd followed her all the way to the harbour. Holly kept walking, knowing he was behind her. She was careful not to bring him anywhere into town where somebody might recognise her and call her Holly.

She'd been registered in the school under her real name, Eva Baker, even while the teachers had agreed to call her Holly, having received a condensed version of events from Alison. Eva was all he knew her as; he never knew their alias. If he found out it was Daly, he might be able to link it to the shop and then to their home. For all Holly knew, he'd already followed her home but she didn't think it had got that far. Otherwise he'd have been waiting for her there, not at the school gates.

She didn't stop until they'd arrived at a secluded spot down near the sea.

Then she turned around and looked at him. He had no choice but to keep walking towards her.

Holly wasn't afraid of him. She'd never really been afraid of him. The stupidity of youth. She'd reserved all her fear for her mother. And then for her child. Never for herself.

But her mother wasn't there that day and her child was no more.

'Eva,' he said. 'How are you?'

'How do you think I am?'

He'd looked at the ground.

'I . . .'

'What do you want?'

'I want to tell you how sorry I am, baby. For what happened. I'm getting help now. I know I had a problem. It was the job. You wouldn't understand. I saw such violence, all the time. It seeps in. It makes you immune. And I was under so much pressure. I think I was having some sort of breakdown. I would never have hurt you if I'd been in my right mind. You know that.'

'A breakdown,' Holly repeated. 'A decade-long breakdown, was it? Wasn't that how long you were hitting my mother?'

'That's different. Grown-ups – people fight. We both loved you. It was never about you.'

'It was about me when you kicked me in the stomach.'

'I was out of my mind. Come on, sweetheart. Tell me how any father would react upon finding out his fourteen-year-old is pregnant? It was the little bastard who'd got you that way that I wanted to kill. I wasn't thinking straight.'

'Oh. I see. But you're all fixed now?'

'Of course I am. I wouldn't be here if I wasn't. I haven't stopped looking for you since she took you away.'

'She?'

'I mean your mother.'

'Are you angry at her for taking me away?'

He took a deep breath. He was desperate not to show her what was on his mind.

'You're my child, Eva. I was angry but I'm not any more. Now I'm just sad.'

Holly laughed, a thin, horrible sound.

'I almost believe you,' she said. 'You sound so convincing. But I don't believe you know what it means to be sad.'

'I do . . .'

'No. The only emotions you understand are hate. Anger. Rage. If you felt sad, you'd have stayed away. You'd have understood.

What did you feel when you murdered your grandchild? It was a girl, did you know? I called her Rose. I know I was young and didn't have a clue what was happening to me, not really, but at that last scan I heard her little heart beating. I saw her sucking her thumb. And they told me she was perfect. She was healthy, a good size. She was going to be beautiful. She was beautiful. They let me hold her when she was born. This tiny little thing, barely the size of my hands. You took that from me.'

He flinched. She thought his eyes filled with tears but it may have just been the wind. She imagined it was all too easy for him to have told himself there was no baby. Just his daughter with a bump that said, *Look, Dad, I let a boy do this to me.*

'It doesn't matter now, anyway,' she said. 'None of it matters. What you did or didn't mean to do. I'm glad you came. I always knew you would, eventually.'

He hesitated.

'You did?'

She'd enjoyed seeing the look of confusion on his face.

'Yes. And I wanted to speak to you.'

He took a step towards her. In hope.

'I wanted to tell you that if you ever come near me or my mother again, you'd better be planning to kill us. You might have got away with it the last time, but not this time. This time, I'll tell everybody.'

'Tell them what?' His face was a grimace now. She recognised it, that oh-so-familiar look of simmering rage, the expression she'd spent the best part of fourteen years trying not to provoke. Holly wasn't playing the reunion game he'd planned and it was riling him.

'I'll tell them that you made me pregnant. That you forced

yourself on me and then you beat me up so I'd lose my baby and there'd be no proof. I never told them who the father was. And now I'm ready to talk.'

Her father's mouth fell open. He was appalled.

'I never touched you,' he said. 'Eva, how could you say that?'

'Easy,' she said. 'I just open my mouth and it comes out. I can even make myself cry, look.' She closed her eyes and opened them and the tears started to spill out.

'I knew if I cried he'd hurt my mammy. So I just did what he said.'

'You . . . you!' His eyes were wide and horrified. 'I never laid a hand on you before that night. You're crazy! Batshit crazy!'

'I know it's all lies and you know it's lies. But who do you think people will believe? You, the man who lost his job after he put his wife and daughter in hospital, or me, the pretty little teenager, who, by the way, is gay and yet got pregnant when she was thirteen?'

She'd thought then he might kill her. She didn't care. He'd get what was coming to him either way and at least her mother would be safe. In any case, Holly had wanted to die ever since they'd taken Rose from her arms. But instead her father had backed away from her, looking at her like she was an alien. He couldn't handle what she'd said.

She'd been triumphant that day, but satisfaction had quickly turned to fear. It was like she'd thrown the gauntlet down. He knew he couldn't get them back. So what if he decided to take her up on what she'd said and kill them both?

Holly hadn't really thought that far ahead.

'Holly? Can I come in?'

'No.'

Her mother came in anyway.

Holly pretended to read the book she'd been holding in her hands for the last hour.

'I just had the strangest two phone calls,' Alison said.

Holly ignored her.

'Lily rang first. She says the cops just came around and took the twins' fingerprints. So I rang Chrissy then and she said they'd already got Cam's. Matt has suggested we have a community meeting tonight.'

Holly raised an eyebrow.

'Where? In the imaginary community hall? Or in the Hennessys' treehouse?'

'I suggested here.'

'What?'

Holly sat up.

'Have you gone totally bonkers? Is that what's happening? You're losing it again? Wasn't the whole point of moving here so that we could keep to ourselves? And now you're getting pissed with the neighbours and offering up our house as some sort of headquarters for crackpots.'

Alison laughed.

She *laughed* at her.

Holly grabbed her mother by the shoulders.

'Mam. I'm serious.'

Holly started to cry. She couldn't help it. Big, huge gulping sobs. She couldn't swallow them. She didn't even have time to wonder what effect it would have on her mother, whether it would start her off too. It was like the pressure of the last few days had popped some bubble in her head.

Holly couldn't see through the tears. But she felt her mother's arms tighten around her as she pulled her in close.

'Oh, sweetheart,' her mother said. 'I'm here. I'm here. Just let it all out. All of it.'

Alison held her like that until all of the noisy crying stopped and Holly was able to breathe, deep, guttural spasms that shook her body.

When she'd calmed down, Alison gently pulled away from her and met her eye.

'This cannot go on. It's eating you up. I can't let you carry this any more, do you understand? That's why I told the police. And it's why we need to tell more people. People need to know what he is. What he did to us. They need to be aware. And then people like Olive Collins won't be able to have power over us any more. If it's out in the open.'

Holly nodded.

'I know. But I'm so scared. After the school.'

'He never came near us, though. It's been over a year now.'

'I have to tell you, Mam. I have to tell you what I said to him the day he found me.'

Her mother frowned. Then she listened. And when Holly was finished, she stared at her with wide, startled eyes, then drew her into another hug.

'It serves him right,' Alison said, speaking into the air over Holly's head, and her voice was cool, determined. 'I don't know where you got that from but it bloody well worked.'

'You're not angry at me?'

'Angry at you?' Alison scoffed. 'I would never be angry at you, love. Sometimes we have to use our imaginations. And he's not going to find us and kill us. I promise you. Can you believe me? Do you believe I'll keep you safe?'

Holly said nothing for a minute. Then she spoke.

'Yes. I do.'

She'd heard something in her mother's voice that hadn't been there before.

The timidness was gone. There was a steel in Alison's words, an undercurrent that said she would kill for her daughter if she had to.

Holly would do the same.

She knew they would keep each other safe.

RON

No. 7

Ron had a shiner. A great big bloody black eye, and he was convinced the bag of frozen peas thing was all a big myth. It was making the side of his face numb but it didn't seem to have brought down the swelling.

Matt Hennessy. Ron had never seen *that* coming.

The one word he would have associated with Matt Hennessy was weak. Ever since he'd started having sex with the man's wife, that's how Ron had thought of his neighbour. Chrissy was gorgeous, but she was one of the saddest women he'd ever met. What kind of man landed a woman like her and let her become so miserable? If Ron had been luckier in life, if he hadn't spent so many years prioritising Dan, he might have settled down with somebody like Chrissy. Somebody who could have made him happy.

Matt Hennessy didn't know how lucky he was.

And never in a million years would Ron have foreseen that onslaught.

And Chrissy had just stood there and watched — after everything she'd said about Matt, all the times she'd told Ron how terrible her husband treated her, how he always abandoned her every time she needed him. She'd obviously told Matt what was going on. How could she!

Ron was fuming. He was humiliated and he was pissed off.

In another life, he'd have been straight over to Olive. Because, say what you like about her, Olive (up until she'd dropped him in it with his exes, anyway) was usually on Ron's side.

Ron stared at himself in the mirror. There was no denying it. He felt really sorry for himself. And more. He felt sorry for Olive. Whatever she'd done, she didn't deserve to die.

Why did she have to go and ruin everything?

For so long, without even realising it, he'd been happy to have just two people in his life. Olive and Dan. She was gone and Dan . . .

Ron choked back a sob.

Had Dan ever even been there?

Fuck. He missed Olive.

LILY

No. 2

When Lily returned from the shops, David was waiting for her.

He was sitting at the kitchen table, a coffee in front of him.

This is different, she thought.

He'd changed his clothes, she noted. Put on a shirt. He looked like he was going to work.

'Holly Daly is upstairs with the twins,' he said, as Lily put the shopping bags down. 'I'd like to go over to this meeting with you, if that's okay.'

'That's absolutely fine, David.' She reached into one of the shopping bags and withdrew two bottles of wine. 'I bought supplies. I see you're already on the hard stuff.'

'I guess we all have our weaknesses.' David narrowed his eyes.

'Indeed,' Lily said. 'Stretching the truth seems to be one of yours. You might want to tell the police what you were doing the night Olive died.'

'It's irrelevant.'

'It's *relevant* that you weren't here,' Lily snapped.

'All I did was go for a walk. You know that. You'd have been with me if you weren't doing that bloody Easter egg thing.'

'But I wasn't with you, David. And you weren't Olive's best buddy, by any stretch. You knew she used to laugh at you. I know you. That would have made you furious. And more to the point, you were really angry when I came back from hers so upset.'

'Right, Lily. I decided I'd kill her because she used to laugh at me. Seriously. Is that what we've been reduced to?'

She placed the wine to cool in the freezer and unloaded the pizzas and crisps, noticing he'd avoided the last part of her point.

'I see,' he said, watching her. 'We're throwing the baby out with the bath water, are we? Moving from vegetarian to a diet of frozen crap.'

'*We* are doing nothing. I'm shopping for me and the children now. You can eat quinoa and buckwheat to your heart's content. That's the amazing thing about being a grown-up. You can make choices for yourself and not really give a damn what anybody else thinks. And, anyway, it's a cheese pizza. See? Not a slice of pepperoni in sight.'

'You're choosing for the kids.'

'We'll let them decide,' she said. 'For once. Wasn't that what Wolf was doing anyway? If we give what Olive said any credence, he will be feasting on live bats by Christmas.'

'I don't understand what's happening to us.' David's voice broke.

Lily paused at the counter, her back to her husband.

'David. It's like this. It's absolutely clear to me that we have fundamental problems in our marriage and we can't continue without addressing them.'

'But I don't even know what these problems are!'

'Really?' Lily sighed. 'You control us. Me and the children. I wanted to take Wolf to the doctor years ago – you insisted we didn't. But it wasn't only your choice to make. And why did you take on all my things – being a vegetarian, gardening? You didn't do any of that when we met.'

'Jesus, is it a crime for a man to want to share things with his wife?'

'No.' She held up her hand. 'Don't. That's what I've been telling myself. I made myself feel bad for hating you for being like me. But that's not what's happened, David. You've twisted it to make it look that way. You fancied the life I'd made for myself and you appropriated it. It made you feel something you needed to feel, I don't know. Don't roll your eyes at me.'

'I'm doing no such thing. You know what, Lily, you sound like a crazy woman. Truly.'

'That's fine. You can say that. Maybe I am being a little crazy. But know this – if you insist you're the perfect husband and I'm the one with all the problems, this is going to get messy. Oh, and by the way.' She turned and faced him. 'I've been thinking about this a lot the last couple of days, and I distinctly remember telling you I did not want to call my son Wolf.'

'What?'

'Yes. I remember. When the twins were delivered, you said, *Oh Lily, look, a boy and a girl. Wolf and Lily May.* And I said, *Wolf? What sort of a name is Wolf?* Now, tell me this, David. What happened between me going off to the aftercare surgery and arriving back on the hospital ward to make you think I'd changed my mind?'

David laughed.

'Are you serious? You were on pain meds. You'd just had a

C-section. You didn't know your own name. You can't remember that. I don't even remember it.'

'Oh, but I *do* remember. That's the problem. And I remember thinking that that was the start of me feeling so depressed. The nurse handed me these babies that had been cut out of me and I hadn't even named them and I was supposed to care for them. I didn't even feel like they were mine.'

Lily slapped her hand on the counter.

'I was postnatal. And you were too caught up in the success of becoming a father to even care.'

'You had the baby blues,' David said. 'It was normal. You weren't postnatal. You filled out that card the nurse gave you and said you were fine, o. What is this obsession with *naming* everything, any-way? Sadness must be depression. A child being particular must be *autistic*. In Nigeria, there is no *depression*. In Nigeria, Wolf would be considered a genius.'

Lily walked over to the table. He flinched.

'You know what your job is, David? It's undermining and spin-ning. Creating a new reality with lies. That's what a hedge-fund manager does. You need to stop doing it to me.'

MATT

No. 5

Matt had chaired many a meeting at his accountancy practice. Sometimes, the partners could be an unruly bunch and he would have to crack the whip. Generally, he was able to keep things under control.

The gathering at Alison Daly's house was more challenging than any meeting of his board.

He'd invited everybody bar Ron Ryan, for obvious reasons. He told his neighbours he'd had a falling-out with the man. Nobody seemed to care. For all his hail-fellow-well-met front, Ron didn't seem to be particularly popular in the Vale.

Matt had toyed with the notion of not inviting the Millers. Even though he'd a good working relationship with Ed, he didn't like his neighbour.

Matt initially hadn't wanted to take Ed's business. He knew the Cork firm that Ed was leaving; in fact, he was friendly with one of the top chaps there. You didn't poach other companies' business if there were relationships there. There was enough to go round.

But the Cork firm seemed happy to let Ed go, and money was

money. Matt had thought it all a bit odd and when, at a conference a couple of weeks later, he bumped into the old acquaintance, he'd made sure to buy him a pint. He'd raised the topic of the Millers over drinks and the fellow had filled him in on the rumours circulating about Ed and Amelia and how they'd got all their money.

Handling Ed's accounts was just a job, that's what Matt told himself. But, if Matt was honest, he didn't think he'd like to have the man inside his home.

In the end, he did tell the Millers about the gathering that night but they'd chosen not to call over. Matt was starting to wonder if that in itself didn't say something.

George Richmond had arrived with a huge bunch of flowers for Alison. It looked liked he was apologising for something, but for the life of him, Matt – and Alison, by the looks of things – couldn't figure out what for.

The Solankes turned up carrying the aura of a couple who'd just had an argument. Matt recognised the signs. And now Lily was getting stuck into the alcohol.

In fact, as soon as they'd all arrived, Alison had popped the cork on a bottle of wine. Her hands, Matt noticed, were trembling. It seemed everybody was feeling a little nervous.

'I can't believe we're starting this now, being a community, just as we're about to move,' Chrissy said.

'What?' Alison said. 'You're moving?'

'Probably not immediately, but yes. I want to work again and . . .' Matt didn't hear the rest but from the strange, pitying looks he was being thrown, he knew Chrissy had blabbed. Perhaps, given his performance with Ron earlier on, she'd decided he didn't mind if people knew.

He'd bloody kill her.

'Women!' David Solanke had arrived beside Matt. He was in a foul mood.

'I don't know,' George interjected. Why had he come, anyway? Matt wondered. He'd never seen George exchange more than two words with Olive. 'I think you pair are lucky. Lily and Chrissy are lovely.'

Matt didn't know whether to thank him or view him in a new light. Was George Richmond after his wife too? Maybe he'd have to watch him now.

Matt looked across at Chrissy. She seemed the least worried of everybody there. She actually looked beautiful tonight. More like herself. Her hair was tied up in a pretty ponytail and her eyes had their sparkle back. There was no denying it, she'd looked terribly unhappy this last while. That was something he'd noticed when he'd lain awake at night, watching her sleep. She didn't seem to be exactly loving her life as an adulteress. He'd told himself that perhaps that meant there was hope for their marriage. And he'd been right.

And while she'd been annoyed that he hadn't *told* her he'd had a go at Olive, she'd seemed sort of thrilled that he had. With that, and him launching himself at Ron.

'Eh, maybe we should call this to order?' he called over the din.

'Ooo-er,' Chrissy said. 'We'd better behave.'

Alison told them to get comfortable on the patio rattan chairs as she topped up the glasses.

'Actually, before you speak, can I say something, Matt?' she said.

'You don't need to clear it through the chair,' Chrissy laughed.

'Ignore her,' Matt said. 'Go ahead, Alison.'

'I just wanted to let you know that I'm happy to have you all over here tonight, even if it isn't in the best of circumstances. This is the first time we've done this at ours, but I really hope it isn't the last. Holly and I haven't had it easy the last few years – actually, no, that's not true – we haven't had it easy in as long as I can remember. Coming here helped a bit but we kept to ourselves for reasons which will be obvious once I explain. The point is, we've been very lonely and I see now that we need our neighbours. We need *good* neighbours. And if Olive's death has one silver lining it might be that perhaps we've all realised that.'

'Hear hear,' Lily said.

George leaned into Matt's ear.

'I thought the silver lining was that she was fucking dead.'

Matt frowned.

'What obvious reasons?' David asked, picking up on what Alison had said.

Alison stared down at the glass in her hand. She hesitated, took a deep breath, then looked ready to speak.

'My ex-husband is a very violent man. I took Holly and ran from him a few years ago but not before he put us both in hospital. She was only fourteen at the time.'

'Oh, my God,' Chrissy said.

Lily leaned across and squeezed Alison's hand.

'Alison, I'm very sorry,' Matt said. 'I'd no idea. Is there anything we can do?'

'Well, I was hoping if you ever saw a man scaling the gates . . .' Alison laughed thinly, but nobody else did.

It was, oddly, George who spoke next.

'If I see a man scaling the gates, I'll beat him to within an inch of his life,' he said.

'Thank you, George.' Alison raised her glass.

'Eh. Me too,' Matt added. 'Is he a big man, your ex?'

'Don't tell me you're afraid,' Chrissy snorted. 'Not after the hiding you gave Ron today.'

'What?' George said.

'It was nothing,' Matt said, before Chrissy could jump in again.

'It doesn't matter if he's big or not,' David interrupted. 'It's the strategy we have for taking him down. There's three of us, one of him. He doesn't stand a chance. Strength in numbers. And if he raised a hand to his wife, then he's a weak man anyway.'

Everybody looked at David.

'Eh, yes, that's reassuring,' Matt said. 'At least you're not suggesting we fling organic vegetables at him. I think I'm far happier to have David the hedge-fund manager on our side than David the hedge-trimmer.'

Lily was blushing. Her and David exchanged a glance, only for a second, but Matt clocked it. Maybe the ice was thawing slightly.

'Anyway, the point of this meeting is less to plan for an eventuality that may or may not happen – sorry, Alison, I promise we will revisit it – but to discuss what's happening right now,' Matt said.

'We'll put it in the minutes for the next meeting,' Chrissy said, and winked at Matt. He sensed she'd made her mind up about something. About him, and their marriage. She wanted things to work now and she'd back him. No matter what.

'As I was saying,' Matt said, 'the point of tonight is to discuss something that definitely *has* happened. We know the police were around today and took the Solanke kids' fingerprints. They already have Cam's and Holly's. And now we can guess why. I spoke to that detective yesterday, Frank Brazil, when he came by for some plastic bags. He has revealed that Olive died from a heart attack but he added that they believe carbon monoxide poisoning brought it on and her boiler may have been tampered with.'

'That's all they found?' Alison asked.

'Shit, isn't that enough?' George said.

'Now, they're not saying one of us did it,' Matt continued, 'but we all know that Olive never had visitors call to Withered Vale. I've let plenty of people in through the gate for . . . most of you.' Matt eyed George, who wasn't Mr Popular either.

'But Olive didn't have friends,' he continued. 'Or family, as you pointed out, Alison. We've had two detectives questioning us all weekend and that has set alarm bells ringing in my head. How many times have the cops made a hames of things in this little country of ours? Every other week there's a tribunal into police corruption of some sort. We know what they're like. When they can't find the culprit – they find a scapegoat.'

'I'm worried they're going to try to pin this on Wolf.' The words burst out of Lily's mouth. They were followed by a sob. 'I punched Olive in the face and Wolf saw me do it. He was in her house loads. I think they're going to say something like he saw me be violent to her and he thought it was okay. But Wolf is not like that. He couldn't plan something like that. He just doesn't have it in him. He's only eight.'

'No kid does,' Chrissy said, leaning around Alison and patting Lily's arm. 'I know Cam can be a right little shit but he's been going through some tough stuff as well. And like you say, Wolf is *eight*. Even the police couldn't be stupid enough to imagine him capable of killing somebody. Oh, and kudos for planting one on Olive. I can't say she didn't deserve it.'

'I . . . I don't know,' Alison interrupted. 'I think Matt has a point. We don't know what the police are stupid enough to think. I don't mind those two who've been asking questions. They *seem* nice. But we can't assume we're dealing with rational individuals just because they carry badges. I'm sorry . . . maybe I'm speaking out of turn. I've just . . . had some bad experiences with cops.'

Her neighbours shrugged. Not one of them could, hand on heart, express confidence in the police.

'Look, let's be honest here,' George said. 'Ever since that woman died, we've clearly all been tearing ourselves asunder with worry. Fine. As it's confession time, I fell out with her too. She was a stupid, vicious woman. But she's gone. And maybe we need to stop thinking about that old witch and start supporting each other.'

'George is right,' Matt said. 'So, what are we going to do about this situation? Because I can see what the police are at. They're trying to get us to turn on each other. Both within our own homes and as neighbours. And to be honest, Lily, I too am concerned that they've taken our children's fingerprints. I'm not sure they'd think Wolf capable of planning to kill Olive – but what if they accused him of messing around with her boiler or something? I don't even know where it is – where did she keep that thing?'

'It was in a cupboard in the kitchen,' Alison said.

Everybody stared at her. She blushed furiously.

'She told me she was having problems with it. She was getting it replaced. Ron was helping her. Jesus!'

'See – there we are again,' Matt said. 'Look, we need to make sure we aren't inadvertently giving the police stuff they can throw at us. Though it's bloody interesting *Ron* fixed her boiler.'

Alison met his eye. They both nodded, slowly, in agreement.

'No, I think she got it fixed properly in the end,' Lily said. 'Remember that van that came in? They knocked and asked me did I want mine serviced while they were here.'

Matt shrugged.

'So, what's the plan?' George said. 'We need to have a plan. Especially to protect the kids. And it will have to be more sophisticated than *I Am Spartacus*.'

'Precisely,' Matt said. 'It's about protecting the kids.'

Matt thought he had a plan. He was about to suggest it and get them all to agree to it. And while he was congratulating himself on how smart he was, he completely failed to notice one of his neighbours watching him quite closely; a neighbour who had carefully considered everything about that evening.

A neighbour who knew that if you were really honest about something big, nobody would ever imagine you were lying about something small.

OLIVE

No. 4

In the last few months of my life, I was very, very unhappy.

But it hadn't always been like that. I have some wonderful memories of my life in Withered Vale.

One of my favourites was playing cards with Wolf. We would set up the poker game and he would slowly strip me of every bit of loose change I had. The child was a numerical genius.

'What would you like to do when you go to college, Wolf?' I asked him one day. 'I hope it's something to do with numbers. Coding, that's a big thing these days, isn't it?'

'I want to make things,' he said.

'Well, writing computer games is making something. And I bet it pays big, too.'

'No. I want to make useful things.'

He resumed his winning streak and I sat back and thought, *you can do anything you want to, Wolf, and you'll be successful.*

During one of our longer games, I taught him how to make hot dogs. So smart in so many ways, so innocent in others.

'You boil the sausages?' he asked, like it was the oddest thing he'd ever heard in his life.

'Yes, you do.'

'Boil them? Are you sure? Because you normally fry or grill them. Why are these different?'

'These are Frankfurters, not the sausages you're used to. You have to trust me, Wolf! Now see when the skin starts to split? That's when they're ready. You keep an eye there, call me if you see them splitting. I'll get the rolls in a minute. And the ketchup. Do you want mustard, too?'

'Why not?' He gave that funny little shrug that said he'd try anything once.

I loved that kid.

I went out to listen at the sitting room window, just to make sure Lily wasn't calling for him. No Lily, but I noticed Lily May lurking about outside my garden. Well, she wouldn't be getting inside the house that day to catch her brother out.

When I went back into my kitchen, Wolf was opening all the cupboards, looking for the condiments.

'Can I have more ketchup than mustard? It's just, Papa says mustard is spicy and might burn my mouth. Just this first time?'

'Whatever you want, Wolf,' I said. 'But you won't find anything in there. That's the boiler.'

He touched it, just once. At the bottom, where he could reach.

'It's very shiny,' he said. 'Ow – it's hot.'

'It's new. Be careful, Wolf. Boilers are really dangerous. Here's the ketchup.'

We set out our tea on the table.

He took a bite and made a funny face.

'This does not taste like sausage.'

'No. They're different. Just give it a chance. They're delicious, when you get used to them.'

'Mm-hmm.' He took another bite. 'I think I like it.'

'Good.'

'What are we having tomorrow?'

'Wolf! I can't feed you every day. I have to call into town tomorrow.'

'Can I let myself in? I'm big enough to use the cooker on my own.'

I laughed.

'You certainly are not, my dear. Promise me you won't go near a cooker unless there's an adult with you.'

'I promise.'

It was one of many pleasant afternoons I had in my house with Wolf.

One of many until his parents broke my heart and I couldn't see him any more.

That's the thing about kids. You can love them, but unless they're yours, Mummy is always the most important person in the end.

ALISON

No. 3

Her neighbours had gone home and Holly had returned from the Solankes and headed straight to bed, but Alison didn't clean up straight away.

Instead, she fetched another bottle of wine from the fridge and returned outside, wrapping the throw from one of the chairs around her shoulders, and settling back into her seat with a glass in hand and an eye on Olive's cottage across the way.

The meeting had gone well, she thought. It had been a good idea to let people into her and Holly's lives a bit more. She'd realised, over time, that their bad experience with Olive didn't translate to all their neighbours being out to get them. They were a group now, on the Vale. They would stand up for each other – with the police and with others. It was useful to know that, should her ex-husband ever turn up at the Vale, she would have David and Matt and George to call upon.

Not that he would, she was fairly certain.

She'd wondered why, after approaching Holly in school that day, her ex hadn't come to their home. Alison hadn't any idea what

376

Holly had said to him. She'd had no idea her daughter could be so strong. So . . . ruthless.

Alison had been convinced Lee was going to arrive on the doorstep one day.

Not because he'd followed Holly or got lucky.

No.

She was worried that Olive Collins would give Lee Baker their address.

Alison had stupidly, irrationally, told Olive her ex-husband's name. That, combined with the fact he'd been a police officer had made it easy for Olive to find him.

That's what Olive had said when she called to the shop the day after Holly had threatened her. *I can contact him. I can tell him where you live.*

Alison hadn't told her daughter. She couldn't. Holly would have had their bags packed in seconds, and not before she'd gone over to Olive's house and done something stupid.

Alison had promised Holly, and promised herself, that her daughter would never have to run again. That she would never have to be scared again.

In the days that followed, Olive's threats had festered in Alison's mind.

It had taken every ounce of willpower to not strangle the woman. If she'd done that, Alison would have been carted off to jail and Holly, under age, would have been left exposed to Lee. Holly wouldn't have even waited until the courts or family services or whoever it was made up their minds – she would have run. Alison knew her daughter.

So Alison had two jobs.

Make sure Olive Collins would never speak to Lee and make sure that if her ex ever did turn up, he'd be leaving in his own coffin.

She'd nearly died when that woman detective had asked her if she was prepared for Lee's arrival. She was convinced, just by the way she'd looked at her, that Emma Child knew Alison had a gun.

Ever since she'd brought it into their home, Alison had felt a strange thrill of both terror and readiness, an adrenaline-filled anxiety that actually made her feel safe and powerful.

Dealing with Olive had been more difficult.

Olive, who she'd once considered a friend. Olive, the stupidest, most selfish, interfering, horrible piece of work that Alison had ever encountered.

Alison had lied to the police. She'd even lied to Holly, but that was just to protect her.

Alison had called into Olive's house that day before she left for the airport. She'd let herself in, with the key Olive had insisted on giving her.

Alison had been convinced, right from that first day, that the police were coming for her. That she'd left a fingerprint or something else incriminating. But, no. She seemed to be in the clear.

Alison raised her glass in the direction of Olive's cottage.

'*You got what you deserved,*' she whispered.

FRANK

'There's just no way, is there?' Emma opened Frank's car door with a question and jumped in, puzzled.

He'd texted that morning and said he'd pick her up. She had her car, he had his, there was no need, but Frank had a feeling this was the pattern that would persist until he retired.

He also got the feeling that, bizarrely, of all the people he'd worked with over the years, for far longer periods and far more closely, Emma Child was the one he'd be seeing the most of when he finished up.

Life was weird like that.

'Anything is possible,' he said. 'Put your seatbelt on. Anyway. Amira was adamant. The fingerprints match the kid's. There were none belonging to Cam and they only picked up one from Lily May, on the television remote. That makes sense, going by what her parents say. She stopped going over there long before Wolf did.'

'So, he touched the boiler. It doesn't mean he taped her air vents, loosened the caps and blocked the flue. He liked the woman, by all accounts, and she liked him.'

'Did she, though?' Frank said. 'Or was he just a weapon in her war with the mother? I mean, I don't have kids, Emma, and even I'm not sure I'd be okay with some child being in my house every day watching TV and eating his way through my larder. Especially if his mother had already expressed a concern about it.'

'Yes, but you're a special case, Frank. Cantankerous. Olive was a very lonely woman, by all reports. Maybe she just enjoyed the company. That's no less plausible than an eight-year-old knowing how to poison somebody.'

'Kids these days. They don't even know women have pubic hair.'

'WHAT?'

'It's just something I heard,' Frank smirked. 'The point is, you can pick up anything off the internet. You were in the treehouse with him. Was he displaying any psychopathic tendencies?'

Emma shook her head.

'Jesus, he's just a little boy. He's not capable of murdering anyone.'

'Now you know that's not true, Emma. Kids kill. And anyway, what if he didn't intend to kill her? What if it was an accident?'

'Eh, the Sellotape?'

'A game that went too far?'

'I still don't believe it. And nor do you. This is us scraping the barrel, Frank.'

They'd arrived. Frank keyed in the passcode at the gate and it swung open.

The neighbours were waiting for them. That's what it seemed like, anyway. The residents of Withered Vale were gathered in a small gang outside the Solankes' house. Most of them were there. The

Solankes themselves, the Dalys, the Hennessys and George Richmond. The adults were talking. The kids were playing on the road.
Wolf and Cam, kicking a ball to each other, Lily May languishing
by her brother's side. There was no sign of lover man Ron or the
Millers.

'Intriguing,' Frank said, pulling the car over to the kerb.

'Very,' Emma agreed.

They got out of the car and approached the small group.

'How's it going, Detectives?'

It appeared Matt Hennessy had been appointed spokesperson.

He was an odd choice, Frank thought. But then, he hadn't
expected to see the man slinging punches at his neighbour yesterday, either.

'Good morning, Mr Hennessy. Folks. We're just here to have a
chat with Mr and Mrs Solanke today.' He nodded at Lily and David.

'Oh, we know,' Matt said. 'We reckon you found Wolf's fingerprints all over Olive's house.'

Frank and Emma looked at each other.

'Mr Hennessy, this is between ourselves and Lily and David. The
footpath is not the place for this conversation.'

'No, that's fine,' Lily said. 'It's just we think we can save you
some time. We spoke to Wolf this morning. We know he was in
Olive's house. We told you that. But Matt said you think Olive's
boiler may have been tampered with. Wolf says he knew where the
boiler was and that he touched it once. So if you've found his fingerprints on it, that's the reason why.'

'Okay,' said Frank. 'We'd still like to talk to him.'

'The thing is,' Matt interrupted. 'None of the kids were near
Olive's that day. Lily May was in with her mum, but Wolf was over

with us. He was playing with Cam, up in the treehouse. After school, anyway.'

'On 3rd of March?' Frank said. 'You remember the exact date?'

'Yes,' Chrissy answered. 'It was a chilly enough day. I made the boys hot chocolate and brought it up to them. I remember. I was keeping an eye. And then Wolf came in and they played on the computer for a while. Then Lily collected him and brought him home.'

Frank looked at the adults assembled in front of him. They'd formed a defensive line. He'd no idea if they were telling the truth or not. And he felt entirely ridiculous, wanting to speak to Wolf.

But he wouldn't have been doing his job if he wasn't asking questions.

'Wolf. Cam,' he called out.

The two lads dropped the ball and sauntered over.

'Wolf, do you often hang out in the Hennessys' treehouse?'

The kid looked up at him.

'All the time.'

'With Cam?'

He was a bit more uncertain now.

'Yeah. Sometimes.'

'Did anybody tell you to say that?'

'No.'

Frank turned to Cam.

'And you, sir. Do you remember playing with Wolf up there a few months ago? Like on the 3rd of March? Your mum says there was a day she gave you hot chocolate and then Wolf went into your house and you played computer games.'

Cam looked over to his parents and then back to Frank.

'Yeah. Sure. I remember. It was a cold day. I think it started to rain. That really freezing rain, you know the sort I mean. Wolf said he was starving. I said I'd ask Mum for treats. We'd been out in the treehouse long enough. I figured she'd feel guilty. She always leaves me out there for ages. Especially when she's knocking back the gin. Then we started talking about WWE. I said John Cena was my favourite. But Wolf said Kevin Owens. I told him Cena could tear Owens' head off and shove it down his neck if he wanted and then Wolf said, not if Owens had a Kalashnikov, which technically . . .'

'Cam,' Matt barked. 'I think that's all the detective needs to know. Chrissy doesn't drink gin.' He smiled nervously. The kid had definitely gone off script. He was writing his own memoirs.

Frank inhaled deeply. He felt sorry for these folks, but he didn't like being made a fool of, either.

Emma placed a hand on his arm.

'That's all we need,' she said. 'Thanks for getting all the facts together for us.'

The neighbours looked at one another, uncertainly. In the cold light of day, their little plan had sounded a lot less convincing than whenever they'd concocted it. Frank suspected drink had been involved.

'Um. Well, great,' Matt said. 'Eh, listen, could I speak to you, Detectives, before you go?'

Frank sucked in his cheeks.

'Why not? We're here now. I'd rather it wasn't a complete waste of our time.'

They followed Matt over to his house, where he brought them into the seventies-style sitting room.

'Not due in work today?' Frank asked, as they took their seats.

'I took a few days off. Figured I could do with a bit of family time.'

'I see. Important, that.'

'Yes.'

'Anyway, there was something you wanted to tell us?'

'Indeed. Listen, you know I'm Ed's accountant? Ed next door?'

'We do.'

'It's just – well, when you told me what you suspected about Olive, about how she'd died, I got to thinking. I believe there's something you need to know about Ed and how he came into his money. It could be pertinent. It's about his father's alleged suicide.'

Frank stared at Matt. There was a sheen of sweat over his upper lip and his eye was twitching. He wasn't stupid enough to lie to them – Matt was a man who knew they could easily check out whatever he told them about Ed. But was there something else at play here? Some sort of diversion tactic?

Was Matt about to throw his neighbour under the bus to protect somebody else? Somebody close to him?

Or perhaps, himself?

Frank withdrew his notepad.

'Go ahead,' he said.

OLIVE

No. 4

I knew, when Ed called over on the 3rd, that something was awry.

I was already feeling very shaky that morning. I hadn't recovered from what Ron had done the previous evening. But I had had the cop-on to set my digital camcorder up on the mantelpiece and, when I heard the knock on the door, I turned it on. I figured if Ron came in and threatened me again, I'd get it on camera. And this time, I'd go to the police. I'd sent pictures of him swilling champagne and driving his nice car to his exes. There was nothing illegal in that. But what he'd done to me was absolutely disgraceful. I needed evidence.

The camera was recording when Ed came in and sat down.

He told me his brother Paul had been in touch to say he'd spoken to me. Then Ed gave me the whole spiel about what a liar his brother was.

What he didn't realise was that Paul had also been in touch with me. He'd written to me with more evidence of his claim. It was unnecessary. I'd believed him the first time we met. I'd already agreed to be his ally and keep an eye on the Millers. But Paul wanted to convince me even more. He said the solicitor who'd changed the will for Ed's father claimed he'd tried to contact Edward Senior again but Ed and Amelia wouldn't put him through. It was standard practice, when somebody changed a will that late in life, just to follow up with a call to make sure the decision was final. He hadn't mentioned it at the inquest because the coroner hadn't asked.

And then Paul said he'd landed the real clincher – he'd started to dig up Amelia and Ed's history in Dublin. It transpired that the business Ed had been running had gone bust shortly before his father fell ill, which he'd never told his siblings about. But Amelia was the real revelation. It seemed she had a record with suicidal patients. She'd cared privately for an old lady in Dublin who had died from an overdose a few months before Ed and Amelia had married. The old woman's will hadn't been changed, but the woman's family reckoned a large sum of money had gone missing from her savings stash, which she had kept in the house.

The police hadn't been aware of that when Edward Senior had died. Paul wasn't even sure his brother had been aware of it.

It was fairly damning.

I didn't mention any of that to Ed. Paul's letter sat in a box at the top of my wardrobe. A box that is still sitting in the police's evidence room, unexamined.

That day, I listened to Ed and just once alerted him to the fact I didn't believe him. I couldn't help it.

Couldn't you have shared out the inheritance? I said, in my most innocent voice.

He nearly choked. He knew I knew.

But then he made his stupidest move. I'd only ever seen Ed and Amelia as friends. God forgive me, I really was that innocent. I'd hoped we could be the best of friends, family even. I would have loved to have gone away with them, spent more time in their company.

I had absolutely no designs on Ed in *that* way.

He read it wrong. Of course, they'd no idea about Ron.

'I was hoping you might come out and join us, Olive,' he said. 'When we get settled, like. It's high time we had a holiday together and we're bound to have an apartment with a spare room.'

Months ago, that offer would have made me beam.

Ed sidled up to me on the couch.

'In fact, I was wondering, Olive, if you would consider maybe popping away just with me sometime. Amelia's . . . well, I don't talk to Amelia the way I talk to you.' He reached out and stroked my cheek. 'She doesn't have your brains. I think we'd get along terrifically if we went off together, alone. And I could spoil you rotten. The things I could show you.'

Then he leaned in to kiss me.

His breath smelled of onions and tobacco and it made me want to retch. I pushed him away.

'Oh, no, Ed,' I said. 'I think you've got this all wrong. I don't feel that way about you. I care too much for Amelia to do anything like that. And, to be honest, I'm absolutely appalled you think so little of me and of your wife that you could imagine I would want to shoot off with you for dirty weekends while she was left behind at home.'

His eyes nearly popped out of his head as he tried to backpedal. I saw the red light on the camera over his shoulder. It was recording merrily away.

'Or is it that you're saying you'd leave her altogether?' I continued. 'Is that it, Ed? Would you dump your wife for me? This is terrible. What would poor Amelia say? I think you should leave. Please. Leave now.'

He got up, his face purple.

As soon as he left, I sat down and typed an email to his brother. I said I'd had a terrible scare, that Ed had come over and more or less threatened me if I revealed the truth about what he'd done to his father. I said he'd invited me to go on holidays with him and Amelia and I'd an awful feeling I'd had a narrow escape. They'd have probably flung me off a cliff or something.

He wrote back immediately and I assured him I was fine.

Obviously I haven't replied to any of the emails he's sent in the three months since. Six unanswered emails and a very concerned sender.

After I'd mailed Paul, I took the sim card out of my digital camcorder and placed it in an envelope. When it looked like the Vale was deserted, I scooted on down to the Millers and popped it in their mailbox. Addressed to Amelia.

I was always very good at getting back at people who'd hurt me.

I'd only left the house for a few minutes.

That's how long it took for Alison Daly to get into my home.

Not that I saw her.

The last person I saw from the Vale was Lily May.

I guess she was looking for her brother that evening. She'd no idea where he was. He certainly wasn't in Cam's treehouse, that's for sure. He was probably hiding in his room, under the bed where she couldn't find him.

She didn't think of that, though. She'd figured he'd snuck into mine again and so she crept out before her parents could grab her for bed.

Even though it was dark, she made her way into the garden. She banged on the door. There was no answer, but that didn't stop her.

Seeing my blinds were drawn, she walked to the end of the window, trampling on my flower bed under the sill. Just at the very edge, she was able to peek in. If the police I'd called had done the very same, they'd have found me earlier. I'd have still looked like me, at least.

I was sitting there, paralysed and in agony, in the throes of a massive heart attack, when my eyes met hers. I sent her a silent, desperate plea, this little girl peering in my window.

Maybe she didn't realise what was happening. Or maybe she did. She walked away.

She didn't like me very much, little Lily May. I probably deserved it.

FRANK

Six months later

The capital's roads were deserted, the light blizzard forcing residents to stay in the comfort of their homes or seek off-street shelter in well-lit, welcoming bars and restaurants.

Frank liked the solitude. He was enjoying feeling like he owned the city on this cold winter's evening.

He made an illegal right turn off the main road. Further on down, he took the left that brought him to the car park behind Dublin's largest prison.

The prison administration was expecting him. Frank had retired in September and his leaving do had been larger than usual. Crotchety, opinionated and often misanthropic, Frank had still been held in high regard. He was one of the country's finest, longest-serving detectives and he'd carry that currency for a couple years more – at least until people forgot his name.

'We have him in the visitors' room,' the young male guard who let him into the prison told him. 'He doesn't know who's coming in to see him. I'll bring you down.'

'Great stuff. That's some weather we're having, isn't it?'

'Shocking. Our shift finishes in an hour. We're all heading up to Darby's. You're welcome to join us.'

'Sorry. I have a date later.'

The guard blushed.

They walked down the quiet prison corridors, through the processing area and towards the public quarters, where the visitors' room was situated.

He was sitting at one of the blue plastic tables, shoulders hunched, head hung low. The grey tracksuit hugged his wide frame in a way that said, *I spend my time in here productively.*

He looked up when the door opened and Frank came in. The guard entered too, but she positioned herself well away by the wall.

'Well, hello there,' Frank said, taking a seat on the other side of the table.

The man looked at him.

'Who are you?' he said.

'Oh, I'm Frank. Formerly Detective Inspector Frank Brazil of the serious crimes squad. Just Frank now.'

The man cocked his head, no closer to knowing anything.

'What do you want with me? I haven't done anything. I'm nearly finished with my sentence.'

'So I hear. It's incredible, isn't it, Anthony? Five years for stalking, breaking and entering, and serious assault. Of a policewoman, too. It makes me question the justice system. 'Course, I know it's phenomenal there was ever a prosecution at all. Our conviction numbers for violence against women are poor, and with you being a former boyfriend and everything. I imagine it was bringing the knife to slash her face that did it. If you'd restrained yourself even a little, you probably would have avoided a custodial sentence.'

The man squinted at Frank and fidgeted in his chair. The years in prison as an attempted murderer hadn't marked Anthony Hall as they should have. He was unbeaten, unbowed. Still handsome, still with all his own teeth. Still a nasty piece of work. Frank read all that on his face.

'Ah. You're a friend of hers. I know my rights. I've done my time. I'm a reformed man. You fuckers aren't allowed to harass me. The screws in here have done enough over the years. My solicitor reckons I should sue the state. Says I'll get a fortune.'

'Sorry, which fuckers aren't allowed to harass you?'

'You lot. Police.'

'Let me just repeat what I said when I came in, Anthony. I'm a former cop. Retired. No longer serving.'

Emma's attacker processed this. He leaned back in his chair, swung an arm over the top of it.

'So. What do you want, then?'

'I am here to give you a warning. A warning to steer clear of that girl when you get out of here. You see, leaving the police has freed me. I can do what I like. I won't be bringing the force into disrepute. And in case you think I'm bullshitting you, let me make a few things clear. I live alone. I have a small number of friends that I keep close and are important to me. I'm old-style – friendship means loyalty, means their battles are my battles. And Emma Child's fight with you is my fight too.'

'You wouldn't lay a finger on me,' Anthony scoffed. 'A former detective? No way you'd risk ending up in prison just to have a pop at somebody who's already served his sentence. That's not how it works.'

Frank laughed.

'End up in prison? Are you daft? You don't spend over thirty years working in the system and not know how to play the system. Whatever I do to you, sonny boy, will never result in me going to prison. The handy thing about being retired is that you have all the time in the world to get creative. And there is nobody more creative than a gamekeeper turned poacher.'

Anthony stared at Frank. He said nothing for a minute. Then he smiled.

'Okay, old man. You don't scare me. Go on, you can go home and tell her you came in and scared the life out of me, that she's grand. I've no intention of going near Emma Child. She's already robbed years of my life. I'm leaving here to start living the rest of it.'

Frank stood up. He pushed in his chair, and leaned into Anthony's ear.

After he'd said what he wanted to say, Frank straightened up again and patted him on the shoulder. The other man was rigid.

The snow had left a dusting on Frank's car. He turned the key in the ignition and let the engine warm up while he rang Emma.

'Hi. Where are you?' she answered.

'Shopping. Picking up some turkey slices for tonight.'

'Turkey slices? Are you kidding me?'

'Well, I can't cook a whole turkey in the next couple of hours, Emma.'

'Just buy a turkey crown, Frank, for God's sake. You cannot give Amira a turkey sandwich on your first official date.'

'This is not a date. It's dinner in my house with you and Ben there as well.'

'We're calling ourselves your chaperones.'

'Aren't we yours?'

'Just buy the damn turkey crown, Frank. I'll be over at 7. I'll cook it. We can have . . . I don't know . . . buy nachos for starters or something. Why are you set on turkey, anyway? Just because it's Christmas week? Nobody likes turkey.'

Frank chuckled.

'I've a curry on, you daft woman. See you later.'

He grinned.

Yvonne next door had cooked the curry for him that morning and given him instructions on when to turn the pot on that evening.

'I'm warning you, don't bang it in the bloody microwave, Frank,' she'd said, standing in his hall after delivering it. 'Here, does Mona know you're bringing your girlfriend over? I see she's smiling away there.'

Frank turned to look at the picture on the wall.

'She's not my girlfriend. But, yes, Mona knows I'm having female company. We had a chat.'

'Good man. I don't want you to take this personally, but she had a chat with me too.'

'Yeah? You know Mona is dead, don't you, Yvonne?'

'Yeah. She spoke to me from beyond the grave. Turns out we don't need a photograph to communicate. Anyway, she said she's seeing somebody in heaven and would you take that fucking shrine down because it's embarrassing her.'

Frank raised an eyebrow.

'Thanks for the curry, Yvonne.'

'Oh – one other thing.'

Frank sighed. This was an awful lot of quid pro quo to save him a few bob on a takeaway later.

'I saw the news in the paper about those two out in Withered Vale, Ed and Amelia Miller. It said a date had been set for the trial for the father's murder. Tell us, Frank, did they do your one in as well? The neighbour?'

'Yvonne, you know I can't . . .'

'Oh, come on. You're retired now, aren't you? You're still pals with that girl, the head detective on the case. You must know everything.'

When Frank didn't bite, Yvonne threw down her last card.

'I'll do a lemon meringue for your dessert. It's a surefire panty-dropper. Even works on me, and I make it.'

'Yvonne, you should be in car sales. Right, well, you didn't hear this from me and you'd better not repeat it to anybody.'

Yvonne drew her fingers across her lips. They were zipped shut, at least until she got back next door.

'Yeah,' Frank said. 'I'm pretty sure they killed Olive. But there wasn't enough evidence to go after them for that. We have them on Ed's father though. We found a letter to Olive from Ed's brother, so we know she knew what the Millers had done – that was probably what did for her in the end. Though she did seem to have pissed off nearly every one of her neighbours.

'Anyway, Paul Miller had dug up enough on Amelia for the case into Ed's father to be reopened and get that pair in the dock. Wait until you see them turn on each other in the stand. They were already talking in the police station. Let's just say, Ed had tried it on with Olive and, somehow, before she died, Olive made sure Amelia knew about it. Ed was loyal to the wife at first, but once he found out Amelia was singing about him and Olive, he started to claim she'd murdered his father.'

'Jesus, it's like Dallas!'

'Worse. Anyway, I'm not sure Olive Collins will ever get justice. Unless you can call it indirect justice.'

'Oh God, that's terrible,' Yvonne said, wide-eyed. 'Well, at least that pair are in the spotlight. Animals. Murdering your own dad? I always thought, though, you should have arrested the whole lot of them up in that Vale.'

'Why's that, then?'

'Leaving that poor woman in her house dead like that, for all that time. What kind of neighbours would do that? Heartless shower, the lot of them.'

Frank smiled.

'They were surprisingly normal.'

Yvonne hadn't believed him.

That was okay. It was easy to judge.

Frank pulled out of the prison car park, his wipers clearing the last of the snow from the now heated windscreen.

Everybody always assumed they were better than the people they heard about on the news.

OLIVE

No. 4

There's this moment, when you die.

You think, *Is that it? Is that all it was?*

All that hope and expectation, all that anxiety and effort.

All that . . . living.

Happiness by calendar. Birthdays, Christmas, New Year's Eve. Oh, and, lest we forget, Valentine's Day. The cruellest joke the gods at Hallmark ever played. We're not all a *half*. Some of us, believe it or not, are whole.

All that waiting. The endless bloody waiting for everything to fall into its glorious place like you'd assumed it all would when you *grew up*.

Life. I've heard some see it for what it is. They're the ones content in the moment, at peace with their insignificant anonymity in this vast world, able to find magic in little things like rain on a summer's morning, snow on a winter's eve.

I get it. We should all be grateful to be alive. Here's the problem: for many of us, life ends up being little more than a damp squib. There. I said it. I'm very philosophical now it's all over. Very *wise*. And oddly accepting.

I didn't choose to be here. That decision was made one Christmas night when my newly married parents, tipsy on hot whiskey, decided to break in the bed springs of their new home.

I didn't ask for life, but I was the one supposed to make the most of it, to join the dots and dance like a performing monkey.

School, job, sex, marriage, children, greed, charity, outrage, resignation, death.

A hamster wheel of expectation.

I never made the cut.

I was never *happy*, not the way I was supposed to be.

And yet, no matter how mundane and ordinary our lives are, in the end nearly all of us are clinging on by our fingernails. It's a cheap irony.

We fear death. We fear the unknown.

But, believe me when I tell you, it's actually a relief when death comes. A funny little moment when you think: *Hello. I always knew you and I would meet. And now you're here.*

It's like visiting New York. You've seen that skyline so many times on television and in pictures, you think you've been there.

Death is like that. Familiar.

That's how I felt, anyway, when it came, unexpectedly and without warning.

I didn't even realise how much I was worrying about it until it happened. Then I was almost content because, once it happened, I didn't need to worry about it any more. I didn't need to worry about anything. Even if it was untimely. Even if I wasn't due to meet it, just then.

It was all over and the real fun could begin.

I often wondered, after I'd upset so many people on the Vale, if any of them would have it in them to kill me.

None of them did.

Even Alison Daly with her single bullet and the little note she left — oh yes, I knew it was her. When I'd told her I could contact her husband, first she went completely pale and then she said if he ever turned up, she'd put a bullet in his head.

Keep interfering in other people's lives and you're getting one of these in your head.

She hadn't even changed the language in her note. I mean, honestly, once the shock had subsided, it just made me laugh.

And yet, of all those I fought with in the Vale, my clash with the Dalys was one in which I knew I wouldn't emerge from covered in glory.

And when the police investigated who'd tried to murder me, I didn't want the fact I'd made threats to Alison Daly surfacing. Seeing the raw, animalistic fear on Alison's face when I told her in the shop was enough for me to realise I had misjudged the situation, spectacularly.

So I burned the note and buried the bullet.

Thing is, she'd no idea how fateful that date would turn out and I've no doubt she's been feeling sick this whole time about that note and what happened to it. I wonder if she'd convinced herself I'd actually been scared enough to run, when I disappeared for so long.

But, no. I had my plan, and Alison Daly's threats weren't part of it.

It was Lily Solanke banning me from seeing Wolf that tipped me over the edge.

Oh, fair enough, that wasn't the only thing.

It had been on my mind for a while.

So many awful things had happened. I'd tried everything to make people like me. To be neighbourly. I could do no right for doing wrong.

I was lonely. I was sad. I guess I was depressed. I had to do something.

No, not kill myself.

I'm not that fucking stupid.

I no longer cared if my neighbours liked me. Being nice had got me nowhere.

I was going to punish them.

I was going to make them pay.

My plan was to make it look like one of them had intended to hurt me. Not just injure me, though – that they had attempted to *murder* me.

And, ha, the irony! The police would interview all of them.

All my respectable, oh-so-perfect neighbours would have their lives opened up and examined, who'd said what to me, who'd fought with me, who'd threatened me and *why*.

Their dirty little secrets would be exposed.

I had my plan, but I didn't know exactly when I was going to carry it out.

Then Ron called over on the 2nd.

At first, I thought everything was going to be okay again. I wanted to cry with relief. Right up until he pulled that stunt with the camera.

I was devastated by what he did. Destroyed. I needed him to apologise. I needed him to beg for forgiveness and to tell me he forgave me too.

And then I thought – a potential bonus – if I nearly died . . . he couldn't stay angry at me, could he? Surely he'd feel guilty? Nearly dying outdoes everything, doesn't it?

I would go ahead with everything the very next day.

Ed calling over cemented it. Knowing the Millers were going away that night just gave me the added impetus. Of all the people I wanted to feel guilty and for the police to investigate – it was that pair. Murdering people and making it look like suicide – well, that was their MO, wasn't it?

Now. I appreciate this all makes me sound a little unhinged. Desperate, even.

But look at it from my perspective. I couldn't see a way out. I was stuck living in that place with those people – feeling threatened and scared and isolated – and I couldn't see a way forward. I didn't want to move. It had been my home long before any of them came. They'd ruined it for me. They'd made me hate a place I once loved.

Something drastic had to happen.

As soon as Ed left I taped up the vents. I wore gloves but even still, I made sure to wipe the tape clean. That's what a murderer would do. I'd read enough books to know that.

That afternoon, I gave the boiler a rub down.

Then I made sure it was leaking.

Later, I sat down with my cup of tea, the telly, and my phone. I pulled the blinds down, unusual for me, but I just wanted to shut the world out for a while. Something else that backfired on me; it was the day for it.

As soon as the carbon monoxide started to make my eyes water and I felt a bit nauseous, I planned to ring the police. I'd done my research – in town, not on my home computer. I knew how much monoxide I could breathe before it became dangerous.

The emergency services would come. I'd probably semi-collapse in the garden and be taken off in an ambulance. Alison, most likely, would come running.

The sabotage would be discovered and everyone would be appalled.

The police would be involved.

And while my neighbours were in the spotlight, being questioned and questioning each other, I'd be comfortable in bed, stuffing myself with grapes and watching the soaps.

Except I didn't know I had a heart condition.

I didn't realise anything was wrong – I mean *that* wrong. I'd a pain in my chest and my eyes were watering. I'd expected to display symptoms. But then I started to feel like I couldn't move. I figured I'd better ring the police, pronto.

I'd barely got my address and the words *I think something is very wrong* out of my mouth before I was seized with an agony unlike anything I'd ever felt. I clutched the phone and the side of the chair as my body convulsed. My heart felt like it was exploding in my chest.

And there was Lily May staring in at me like some useless, spiteful doll. How I wished in that moment that I had been nicer to her. That I had, just once, favoured her over Wolf. And she might have run for her parents or screamed or done something, rather than just watch me then skip off home thinking, *serves her right*.

I'd no idea I was going to die.

How could I have?

And the absolute waste. I failed, spectacularly. The people I wanted to turn against each other, the people I wanted to suffer, are stronger and more united than ever.

And the people I wanted love from finally realised they were actually fond of me, but it didn't matter any more.

When they buried me, everybody from the Vale, bar the Millers, came. Ron didn't stand with his neighbours, but he brought a single rose. He waited until everybody had started to move off and threw it on my coffin, his eyes watering.

Wolf ran back and the two of them stood there for a minute.

'Do you miss her, too?' Wolf asked.

Ron hesitated.

'Oddly enough, I do, little man. I wouldn't have wanted anybody to harm her, not like that. Even if I didn't tell her. You were her buddy of sorts, weren't you?'

'She was my best friend,' Wolf said.

Ron placed his hand on Wolf's shoulder.

And they both walked away.

ACKNOWLEDGEMENTS

And another story makes its way out of my head and into a book, a lovely new book! None of it could be achieved without the excellent advice and guidance from some very special people:

My agent, Nicola Barr. Editor, Stef Bierwerth. Book boss, Rachel Neely (after a point, we just do what you say, Rachel!). And all the fabulous teams at Quercus and Hachette Ireland.

My early readers, who take these shocking drafts and tell me what shines and what – well, let's not worry about that. Especially, this time, Jane Gogan. Thank you, Jane, for offering so much of your time and support, in everything.

Family and friends who know writing has taken over my life but are still there, team Jo. Love you all. And miss you, too, Willie, the best stepdad I could have had.

The bloggers and reviewers who, especially with my last few books, have really got behind me and cheered my stories on. Thank you so much.

Chris Whitaker. The day will come. Thank you for the read. Now, for the love of God, somebody make us rich and famous.

Martin and my four (growing) little ones. I'm writing these acknowledgements in the worst weather we've seen since I was born. We're snowed in, but where else and with who else would I rather be? Nowhere and nobody.

And you, the reader. Aged four and a half I read my first Enid Blyton. My heart was won by the written word. It's been a lifelong affair. If I can give anybody the gift of a good story, a gift I still treasure when I snuggle up in the chair with a book at night, then my job is done. Thank you for giving me a chance.